I0708732

N
W
E
S

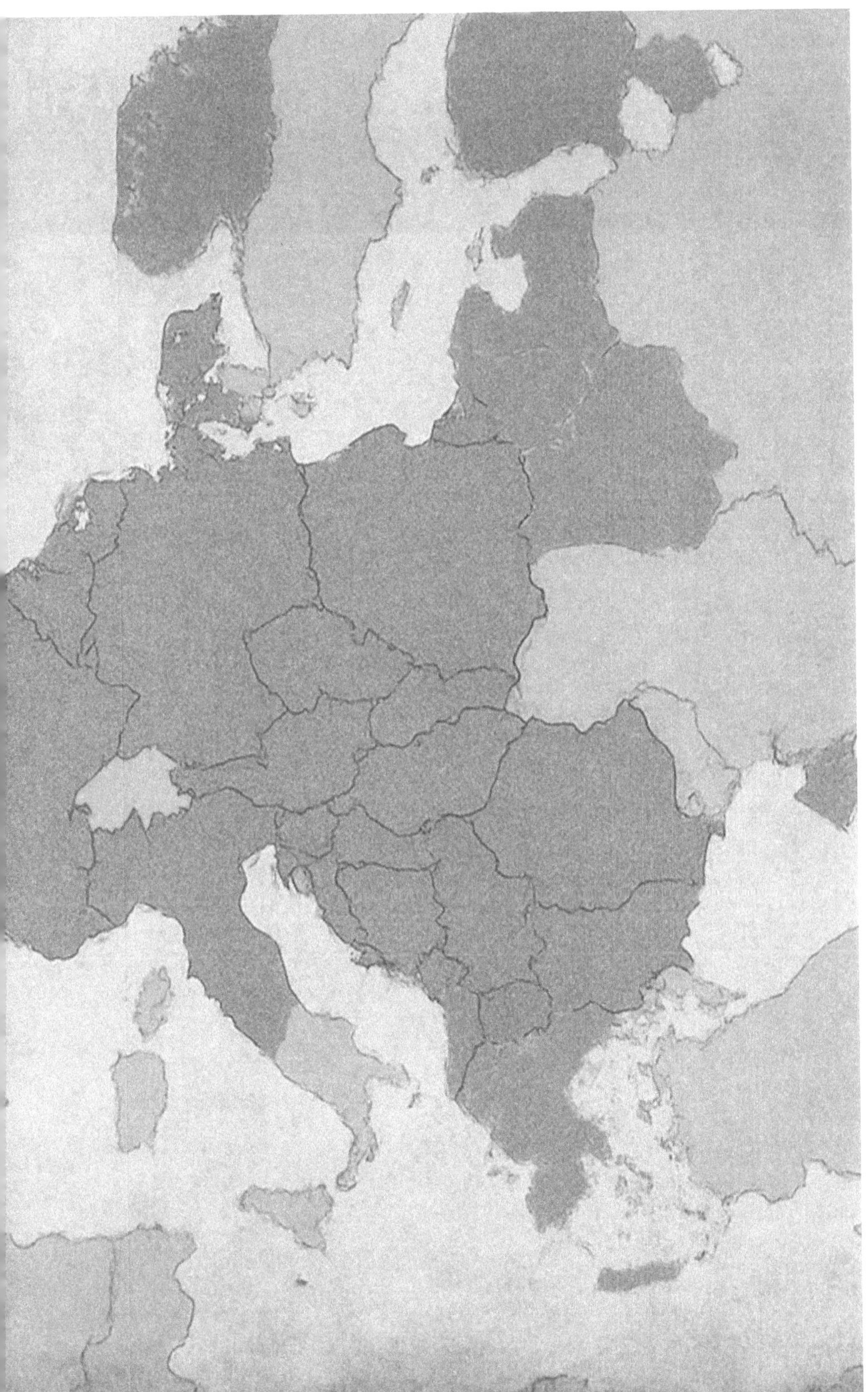

Also by Jack J. Wyatt:

Lions in the Water
Blood Stone Mountain
Scorn

BROKEN CASTLE

JACK J. WYATT

This book is a work of fiction. Many characters, places, and events are the product of the author's creation. Where past historical names or events are used, the author relied on research to portray those as accurately as possible. Any conclusions drawn from these characters, fictional or otherwise, is a matter of speculative creative license taken by the author for the purpose of entertainment.

Copyright © 2025 Jack J. Wyatt, Unrest Adventures LLC
First Edition, May 2025

Any use, including photocopy, scan, electronic transmission, or other unauthorized distribution, is strictly prohibited and discouraged. If you would like permission to use material from this book (other than for review purposes), please contact JackWyattBooks@gmail.com. Thank you for your support of this author's work.

Library of Congress Control Number: 2025911305

Paperback ISBN: 9781734108385
Hardcover ISBN: 9781734108378

BROKEN CASTLE

For Cliff— who fed every stray dog he ever met, savored the drum of falling rain, and volunteered for the war.

The truth was never lost.

It was just never meant to be found.

— Unknown

ONE

Ellis Martin shoved through the terminal at Hartsfield-Jackson into the rain. His suit was soaked, the trip a waste. Five weeks chasing down a cryptic old telegram, and all he had was a splitting headache and a pissed-off wife. He reached for his phone—shit.

His duffel. Shirts, sneakers, but no cell. He'd shut his eyes for only a few minutes during the flight—the damn thing was probably wedged in the seatback of 23B, halfway to Boise or Baltimore by now.

Linda would kill him—he'd promised to call the second he landed. "Ellis, you're not twenty-five anymore, and caffeine isn't a food group."

He never should've taken the case—but a fat retainer had sucked him in. Simple legwork and research. Bullshit. The telegram was a relic, dragged in from a world when rivets and steel ruled—before influencers, hashtags, and online horseshit. But solving the message? The trail was too dated, too bizarre. And now he'd lost his damn phone.

His loafers squeaked through the garage. He'd kill for a beer, a burger, and dry socks—hell, anything dry. But first, his car and home before Linda got worried and called every hospital in Atlanta.

In the parking garage, a white van rolled in behind him, slow and quiet. Ellis clocked it but kept scanning for his Audi.

The place was mostly empty—rows of concrete and dull light bounced off the wet surfaces.

From an outer crossway, a woman in an arm sling stumbled in from the rain. She slipped and hit the concrete hard.

Ellis hurried over. "You okay?"

She cradled her injured arm, blonde hair plastered to her face. "I'm fine."

He helped her to her feet.

The van idled close.

She shot him a look, turned, and vanished into the shadows.

No thank you. No glance over the shoulder. Just gone.

Ellis frowned. People were fucking weird.

Behind, the van's engine growled.

He jabbed his key fob, but nothing chirped or flashed. Was this the wrong level? Where the hell was his damn car?

The hiss of rain echoed around him.

"Good evening, sir."

Ellis flinched, hand shooting to his hip—coming up empty. Reflexes.

A guy stepped from the shadows, late twenties, six-two or three, scruffy beard, wearing a faded trawler hat and a patch on his jacket that read Ground Transportation.

Ellis forced a tight smile. "I think I might be on the wrong level. Can you point me to the stairs?"

"The stairs?" He gave a crooked smile. "This way."

Ellis followed. The strange van slithered behind—its driver determined to park at this level.

The attendant's tone was smooth. "How was your flight, sir?"

"Fine," Ellis grunted. He hated pointless chatter.

The man glanced at his duffel. "May I take your bag?"

Ellis was fifty-one, drank the occasional Scotch, and his brown hair was thinning a bit—but he was in good shape and far from needing that kind of help.

His nostrils flared. "Thanks, I got it."

The two trekked deeper, past rows of cars as the downpour outside grew.

The attendant tipped his cap. "Should stop raining before long."

Ellis rubbed an eye. Thank you, Mister Weatherman.

They approached a dark corridor. Something was off. And wasn't this area self-park?

"I don't see the stairs."

"Just ahead, sir."

Tires squealed.

The van roared forward. Its door flew open.

Ellis spun—too late.

Arms locked around his ribs, crushing air from his lungs.

Hot breath struck his ear. "Don't fight me!"

What the fuck was going on?

Ellis dropped his bag, twisting hard. Adrenaline surged. He slammed a heel into the attendant's shin—the grip loosened.

Ellis broke free.

A man from the van gave chase.

Ellis bolted toward the rain.

A crack split the air, barbs punching into his back. His jaw locked, teeth gnashing. Fifty thousand volts fried his spine, slamming him to the concrete.

TWO

The short text dangled a job Jadene Bowman desperately needed. Please arrive at Sinclair Whitmore's estate—7 p.m. sharp. That was it.

Night dropped as the Camry veered onto a narrow road. She clutched the wheel. Her tiny firm wasn't a year old and survived on fraud and missing inventory cases. A client like Whitmore could really change things.

She bit her lip. Was this position real, or a waste of time? She'd dug out her old navy skirt-suit, fixed the scuffs on her heels, and tied her brown hair in a tight ponytail. She looked like an FBI agent. "Dress for the job you want, honey," her mom used to say. Jadene sighed. If she knew the dreadful irony.

After a mile of holly trees, a gate wrapped in kudzu appeared in the headlights. She reached for the intercom, but the entrance creaked open. Someone inside was waiting for her.

Beyond the gates, the drive twisted uphill.

Pressed for time, she'd scoured the internet for information on Whitmore and his businesses. A tech tycoon with no social media presence—his wealth hid him from the world.

She flicked a glance at the rearview. How many others got that same text as her? Likely plenty—all seasoned PIs with better credentials. Would they give her a shot? Or was she here to fill some quota?

The embankment leveled.

She gasped, "Oh… my God."

A towering estate loomed—three stories of black iron and sandstone. White roses bordered a circular drive. At its center, a marble fountain—the size of a swimming pool. It was overwhelming. The place was lit up like a fairy tale.

"Shit!" She jerked the wheel. The Camry missed the fountain by inches. "Nice going, Bowman."

She parked well short of the entry, ditched her phone, and took only her leather notebook and pen. A professional look—and if the job was over her head, she could scribble some doodles before they kicked her out. She opened her door and stepped onto the drive's bumpy cobblestone.

"Miss Bowman." A man emerged from the entrance.

"Hello," she shouted, minding her balance.

"He's anxious to see you."

She was anxious not to fall on her butt. She should have worn her flats.

Tall and broad-shouldered, a man in dark slacks and a maroon tie welcomed her with a brisk nod.

She shot out a clammy hand. "Jadene Bowman."

"And I am Wes." He ignored the handshake. "This way, Miss Bowman."

She widened her eyes. Mahogany floors ran wall to wall in every direction, and the foyer was large enough to host a banquet or a battle. A grand staircase led to the upper floors.

Her nerves tightened as they moved down a long corridor. Wes slowed near a nook.

"You can lay your jacket on the chaise if you'd like."

She froze. "Do what now?"

"Mister Whitmore is in the keeping room. It's pretty warm in there." He pointed to an odd couch. "The chaise lounge here, you can—"

"Oh, yes, of course. I didn't hear you the first time," she lied.

A comfy velvet lounger. She removed her jacket, placing it on the long cushion.

Wes opened a set of giant wooden doors. She held her notebook and entered the passage.

Holy shit. This "keeping room" was the size of a concert hall. Towering bookshelves flanked a massive fireplace, and a family of chandeliers glowed above. Hung on the walls, huge portraits of seascapes, landscapes, and people she didn't recognize.

Two men spoke by the giant fire. A middle-aged one with slick hair stood, arms crossed, a faint smile on his lips.

"Understood. Of course, sir," he said.

The other man. She could hear the deep tone of his voice but not his words. He faced away from her in a high-backed chair.

Wes leaned over her shoulder.

"Iverson snuck in before you. Company business. But you're up next."

The conversation ended. Iverson marched across the gallery, forehead creased.

Wes stepped toward him.

"I thought we'd agreed on making appointments from now on." His tone sharp.

Iverson flashed his bleach-white smile. "Always a pleasure, doorman." He whisked past, vanishing down the corridor.

Wes didn't move—but his jaw tightened. "Scumbag."

Jadene pretended not to hear him.

Wes turned, grinning. "Are you ready?"

She had the sudden urge to pee but nodded instead.

He straightened his tie, stepped inside, and announced, "Miss Jadene Bowman, of Bowman Investigations."

Her cheeks warmed. Her "agency" was a downtown shoebox with a tacky neon sign that once flashed "Bowman PI." At night, it looked like she ran a cocktail lounge—or a strip club. She'd yanked the plug after eyeing it from the street, but the damn sign still hung in her window like a pink scar that wouldn't heal.

A seldom-visited webpage featured her college headshot and contact details. Her business scraped by on insurance and workers' comp investigations, but even those were drying up.

She'd met clients before—but none like Whitmore. Her background check turned up a single photo, buried in a defunct business journal from twenty years ago. It also held the only direct quote from the billionaire. After a closed-door Senate hearing, a reporter fired off three questions in one breath, shoving a mic into Whitmore's face. His response? "No comment, asshole."

Jadene smoothed her blouse.

"Over here, please," a commanding voice called. On the far side of the colossal room, a hand rose from the chair, summoning her forward.

Her pulse quickened.

It was the mysterious Sinclair Whitmore.

THREE

Jadene's heels clacked on the polished wood until a sprawling Persian rug—probably worth more than her college degree—softened her steps to a dull thud. Aged mahogany and old books scented the air. The giant stone hearth crackled.

She moved deeper into the room, toward the sitting area.

Sinclair Whitmore, silvery-gray hair, dressed in a pullover and trousers, sat gazing into the fire. Even in stillness he radiated an undeniable presence. He leaned forward, rolling a golf ball beneath his bare foot, like a cat toying with its prey.

She considered offering a handshake, but didn't want to interrupt his peculiar ritual. Instead, she settled into a chair, crossed her legs, and placed her notebook on her lap.

"You have a lovely home," she offered.

Sinclair gave a nod without looking at her.

So much for "anxious to meet her," she guessed.

Wisps of smoke curled upward, scented with oak. The dim light was intimate—like a small bistro, despite the grandeur.

Wes stepped forward with a tumbler of whisky for Sinclair. "Anything for you, Miss Bowman?"

She'd been so nervous before the interview, she hadn't eaten. Half a glass of wine would knock her flat. However, the big guy could carry her to that comfy chaise lounge and let her sleep it off. Then again, passing out might not make the best impression for the interview.

"Nothing, thank you." Jadene smiled politely.

Sinclair turned to Wes. "She's signed?"

Wes gave a firm nod.

They'd sent a non-disclosure attachment with the text. She'd perused the NDA—language she'd seen a thousand times working fraud cases. It instructed her not to discuss anything shared in this meeting with anyone. She returned the electronic form with her virtual signature, half expecting the entire ordeal to be a mix-up.

Sinclair leaned back, steepling his fingertips. His baritone voice finally addressed her. "I believe you know who I am?"

Sinclair Theodore Whitmore. Sixty-nine. Princeton grad, engineering. Worth north of $33 billion. He'd built two empires—one supplying microchips, the other manufacturing advanced aerospace machinery, rumored to lead the race in deep-space mining. One blog even claimed he'd developed a drill-bit alloy so dense, it was ten times stronger than diamond.

However, Sinclair's romantic ventures were less fortunate. Married and divorced three times, he once bought an island in the Caribbean for his second wife as a birthday gift—although court records later revealed he'd done it to keep her as far away from him as possible. His third wife didn't last a month and didn't receive an island.

He'd fathered three children from his first marriage. One daughter and two sons. Each a Princeton alum like himself, with two of them now company officers who ran the day-to-day operations of his technological empires. His youngest son was a mathematics professor at MIT.

"Yes, Mister Whitmore, I do," she said. As the two sat, a strange energy grew from Sinclair. He was preoccupied with something, and it wasn't her.

Pausing his game of foot golf, he motioned to the man in the tie. "And you've met Wesley Holt, trusted confidant and advisor."

Fascinating titles. Nowhere in them was anything like servant or butler. But from his size, the guy would have no trouble buttling anything.

He approached. "Please, call me Wes."

She didn't get a good look at him outside—the minefield of cobblestones in the driveway had demanded her attention. Wes was in his mid-thirties, handsome, and well-built, with neatly parted hair. Easily over six feet, with a jawline as sharp as his shirt collar.

She offered her hand again. "Jadene Bowman."

This time, he took her palm.

His grip was firm yet gentle. A pale scar ran from his thumb to his wrist—an odd contrast to his otherwise polished appearance. Scars held stories, and she'd seen enough to know the quiet ones were the ones to watch.

Wes caught her staring and released his grasp, moving to stand by the roaring hearth.

The room grew quiet.

Jadene assumed this was the time she should provide her qualifications for the interview. She opened the journal to fish out her credentialing and licensing information when Sinclair rose from his chair.

Fit, not frail. Hardened lines cut across his face. Despite his age, he moved like a man twenty years younger. Average height, but his posture was straight and strong. He didn't hunch or stoop—which many his age did as time caught up with them.

"Wes, a moment?" Sinclair said.

The two left her by the crackling fire and had a conversation on the room's far side.

They were likely discussing her. She didn't have the usual law enforcement pedigree—she was a civilian turned detective. Her palms moistened. It was dark outside and she was likely the final contender for whatever job this was. As seconds passed, though, it seemed Sinclair had made his decision and shortly they'd send her on her way.

Wes stepped to her side. "It was nice meeting you, Miss Bowman."

Her shoulders slumped. That was the shortest interview ever, but at least they were quick and polite. She offered a flat smile and counted her wins.

First, the invite wasn't a mistake. They knew her name, and no one tossed her into that giant fountain outside. She'd met Sinclair Whitmore. And although he'd only said a few words to her, at least one of them wasn't "asshole." Small victories.

She'd compliment Sinclair's lovely home again, thank them both for their time, and offer to see herself out of this giant maze. She slipped the notebook under an arm and uncrossed her legs.

Wes raised a palm. "No, no—I'm needed elsewhere." He glanced at Sinclair, voice lower. "Just remember—he's got a good heart."

Jadene stiffened. Was that a warning or a blessing? Before she could ask, the handsome Wes vanished from the room.

Sinclair returned to the area and reseated himself.

The fire crackled as Jadene bounced a knee. Flipping open her notebook, she withdrew her CV again and offered it to the sockless billionaire.

"I don't need that." He locked eyes with her. "You'd have never made it past the gates if I didn't know all about you."

Her breath caught—not from flattery, but from the eerie sense that her life had been read like a case file. Every failure logged. Nothing hidden.

She came to prove herself—but this felt like judgment.

FOUR

At first, Ellis thought he was dead. Bluish light lapped at the edges of his vision, murky and opaque, like the depths of an ocean trench. He was lost in a forest of messy thoughts. Was this the afterlife, heaven, hell, or someplace worse?

Chilly, dry air drew in and out of his lungs. Beneath him, something vibrated—clicking in a tempo he almost recognized. A steady hum, then a clack. Every few seconds.

If he was dead, maybe reincarnation was real. Would he come back as a tree frog or something more bizarre?

Numb. Weak. Limp. It was a dream he couldn't wake from—barely lucid with no control, like a puppet with its strings cut. His fingers twitched, but the response was distant—as if they no longer belonged to him.

The vibrations slowed.

A clang. A sudden shake. A whoosh of air. Someone, or something, drew near. The rank scent of stale cigarettes crept over him—sharp and biting.

Had he been abducted by chain-smoking aliens?

"Grab his legs."

Ghostly voices floated around him.

"Flip him on his stomach. Hold him steady."

Steady for what? Ellis tried to calm himself, but nothing made sense. His heartbeat was frantic. They wanted him still, not to move. His eyelids fluttered. Was this a hospital? Had he been in an accident? Did he fall? Had his heart finally fought back? Linda was always telling him no cigars and never more than one Scotch. Linda. Yes. He needed to call her—she'd be worried.

Cold hands pressed against his skin as the air shifted around him.

Sudden memories flashed, hazy and incomplete, like a broken reel of film flickering in and out of focus. The airport. The parking garage. A woman in an arm sling, slipping. The attendant in the hat. A circling van. That excruciating shock—the cut on his tongue—and then nothing.

The cigarette stink hit him again. Someone seized his wrist— rough hands, calloused. A needle, sharp and swift, pierced his skin.

"Can't give him too much." The smoldered stench of the man's breath hit Ellis like a punch. "Don't want to kill him."

The sting was real enough. But it was like he was trapped in someone else's body, disconnected from the pain. A firm grip held as an icy burn spread from the injection site, snaking through his arm. Christ in Crocs. A mystery drug. Not good.

"Nice and easy." The smoking man's gruff voice hung over him like a swinging blade, threatening to lower and slice him in half. What the hell had they injected him with?

Shadows swam, turning to blots. Then came the spins—slow at first, then gut-wrenching. Bitter metallic coated his tongue. Holy hell. Vertigo with a side of nasty.

"That should keep him."

Keep him? Keep him where? For how long? Was this a nightmare? He tried to move, but his limbs refused. Numbness seeped deeper, drowning him in helplessness. A wave of dread pooled in his gut. His breathing grew shallow. His mind clawed at consciousness, trying to break free, but everything pulled him further under.

Another whoosh of air. Something stiff and mechanical clicked, followed by a grinding rumble. The vibrations sounded again, and the world around him shifted.

He was weightless, tumbling through an endless pit. His thinking spiraled, lost in some strange unknown. But he wouldn't—couldn't give in. Not like this.

Images of Linda appeared in his messy mind. He wasn't done. Not yet. He had to claw his way out of whatever this was.

Somewhere beyond these shadows, dawn waited—with answers. An end to this bad dream.

He had to reach it, even if everything inside him screamed to give up.

FIVE

"Twenty-nine, college educated, never married." Sinclair's words came deliberate, like bullet points in a lecture.

Jadene slipped the résumé into her notebook, her grip tightening on the chair's armrest.

"You attended college on a swimming scholarship, competing through your junior year." His sharp gaze pinned her. "I understand you were excellent."

She had been—a lifetime ago—winning state in the 200 meter, even making Nationals. A memory flashed. Her mom's proud face, the podium beneath her feet. A lump grew in her throat.

"After earning your MBA, you worked in the private sector at a legal firm—contract management. But only for a handful of years?" He arched a brow. "You turned your back on your degreed career to pursue detective work?"

Jadene swallowed. She hadn't turned her back on it. She'd been laid off without warning. The email cited "right-sizing" and "streamlining," corporate jargon that still curdled her blood.

Yet, given the turmoil of her life at the time, shuffling through emails and pecking out PowerPoints became increasingly meaningless. She enjoyed legal research, sure, but she craved autonomy. A way to earn money where nobody could fire her when their quarterly numbers didn't add up.

At first, true-crime docs and old case files were a way to cope—a distraction. But over time, they sharpened her observation and gave her a lens to reinterpret the world. For her, this wasn't entertainment. It was a path forward.

A year ago, she earned her investigator's license and opened shop—just her, a cramped office, that gaudy neon sign, and big dreams. Though she wasn't sure she'd made the right decision leaving the nine-to-five world.

She straightened, turned from the fire, and provided her practiced answer to Sinclair. "It's something I wanted to do, and I saw it as an opportunity to challenge myself."

"Pretty gutsy," Sinclair said. "How's that working out? Is the thrilling world of private investigation everything you'd thought it could be?"

She winced, shifting in her chair. Business was not good.

The reality of the PI job wasn't at all the adventure she'd hoped for. It took time to build a reputation and generate a clientele. She understood that. But she promised herself that thrilling cases were just around the corner if she could keep her business afloat. Dicey surveillance. Missing persons. Chasing down a crafty executive who'd escaped with millions from the company coffers. Exciting cases, she often dreamt, would soon come her way. However, in eleven months, only one job had come close to stimulating.

A woman alleged her spouse was cheating. After tracking the husband's phone and tailing him for eight mind-numbing nights, she found that his excuses for working late turned out to be so he could drink beer and play video games with his buddies until 3 a.m.

Weirdly, rather than laughing in relief, the young man's wife screamed, cried, and started packing his things. Jadene figured the poor guy would have been better off if he was caught with another woman.

Her other clients were businesses looking to outsource worker depositions to avoid paying claims. Or, they wanted her to claw through paperwork and trace missing funds and inventory.

But thus far, there'd been no espionage. No suspicious characters in dark suits to follow. No hidden staircases. And no climactic crime reveal.

Ironically, she still spent most of her days clicking through emails and shuffling through paperwork. The money was awful, and if something didn't change soon, she'd be done.

Despite the warm fire, a chill lashed her naked ankles.

"It's… challenging," she offered.

Sinclair stroked his chin. "Same shit with a different view?" he said dryly.

Her stare broke. That was precisely how she felt, and it disturbed her deeply. Had she become a paper-pusher with a slightly nicer business card? Did she rush into this whole thing? Had she overreached? Had grief pushed her into it?

It was the same shit, and soon, she'd have no view.

Jadene's doubts hung in the air as Sinclair eyed her, silent.

Six

If there was a job here, Jadene wanted it—needed it. She stared at the rug, waiting for him to speak.

Sinclair looked her over, then cleared his throat.

"My comment was insensitive," he said. "Running a business is difficult, as I know." He grimaced. "Please understand that social warmth does not come easy for me."

Jadene lifted her gaze.

"One of the ex-wives called it emotional detachment." He raised his hand sharply. "Or, her shitbag lawyer did."

She huffed a chuckle.

"But my late father taught me to get right to the point, that emotions and feelings cloud decision-making." He kicked the golf ball with his barefoot, and rose.

Jadene feigned a smile, guessing Sinclair's father had been a real piece of work.

"That philosophy allowed me to make an industry but not many friends," he confessed. "I've always been more comfortable with nuts and bolts than people. Which is why these kinds of one-on-one meetings are usually the duty of Wes."

She offered a slow nod.

Sinclair made his way to a bookshelf, fingered a volume, and tilted its hardcover to inspect its spine. He let the book fall back with a soft thump, then moved on to another section, plucking out a hardcover and thumbing through its pages.

"Science and engineering are my comfort zones." He peered down at the book. "But let's try to find a middle."

Jadene wasn't sure if his statement was aimed at her or the pages he was studying.

"Chemistry intrigues me." He squinted—as if connecting an intricate web in his mind. "Like how simple elements shape our daily tools."

He was switching subjects, albeit to a random one, but the change allowed her to put his earlier insult aside, and refocus on why she was here in the first place.

Paging through the novel, he squinted. "The common pencil, for instance. Do you know what the first type was made of?"

She frowned. "A writing pencil?"

"Yes."

Was he testing her?

"It was made of lead," she said. "No, wait, carbon."

"Close," Sinclair grinned. "Graphite. And modern pencils are made of graphene—but we don't need to get into that."

Why pencils? Strange topic, but he was an aerospace engineer. His mind worked differently. She'd try to hold interest in whatever subject he spoke about and do her best to keep up with him.

Sinclair turned a page and studied the words.

"While graphite does look similar, pencils were never made of lead," he said.

Why tell her this?

He examined the ceiling. "And did you know that in the mid-18th century, an Englishman discovered that rubbing caoutchouc—a milky tree sap—over penciled graphite marks completely removed them from the paper?"

Jadene did a double-take. "He invented the eraser?"

Sinclair bowed. "Correct."

Okay, but where was this all going?

Sinclair continued, "As people embraced this new way to rub out their mistakes, the act became so widespread that the tree sap itself was renamed."

"The tree sap?" She blinked. "Changed its name to what?"

Sinclair smirked. "To rubber, of course."

A bit nerdish but interesting. But why the lesson?

"Though beyond erasing pencil marks, and a handful of other uses, rubber had limitations." He stepped toward her. "It was unstable, cracked, and melted with fluctuations in temperature. But this is where our elements come into play." He lifted the book and tapped its cover. "A twist of fate, really. A failed hardware salesman accidentally dropped a sulfur-rubber mix onto a hot stove, triggering the discovery of vulcanization."

From pencils to a chemistry lesson. She kept his gaze but was lost on why he was telling her all this.

"Simple chance can thrust us forward." He circled the rug. "And durable rubber had many applications, car tires and such. However, the first was to replace the soles of shoes. Their bottoms at the time were often made of hardwood and leather. With this new, softer rubber on the soles, there was no more clickety-clack." He grinned, eyeing her shoes.

Jadene's cheeks reddened. She should never have worn her heels. He was poking fun at her with this long-winded story. Or was he?

Sinclair went on, "This vulcanized, gummy elastic created a much quieter shoe." His finger shot up. "Straightaway, police adopted the footwear to patrol the streets—undetected by criminals." He curled the corner of his mouth. "And this is how your profession got its moniker."

She drew in a sharp breath. She had no idea, but now it made total sense. She nearly shouted, "Gumshoe?"

"Very good." He snapped the book shut. "These days, we use more synthetics—styrene and whatnot—and precise heating methods. Those rubber-soled shoes have become much quieter." He smirked. "They also have a new name."

She smiled ear to ear. "Sneakers?"

Sinclair winked, reshelving the book. "Just a bit of fun."

Jadene was astonished. Had he gone into all of that just for her? She'd likely never remember any of his story, but a sense of ease came over her for the first time since coming here. Sinclair was complex. He could be cold, nerdy, and charming all at once. She was fascinated.

The billionaire strolled to a side table, opened a tiny tin, and withdrew a weathered paper from its insides. He scanned the old document, returning to his chair next to her by the fire.

He looked at her, his expression hardening. "Now, let's see if you can be the great gumshoe we both want you to be."

SEVEN

The fog in his mind lifted, Ellis's sight sharpened, absorbing his surroundings. A wave of nausea curled his gut. He took a steady breath to calm himself. Either they hadn't given him too much, or the troops in his liver were mounting a heroic defense.

Above, a germicidal LED—the lab-and-hospital kind that kills bacteria—bathed four metal walls in bluish light. A steady hum came from a built-in, box-sized cooler in front.

He was not dead. He was not in purgatory.

He was inside a moving icebox.

And someone wanted him cold, quiet, and forgotten.

The road beneath clacked at its joints.

Behind his back, a nylon cord dug into his wrists.

Those men at the airport—that asshole attendant and his van-driving buddy—had snatched him. They'd put him in the back of this vehicle. But this was no standard van. It was a refrigerated truck.

The van's freezing compartment was the size of a garden shed, with metal shelving fixed to its squared walls. The type used to transport those shitty airline meals, he guessed. Now, he was trapped inside its chilly prison.

The tires hummed along the roadway.

Turning sidelong, he attempted to loosen the bindings, but they wouldn't budge. A stinging throbbed his forearm. An awkward inspection revealed two puncture marks on his skin.

If it were propofol, he'd remember nothing. No, those bastards pricked him with something else. Some other sedative. Midazolam or fentanyl. Street shit, no doubt.

He wobbled to one knee, pressing his back to the shelves. He ran his fingers over the cold, hard wire, searching for a loose spine or sharp edge.

They'd snagged his fleece and duffel. A void in his rear pocket told him those assheads had also taken his wallet. His muscles tightened. If he'd only been able to make it to his car, he'd have shown these kidnapping clowns the business end of his Glock.

Frosty, thin metal bars met his fingertips.

Why had they taken him? What was the motive? If this were a typical mugging, they'd have swiped his wallet and keys, and he'd be nursing a black eye and a few sore ribs right now. No, they wanted him. But why?

The vehicle slowed.

Should he shout? Fat chance anyone would hear him. The insulated walls inside this van had to be four inches thick or more. On top of that, the corners were gasket-sealed to keep in the cold. A panic struck. Shit, he'd better conserve his air.

The van turned.

The clacking roadway went silent.

The ride grew smoother. He figured they'd left the interstate. But where were they going? How long had he been out? Hours? A day? It couldn't be a day, could it? If so, he'd be a popsicle by now.

On his backside, he found a shelf edge. He rose, hunched, and scraped the nylon cord against a nubbed spike.

The truck braked rapidly, throwing him off balance.

Ellis tumbled forward, striking his head on the chiller.

An icy pain jolted the side of his skull. Blood dripped.

Fuck. A kidnapping and a concussion—awesome.

But the cooler took the worst of it. A massive dent marred its side.

Thud, thud.

The condenser's fan grated inside the cooler, blades hammering for space.

Warm blood dribbled down Ellis's cheek.

The thumping stopped. Smoke grew from the chiller, snaking upward into the UV light. Something popped. A yellow plume flared from the fan's grille.

The cooler buzzed its final tune. More smoke rose from the mechanism, gathering on the truck's ceiling.

Ellis was in trouble. This wasn't a lot of space.

"Hey!" he yelled. "Hey! There's smoke!"

The vehicle kept moving.

He kicked the van's wall.

No response.

Burning fumes floated about.

"Hey! Hey!" he screamed.

Smoke billowed from the cooler.

Ellis coughed, gagging for breath. He couldn't stand fully upright but shuffled back, using the little space he had. With seven feet of runway, he threw himself forward, slamming a shoulder into the wall.

The crash threw him off his feet.

The truck came to a stop.

Ellis pressed his cheek to the floorboards, sucking in shallow breaths beneath the smoke.

A rattle and the tug of a lever came from outside.

The truck's rear hatch creaked open.

Hands bound, he gasped for the fresh air.

"The fuck was that?" a man said.

Ellis tried to focus on the face, but it was far too dark to profile the man's features. However, it sounded like stretch—the asshole parking attendant in the hat.

Outside, the dashed line of the roadway glowed in the van's brake lights. There were no cat's eyes—no reflectors—dotting the asphalt. They were on a two-lane route. Unfortunately, he didn't see any street lights or signs.

They were somewhere remote.

"Fucking smoke?" said the other man. "Damn fire in there or what?"

"Yes!" Ellis yelled from the floor. "Luckily, I'm still breathing, you dipshits!"

Behind his two shadowy captors, bright lights beamed.

A vehicle appeared and slowed as it neared the van.

The two turned toward the headlights.

Ellis wrenched his wrists, but the cord wouldn't budge. He rose to a knee, focusing on the duo hindering his escape.

Their attention held on the approaching car.

His chest drummed. The van's rear was two or three feet high—enough of a drop for surprise. Should he charge? If he timed things right, he could bowl both men over before they turned around. But would it be enough? Without the use of his arms, could he make it to the other vehicle and safety?

Should he call out for rescue? Would the approaching driver be smart enough to stay in their car and avoid getting tangled with these two idiots?

Brakes squealed. The oncoming vehicle was a large, older truck. It stopped several lengths behind the van.

Through the open hatchway, Ellis glared at its lights.

The other vehicle's door opened.

Ellis scrambled to his feet, stumbling forward. Tall trees stood in every direction. They'd taken him far out into the boonies. Likely, nobody else was around for miles.

A shadowy figure approached—whoever it was had no idea what they were walking into.

Ellis had no choice. He planted a foot and readied to charge.

The distant man hollered, "He's awake?"

The shorter kidnapper nodded.

Ellis dropped his head.

A silhouette hovered in the headlights. "We're almost there," the newcomer grunted. "Put his ass in the cab with you two."

EIGHT

A flicker crossed Sinclair's face as he studied the crumpled paper.

Jadene settled into the chair, watching him closely. Was that a love note? Did he need her to find somebody?

Sinclair took a slow drink and turned to her.

"My father ran a small grocery store in the middle of nowhere, Pennsylvania," he said.

She'd learned about his current corporations, but nothing about his past. Most of what she'd found online was unsourced, tabloid nonsense about his personal life.

"Believe it or not, had it not been for my scholarship, I never would have gone to college myself," he said. "You see, I do not come from money."

She couldn't wrap her mind around it. The estate, this room—she assumed a large part of it came from generational wealth.

"My father wanted me to take on the family business, of course." He chuckled. "He tolerated college but considered it an interruption."

"An interruption? But you went to Princeton?"

Sinclair lowered his chin. "I could have invented fire, but a father's want for his son to take over his life's work is a strong tradition."

"What did you do?"

"After college, I came back home and made good." His eyebrows raised. "I woke up at 5 a.m., minded the shipments, kept the shelves stocked, and worked with the suppliers… until my father died of a sudden heart attack a year later."

A stab hit her chest. "I'm so sorry."

"It was fate." Sinclair shrugged. "My father was a good man, and there's nothing wrong with a noble life. But I had other dreams." He tilted the whisky to his lips. "So, I tallied up the assets, two trucks and a half-mortgaged store, and sold everything."

She didn't know this about him. "You did?"

"At twenty-five, my focus had shifted. Technology called to me, and I'd already filed a few patents." He scratched a cheek. "I was a risk-taker. And, as you know, only when we take risks do we find out what we're truly made of. Leap of faith, as it were."

She gave a slow nod. Her leap of faith would have her sleeping in her car before long.

Sinclair set the whisky aside. "I put every last cent into the development of semiconductors."

She inched forward. "Right. I read about this. Your components revolutionized the cellular industry."

He laughed. "Well, that revolution came at the expense of many, many sleepless nights. You must understand, at the time, there were dozens of R&D companies like mine all over the world, vying for the business of maybe three emerging cellular companies."

It was strange for her that there was a time when cell phones didn't exist. "Really?" she said.

Sinclair swept a hand outward. "It was a goddamn race. One where the winner got everything, and the losers went bankrupt."

She couldn't imagine that kind of pressure. Oddly, none of this appeared to be part of the interview, but she was learning so much about the man.

"But you succeeded, and it paid off?"

"It did. And I've parlayed since. But all I have worked for, and my father before me, I'm not positive… it's not…" He gripped the torn sheet, lowering his head.

The fire crackled.

"In many ways, this skipped a generation," he said.

"Skipped?" She perched on the edge of her chair. "How do you mean?"

Sinclair's gaze lifted. "My father, Nathaniel, was a good man, but consumed by his store. I didn't spend a lot of time with him." His forehead creased. "And he and his father, Arthur, never spoke to one another."

"Your father and grandfather?"

"They had a major falling out."

"A fight? About what?" she pressed.

He sipped, then set the tumbler on the table. "I was never clear on the matter."

That answer was curious and she made a note. "Did you and your father ever discuss it?"

"No. It all happened long before I was born." He returned his gaze to the flames.

"Did you know your grandfather well?"

Sinclair's normally confident words came low and cracked. "I met Arthur only once… on his deathbed, when I was seven years old."

"I'm so sorry." Another stab hit her chest and she cupped her hands. Yet something else struck her. While he'd branded his father's death fate, his expression was a blend of grief and regret—as if the loss of his grandfather had cost him something. Something he wanted to reclaim.

"You'd said the incident skipped a generation," she said. "What did you mean?"

Sinclair stared into the flames. "What I share comes from Arthur."

She blinked, startled. "Your grandfather?"

"Yes." He hunched, as though burdened by an invisible weight.

He was upset over whatever this was. She tried to compile the facts. A fight between a father and son, the basis of which Sinclair claimed not to know about. And this whole story—this mystery—hinged on a single encounter Sinclair had at age seven.

"Some of this could be difficult to understand," he confessed.

Jadene wasn't sure where this was heading, making it hard to form the right questions. From his expression, this was a past he'd not revealed to many—and she didn't want to push him.

Ice clinked in Sinclair's glass. "Arthur was a telegraph operator in the service. Overseas, during the war."

She pursed her lips. The term "the war" didn't exactly narrow things down for a 29-year-old. But she didn't want to seem stupid and tried to work around the gap.

"Oh, where was your grandfather stationed?"

"At one of the outposts," came Sinclair's reply.

So much for the indirect approach, she guessed.

"But when I met Arthur, for the first and last time, it was under sad circumstances." His eyes—which moments before had held hers so intently—shifted downward. "Arthur was not well. Mentally, you understand. He was drifting in and out."

Jadene scribbled in her notebook. His grandfather could have been suffering from a severe fever or dementia.

Studying the patterns in the carpet, Sinclair continued. "Nathaniel, my father, for reasons I never fully understood, found it unbearable to be in the same room with Arthur. Even in those last moments." Fingers brushed his chin. "In my grandfather's final hours, my father told me to say goodbye to a man I'd never known."

A knot tightened in Jadene's stomach. A child, so young and naïve, thrust into the face of mortality was crushing. She wanted to reach out and hug the barefoot billionaire.

But Sinclair's gaze lingered on the rug, lost in the haunting memory.

"I was alone in that room," he said. "Arthur's chest rose and fell with each rattling breath. I was young. I didn't understand death. I didn't... I couldn't know." His voice cracked. "Arthur, this strange man... he lay there, so still. I was confused. I wondered if I should try to wake him up."

He must've been petrified. She clenched her fists. How could a father leave a boy like that? She opened her mouth—then closed it. Emotional detachment? It was no wonder he kept people at arm's length.

The fire snapped and hissed. Sinclair's next words came rushed, as if trying to get through the moment.

"The room was quiet except for his gasps. I approached his side. I wanted to touch him. I don't remember why. Maybe to see if he was still warm? I don't know. It was like a force drew me to him."

A chill coursed through Jadene.

"My grandfather's wrinkled, gray cheeks. I reached out..."

Her chest tightened, taking in his words.

"A heave. A cough. And then his eyes sprang open and he grabbed my wrist."

Jadene swallowed.

"I didn't know if he knew who I was. He uttered: Loyal, not lost. Mumbling it over and over. The desperation in his face, I cannot describe."

The notebook slipped from her lap, crashing to the floor.

Sinclair pinched the document between his fingers. "He slapped this into my hand and made me promise something."

She brought her fingers to her chest. "He made you promise what?"

Sinclair pressed the crumpled half-sheet into her palm, his eyes dark. "He made me promise I would find this."

NINE

Squeezed between two assholes in the van's cockpit was no better. Ellis had traded coldness and suffocating smoke for the stench of body odor and silence.

The vehicle rumbled down the dark road, jarring him with each pothole. He sat at an uncomfortable incline with his hands still bound behind his back. In the van's sideview mirrors appeared headlights from the pickup truck, piloted by the man who'd ordered him inside this unpleasant cab. Ellis didn't see the guy's face, nor could he clearly describe the vehicle. They'd dragged him from that freezing prison into his seat by the scruff of his shirt.

As for these two idiots, he'd already met one of them. The tall parking attendant in the hat was crammed alongside him in the passenger seat. He scratched at his scruff, said nothing, and stared at the road.

The driver—he'd never seen him before. Twenties, buzz-cut, medium-build. He wore a black jacket like his partner, with dirty jeans, and desperately needed a shower. He also liked to pick his nose when he thought Ellis wasn't watching. The moron was also wearing his company identification badge, which dangled by a plastic lanyard around his neck. The ID didn't have his name, but a logo showed he worked for *Tress Food Services, LLC.*

Ellis had no idea where they were going, but no other vehicles except the pickup tailing them were in sight. The road ahead was a black void—no signs, no mile markers. He'd seen a stop sign twenty minutes back, and now the asphalt's yellow divider was fading into nothing. He suspected more potholes would emerge before long.

Tall pine trees lined the sides of this forgotten route. He guessed they'd traveled south from Hartsfield and were now far from the city where cell coverage became questionable. Not that it mattered—he'd lost his damn phone long before this all began.

But the big questions gnawed at him. Why was he taken? Was it revenge? An old bust coming back to haunt him? During his two decades on the force, he'd put away his share of shitbags. Any one of them could be behind this. However, figuring out which of those jackals might have it in for him was a lineup longer than the pub queue for urinals on Saint Patrick's Day.

If they were driving him out here to kill him, they could have dumped his body miles ago. Tossed his corpse in the trees anywhere along this road—where nobody would ever find his remains.

He gazed through the windshield, out at the black road, and raised an eyebrow. Were they looking for a clearing? A place where giant buzzards could circle in to pick the meat from his bones—and nobody would ever find his remains.

Whatever this was, it was personal. Ellis was sure he would never return alive. Nobody drives a victim miles and miles out into the middle of nowhere, beats them up, and then drives them back home. This wasn't dinner at the in-laws.

And it left Ellis curious. Why the long outing? They didn't want him dead—yet. Full of questions, he tried to get chummy.

"Hey guys, where we headed?"

The driver grumbled, "Fuck you."

Laughter erupted from the man mashed against his side.

Ellis fixed his gaze on the empty stretch of asphalt. He was a retired cop, living a quiet life in the suburbs with his wife. The PI gig was supposed to be a side hustle—something to keep him occupied in retirement. Good money, but he and his bride were doing fine on his pension. They'd whittled their life down to the basics, weren't trying to impress anyone, and just enjoyed each other's simple company. They had a modest three-bedroom with a hot tub and grill—amenities they used occasionally in the summer. It was a no-frills life, but lately, he hadn't enjoyed any of it.

Cases stacked faster than he could close them. For every job he wrapped, two more came crashing in. Linda was always saying he cared too much about his clients for his own good, but Ellis couldn't help himself. It was just who he was. Still, she was right—he needed to slow down.

He was planning on surprising his wife with a week in Puerto Rico this winter. Linda loved the ocean, so he'd planned to splurge on a four-star hotel right on the beach. Besides, it'd been years since they'd taken a real holiday together.

However, he was far from the sand and enjoying a cold beer. Though, he considered, moments ago, he was asphyxiating on smoke in the back of this wagon—so things were definitely looking up.

The food van's console contained no clock. It was equipped only with analog indicators for speed, fuel, oil, and other basic gauges. Cheap components likely standard on every airport service vehicle, Ellis figured.

Outside, there was no moon, and blackness enveloped everything. Now that his mind was clear, he figured he'd been confined in the rear cooler for two or three hours since his abduction from the airport. But there was no reliable way to tell time or confirm his hunch that they were heading south. And without any markers, he couldn't pinpoint their location.

Neither man beside him had a weapon he could see, but the spent taser they'd used to subdue him sat on the dash, its wires hastily coiled around its base. Nothing in the cab was suitable to start an attack with.

However, even if he could get free of his restraints, launch the parking attendant out the door, and overtake the driver with an elbow across the nose, that still left whoever was following them in the pickup. And that person might be armed, making any mutiny pointless.

A side road appeared in the headlights. A passage split the tree line. The van slowed. The unpaved path was muddy but not saturated.

As smelly turned onto it, Ellis wished he had the use of his hands so he could torque the wheel and flip the truck. But even if he could, then what? They'd drag him into the woods and make him dig his own grave, that's what. No, it was better to play this out. See where they were taking him and what they wanted.

The van bounced down the grimy road as the pickup behind followed. The two vehicles slowly snaked up the dark hillside for several hundred yards until the tree line broke again.

Ahead, dark vines draped a dwelling. It was an old cottage—a hunting cabin. Made of wood and exposed cinderblock, the isolated lodge appeared abandoned. The van plowed through a patch of tall grass and stopped.

Buzz-cut and his sour stench got out while Ellis and his seatmate remained inside.

A man materialized in the van's headlights. It was the pickup truck driver. Wiry build, he wore muddy work boots and carried a long knife.

Ellis wasn't positive, but a second person, possibly moved about the cabin's dark entry.

"Bring him out," the pickup truck man shouted.

The passenger door opened. The parking attendant grabbed Ellis by the neck, jerking him from his seat.

When his toes reached the ground, his abductor torqued his wrists upward, bending him at the waist. He was frog-marched to the front of the van. Time to meet the boss, he guessed.

A hand clawed his hair, yanking him upright.

The pickup truck driver, the two from the van, and Ellis stood in a wide circle in front of the headlights.

"Safe and sound," Smelly said. "Just like you wanted."

"Yeah." Parking attendant tugged Ellis by the scalp. "Where's our cash?"

A blinding flash came from the cabin's doorway.

Smelly hit the ground.

Ellis buckled at the knees.

The second bullet struck the parking attendant in the forehead with perfect aim. No last words. Just a red hole and dead air.

Ellis closed his eyes and said goodbye to Linda.

A rough hand hoisted his chin.

"Now you know not to fuck with us."

Ellis held silent, his constrained hands trembling with adrenaline.

The wiry man raised his long knife, spun him around, and sliced through the bindings at his wrists.

"If you run, I'll kill you. Got me?"

A shiver shot down Ellis's spine.

The man yanked him back around to face him.

"Not gonna say it again. Do you got me?"

Fear needling his core, Ellis gave a slow nod.

They'd dragged him here, to parts unknown, for reasons he didn't understand, and now two men lay dead at his feet.

The wiry man over him slid the knife back into its sheath. "C'mon, dickhead, you've got work to do," he said.

TEN

"Careful. It's very fragile," Sinclair cautioned.

The yellowed paper crinkled between Jadene's fingertips. A musty scent rose from the document, and the bitter tang of an old penny coated her tongue.

Almost a third of the sheet's upper half was torn away. What remained, though, contained faded, typed lettering.

TELEGRAMM   KRAK (tear)

NL 17 JAN 1945

URGENT STOP BROKEN CASTLE STOP DAKOTA FREE BLUE STOP WHISPERING WEST STOP BAY OF THE MONTEBELLO STOP LITTLE RANCH STOP HERMANN STOP DOUBLE SAFE HAVEN STOP POWODZENIA

She'd heard of these old wired communiqués but never seen one. A physical telegram, printed longwise, across the width of the old, torn sheet.

She pointed to the four letters in the upper right corner.

"What's that word?"

"Kraków, Poland," Sinclair said, his voice measured. "That's where this dispatch originated."

"What is this? I mean…?"

"It's a coded message, intercepted during the war."

She read the words again. An 80-year-old telegram? None of the phrases made any immediate sense, and she wasn't even sure where to start.

Sinclair lifted from his chair, stepping barefoot across the carpet. He stopped and eyed her.

"Before we move on to the next part, I remind you of the NDA and your confidentiality."

She was already bound to secrecy as an investigator. She would never break it—not in this case, not for any client.

"Many of the details I've already shared have not been disclosed to anyone but you." He clasped his hands. "And should I hear a whisp of them in the media, you'll face a team of lawyers who share the collective humor of a hemorrhoid."

She fought a chuckle. But she'd assumed this was an interview? What was he saying? What was happening? The fluttering in her stomach returned.

He glared at her. "Do you understand?"

She nodded.

"I need to hear you say it."

With a dry mouth, she managed, "I understand."

"Good." Sinclair fixed his hands to his hips, his words coming rapid-fire. "You're here because I need someone who won't quit. Who's sharp, relentless."

Goosebumps spread across her arms. Was she hungry and dedicated? Yes and yes. Would she quit? She didn't have that choice. But on its face, the telegram's message made no sense. It was almost a century old with bizarre phraseology. She was already struggling, trying to figure out how to decipher it.

Sinclair's chin rose. "You're young, intelligent, and attractive."

Usually, those bullet points would have made her cheeks redden. But too much was swirling in her mind right now for embarrassment.

"And I believe you'll do well if you accept my offer."

She jerked her head. "Your offer?"

"I will give you five days."

"Five days?"

"Five days to bring me answers."

"Answers?" She winced. He had to be out of his Ivy League mind.

"I hid this note from my father for decades. I never brought up the subject of Arthur because it was too explosive. But I need…" he paused. "I must understand."

"You want me to find—?"

He shot up a hand. "I don't expect you to solve the riddle, no. Not even I could do that."

Jadene was confused.

"I need to know who Arthur Whitmore really was."

This was about Arthur? Was it some kind of family secret? And if he couldn't solve the riddle himself, what did he expect of her? Before she could ask any of these, Sinclair fired off his terms.

"Now, to our deal." He paced the rug. "For the next five days, this is all you do. No distractions. Can you commit?"

Jadene straightened in the chair. At the moment, she had absolutely no other cases. Sadly, not even a call to return.

She flashed a wide smile. "You'll have my full attention."

"Excellent. Now, as to your fee. To cover your time and expenses, I will pay you $2,000 each day."

That was four times her usual charge. She could sure use that glass of wine now.

"I cannot emphasize the importance here." He pointed to the document. "The answers speak to the foundation, to my family's reputation."

She narrowed her eyes. "I don't understand."

Sinclair flexed his cheek muscles. "Digging into Arthur's character. I know this won't be an easy case. I've asked you not to quit, not to give up. And I've told you how vital it is to me that you don't." He raised a finger. "Yet, I've always found if I want the most from someone, I must offer an incentive."

"An incentive?" She blinked. "What did you have—?"

"We'll talk numbers when the time is right." He took a slow sip. "And if you do what I ask, you will be well compensated."

Sweat gathered around her neckline.

Sinclair paced to a side table. There, he drew out a second sheet of paper, though this one was white and untorn.

"This is a duplication of that message, as I will keep the original." He exchanged documents with her.

The photocopy Jadene received was indeed exact. It even showed the faint lines of the original's upper tear. She scanned the telegram's words, hoping some meaning, some phrase would make sense. But nothing did.

Across the room, a figure appeared in the passageway. It was Wes Holt.

Sinclair refolded the yellowed document and placed it into its tin. "I'm off to London tomorrow for business. When I return, we will meet again."

She stood. "How do I reach you if I need to?"

Sinclair motioned to the man in the tie. "Leave a message with Wes. He'll know how to find me."

She still had so many questions but gathered her things as the suited man came to her side.

"If you need, my resources are at your disposal," Sinclair said. "But the clock of your investigation starts tomorrow morning."

"Miss Bowman." Wes extended a palm. "Won't you please come with me?"

Jadene approached Wes as Sinclair returned to the hearth.

"I'll see you at the end of the week," Sinclair said.

Wes escorted her toward the arched passage.

"If there's more to that message…" Sinclair called, his voice softer now. "Then maybe there's more to him than I ever understood."

Jadene slowed near the threshold. This wasn't just about decoding a telegram. It was a man reaching back through decades of silence, trying to make sense of someone he never really knew. Maybe trying to understand him. Maybe just trying to look him in the eye.

Sinclair settled by the fire, nudged the white ball under his foot, and resumed his quiet game.

"You'll hear from me soon," she said.

ELEVEN

The air was thick with the scent of decaying leaves and damp earth. A blinding flashlight shone on Ellis's face.

"Both of them. C'mon, let's go!" the man shouted.

With effort, Ellis hooked his arms under the corpse's armpits. The smooth fabric of the man's polyester jacket was slick against his skin. He dragged the heavy body backward through a thicket of tall, thorny palmettos to a ridge, the tiny spikes slicing at his limbs.

At the cliff's edge, he gave a quick nod before heaving the lifeless man over the side, down into the steep gully. The body barreled through the wild foliage, snapping branches, rustling leaves, and rolling down the uneven terrain until it ended with a horrible thud.

"Now the other!" came the command.

The flashlight beamed on the second body. Ellis returned to the area, his heart pounding with exhaustion. Bending to a knee, he fixed his grip and hauled the deceased parking attendant down the same thorny path. He offered a nod of respect, shoved the body over the cliff, and the same sickening echoes rose from the ravine as it tumbled to a halt.

Grateful for the cover of night, he was spared the sight of the carnage below. He guessed the ravine was at least thirty feet deep, and wondered if he would be joining those two before long.

Drenched in sweat, Ellis took a moment to catch his breath. Even under the stars, the southern air was a stifling 85 degrees with oppressive humidity. He wiped the wetness from his forehead with the bottom of his dirty shirt, wondering what was in store for him next.

"Get your ass back here," the wiry man barked, aiming his flashlight in Ellis's eyes. His voice was raspy, punctuated by loud snorts as he cleared his nostrils.

Ellis still hadn't seen his face. But the man wore jeans—not fancy designer ones. No, these were old Levis. On his feet were well-used steel toe boots, and the rattle of keys came from his hip.

The two dead men who'd kidnapped him from the airport had worked there. At least the driver had, but Ellis would bet the pair. They'd become disposable once they'd completed their mission and brought him out here. Whoever fired the gun from the cabin's doorway showed no reluctance.

Ellis trudged through the bushes, blood trickling from scratches on his arms and neck. His captor shined the flashlight in his eyes. As Ellis passed, the jerk struck him mid-spine with the butt end of his knife. Ellis crumpled to the ground.

His attacker chuckled.

From below, Ellis caught sight of the pickup driver's face— mustached, about twenty-five, wearing a silvery oval belt buckle he probably never went without. In his hand was a serrated buck knife.

"Get your ass up!"

Exhausted, the coolness of the earth was nice. If Ellis had the strength, he'd wrench this shitbag's ankle, yank him to the ground next to him, and force-feed that oversized crotch medallion down his throat. But he rose slow, the ache in his back smarting from the jab.

Belt Buckle directed with his knife. "Let's go, dickhead."

Without a word, the two trudged back to the run-down cabin. Ellis scanned the area, taking in everything he could in the darkness.

The airport food van remained parked in the muddy drive, looking as out of place as a tuxedo at a dive bar. Adjacent to that vehicle sat an old Ford Bronco—not a pickup—weathered and worn, with freshly bent grass behind its tires. It was the same vehicle that had followed them from the airport, driven by the Belt Buckle-wearing asshole behind him. There didn't appear to be any other vehicles in the area.

As they approached the cabin's doorway, the flat of the buck knife slapped Ellis on the shoulder.

"Inside, now!"

Ellis turned the rusty knob, and the wooden door squeaked open. Inside was a wooden table with two chairs in the main room, a stove and sink against the far wall, and three doors—two on his left, one on his right. A bath and two bedrooms, he guessed. It was the standard configuration for every creepy cabin he'd ever been inside. Strewn about were several cardboard boxes, some open, others sealed with bands of duct tape.

The knife pricked his backside. Ellis shot forward half a step.

"Over there." Belt Buckle commanded him to a door, and Ellis entered. It was a bedroom, but instead of a bed with soft pillows and a comforter, there was something unusual. A cage, roughly four feet in height, constructed entirely of rebar. It was large enough to hold a bear—or a human.

"Get in—now."

With the knife at his back, Ellis crouched and stumbled inside. There wasn't enough headroom to stand. Behind him came the screech of metal. The hinged rebar door clanged shut. Belt Buckle fixed a shiny padlock to its latch.

"That should keep you, dickhead." Nicotine stains blotched his toothy smile.

Two men were dead. Shot and dumped into a ravine. Ellis had been a cop for twenty years—he'd seen worse. But not like this. Not as the one disposing of the bodies. His hands stank of blood—and of guilt he hadn't asked for.

He dropped his head, gut clenched. Hunger gnawed at him, thirst burned, and his limbs trembled with fatigue. He was trapped—caged, hell-and-gone from civilization.

He had to find a way out. He had to get back to Linda.

TWELVE

Jadene's downtown apartment catered to young professionals, with comings and goings at all hours. She'd see other residents in passing, supply a wave or a quick hello, but nothing beyond that. When she'd moved in after college, she'd convinced herself that the lodgings were only temporary. That was six years ago.

Her place had a bed, a kitchen table—used chiefly for drying her delicates. She also had a small desk for her computer. The apartment was relatively inexpensive for the area, but it had a large pool—mainly unused—and offered keyed access at any hour.

After her morning swim, she showered and spot-shaved. As usual, she didn't bother with breakfast. She slipped into a light-blue sundress, grabbed her laptop, and headed out.

Last night, after the meeting with Sinclair, she'd raced back to her place and attempted several queries using different internet search engines. However, despite pecking at her laptop until 2 a.m., she'd made no progress.

Little Ranch? Texas, and thousands of results. *Dakota Free Blue?* A bunch of links for health food and health insurance. Every isolated phrase was like this, returning page after page of nonsense onto her screen.

Outcomes using only single words were so varied that getting anywhere without more context was impossible. She tried mixing and matching phrases and words, thinking those might be a code within a code. But after each try, the search engine gobbled up her input, and the results were unkind.

The first line, *Broken Castle*, made no sense—just as the rest of the passages. Still, she wondered if it referred to an actual castle. Surprisingly, she'd learned, Kraków had several medieval structures, and she browsed through a bevy of photos, but soon grew weary and concluded it was likely a waste of time. With only a few days to work this case, she couldn't afford time-consuming rabbit holes like this.

So far, the only meaningful word in the message was *Powodzenia*, a Polish term meaning "Good Luck." Fitting for the time, it was a typical farewell between Allied forces during World War II. But it didn't take a PI to solve that riddle. Any six-year-old with a tablet could have done it—and Sinclair Whitmore would expect much more for his $10,000.

Leaving her apartment, a mile's walk took her to the business district. Bowman Investigations was sandwiched between Sean's Vape Shoppe and Pay-As-You-Gab-Mobile.

Before she'd moved in, the space had sat vacant for over a year. During that time, her mindful landlord, Stan Roseman, had closed the air vents to save on heating and cooling during its long vacancy. This left the uncirculated 400-square-foot space stinking like an old basement. It had taken her a full week to clear the cobwebs, paint the walls, and scrub down the sea-blue carpet.

Now, the candled aroma of Tiki Paradise filled the office—a fragrance reminiscent of an exotic vacation she'd never had time or money to take.

Once inside, she made her way to her desk, plugged in her laptop, and scanned the telegram's photocopy for the thousandth time.

TELEGRAMM   KRAK (tear)
NL 17 JAN 1945
URGENT STOP BROKEN CASTLE STOP DAKOTA FREE BLUE
STOP WHISPERING WEST STOP BAY OF THE MONTEBELLO
STOP LITTLE RANCH STOP HERMANN STOP DOUBLE SAFE
HAVEN STOP POWODZENIA

Sinclair's tight timeline worried her. Why only the five days? It didn't take an aerospace engineer to understand that making significant progress in such a short period of time was next to impossible. Then again, this could be how things worked in a billionaire's world, and he didn't care.

She massaged a kink in her neck. This was pointless unless she could understand more about the circumstances of the time. She had the date and location—but nothing else in the telegram made sense.

Across the top of the photocopy she scribbled Sinclair's name. It was a reminder of the man it was all about—and the one who would inevitably laugh in her face when they met at the end of the week, and she'd uncovered nothing.

Her mind wandered. Yesterday, she'd tried to mask her astonishment, hoping neither Wes nor Sinclair would sense how foreign that world was to her. The billionaire's estate. The grounds, the home, the magnificent furnishings—she'd never seen anything like that mansion before. Everything was so elegant, and the entire place was like a museum.

Growing up, she and her mother were never more than a missed paycheck away from proper white trash. She hadn't realized this, of course, not until high school. That's when the other kids started showing up wearing expensive designer jeans and palming the latest cell phone. They drove new cars. She took the bus. They went on summer vacations. She swam at the town pool. It was just how things were.

But that lean upbringing taught her to stretch every dollar. She and her mother always made the most of whatever cozy place her mom could afford, and Jadene never complained. Even today, she avoided expensive clothing, didn't accessorize with needless jewelry, and purchased her lipstick and eyeshadow at the drug store.

Sinclair Whitmore's case was a gift, and she was still shocked by his generous retainer. However, after paying off her debts and sticking to her usual tight budget, the money would only keep her PI business afloat for the next few months.

And solving his case was another matter altogether. She stared at her screen, raising a finger to her chin. Nothing in the old telegram made any sense, and the internet was useless. This case would be a grind.

But was it the timeline, or was she out of her depth? Adjusting her sundress strap, she moved to the office window, her mind circling another worry.

Sinclair was disgustingly rich and could hire anyone he wanted. In fact, he could employ a team of investigators around the globe. They could decode this telegram, transmit their findings over one of the many satellites Whitmore Dynamics blasted into space each month, consolidate them at some secret headquarters, and provide him with robust, beautiful results.

Why her? It made no sense. She was a single woman with no real experience and barely a business. What made her special? If this was pity, she didn't know whether to feel insulted or seen. Maybe they'd picked her because she was a nobody.

Gazing through the window, she drew a finger on its pane, her exhausted mind drifting back to when she was a girl.

Her mother's daily 12-hour shift ended at 6 a.m. By the time she got home, there was only time for a quick chit-chat and a kiss before Jadene left for school. But one morning came a surprise.

"The diner made too much," her mother, Victoria, said. She grabbed two plates from a cupboard. "We've got to eat it before it goes bad."

Jadene was ten years old. A year before, she'd outgrown the need for a sitter, and the savings allowed them to move into a two-bedroom townhouse with a community pool.

"But the bus?"

"I'll drive you to school today," her mom said, pulling a small pint of ice cream from the freezer. "Sit down, it'll be fun!"

She couldn't contain her smile. It was rare on a weekday when she spent quality time with her mom. Two slices of warm apple pie appeared, each crowned with a scoop of vanilla. Jadene savored every bite, not wasting a single crumb or spoonful. They talked about school and boys and made plans to buy her a new bathing suit that weekend.

She lifted her finger from the windowpane, a sad smile brushing her lips. Apple pie still lingered on her tongue—a memory so warm it barely felt real. Before Sinclair. Before this career. Before everything started tasting like doubt.

The tiny bell to her office door chimed, and she snapped from her daze.

Thirteen

Seventy-year-old Stan Roseman hobbled about the entry. Tall and skinny, Jadene feared a strong wind would blow the poor guy into the next county.

Her office entry could be problematic, especially for Stan and his cane. The door's hydraulic assist was malfunctioning and caused the weighty entrance to slam shut if not held properly. If the heavy door smacked Stan's butt before he made it through, he'd launch like a pinball, rocketing across the office. She'd never forgive herself or the sight of it all.

Jadene raced to the doorway.

Stan cracked a smile. "How's my favorite tenant?"

As always, his dress was impeccable. Silvery trousers, a collared long-sleeve, and a matching vest. It had to be 90 degrees outside, but this didn't seem to affect Stan.

"I'm good. How are you?" Smiling, she held the door as he passed. She'd texted him last evening and wanted to square her rent on the place. It wasn't unusual for Stan to visit his tenants monthly to check on his properties, but this was a special visit.

"Apologies, my dear." Stan eyed the pneumatic. "The replacement hasn't arrived yet." He stretched a hand to the glass door's upper frame. "I called the company yesterday and was assured by a friendly robotic voice that the parts were on the way."

Jadene laughed. "That's comforting."

Stan shuffled from the entry. "Yes, my heart was warmed as well."

Jadene giggled again.

Stan pole-stepped past the four chairs in the empty waiting area and headed toward her desk.

"Love the wall color," he said. "Goes well with the carpeting. What did you say its name was?"

"Shetland gray," she said. Despite the name, the walls were nowhere near gray as white. But the color opened the small space and paired it nicely with the carpet.

"Ah, yes. Shetland gray." Stan eyed the walls.

The two approached her desk.

He touched her arm. "Are you sure you can afford this right now?"

Jadene smiled. "I have a new client, and I really appreciate your understanding." She brought up the payment app on her cell.

"Very well," Stan said.

Behind the two, the bell chimed again and the office door wedged open.

"Good morning!" sang a voice.

Jadene glanced up from her cell. Oh yeah, Lilly.

Stan had let Jadene float on rent for the last two months. Like most, Stan knew her business had ebbs and flows, but he liked what she'd done with her space and said she was adding value just being here. However, Jadene thought he was being too generous.

The second time she was late with her payment, she'd felt horrible taking advantage of him. That's when she'd offered a solution to one of his problems.

Lilly Weller was Stan's great-niece. An attractive, perky 19-year-old Jadene hired as an intern for the summer. Jadene didn't need the help but had taken on the girl to buy some goodwill with Stan. Lilly showed up on "Lilly time" four days a week.

Stan was concerned about Lilly's maturity, and for good reason. On her first day, Jadene had to explain to the junior college student that it was inappropriate for Lilly's boyfriends to hang around inside of her office all day.

However, even after that talk, Jadene still caught her suitors strolling outside the window for a glimpse—or lurking on the sidewalk—pouting like a starving puppy.

Still it wasn't the boys that bugged Jadene most—after all, Jadene was 19 once, too. But Lilly had brains in her head and was a whiz with technology. Yet, she carried herself with a cutesy-airhead personality and hadn't shown any genuine interest in anything but her cell phone.

"Good morning," Jadene said, despite it being past 11 a.m. Because Stan was here, she decided against reminding Lilly of the large pink smartwatch dangling around her wrist.

Dressed in tight black Capri pants and a low-cut blouse, Jadene suspected the majority of Lilly's actual morning was spent either texting her boyfriends or prying herself off one of them. Amazingly, Lilly had found the time to curl her long blonde hair, apply her false eyelashes, and coordinate her outfit—though it was still too revealing.

"Hi, Unky!" Lilly chimed.

Stan sighed. "Hello, pumpkin."

Stan had also confided that Lilly's mother wasn't the best role model. Currently, she was dating a singer or a drummer, and was off with the band touring the coast. Stan was hoping that by working in this office, Lilly could break the cycle of selling herself short. He wanted her to gain a bit of self-esteem and develop a sense of purpose. Though, so far, neither had emerged.

Lilly wandered to her desk, set aside her things, and brought up her phone. Unless Jadene gave her something to do, Lilly would remain there until 5 p.m., scrolling and texting through the endless list of hearts she intended to break.

But for Jadene, Lilly was a small price to pay to help keep Stan happy. After all, she'd lucked out having this man as a landlord. Any other owner would have tossed her out on her butt for missing rent. And, without a physical location for her business, her dream of becoming a serious PI was over—and she could say goodbye to her Shetland gray, Tiki paradise of failure.

But while she was flush, she needed to make things right.

Jadene thumbed her payment while Stan hid his disappointment about Lilly, admiring her work area.

Seconds later, Stan uttered something strange.

"Where was she headed?"

Jadene didn't break from the mobile's screen. "Headed?"

"Your Dakota. Where was it going?"

Jadene froze. "Dakota?"

Stan motioned to the photocopy on her desk. "Your message there, Dakota free blue."

Her stare swept from Stan to the telegram.

"Dakota free blue?" A prickling danced up her neck. "Stan? What are you saying?"

"Your flight there."

"A flight? You mean an airplane flight?"

"Yeah."

"Stan, what makes you think that?"

He sported a wide grin, steadied himself without the cane, unbuttoned a cuff, and rolled up a sleeve. A faded green tattoo appeared on his forearm. It read, "Bell UH1 1969."

Jadene took in the image. "What is that?"

"Vietnam. I served as a medic on a Huey. Two tours," he said proudly. "This used to be a fine helicopter. Though her blades sag a bit nowadays." He fingered the ink on his skin, chuckling.

"You were in Vietnam?"

Stan nodded. "In 1971—my last month of enlistment—our Chopper's tail got sniped. One hell of a shot. Struck the nut and tore the rotor right off." He tongued a cheek. "We spun in circles, and our bird came down hard."

"Were you all okay?"

Stan reached down and touched his leg. "We survived, but the wreck shattered my tibia." A soft grin crossed his lips. "Doctors didn't put me back together quite right. But it was war, you understand? They patched me up the best they could and sent me home after that."

Jadene touched her chest. Who would have ever guessed skinny Stan, her kindly landlord, was in the service? Her cheeks warmed.

"As I was saying, that phrase on your message there, free blue. It's slang for takeoff." He gripped his cane to steady himself.

"Takeoff?" Jadene had almost forgotten where this all started.

"Right. The C47 Dakota. Hell of a plane, really."

She was dumbfounded. Dakota didn't refer to a place, no. It referred to an airplane. This changed everything.

"They called her the Dakota." Stan pointed to the telegram. "But it's one of those terms where each letter stands for something."

"Acronym," Lilly shouted, pecking away on her phone.

"Right," Stan said with a speck of pride. "Short for Douglas Aircraft, Transport—or something along those lines."

"Transport aircraft?" Her skin tingled. "And you say this means it was taking off?"

"Yes, dear. Dakota free blue." He scanned the telegram again. "World War II, 1945, it looks like your bird departed an air base from… err…"

Excited, Jadene pointed to the dispatch's tear line.

"Kraków. From an air base in Kraków, Poland."

"Ahh ha."

"Does any other word or phrase in this message make sense?" she pleaded. "Anything at all?"

"Sorry, dear," he shrugged. "Not my war, I'm afraid."

Jadene let out a quiet huff. But he'd supplied her a clue.

Stan eyed her. "I gather this is important to your business?"

"Very. I've been working on deciphering these phrases and I can't get anywhere."

"I might know one fellow who can help." He swished his tongue. "Name of Tom."

"Really?"

"Yeah. If he's still around."

Her tone softened. "You mean he might have passed?"

"No, no. Not this son-of-a-bitch." Stan smirked. "I mean you might be able to catch him, if he's still here in town."

A lead? If one of Stan's buddies turned out half as helpful as Stan was, that would get her closer to solving this riddle.

"Tom?" She tried not to sound too anxious. "Where can I find him?"

"Not far," Stan said, raising a brow. "Usually at O'Malley's."

O'Malley's was a dive bar right around the corner from Gab-Mobile, about a block away.

"Good man." Stan squeezed his cane. "Special breed."

"Do you think he'll be there this evening?" she said. That would give her enough time to wrap up here, usher Lilly off to one of her beaus, and return to her apartment to freshen up.

"Evening?" Stan laughed aloud. "I'm afraid if you waited until then, you'd be too late."

Her lips rounded in confusion.

Stan angled a nod. "If you really want to see him, I'd go now."

"Now?" she blinked. "To O'Malley's?"

Lilly glanced up from her phone. "If you're going out, I can watch the office!"

"Wonderful." Stan leaned toward Jadene, whispering, "Holly Golightly here can watch the office for you."

Jadene frowned. "But you're saying I should go to the bar right now, Stan? It's only noon…"

His cane tapped toward the door. "Yes it is, my dear."

FOURTEEN

O'Malley's was a quiet place for regulars, except on Friday and Saturday nights when the waves of local college kids would flood into the tavern, demanding Jello shots.

Rocco O'Malley would accommodate the noisy undergrads, secretly raising the price from $2 to $8 apiece as the night rolled on. Anyone who complained received a lecture on supply and demand from the 19-1 boxer and his son "Rory" Junior.

Jadene enjoyed the occasional drink. O'Malley's had a nice Italian Montepulciano, and she'd always wanted to visit Italy. Or anywhere, really.

That afternoon, young Rory was tending to rounds in the dimly lit bar, while half a dozen patrons sat on various stools clutching their drinks.

Jadene adjusted to the light. A couple chatting at a nearby table sipped cocktails while another man sat alone in a corner booth.

"Hey, Miss Jadene." Rory beamed. "What brings you in so early?"

Her brow furrowed. Well, business sucks, and if I can't crack an 80-year-old telegram given to me by a billionaire, I'll have to close my doors in another couple of months. But fine. How's your day?

Brushing those woes aside, she straightened her dress and approached the rail.

"Hey, Rory. I'm looking for someone."

He flashed a broad grin and flexed his biceps. "Is he a strapping 23-year-old working at his dad's bar?"

"Ha, ha." She smiled. Rory was handsome and had his pick of undergrads every weekend. She was a bit taller than average, had her mother's olive skin, and kept herself toned by swimming. She didn't mind the light flirting, especially on rough days, but suspected young Lilly was more Rory's type.

Besides, dating at her age usually brought two types of men. The damaged and the adolescent. Her last boyfriend, Curtis, worked in Midtown and was the typical self-centered bachelor who aimed to land a trophy wife. Someone to depend on him, hang on his every need. As a lawyer, he had his pick, of course. Though, one evening, when she was running late for their date because of a case she was working, Curtis had texted her, "Right, you're still playing detective. LOL."

She'd done no dating since, focusing instead on building her business and taking on every job that came her way.

Rory's fast hands yanked a wineglass by the stem and angled a pour before she could stop him. He pushed the glass toward her without a word, dabbing an errant drop from the bar's surface with a rag.

"Who you looking for?"

"I'm not sure what he looks like, but his name is Tom. I'm guessing an older guy, like 70s. Any idea?"

Rory halted his wipe, and his forehead lifted in surprise.

"Are you in trouble?" he said.

"I just need to talk with him if he's around?" she said, curious about his remark.

Rory shot a look to the tavern's far corner.

"It's about something I'm working on," she said.

Rory snatched a pint glass from beneath the bar, bent a tap, and streamed a beer. He skated the drink next to her wine.

"You'll need this," he said, lowering his voice. "And you'd tell me if you were in trouble, right?"

"Yes, Rory. It's just business."

"Well, the Tom I know is younger. But I think he's the one you want." He motioned toward the distant booth. "Over in the back there."

She reached for her drink and the extra beer.

Rory's large hand unexpectedly clasped hers.

"You promise, right? Just business, no trouble?"

"Promise," she said.

She knew Rory and his father. Not well, but something had this kid's radar up. Was Tommy a threat? Was she walking into danger?

Rory's hand slipped from hers. "He's a good man. Peculiar, but a good man."

A good man—both Stan and now Rory had said the same thing. Uneasy, she thanked him, took both drinks from the bar, and approached the booth.

The lighting in this section was especially dim. But the man in front of her wasn't who or what she'd expected. Forties, military-cropped salt and pepper hair, with a strong face. His split-collar shirt showed him fit without being bulky.

She wasn't sure she had the right person. This guy was far younger than she'd anticipated. She was about to return to the bar when the stranger peered up at her.

"Jadene Bowman?"

His accent surprised her. It wasn't American and sounded European. Scottish or Irish, perhaps.

She set the two drinks on the table. She wasn't surprised he'd recognized her, knowing Stan had probably called ahead on her behalf.

"And you're Tom?" her voice cracked.

"Tommy." He raised from his seat, grinned, and extended a hand. "Named for my American great uncle, Thomas Baker. Pleased to meet you."

His eyes were near black. Despite his rigid forearms, he held her palm without squeezing. However, he paused, looking her over. It wasn't creepy or off-putting—but almost as if he recognized her.

"My apologies. I don't have a lot of time." He stretched an arm toward her seat. "Business finds me in half an hour, so I must ingest my vitamins while I can." He raised his drink and winked.

Jadene sat opposite him in the booth.

"I understand you've come across an interesting message of sorts?" he said.

She pulled the photocopy from her clutch. "Yes, I'm a PI and was hired to unravel this…"

Tommy plucked the paper from her hand before she could finish.

Diving right in. All right, she'd go with it.

"The top section there, where the scan cuts off. There was a tear on the original, and the man I got it from says the communication was sent from Kraków."

Tommy stroked the stubble on his chin as he read.

"Stan Roseman, who referred me to you, says the phrase "Dakota free blue" refers to a plane flight. And that, I think, would mean the aircraft left from Kraków. But I don't know what the rest of the message means."

Tommy swigged the remains of his pint, and reached for the drink Jadene had brought him.

"Quite the mystery you have," he said.

Despite the early afternoon, Jadene sipped at her wine. It relaxed her and helped take her mind off whatever bedlam Lilly could be getting into back at the office. But, as seconds of silence passed, she grew restless.

"What do you think?" she asked.

Tommy's gaze rose to hers. "If this was a coordinated incursion, it didn't come through Bainbridge. Possibly the eastern front offensive. But given the whereabouts of troops during that period, it wouldn't make any tactical sense. Though, perhaps they'd…"

Jadene shifted her head slightly.

Tommy narrowed his eyes.

A silence swept between them.

The pint stopped short of his lips. "How much do you know of our Second World War?'

Her brow tightened. History wasn't her strongest subject in school. She was well read, but her preference was more classic literature, as nonfiction rarely appealed to her.

Averting his gaze, she said, "I mean I know who fought whom, and the bomb, and…"

Tommy's words came crisp, like a warning. "To understand this period and the events behind this message you have here, we should discuss a few things."

"A few things?" She'd come for a quick tip on the telegram, not a full-blown history lesson.

Tommy checked his watch. "We've not much time, but you'll need a proper quick lesson to set the stage for all this."

A proper quick lesson? Strange phrasing.

"Some may be refresher but you must understand the true complexity of the past." His finger stabbed the photocopy between them. "And to get to the bottom—the context here—we need to scrape away the bullocks."

An eager weight came in Tommy's words. An undercurrent from someone who knew of things they rarely shared with others. Jadene sipped her wine.

Tommy rubbed his chin, reexamining the message. "But if this were a lone aircraft, that tells me it had to be some type of retrieval mission. They weren't dropping bombs."

"How do you know?"

He tapped a finger on the table. "Because your C47 wasn't equipped with any weapons."

"None?"

"Nothing to defend itself."

Every war plane she could recall had guns under the wings, like in the movies.

"This wasn't an attack craft—that wasn't its purpose." Tommy shook his head. "And if it flew into Kraków on this date, then you'll need to prepare yourself."

"Prepare? What do you mean?"

"These men on this plane, they likely died."

She wasn't surprised. "Yes, it was a long time ago."

"No, they probably died doing this."

A knot grew in her stomach. "You think so?"

He peered into his pint. "It would be a bloody miracle if any of them survived."

Fifteen

Tommy circled a finger overhead.

Rory called from the bar, "Gotcha, boss."

"Oh, no," Jadene said. "I'm good here. But thank you."

Tommy ignored her. "First, your context."

"Okay?"

His voice had a cadence, a rhythm. His unusual accent absorbed her.

"This was a dangerous time, and you must recognize something."

The wine held in front of her lips. "Sure, yes."

"Collective memory is peculiar. Time and opinion erode truth, and people cling to the latest reality they're raised on." His cheek muscles flexed. "You see, life has gotten much softer since. But you must understand that the world rid itself of absolute evil in 1945."

She understood this but nodded anyway.

Yet, Tommy pressed. "This isn't hyperbole. Not some figure of speech, Jadene."

The use of her name sent a shiver.

"The atrocities of Hitler and his Wehrmacht forces were beyond comprehension. Fascism and extremism at its worst, you see."

"Yes, I understand."

"No offense, but I don't think you do." He set his pint on the table. "Life was lived by different rules back then."

Her lips parted, but no words came.

"But, first, let's back up."

"Back up?"

"To the beginning." Tommy lifted his pint, swallowed a swig, and wiped his lip. "Hitler's Nazis fancied themselves heirs to the Holy Roman Empire."

"Roman?"

"Not Caesars' Rome—no." He thumbed the rim of his glass. "The Holy Roman Empire came centuries after the actual fall of Rome."

"Why did they call themselves—"

He raised a palm. "That label wasn't just tradition. It gave them power over the Church."

"To intimidate them?"

"Precisely. This new domain had German origins and began around 800 A.D. At its height, the realm stretched from the Netherlands to Italy." He raised his pint glass. "And the Holy Roman Empire held power over those regions for one thousand years."

"Really?" She genuinely didn't know this. She'd never found war documentaries interesting, but hearing it in a hushed bar from this intense man was surreal.

"But things changed. In the 1800s came a sharp little man who ended the thousand-year reign of the German Nation."

"Sharp little man? You mean Napoleon?"

"Exactly. He crushed the empire and reshaped Europe."

She was intrigued.

Rory appeared with two more drinks.

Tommy flourished a palm. "Cheers, my good man."

"Everything okay here?"

Jadene smiled. "Yes, and thank you."

Rory lowered a nod and returned to his tap station.

Tommy cupped his pint. "However, in the years after Bonaparte's toppling, angry Germany recovered. Slowly, they started to regain control over some of these territories." He swigged. "But by then, you see, Europe was divided."

"Divided? How?"

"Britain, France, Russia, and Serbia held a strong coalition against them." He bobbed his head. "And when a 19-year-old Serb shot an Austrian in the neck, the German empire would crumble once more."

"Wait, wait." A vague memory surfaced. "That was the beginning of the First World War, right? The duke, the assassination?"

"The Archduke, yes."

She'd all but forgotten about the telegram itself. The man spoke like an obsessed professor, determined to share every detail.

Tommy raised a finger. "Empires jostling for control over Europe, fractured by gunfire, sparking the first global conflict in history." His eyes held hers. "But even after losing this war, Germany was not finished. They were desperate to regain and rule these territories." He cocked a nod. "So, they tried a third time."

"A third time?"

Tommy raised a brow. "The Third Reich."

"Shit," she huffed. Eighteen years of schooling and a stranger in a bar put this all together for her in minutes.

He tapped the telegram. "In September of 1939, Hitler's first target was Poland."

A chill struck her.

"And with each victory came confidence. By 1942, Nazi Germany strangled Europe—France, Greece, Norway, even deep into Soviet soil." He drew a loop in the air. "Those forces controlled nearly everything."

"Hitler controlled everything?" She half wanted to ask Rory for a pen and notepad. No one had ever summarized the rise and fall of empires over afternoon wine to her before. She tucked a loose strand of hair behind her ear, trying to remember everything.

"Yes. But you must understand fascism isn't a man. It's a plague. And wherever Nazis marched, it festered." His expression went stiff. "Gestapo and SS bullied the population. They arrested, interrogated, murdered—"

Jadene shuddered. "No one was safe."

"It was the extinction of freedom." Tommy's gaze drifted downward.

A sadness welled in her chest.

"Wives and husbands couldn't confide in one another. Children informed on parents, sewing complete distrust at home." He paused. "This ensured the only loyalty was to the Nazi party."

Jadene sank in her seat. "Turning in family members. I remember reading about that once." None of it was real to her, the cruelty. Who could do such a thing?

"It was a wickedness the world had never seen. Many German civilians did what they needed to survive, helpless against the unfolding nightmare of the Nazi party." He gave a hard tsk. "Many who resisted fell victim to impulsive, public executions."

A breath caught in her throat. "My God."

"God was busy with other things, I'm afraid." He scratched the stubble on his chin. "Hitler's disdain emboldened his forces. They ran without honor, taking anything they wanted from anyone."

Jadene swallowed.

"And they took many lives." Tommy shook his head. "But we never knew how unconscionable man could be until that war. Until the smoke, the secrecy, and the half-truths were lifted."

A chill grew inside of her.

"Only after the war did the world see the horrible reality—death camps, mass graves, the scale of it all."

Her face went flush. She was without words.

"Hitler created a social sickness in his followers, dehumanizing his enemies."

She'd never understood how so many could be complicit in that dreadfulness.

Tommy drew a long sniff. "And they were well on their way to global rule until 1944."

"What stopped them?"

"That's the remarkable part." He took a sip, his stare unwavering. "The world's fate rested on a generation already broken. Starved by the Depression… and hardened by survival."

Sixteen

Rory appeared with another pint for Tommy, but nothing for Jadene. She was already tipsy from the first glass and nibbling on her second. Tommy drank his beer like it was water.

They were seated in an isolated booth, apart from the main area. The couple at the table had finished their cocktails and left. Only one patron remained at the bar—sitting quietly on his stool as Rory returned to mind the taps and shine the glass and stemware.

Tommy took another gulp and picked up where he left off. "When the Soviets kicked off their offensive, the Führer's plans unraveled."

She leaned forward, the wine glass forgotten in her hand.

"The tide turned with Hitler's Atlantic Wall." He eyed the ceiling. "Twenty-four hundred miles of shoreline, from France to Norway, fortified by Nazi troops."

"Twenty-four hundred miles?"

Clatter came from the bar. A patron knocked over a stool, then supplied a loud apology to Rory.

The young bartender shot out his hand, glaring.

"All right, all right," the man said. He fished keys from his pocket, surrendering them to Rory.

Tommy didn't even flinch. "The Germans dug in all along the English Channel." He swirled the remains in his glass. "Less than a hundred miles from England's front lawn."

"They were that close?"

"The Allies were desperate to keep them at bay, and leadership probed for the weakest link in the Führer's barrier." He narrowed his eyes. "And the massive Allied assault to come was called D-Day."

Another recollection surfaced. "Right. They called it D-Day to keep the real date a secret in case of leaks."

"Precisely." Tommy cocked a nod. "The soldiers only knew mission objectives, not the timing. Not until troop movement was underway." He gulped a sip. "And when they crossed the channel, those brave men fought a true battle, not just of arms, but of will. It raged for 80 days and nights. Planes, bombs, and guns. Relentless carnage between Allied and Axis powers that cost nearly half a million lives." He dropped his gaze. "A battle equally devastating to both sides."

She eyed her drink. Half a million dead. That scale of destruction was impossible to grasp—a city of people gone in a single battle. Her throat tightened.

"But with Nazi focus elsewhere, somebody noticed," Tommy said.

A frown formed. "I don't understand."

"The Soviets—our Allies at the time."

"And they planned their own invasion?"

"They knew Hitler had overcommitted his troops on the Normandy coastline, and those crafty reds took advantage of it."

"How?"

"Came in fast from behind." He slugged his drink. "Weeks into the battle at Normandy, with most Nazi attention pulled twelve hundred miles northwest, the Soviets drastically ramped up their forces. Turned a game of pattycake into a hurricane of artillery.

The reds stormed from Belarus into Nazi-controlled Poland." He chuckled. "Those German bastards never saw it coming."

"And they kicked their ass?" she said.

"Every bloody cheek. Sent them running for Berlin. And the target they struck put the proverbial noose around the Führer's neck."

"What was the target?"

"A Nazi stronghold. A place Hitler's forces gathered between battles to rearm and recharge." His eyes locked on hers. "Over two million Soviets attacked, killing or capturing a half-million of Hitler's men in one go."

Her foot bounced under the table. The detail he shared was overwhelming.

"It wasn't a bomb that ended World War II, you see. That's how the Americans ended their war with Japan. No, for the world, the decisive blow to the head of the snake, the Nazis, was the Soviet Union's capture of Berlin in May of 1945."

Rory came with another pint. Tommy drank half of it before he spoke again. Jadene barely touched her glass.

Refreshed, Tommy resumed. "We know Germany lost hundreds of thousands of men at Normandy. The same occurred during the Soviet offensive on the Nazi Army Group Centre."

Jadene waited as he pondered something.

"If I recall, the remaining Nazi armies were now fighting for their existence in Western Europe." He gulped. "As well, with American troops now in the war, the weakened Nazis could no longer launch any successful offensive."

She clutched her glass with both hands, absorbing each word. War—and the decisions behind it—was more complex than she'd ever imagined.

"When Soviet forces started to move in the direction of Kraków, the weakened Nazis weren't so keen on fighting, you see."

"So they ran like the others?"

"Most Nazis high-tailed it back to the motherland. And that brings us to the meat of things." His focus returned to the telegram on the table.

Jadene didn't move.

"Now, the Soviets didn't liberate Kraków until January 19." He squinted. "Your communication here is dated the 17th, which left two days. A gap where your aircraft possibly took advantage. But two things puzzle me."

"They do?"

"First, C47s were used chiefly to deploy paratroopers. But with the Soviets moving in and the Germans in retreat, there was no reason to do this."

"And the other?"

"This word here, whispering."

The *Whispering West* phrase had confused her, too.

"That term in warfare usually refers to a privy, to a secret."

A chill raced up her neck. "Really?"

"Perhaps a secret base, or it concerns the flight itself—I can't be sure."

"You think so?"

Tommy fingered his pint. "My guess is to find where your C47 fled to, you'll need to dig for the flight logs—if any exist at all."

Jadene made a mental note.

A stocky brown-haired man entered the bar. He didn't order anything but glanced in their direction. Tommy acknowledged the man with a nod, before his attention returned to Jadene.

"These two days, the 17th and 18th, a sliver of time, you see. And this territory of conflict was not safe by any means. The Nazis were in retreat, and the Soviets were storming in from the East. There were men and artillery everywhere." He finished the last of his pint and grabbed the new one. "Any flight into Poland would have been a near-suicide mission. Unless…"

A fluttering came to her chest. "Unless?"

Tommy scratched his temple. "Kraków was in the heart of Reich territory, and the Nazis were everywhere, for hundreds of miles." He thumbed the edge of his beer glass. "Even if your plane landed and managed to take off again from Kraków, heading east toward the USSR… the Soviet forces weren't the best partners during the war."

"Not the best partners?"

"Truth is, they were never real allies—just convenient ones. As soon as the war ended, Russia carved up what was left of Germany—took Berlin, then split the country in two."

Another memory clicked. "East and West—"

Tommy nodded. "East was theirs, and they ruled it with an iron fist. KGB, secret police, breadlines, propaganda. Turned Berlin into a wall-divided ghost town. Cross the wrong street, you caught a bullet. Stalin hunted scientists, artists—scoured the ruins for anything of value." He swigged. "Another part no one likes to talk about."

Jadene sat back, absorbing it. She'd always thought of the Allies as a united front—good versus evil. But history wasn't textbook clean.

"No, your aircraft could not have flown over Russian territory." He scratched his temple. "My guess is they'd have fired on anything not scribed with a hammer and sickle."

"Shot it down?"

"Your C47 would have met with a wall of artillery in every direction." A finger touched his chin. "Every direction, but one."

"Which?"

He leaned forward, his cadence slow. "That's what leaves me curious. It would have taken absolute balls of steel to split the seam and come in from the north."

"You mean Sweden?"

Tommy laughed. "Not a chance. Back then, those blue and yellow swine were catering to both sides. They'd have never assisted any Allied operation. No, my guess is the UK for takeoff."

"United Kingdom?"

He guzzled his pint, belching softly. "If that aircraft could avoid the flak between Norway and Denmark, Hitler's forces were in chaos at the time."

"Retreating from Kraków, right," she said.

Tommy paused and tongued a cheek. "But why do this? Why fly a defenseless aircraft here and go through it all?" He lifted the telegram, scanning the page.

Jadene held.

Eyeing the telegram, a wide grin grew on Tommy's lips. "You crafty bastards."

"Crafty?"

The brown-haired man at the bar raised his arm, signaling to his watch.

"My apologies, Jadene, but I'm on the clock now." He lifted his chin. "Yet, a word of caution."

"Caution?"

"If you're to see this through, remain guarded."

"What do you mean?"

He slid the telegram back her way, a shadow crossing his face. "The deeper the briar, the thicker the thorns. And there's an iron truth you must come to understand."

"A what?"

"In war, the beaten and conquered never forgive, Jadene. Never. For many, the wounds still run deep."

She tensed.

"Amigo?" the man called from the bar.

Tommy rose from his seat.

"Wait, I…"

He flicked a glance to the telegram, then back to her. "Do you have a weapon?"

"A weapon?"

He didn't smile. "Get one."

"Why? What's—"

"Because your men on that C47 aircraft…"

"Yes?"

Tommy anchored his gaze to hers. "They took something."

Goosebumps shot up her spine.

"There's no other reason for this."

"What did they take?"

Tommy slugged the remains of his pint. "Something the Nazis possessed but the Allies didn't want the Soviets to have."

Her thoughts spun.

"I hope we meet again, Jadene."

With that, he and his colleague vanished from the bar.

She sat for the next several minutes, unease curling in her chest. A thumb tapping her wine glass.

SEVENTEEN

This was a cargo plane, after all. But what in the hell could be so valuable it was worth risking lives over? Who, or what, was on that plane?

Jadene raced back to the office, passing Lilly's empty desk. She couldn't shake Tommy's precise knowledge of every event, every date.

At her laptop, she reviewed the information. Two major battlefronts—one raging inward from the East, the other storming from the West—a strategic masterpiece. Hitler's forces were squeezed back into Germany from both sides.

She smirked, remembering Tommy's words. The Nazi retreat from Kraków wasn't just a retreat. Those stupid bastards were running for their lives. And, as Tommy said, it created a sliver of time when the C47 Dakota Skytrain could have flown into the region.

Gnawing on her lower lip, the next objective was clear. She'd traced bank accounts, credit card purchases, online activity, inventory, and even a cheating spouse—but never an airplane.

A hard click echoed behind her. Lilly wandered from a back room, her blouse misbuttoned.

"What'd you find out?" she said, trying to appear nonchalant.

With so few days before the deadline, Jadene needed help to crack this telegram. Scolding Lilly for her tryst could wait. Whoever Lilly was with had already fled out the back door.

"Get on your computer," Jadene instructed. "Find out how many C47 Skytrains were manufactured. I need an exact number, if possible."

"Skytrains?" Lilly said.

"It's an airplane, you'll see."

Lilly had a good memory and took direction well, especially when it came to actual work.

While Lilly researched, Jadene hunted for possible air bases for the C47. The plane's takeoff point was crucial. Without it, she was nowhere.

She ran a search of air bases in the United Kingdom. The query returned a barrage of results. She learned that wartime airstrips were often hastily constructed with pickaxes and shovels. Runways were created out of necessity rather than convenience. Closing her eyes, she groaned. Accounting for all these bases was impossible. Many probably hadn't survived the war.

Then, something struck her. She was approaching this wrong. She needed a different angle.

"Lilly," she said. "Make sure to include only C47s manufactured up until 1944. And I'll find out how long of a runway the plane needed for takeoff."

"Two thousand," Lilly replied.

Jadene looked up from her laptop.

"Two thousand feet, minimum," Lilly said, twirling a lock of her hair. "But 3,000 or more if it's loaded. Plus, the plane was unpressurized. It couldn't fly above 10,000 feet without oxygen masks."

Jadene shot her a strange look.

"What?" Lilly said. "I didn't know what a C47 Skytrain was until a minute ago. All this stuff came up, so I read it."

Jadene chuckled. "Good work, Lilly."

Next, Jadene crafted a new search: air bases completed in 1944, with runways of 2,000 feet or longer, in the UK.

She hit enter. Three results returned: Lakenheath, Mildenhall, and Brize Norton. Each had a sufficient runway, and each was operational in January 1945. She studied the information.

"All right," Lilly called out. "About 11,000 of those planes were built. By 1944, around 3,400 were produced."

"Thank you," Jadene said, engrossed in her screen.

Lilly sprang over to her desk. "What's this for?"

Jadene scanned her search results. Mildenhall Airfield handled mostly bombers during the war. She'd skip it for now. Brize Norton was used primarily for training. The C47 probably didn't take off from there.

That left Lakenheath Royal Air Force Base.

"Bring up a map of Suffolk, England," Jadene said. "On the big screen."

"Sure, boss." Lilly rushed back to her laptop.

The 60-inch television was meant to entertain waiting clients and until Lilly showed up, it was either tuned to the weather channel or switched off. Bored one day, Lilly had figured out how to beam her laptop's image to its surface, which amazed Jadene.

Aiming a remote, Lilly said, "There you go."

A high-resolution map appeared.

"No, wait. Go back out, and left a bit."

Lilly did as instructed. Jadene stood in front of the large display, eyeing Western Europe end to end. She imagined the Dakota's escape in 1945. Over water, from northern Poland, past Germany, through the passage between Norway and Denmark.

Tommy said it would be nasty. At a maximum of 10,000 feet, the Dakota had to rip through that strait going full speed, dodging artillery fire, and somehow descend into Kraków's airspace.

Jadene pressed a hand to her cheek. The pilots had to be the best. Brave, lucky, with absolute balls of steel. And the aircraft had to do this twice—once fighting into Kraków and once fleeing.

She scanned the topography. If they reached the North Sea and dodged the Nazi navy, they'd be home free, returning to Lakenheath Air base.

But why would they fly into one of the most warfare-riddled places on earth? What were they after?

"Lilly, zoom in here, would you?"

"Suffolk again?"

"Yes, please."

Once more, the peculiar stranger in the bar was right. Lakenheath RAF appeared the best place to begin. But if the Dakota took off from there, she needed proof. Would the flight logs exist online?

Locating one flight and tracking one plane—which may or may not have taken off from Lakenheath—was daunting. Jadene rubbed an eye. She needed help, but what could she tell Lilly?

Turning to the girl, she said, "Lilly, we need to search for something."

Lilly perked up. "What is it?"

Jadene brought out the photocopied message. "It all begins with a telegram."

Lilly frowned. "Oh, I don't use that one. My friends and I are on—"

"It's not a phone app, Lilly. It's how long distance radio communications were sent decades ago."

Lilly tilted her head.

"Each letter of the alphabet was assigned a configuration, decoded on a typewriter."

"The dots and dashes thing?"

"Yes, Morse code. The dots and dashes thing." Jadene held the page. "This is one of those messages from 1945. I'm not sure how all these phrases connect, but they do."

"Really?" Lilly said, excited.

"Yes." Her enthusiasm surprised Jadene. "Make yourself a hard copy."

Lilly flashed a picture with her phone. "Okay, sending it to the printer."

Jadene stepped away to retrieve water from the minifridge in the back office, letting Lilly marinate with the message as she did so.

She knew deciphering the entire telegram would not be possible. It was a different world back then. But if *Dakota Free Blue* was a flight and they could find the tail number, they could trace the plane. And that could lead to Arthur Whitmore himself.

But if they couldn't find any record, they'd get nowhere—and that meant she'd never be able to answer Sinclair's questions about his grandfather.

Returning, she set a bottle next to Lilly.

"All right," Jadene began. "We're looking for a plane that might have landed in Kraków, Poland."

"An airplane?" Lilly said.

"Yes."

"A German airplane?"

"No, this communication shows an aircraft took off from Kraków. We need to find where it went."

"This telegram went out over radio waves, right?"

"Yes, but this…" Jadene sighed. She may have to back up and start all over, Lilly wasn't following everything she was saying. "This was World War II, and…"

Lilly turned. "Jadene, I know what war this was and I know what you're saying. But what I'm saying is that this message is German, right?"

"No, it's…"

"Because at the top it says telegramm with double m's. That's the German spelling."

Jadene blinked. "Double m's? What?"

Lilly pointed to her screen. "I searched the words in the message."

"When?"

"When you showed me the thing like a minute ago. You walked away, got us water…"

"Wait!"

That spelling had never occurred to her. She assumed "telegramm" was an older or British rendering of the word—like shoppe or theatre.

"What's wrong?" Lilly asked.

Jadene replayed her conversation with Sinclair. Arthur, his grandfather, a wartime telegraph operator. The confused words of a dying man.

"Jesus Christ…" The color drained from her cheeks.

"Jadene, are you okay?"

Nathaniel Whitmore couldn't stand to be in the same room with his father, Arthur. Now it all made horrible sense. No wonder Sinclair hadn't assigned this investigation to a team. He sought out Jadene and her quiet business, insisting on that iron-clad NDA.

A coldness swept through her.

Was she okay? No, no, she wasn't.

Arthur Whitmore, Sinclair's grandfather, was a Nazi.

Eighteen

A light snapped on. Ellis stirred. Murky shadows danced in his vision. How long had they kept him in pitch black? Days? A week? Time was a blur.

The steel cage holding him was a web of finger-thick steel rods, welded at every joint. Even beneath him, round and ribbed metal pressed into his back and sides when he tried to lie down. The only bearable position came when he'd removed his shoes and sat on them. The loafers shielded his rear from the constant agony of the grooved rods.

In the cage's far side was a fist-sized hole in the floor, accompanied by a roll of toilet paper. They'd provided him nothing else for comfort or warmth. He sat with his legs bent, arms wrapped around his knees, like a cornered animal, shivering and sore.

A woman entered the doorway.

Ellis lifted his head.

She was five-nine or ten, with long, jet-black hair. Mid-thirties, fit and striking. She stepped toward his cage, cradling something in her hands.

"Eat this." Kneeling, she slid a bowl through a gap under the cage door.

Warmth radiated from the wooden bowl. What had she brought him? It didn't matter. Until now, they'd given him only water. He was starving and would eat whatever this was. Reaching for the meal, his hands trembled. Careful not to spill anything, he brought the bowl to his lips.

Tomato and teeny bits of crusted bread struck his tongue. He hated tomato, but right now, this was the best fucking soup he'd had in his life. Starving, he savored its flavor.

The woman's stare lingered.

Deprived of sleep, Ellis slurped another gulp. He needed all the nourishment he could get. When they'd left him alone in the dark, he'd focused on Linda. How much time had passed since he'd last seen her? She had to be out of her mind with worry by now. He needed to find a way out of this, no matter what it took.

The woman lingered, watching him swallow the soup. Her hazel eyes—was there something in them? Was it pity? Kindness? Ellis gripped the bowl.

If she was afraid of Belt Buckle, he could work that, cultivate her compassion. She might be his ticket out of this death coop. But, like easing a confession from an accused, he'd need to start slow.

"What…" his voice rasped. "What's your name?"

She swept hair from an eye and spoke softly.

"My name is Rena."

Ellis set the bowl at his feet. "I'm Ellis Martin. Do you know why he took me?"

Rena shot a glance toward the doorway.

"Please," he said. "Why am I here? What does he want?"

She blinked.

He eyed the bowl at his feet. "Thank you, I was so hungry."

She reached for the cage, her expression turning fearful. "Please cooperate. I do not want to see you hurt." She brushed her fingers against the rebar. "He is very dangerous."

"What does he want? Why am I here?"

Her expression fell. "I… I do not know why he brought you here."

Footsteps stomped toward the room.

"The bowl." Her words panicked. "I need the bowl."

Ellis grabbed the dish, gulped its remains, and slid it back through the slot.

She seized the dish and rose.

Ellis whispered, "I can help you."

Her lips parted, and she stared at him.

Ellis frowned. She was in trouble. He'd seen it so many times over his career. This was a damaged woman. Whether by physical or emotional abuse, or both, she was afraid of Belt Buckle. Afraid of what the man would do if he caught her consorting with his prisoner.

Ellis had to work fast. He didn't have his usual advantages. There wasn't enough time to build a proper rapport. He was locked in a box after all. But the basics—empathy—it was in her eyes. He'd also remained compliant, establishing trust. She'd responded by telling him her name. And, when she'd asked for the bowl, he'd given it to her without resistance.

But would it be enough? Did they have common ground? Should he wait until they establish more of a bond? Like he had when he'd questioned suspects?

No, there wasn't time. If Belt Buckle was as psychotic as he figured, every meeting with the man could be his last. Why was he here in the first place? He didn't have the luxury of finding out. He needed to get out of this fast if he wanted to stay alive.

He clenched the bars of the cage with both hands as the footsteps outside drew closer.

Rena shot a glance to the doorway, then back at him.

"I can protect you," he said softly.

The woman rose an eyebrow.

"I'm a police officer," he said. "I can end this."

She touched her chin. "Really?"

Ellis crouched, felt for his shoes, returning to his squat. His instincts hadn't failed him. She was terrified, and he could use that fear. It would save them both from the madman who held them.

"Yes," he said confidently. "But you have to get me out of here, okay?"

It appeared she wanted to say something, but got to her feet instead.

"I can help you," he pleaded.

As she stood, a curious expression overtook her face. Her lips smiled, but her eyes did not.

Nineteen

Wandering to the front office window, Jadene stared out at the street, watching the occasional car pass.

What did she know for sure? Was her conclusion the right one? Did the facts line up? Or had she spooked herself?

Clutching her elbows, she drew a deep breath.

Could Arthur have gotten this message by other means? Yes—he could've found the document. That was also possible. Yet, the fight between father and son? Sinclair had said it was a major falling out. Something that happened long before he was born.

Jadene cupped a hand to the back of her neck. There were a few things that could rip a family apart. Finding out your own father fought for the Nazis had to be on that list.

The rift between the two men. A clash that Sinclair claimed not to know the basis of—because he was never clear on the matter. Was that true? Or, did Sinclair know about his grandfather's past? Had he not told her because he knew there was no way she'd have taken the case?

This was all possible—and the most likely answer.

Lilly called, "Jadene?"

Staring out at the quiet street, Jadene cradled her arms, wondering what she should do now.

A hand touched her shoulder.

"What's going on with you?" Lilly said.

Jadene blinked, pulled back to the moment. She'd have to figure this out later. It was too overwhelming. For now, she'd move forward.

"Sorry, I'm just overworked, I think."

Lilly stared at her strangely. "Did you want to locate that plane you were talking about?"

Jadene's expression shifted to a smile. "Right, yes. Lakenheath."

Both returned to their desks.

Jadene took a swig of her water and capped the bottle. "Okay, we're after a C47 that would have taken off from Lakenheath air base on January 17th, and—"

"Fifty-two."

"What?"

"Fifty-two flights left that day."

"How did you figure that out so fast?"

"Easy." Lilly pointed to the Big TV and a mirror image of her laptop appeared. "I found these sites. Old guys love this airplane stuff, so they post stories and pictures, and other details." She shrugged. "I guess it's their hobby or something. But I got this one off the Royal Airforce Archive."

Jadene approached the large monitor. "And these were all C47s taking off that day in 1945?"

"Yes."

Jadene hesitated. "How many returned?"

"That day?"

"Yes."

Lilly's fingers flew across the keyboard. "Twenty-three. No, wait. One of those was an L-4."

"Twenty-two returned, then." Jadene touched her neck. "Less than half."

"Do you think they landed at other bases?"

Something struck Jadene, and she fell quiet again. Beyond her conversation with Tommy and the dreadful atrocities he'd shared, she'd been able to stay mainly analytical since—keeping her feelings in check. But now, an ache in her heart swelled.

These flights from this air base, and countless others during World War II, were dangerous missions taken on by young, courageous men. Many of them still in their teens, risking their lives in a war she'd only recently come to understand. Brave souls fighting for every inch forward against an enemy in a strange part of the world.

She caught a breath.

Fifty-two flights left Lakenheath and less than half returned. Did they land at other bases? Or had they met with a tragic end?

And the fact Sinclair's grandfather could have been on the other side—the enemy. It was hard to stay unaffected. But at this moment, she had to put her emotions aside. She wouldn't share any of this with Lilly. Not right now, it was just too confusing. She needed to figure things out herself first.

"Okay, can you write down the flights that returned so we can split them up and try to track them?"

Lilly struck a key. "It's on your laptop."

"What is?"

"The list." She smirked. "Your half of it anyway."

Jadene chuckled. "Well, all right then."

Lilly had taken on a strange focus, delving into her work like a girl on a mission. She wasn't toiling on her cell. It was refreshing. Jadene was glad she was here to help.

For the next hour, they surfed sites, many put together by volunteer aviation buffs who'd transcribed an array of flight logs from World War II. Several included photos and stories.

Jadene read every flight, every detail—silently honoring each mission with her attention.

Whenever her eyes grew watery, she'd look at Lilly—pecking away at her keyboard, humming to herself—and borrow her resolve.

The two compared takeoffs, landings, and times of return, working feverishly to weed out the list of two dozen.

Jadene was entering the next flight number from her list when Lilly's humming suddenly stopped.

TWENTY

Rena glared down at the caged Ellis. His abyss—cornered, confined, and desperate—the walls steep and slippery. It was easy to know the want of any imprisoned man. Every action rooted in self-preservation, eager to bargain for release.

Here, the true nature of the spirit emerged. Great ones foster defiance, a decided will—fighting with impossible strength until they either triumph or die. But those individuals were exceptionally rare.

Most often came the weak. Those who flounder and grasp at anything—who reach out to anyone, including a complete stranger—in their attempt to claw their way to freedom. This was the misplaced hopefulness in Ellis Martin's face. She relished watching it fade.

And she could have played along, pretending they were equals trapped in the same circumstance, needing each other to break free. It would have been a game of simple manipulation to see if she could make him reveal his secrets willingly. But her quest was far greater than outwitting a trapped man. And, this was no game.

"You are Ellis Martin," she said.

The man in the cage matched the suited man's description and the photo on the site. Broad shoulders, medium build, with a touch of gray at the temples. He carried his years well, showing no signs of indulgence or excess. That was fine—she had no intention of pressing him there.

A glint grew in his eyes. "Yes. Can you help me?"

She ran her tongue over her teeth. Ellis Martin didn't know it yet, but he was here to help her.

"I would not think an ex-cop would suffer from prosopagnosia," she said. "But props can be effective tools."

Ellis inched forward, hooking his fingers through the bars.

"Perhaps if I was still wearing that arm sling?"

"What?" His voice groveled. "The airport. You fell?" He eyed the ruby ring on her finger. "That was you?"

Rena launched a fiendish chuckle. "Courteous and gentlemanly. And yet, at the same time, you did not see me." She crossed her arms and stepped closer. "I was on your flight. I wanted to make certain my men did not act on the wrong target."

Barred shadows crossed his face, and hope faded from his eyes.

"That's right," she smirked. "My men."

He let go of the rods and recoiled like a wounded animal.

"Though, it was adoring when you offered to rescue me from here." She giggled. "The hero to my Vasilisa."

"What the fuck is this?" His fist struck the rebar. "What do you want from me?"

She was making progress. Ellis Martin was processing the weight of his predicament, moving from disbelief to anger. The glint in his eyes was no more. Instead, there were daggers. Her lips twisted into a smirk.

"We are not there yet," she said. "But soon enough."

Ellis shouted, "Lady, I'm not playing. I have people, and they'll come looking for me. You'd best let me go before this all gets real dangerous."

Kneeling, her voice dropped to a whisper. "I would not worry about me. Why do you think I brought you here?" She fingered the rebar. "Why do you think you're locked in this cage?"

He glared.

"I knew who I was taking," she said.

He slumped his shoulders.

She returned to her feet. It wouldn't be long before this man begged to help her.

"What do you want?" Ellis said. "Money?"

"No!" she snapped, her eyes flashing with intensity. "I want repayment!"

He lunged at the bars. "What did I do to you? Lock up your druggie boyfriend?"

Rena took a step back. She'd revealed too much—too much for now. The seeking had to be handled gingerly, slow like a careful stewing.

"Tell me what you want!" Ellis yelled. "Or let me the fuck out of here!"

She drew a long breath, eyeing the ring on her middle finger. Soon, this man would process his misery, and that's when she'd strike. But not now. Not with the heat of hate welling.

"You will understand in time," she said coldly.

"This is kidnapping, you know that?"

Rena turned and left the room. But she quickly returned with a small, boxlike device.

Ellis peered at her from the cage.

She inspected the device, set it on the floor, and pressed a tiny button on its upside.

"Something to keep you company," she grinned.

Twenty-One

"Wait… wait!"

Jadene glanced up from her laptop.

"I've got it!" Lilly cried.

"Which one?"

"It's two planes."

Jadene frowned. "Two?"

"Look," Lilly pointed. "The first flight, number 41-978, left Lakenheath on January 17th. It returned six hours later."

According to the satellite map, the round trip from Lakenheath to Kraków was approximately five and a half hours.

"Right, but—" Jadene began.

"No, no. Check this out. The flight log says this plane was damaged when it returned."

"Damaged?"

The Big TV's screen scrolled. "And there's this second designation in the log that says A-O-G."

"And that means?"

"Aircraft on ground. But they only do that when a plane has to be taken out of service. This probably means it was damaged."

"Lilly, how do you—?" Jadene paused. "Never mind."

"In all these searches, I've never seen another entry like this one," Lilly added. "The thing probably barely landed."

"Barely landed?" Jadene frowned. Could it have been damaged by a mass of anti-aircraft fire?

Lilly shot up a hand. "But there's more!"

Jadene tapped her foot. "More?"

"Not only is this the only aircraft with both of these log designations that day, but…"

Another of the log's handwritten images appeared on the screen, and Jadene hopped from her desk.

"This is where it really gets good," Lilly pointed. "Flight 41-978 TSFR to 42-056."

Jadene sharpened her gaze. "A transfer?"

"Right. They switched to another aircraft. Whoever or whatever was aboard the original plane was moved off and put on another."

Jadene nodded slowly. It did make sense if the Dakota Skytrain was unflyable, as the log had indicated. "Tell me about the other airplane," she said.

"This new one had four engines."

"Four?"

"Yes. It was a C54 Skymaster. They used it for extended hauls during the war."

A picture of the aircraft flashed on the Big TV.

But Jadene was puzzled. All of the war's major battles were happening in Eastern Europe during this time. However, why was this plane headed west, away from the action? She tapped her water bottle.

"Does it say where the C54 went after that?"

"According to the log, our Skymaster headed to Lajes Airfield." Lilly smacked her lips. "It's this military base on an island in, like, the middle of the Atlantic. Part of Portugal, and used by the Allies during the war."

"And it landed there?"

Lilly clicked her keys. "That's the weird part."

"Weird part?"

Lilly motioned to her screen. "I can't find anything. I mean, I found stuff about Lajes and most of its logs, but nothing from January 15 through January 22 in 1945. It's like that week doesn't exist. I can see, like, everything else. Dates and stuff. But not that single week."

"How can that be?"

"Even this National Records site, which is supposed to have everything. I can't find it. Plus, the site keeps pointing me to this archive."

"Archive?" Jadene asked.

"Yeah. It's this place over in Montgomery where they keep the physical records. Like the controller flight books."

"Alabama?"

"Yeah." Lilly aimed a finger at the Big TV. "But check this out, too." On the large screen, a map appeared. "If that plane did all this, I mean, flew from that base in the United Kingdom all the way to that island—"

Jadene stepped toward the monitor. "Then it was headed west, in a straight line."

"Yeah. And if it landed at that air base place in Lajes, I don't think it stayed there. I think it stopped to refuel and—"

Jadene touched a finger to her chin. "And the aircraft probably kept flying west."

Thinking back, the telegram's *Whispering West* phrase appeared to confirm it. But where was the aircraft going?

"I can't prove it, though," Lilly said. "I'm stuck."

"Stuck?"

"I can't find anything online." She twirled a lock of hair with one hand, typing and clicking with the other. "And there's only one way to know for sure," Lilly said.

Jadene stared at the screen's flight path.

Lilly smirked. "Alabama's not that far, you know?"

Jadene shifted her jaw.

On January 17, 1945, a Dakota C47 Skytrain took off from Lakenheath Air base in the United Kingdom. It returned to the same air base six hours later, damaged and unable to fly again. Its six hour trip was the precise time it would've taken to fly into Kraków and back.

Dakota Free Blue?

Whoever or whatever that battered C47 picked up was moved onto a bigger C54 Skymaster, which took off with the payload on the same day. According to the log times Lilly had shown her, the switch between those two planes took only twenty minutes. That seemed suspiciously efficient, especially for the military in a green zone, well away from the action. What had they taken?

The departure log at Lakenheath showed that larger four-engine aircraft flew 2,000 miles west to Lajes Airfield—a Portuguese island territory in the middle of the Atlantic Ocean.

But Lilly found no record of the C54 at Lajes. Not online, anyway. No way for her to know if the aircraft made it to that air base, or where it was headed after that.

"How far is the drive to that archive?"

"Two and a half hours. Max Air base. It's this huge records center," Lilly said, excited. "You can track down that plane, and I'll watch the office!"

Jadene wet her lips.

Yes, she would travel to Alabama to that records center.

Yes, Lilly would watch the office.

She narrowed her eyes on the screen.

Because according to the flight's westward path, that large C54 Skymaster, and its mysterious payload, were headed directly to the United States.

TWENTY-TWO

In suffocating darkness, Ellis counted the seconds, bracing for the noise. He clamped his hands over his ears, shoulders rigid with tension.

Chirp! Chirp! Chirp!

The sound tore through the silence, sharp and relentless, like a dying smoke detector. Even with his ears covered, the shrill blast knifed through his senses, rattling his skull.

The boxy device blared its shrill tone every ten minutes. Ellis quivered, his head pounding. They'd barely fed him, and the relentless lack of sleep left his thoughts scattered. Still, his weary mind resumed the count: thousand one, thousand two… just as it had for the past twelve excruciating hours.

Footsteps—the first sound beyond the device in forever—approached. The door opened.

Ellis lifted his head.

A finger flicked a switch. Light blazed, stabbing his pupils.

"Turn that off," Rena demanded.

Heavy boots approached, and a hand silenced the boxy device.

"I want to see his face," she said. "Open it."

The steel cage door rattled. Keys jingled near his ear. Belt Buckle unfastened the lock, the door creaking open slightly.

Ellis was far too weak to mount an attack. He couldn't focus. His body trembled. Even if his strength returned, he was still stuck—this godforsaken cabin miles from anywhere, and no one coming.

The scent of perfume drifted nearby. "Are you with me?"

He blinked, his vision clearing a bit. Was he still alive in this cage? Just barely.

"Answer!" she said sternly.

Crouched in a corner, Ellis raised his eyes.

"Very good."

Ellis forced his sunken gaze to meet hers.

"My help comes with conditions," she said with cold authority. "I need you to do something for me. Do you understand?"

Weak but alert, Ellis uttered, "Yes."

She knelt, tossing an object toward him.

The plastic bottle bounced before it rolled to his muddied shoes. Grabbing the container and twisting off its cap drained what little power his hands had left. He gulped it down.

"I have provided. Now, you must do the same."

Ellis finished the bottle.

She held up something in her hand. "What is the passcode?"

His voice came out scratchy. "Passcode?"

"Yes. What is it?"

He stared at the object—and gasped.

One Sunday, Linda asked him to bring her "dirt" to the garden. She was planting pansies—purple ones, her favorite. Earlier that week, they'd visited the home and garden store, where some strapping 20-year-old loaded two 50-pound sacks of fertilizer into the trunk of their car.

Not wanting to be outmatched by a kid—and despite the aches of an aging ex-cop—Ellis hauled a heavy bag to her planting area. But the sack slipped from his shoulder, and his phone tumbled from his pocket, landing just in time for fifty pounds of sacked shit to crush the screen.

The phone in Rena's hand bore those same cracked scars. He hadn't lost his cell. This fucking woman had stolen it during the flight—likely when he'd nodded off for a few minutes.

Now she wanted his passcode.

"Tell me," she demanded.

In her other hand was the phone's battery.

They'd zapped him with a taser, kidnapped him at the airport, drugged him, and held him at knifepoint while he disposed of two bodies. Now, he was their prisoner.

But he had to be strong and think. They needed something. This gave him leverage. Not a lot, but he had to use it to his advantage. He'd waste the opportunity if he gave up his passcode without negotiating something for himself. No, he needed food, more water, and sleep. Right now, it had to be food—he had to stay alive.

But the passcode? He could tell them his phone required a biometric—either a thumbprint or his face. They'd have to give the device to him, and when they did, he'd dial 911 from inside the protection of his cage.

No, no, no. These two would have thought of that already. Either this woman or Belt Buckle had tried this when they drugged him earlier. His phone needed only a passcode, and they knew it. But he still had leverage. He had something they wanted.

"Food," he rasped.

"You will get food once I have your passcode."

No way. Once she gets it, she'll give him nothing. He torqued his head. But why did they want his passcode? Money? He still used a walk-in bank and a checkbook. They couldn't steal anything using his phone because he had never set up online banking. He didn't trust ones and zeros with his cash. Besides, he and Linda weren't rich.

Were they after one of his contacts? Would Rena call someone and force words into his mouth? But who? Almost everyone in his social circle was a retired cop. That'd be stupid.

Holding the two pieces of his phone in her hands, Rena's scowl deepened.

For Ellis, a sudden thought struck. Whether she wanted him to make a quick call or send a text, the moment she reconnected the battery, the phone's GPS would broadcast his location. It didn't matter if the battery was connected for two seconds or two hours, once it pinged a tower, bam! Linda would see the pin on her map! Police would track these jokers to this shitty boondock cabin! His position transmitted instantly!

He nearly laughed aloud. Cops would swoop in from every direction. A squadron of flashing red and blue, excited K-9s, snipers, and choppers thundering overhead. And along for the ride—no doubt—a few of his old chums, loaded for bear, determined to rescue their buddy.

These fucking idiots had no idea. They were going down and didn't even realize it.

"Food!" he shouted with a cough.

Rena stood stone-faced as he glared. She marched out of the room, returning moments later, tossing a sandwich into his cage.

Ellis smiled to himself. Leverage, bitch.

"What is your passcode?" her voice came hard.

He held the cellophane-wrapped, store-bought sandwich in his hands. Ham, cheese, even lettuce. But no price tag—they'd ripped it off. Smart because it would've given him an idea of where he was. But that didn't matter, the police were coming.

Rena raised the pieces of his phone. "Passcode."

Ellis took a bite of the sandwich and tried not to smirk. You and your dipshit pal will be in steel bracelets soon enough.

"Now!" she shouted.

"Five, two, three, nine… one," Ellis said, feigning fear. Now, go on, put the battery into the phone, you fuckhead.

Rena turned to the doorway. "Did you get that?"

Standing outside, Belt Buckle's grizzled voice, tinged with too many cigarettes, answered. "Five, two, three, nine, one."

"Good," she said. "Drive 30 miles north, reconnect the battery to this phone, then send that text we talked about."

Ellis stopped chewing.

"If the passcode does not work, continue north." She pivoted to Ellis. "And kill his wife."

Ellis lunged at the bars, screaming. "No!" A vice gripped his heart. "You're fucking dead! Both of you!"

But Rena struck the light switch and slammed the door, leaving Ellis—and his shrieks—in complete blackness.

Twenty-Three

In the morning, Jadene made her way down to the county library. Of the seven phrases in the telegram, she'd uncovered only one solid lead—and if it didn't pan out, she'd be right back at square one. Though, while she'd picked up a few interesting factoids combing through the archive's musty shelves, she was not able to crack any of the telegram's other phrases. By mid-morning, her only hope was to push forward with what she knew—or thought she knew.

On the long drive to Alabama, Jadene mulled a detail she'd missed early on. Investigations were all about the tiny things, the little stuff. During her conversation with Sinclair, when he'd handed her the telegram, he'd said it was "intercepted during the war." She should have picked up on it then, but didn't.

Intercepted meant that Arthur, Sinclair's grandfather, was not among the Allies. He was a radio operator for the other side. This may also be why the top half of the dispatch itself was torn—to hide its origin.

She decided not to let this fact sway her from her duties. It wasn't Sinclair's fault who his grandfather was, and she couldn't blame him for not disclosing his roots outright. But it reminded her that she needed to remain conscious of all details.

Exiting I-85, she steered the Camry toward the Max Air base gatehouse. A good-looking young man in full uniform checked her ID and provided directions to the research building.

"If you get lost, pretty lady, you come back and see me, all right?" he winked.

Jadene returned a quick smile before speeding away.

Max Air base was a sprawling campus tucked among Montgomery's ample green spaces. As the Camry sputtered onto Chennault Circle, she was thankful no dash lights had gone off in the ten-year-old car during the drive.

Ahead, she found the Historical Research building and a parking space. The facility was open to the public, and she'd memorized the tail number she was after, but in the back of her mind lingered the strong chance none of this would pan out.

The hunt was over if this facility didn't have the log or she couldn't find an entry referencing the tail number. She had absolutely nothing else to go on.

She tucked her notebook under an arm. Dressed in a lilac blouse and jeans, she pocketed her phone and made her way up the facility's brick walkway to the building's entrance.

Inside, the research area felt like a library, but its open spaces were lined with file cabinets instead of bookshelves. Overhead, a complement of fluorescents lit the quiet area nicely for visitors.

She approached the information desk and was met by a distinguished woman with long, gray hair.

"May I help you?" The woman's lanyard read Dottie. She wore sparkly cat-eye glasses, that perfectly matched her gold chunk earrings.

"Hi." Jadene smiled warmly. "I'm looking for information on a flight."

Dottie frowned. "We're not an airport, dear."

Jadene stiffened.

"That one never gets old," Dottie giggled. "Unlike me, oh my goodness. I was 20 with blonde hair and a tight caboose just yesterday." She rolled her eyes. "Can you believe it?"

Chuckling, Jadene said, "Well, you look great, and I love those earrings."

"Oh, thank you, dear," Dottie brushed the gray hair from her lobe. "Now, what can I help you with?"

"I tried searching online but couldn't find anything. And I'm looking for a tail number of a military flight."

"What year was the flight?"

"Nineteen-forty-five," Jadene said. "January."

"Ahh, a World War II bird," Dottie replied.

Jadene crinkled her nose. "And it landed at Lajes Airfield. Took off about an hour later?" Although it wasn't a question, she toned it like one and waited for Dottie's reaction.

The refined woman stroked her chin. "That would be a refueling stop, especially on that base. I know we used the Azores during the war." She dipped her head. "Let me see what details I can scrounge up here."

"Thank you, thank you so much."

Dottie typed away on her keyboard. A minute passed before she spoke. "I know we have Azores records, but that one doesn't appear to be online. There seems to be a hard copy in the physical archives, but it's been marked "special" by Karl."

"Karl?" Jadene asked.

Dottie leaned over the counter so only Jadene could take in her words. "Our previous curator took ill a few weeks ago."

"I'm sorry to hear that," Jadene said.

"Karl Riggins, our new curator, is kind of a stick in the mud. He's been strict about some of the older logs." She shrugged. "It's a bit odd, but I guess you need those types to run this kind of records office."

Jadene tapped the counter. "I totally get it."

Dottie's attention shifted to her computer. "It does seem like we do have it. Although, that date range is one of few we've not scanned and put on the website just yet."

"But it is here?" Jadene said.

"I believe so." Dottie's expression suddenly changed. "Oh, no. Unfortunately, we only have a single, hard copy I'm afraid. And because it's an older log, viewing is by appointment only and must be approved by—"

Jadene sighed. "The stick in the mud?"

"I'm sorry, but he's at lunch for another 30 minutes or so."

Jadene was nowhere without that log. It was her only lead. And, if Karl was as overprotective of the physical logbooks as Dottie led on, he may not let her see it at all because she hadn't called ahead.

Dottie, though, was kind and friendly. If Jadene could persuade her that she needed a quick peak, then Jadene could get what she came for and be on her way. But to do that, she'd have to dig deep into her bag of investigatory tools and pull out the oldest one.

She lowered her eyes. "Tom, my uncle. Well, technically my great uncle. But he flew C47s and C54s during the war. That's why I'm here." She touched her nose. "He, well, he went MIA after his last flight, and I just… I came from Atlanta, and I wanted to…"

Dottie reached across the desk and touched her hand. "I'm so sorry, dear."

Jadene's sullen expression held.

Dottie glanced over her shoulder at a clock on the wall. "Please, dear, take a seat at one of our research tables. I'll be right back."

Jadene's features softened. "Okay."

TWENTY-FOUR

Oak tables and matching fabric chairs stretched the research area. Though, but for two individuals sitting at far off computer terminals, Jadene was the only one in the area.

She found a table and sat.

In less than a minute, Dottie returned with a book. "You said he flew C47s and C54s?"

Jadene nodded.

"Special planes." Dottie smiled. "Not as celebrated as the fighters and bombers. But hauling craft were far more precious than attack planes. They fed the front lines with troops, supplies, and munitions." She raised her head high. "Without the Gooney, there'd be no victory."

"Gooney?" Jadene said. Of course, she already knew the C47's many nicknames, but she hoped by keeping Dottie talking, she wouldn't press for more details about Jadene's "great-uncle."

"Gooney Bird. That's what our boys called it. We think it meant good luck. And overseas, the British called the C47 the Dakota. Did you know that?"

Yes. And a couple of those pilots flew straight into Nazi-occupied Kraków for some reason, escaped with their lives, returned to Lakenheath, and then sped off to Lajes in a C54. And I'm desperately trying to figure out where they landed so I can keep my PI business. So if you could show me those flight records that would be great.

But Jadene smiled as Dottie opened the large picture book she'd brought with her, pushing the hardcover toward her.

"Looks like a Pit Bull, doesn't it?" she said.

Jadene had only seen one photo of the C47 before, and scanned the black-and-white images carefully. Pit Bull truly fit the C47. Made of cold steel and rivets, even on the runway, the squatted aircraft looked like a hungry beast ready to pounce.

"They built thousands. My grandfather said they filled the skies during the war." Dottie turned the page to reveal more photos of the aircraft. "Its top speed was around 225 miles an hour, which was quite fast for the time. And, with crewed oxygen, she could soar the skies at almost 25,000 feet."

"Was that high enough to avoid anti-aircraft fire?"

Dottie laughed. "Oh, no, dear. Even then, flak was deadly up to 40,000 feet."

"Flak?"

"Fliegerabwehrkanone—which is German for anti-aircraft cannon fire, dear. Artillery with proximity sensors, which exploded at altitude. Flak turned the skies into an elevated minefield, making it very hairy for our heroes to fly through." Her lips went crooked. "Nowadays, of course, that word is more commonly used as a dumb downed expression."

Jadene shook her head. "Expression?"

"You know, dear," Dottie said. "Like when someone at the office says, "Bob's going to catch a lot of flak for that bad sales report"— that type of usage."

"You're kidding me? That saying comes from exploding anti-aircraft fire?"

"A shitty comparative, really. It minimizes what our boys went through." Dottie flipped a hand outward. "As if Bob's bad report condemned him to obliteration at 10,000 feet."

Jadene shot a laugh.

Dottie rose. "I'll be right back, dear."

Jadene perused the pictures and read the commentary. Born from the Douglas DC-3, the C47 offered duty, no comfort. Under each wing, like a coiled muscle, roared a Pratt and Whitney 1,200-horsepower engine. Both motors torqued a three-blade, 12-foot propeller.

She flipped more pages and found the C54 Skymaster.

If the twin-engine Dakota Skytrain was a Pit Bull, then the longer and more powerful C54 Skymaster was a Rottweiler.

The four-prop aircraft was based on the bigger DC-4. Its design, engines, and raw, unrefined strength—Jadene could almost feel the aircraft's immense power by looking at the book's photos. Both planes were artifacts of a different time, she considered. When war was more meat-grinder and less drones and smart bombs.

Dottie returned moments later, cradling a lunchbox-sized container. Gloved in white mitts, she set the gray box on the table and retook her seat.

"This is one of our oldest selections," she said, opening the lid. "I'm not supposed to handle these myself. But you've come all this way, dear. I don't think us having a look-see will do any harm."

"Thank you so much," Jadene smiled.

Dottie lifted a three-ring leather binder from the inside, supporting its spine with gloved fingertips.

"There must be something special about this log," she said, setting the binder on the tabletop.

"Why do you say that?"

"Well," Dottie began. "It's not part of the cleaning rotation. Karl prefers to do that himself. And, like I said, it's a log he didn't want scanned."

The aroma of musty leather struck Jadene.

"Because it's very fragile, I'm guessing?"

Dottie gave half a nod. "I'm not sure. I've seen others of this era that we have digitized, and they're no worse for wear, honestly." She edged the box aside. "But who knows for sure. Karl is just very particular."

Dottie had used the word "particular" twice when referring to Karl. Jadene guessed that's why the man had the job in the first place. Wardens of historical documents like these needed that quirk, she figured.

"Dear, what was your date again?" Dottie asked.

Jadene leaned in. "January 17, please."

Dottie turned its yellowed pages. "Mm-hmm."

Hand-scribed with names, dates, numbers, and codes. There were also tiny notations on many paged entries.

Most of the ink inside its pages was black, with some red, blotchy in places, and weathered with time. The flight register also contained handwriting and printing, indicating more than one person used it—which made sense—Jadene only hoped one of those people had recorded the detail on the flight she was searching for.

Dottie halted her page-turning. "Here we are," she said. "What flight number were you looking for?"

Jadene rubbed her hands together beneath the table. "It was a flight from Lakenheath, England, 42-056."

Dottie examined the entries, turned a page, and then another with the tips of her gloved fingers.

Jadene held her breath.

Dottie pointed but did not touch the page itself. "Here we are. Tail number 42-056."

Jadene gazed at the entry, a tremor slipping down her spine.

"Oh, oh my," Dottie said. "Interesting."

"What is it?" Jadene said.

Dottie's expression turned grim. "I'm afraid you've come all this way for nothing, dear."

Jadene lowered her brows.

"I'm sorry, but the pilot wasn't your uncle Tom."

Jadene dropped her shoulders. Oh shit. She'd forgotten about good old uncle Tom.

TWENTY-FIVE

Jadene was trapped. Sitting beside Dottie, she tried to catch a glimpse of the flight log, but the musty paper was just out of view. She was desperate to see whatever name was written there. If only Dottie would shift her arm, Jadene could catch a glimpse and weave another lie—something convincing, like the pilot's real name being Joe or John, with everyone in the family calling him Tom.

However, without that detail, she was stuck. Her mind raced. She needed to keep Dottie engaged, to make the narrative seamless. She had to determine the aircraft's destination. She couldn't continue her investigation without it.

Jadene rubbed her nose, searching for an angle. "There's something about this plane. I don't know what yet, but it feels important—to my family, maybe even to the war."

Dottie fiddled with the page. "All right, then. If your uncle was linked to this pilot, that would be extraordinary."

Jadene leaned forward. "Extraordinary?"

Dottie pointed to the entry. "Because we've got ourselves a real maverick here."

"A maverick? Who?"

Dottie's face lit up. "Captain Gabe Gabreski. An exceptional pilot. But really, all of these men were."

"Fearless?" Jadene asked.

"Oh, no, dear. I'm sure all of these pilots were plenty scared. But back then, boys had a sense of purpose—passion, duty, and determination. It's hard to describe." Her smile widened. "They didn't join for money or recognition. They believed in protecting the ideals of this nation. It was grit and pride. Our world was different back then." Her expression soured. "Nowadays, people are glued to their gadgets, and this kind of country-first guardianship is lost."

Jadene nibbled the inside of her cheek. Tommy had said something similar.

"But Gabreski was a testament to persistence." She returned her attention to the log. "Did you know he almost flunked out of flight school?"

Jadene leaned in, pushing past her rising impatience. She needed Dottie to keep talking. "Really?"

"I'm not the expert, but Gabreski was born in Pennsylvania. Although he got into aviation in college, he wasn't the best pilot."

"Not the best? Did he crash or something?"

Dottie gave a short, breathy laugh. "Not that I know of, but he almost flunked out of Notre Dame his freshman year. Too much fun with the boys." She mimed a drinking gesture, rolling her eyes.

Jadene smirked at Dottie's gesture.

"His flight instructor said he didn't have the pilot's touch."

"Did they kick him out?"

"No, but they were ready to." She scratched her nose. "It took time, but Gabreski eventually got his shit together."

Jadene chuckled at Dottie's colorful language.

"He enlisted in the US Army Air Corps in 1940."

"And that's when he started flying in combat?"

"Oh, no. War pilots need to earn their combat wings first. This isn't Delta Airlines."

Jadene gave a quiet snort.

Dottie continued, "They ran him through hell—formation flying, aerial tactics, even fixing his own bird."

"Really?" Jadene's last boyfriend couldn't change a tire.

"Absolutely. Stewardship was vital. Gabreski loved flying, but he faced challenges in the Army Air Corps."

"Oh?"

"His instructors put him through a check ride, which is like having a chef watch you cook to ensure you don't burn the kitchen down."

"He was that bad?"

"He struggled with takeoffs and landings. And he and his airplane had a tendency to wander out of formation, like a balloon caught in a windstorm."

Jadene laughed. "Did he pass?"

"Barely." A frown tugged at Dottie's lips. "Then again, maybe his instructor was too terrified to ride with him again."

"Certified out of fear?" Jadene's lips curled at the corners.

"Probably," Dottie said, eyes twinkling. "But Gabreski wasn't one to quit. He moved on to advanced training, right here at Max Air base." Pride twinkled in her eyes. "In 1942, he convinced his commanders to let him fly for the Polish command." Her tone softened, reverent now. "It mattered to him, flying with men who needed someone to believe in them."

"The Polish command?" Jadene asked, suspicion flickering.

"Our Polish Allies lacked experience, and Gabreski spoke fluent Polish. He believed he could help. His commanders agreed, and he went to the UK." She touched Jadene's arm. "For two years, he flew 20 missions, downing over 30 enemy aircraft—more than any other Allied pilot."

"Wow."

Dottie smirked. "Not bad for a wandering balloon, right?"

"Not at all," Jadene replied, wondering if Gabreski had flown the C47 into Kraków. As the log confirmed, he'd flown from Lakenheath to Lajes. Could he have piloted both the Skytrain and the Skymaster? Given his record, it was possible.

Just as the pieces began to click, the air around her changed—thick with the weight of someone watching.

"Dottie?" a voice called behind them.

She rose. "Just a moment, dear."

The logbook remained open. Jadene couldn't decipher the notes and symbols next to Gabreski's entry and would have to wait for Dottie's return. Meanwhile, the conversation behind her grew louder.

"Is that one of the Azores?" a man said sharply.

More discussion followed.

His voice raised. "Atlanta?"

Something was off. Jadene doubted her sob story would work a second time on whomever this was, and without the logbook information, her investigation would hit a brick wall. She was so close.

Her stomach tightened. She discreetly snapped a few photos of the logbook with her phone.

"Excuse me?" a voice called.

She slipped her phone into her blouse and turned. "Yes?"

Karl Riggins wore no identification. His name was stitched into his burgundy blazer. The bald, fit man peered down at her. "That log is delicate. My associate should not have shared it."

"I didn't mean to cause trouble," she said with a concerned expression.

Dottie stood behind the curator, looking apologetic.

Karl reached for the log. "I understand you're researching a relative?" With his bare hands, he closed the book and placed it back in the gray box. "If you provide your name, I will assist."

She stood abruptly. "I was just leaving, but thank you." The phone slid down the inside of her blouse. Her heart kicked. The phone snagged at her waistline, still hidden—barely.

Karl clutched the box. "What's your name?"

Jadene grabbed her purse, turned quickly, and headed for the door. "Dottie was very helpful," she said.

Outside, she hurried through the parking lot to her car. With only three days left, there was no time to explain things to that Karl character—who didn't seem nearly as compassionate as Dottie. Besides, she had what she needed.

The C47 Dakota Skytrain had taken off from Lakenheath and landed in war-torn Kraków. Who or what the aircraft carried was still unknown, but whatever the cargo, it did return to Lakenheath. She also believed Gabreski piloted that plane. Upon landing, he switched to a larger C54 Skymaster, likely transporting his passengers or cargo from Kraków on a new flight path to Lajes Airfield before heading west over the Atlantic.

Important questions lingered. Where did the C54 land? Who or what was on board? And, finally, how did it all tie back to Sinclair's grandfather?

A uniformed guard waved as she exited Max Airfield's gatehouse, but Jadene sped past without a glance.

She ran a hand inside her shirt and pulled out the phone. If the truth was anywhere, it was in those photos—and she was running out of time.

Twenty-Six

"Please, no," Ellis begged.

Rena raised an eyebrow, her finger hovering over the device.

"You don't need to turn that on," he said, his voice cracking. "I've given you what you asked for."

She stood in silence, her expression unreadable.

He gazed up from the cage. "What did I do to you?"

Yes, he was still bone-tired, but the sandwich had refreshed his brain. His thoughts snapped into focus, a plan forming. He needed to gather every scrap of information about her, then drive a wedge between her and Belt Buckle. A gamble, sure—but his only move. He'd used this trick before, pitting one thug against another in countless interrogations. It worked then. Maybe it could work now.

"I don't know what you want unless you tell me," he said, calculating his tone. "Or should I be asking your partner?"

Rena's glare hardened.

Ellis blinked, trying to appear fragile. This entire ordeal—his taking, imprisonment, isolation—she was trying to break him down. And he would feign brokenness if it sped things up. Besides, he fucking hated that chirping noise.

Rena was about to say something when a vibration came from her pocket. Fishing out the device, she swiped its screen.

"Yes?" she said, holding her glare on Ellis.

Ellis wanted to yell, get the attention of whoever was on the other end of the call, but quickly dismissed the idea. The caller probably wouldn't understand anything he shouted, and she'd play it off—getting him nowhere. Besides, he didn't know where he was.

Instead, he tried to listen to her call.

"When?" Rena turned away.

Ellis eyed her, trying to pick up anything from the conversation. A thin male voice echoed on the other end, though it wasn't loud enough to make out any of the words. Who was she speaking with? Belt Buckle?

Why did they want the passcode for his phone? What would they gain by using it? Were they trying to contact Linda? Would they try to coax her here? Was that what this phone call was about? That'd be a mistake, he smirked. A mistake he'd hoped they'd make.

Thirty seconds passed before she spoke.

"No. I will take care of this," Rena said matter-of-factly.

He stayed hunkered in the cage, sneaking peeks as she paced by the doorway. The room he was trapped in had no window and only a single door for entry. The walls had cedar slats, and the place stank of dampness. In the ceiling, a single socket with a bulb lit the small room.

"I need the description," she said to the caller.

No name or pronoun. Was she making reference to a person? Was it him? Had the media released his missing person photo? Was there an Amber alert? Wait, those were for kids. A Silver Alert, then? But he wasn't elderly, and they wouldn't use that, would they?

Shit, two decades on the force, and it took his own kidnapping for him to realize this gap. Okay, he wasn't a child, and he wasn't elderly. Maybe a Goldilocks Alert? But why would she ask about his description? Yeah, it wasn't making much sense.

Rena wandered outside the room, phone to her earlobe.

He narrowed his gaze. Description—was she talking about a vehicle and not a person? Had they spotted the food truck that kidnapped him? Traffic cameras, possibly? Could they have followed him down here? Yeah, he doubted it. The last several miles were on an unpaved country road. Had they identified the two assholes that grabbed him in the parking lot? Not that it mattered—both were face-down in a ditch right now.

He tapped his thumbs on his knees. Rena and Belt Buckle were dangerous and wouldn't let him go. Linda was the reason he had to survive this. She would be out of her mind with worry, but she was strong. She would have alerted his friends on the force, who would be hunting for him. He had to buy them time. Or, he needed to find an escape before they threw him down the gully outside.

He held in the cage's corner. Would they move him somewhere else if the cops were on the trail? Did he have the strength to overpower them if one of them opened the door again? He had to. Otherwise, he was dead.

But direct confrontation with Belt Buckle was a death wish. The man had the advantage of strength and familiarity with the woods. Ellis was also smart enough to know there was no use trying to outrun a bloodthirsty redneck and his knife.

However, Rena was the real threat. This wasn't her cabin. These men weren't her usual clique. But she was the mastermind. That cold fixation in her eyes went beyond greed. It was personal. He could see it. She'd kill anyone who stood in her way.

He gripped the cage's bars. Did he have enough time to create distrust between this woman and Belt Buckle? Could he turn one against the other? Would one of them side with him? What if the plan failed? Too much could go wrong.

He needed an edge, any edge. Beneath him, the thick leather lace of his shoe dug into his hindquarters.

He shifted his jaw, an idea flickering. The rebar was wired in cross sections with no gap big enough for his hand to slip through. He'd tested them all, scraping his knuckles on the ribbed bars. But the joints were tac-welded. Every one of them.

He slid a hand under his hindquarters. Two shoelaces, both leather. But what could he use as a twist?

Rena reappeared in the doorway.

"Yes. Thank you," she said, clicking off the call.

Ellis refocused on her. Who was she talking with? Not Belt Buckle, there was no way she'd be that courteous to that asshole.

"Interesting," she said, her frosty gaze turning toward him.

Ellis stayed low in his corner, fingering a lace on his loafer.

"Your usefulness has come to an end," she said coldly.

The light clicked off, the door creaked shut, and the room sank into silence.

TWENTY-SEVEN

The late evening air was crisp—the low hum of the city quieter than usual. With more research ahead, and her apartment's Wi-Fi still unreliable, Jadene drove downtown to her office.

Lilly had left for the day.

Armed with the Gabreski lead, she needed to pinpoint where that Skymaster landed. If it crossed the Atlantic into the U.S., it should've touched down at an East Coast base.

She typed the query. Hit enter.

Results filled the screen.

In 1945, the East Coast was lined with military airfields, stretching from Key West to Newfoundland. Worse still, there were hundreds of active bases in between.

Overwhelmed, she dropped her head into her hands. For the next three hours, she combed through the list, cross-checking each airfield and poring over every log she could access.

Outside, the glow of streetlights bathed the quiet commercial district. Storefronts and canopied walkways had all gone dark—except hers.

From her desk, she glanced at the oversized Bowman Investigations sign glowing garishly in the front window. A neon-pink eyesore she'd once ordered with pride, imagining herself a real-life super-sleuth. Now it just embarrassed her.

She scrolled through line after line of faded handwritten entries. Bombers like the B-17 and B-24—massive, high-altitude giants—took up most of the space. Then came the fighters: P-51 Mustangs, P-47 Thunderbolts, F4F Wildcats, F6F Hellcats. Next were the utility and transport craft—the B-25 Mitchell, the C-47 Skytrain. Her eyes ached as the entries piled on.

Jittery and drained, she reached for her mug, ready for a third refill, when an entry caught her attention.

C-54. Lajes.

Her mug tipped, clattering to the desk.

January 18, 1945. 3:21 a.m. A Skymaster had landed at Hunter Army Airfield, arriving from Lajes.

Heart pounding, she pulled the laptop closer, foot bouncing beneath the desk.

The pilot's name was in the record.

Gabreski.

Her mouth went dry. "Oh, my God."

She brushed her fingers against the screen, stunned. She had tracked an 80-year-old military flight from England to Kraków, Poland—deep in Nazi-occupied territory where the Soviets had begun to press in. Chaos reigned across the region. Somehow, amid that, the flight made it to Lakenheath in the UK. There, passengers and cargo were transferred to a Skymaster, piloted by Gabreski—a man known for guts, grit, and flying through hell.

He took the plane west, over the Atlantic to the Azores, landing at Lajes Airfield—a crucial mid-Atlantic refueling base.

She grinned.

And now, she'd confirmed it had reached Savannah's Hunter Army Airfield.

Excited, she scrolled further.

This was huge. But it raised new questions. Who had Gabreski flown from Kraków to the States? Would the log list passenger names? Could Arthur Whitmore himself have been on board?

Her smile began to fade.

There were no names listed. No cargo details. No personnel offloaded.

Loyal, not lost. But she was lost—and puzzled.

Only one entry stood out.

A new pilot.

Collin Buckley. No rank. No military designation. The log simply noted that Buckley took over the aircraft. Twenty-four minutes after landing, the Skymaster took off again.

Another refueling stop.

She leaned forward, narrowing her eyes. If no one deplaned, that meant the passengers were still aboard. That meant the trail continued. And now that the plane was within the continental U.S., maybe—just maybe—tracking it further would be easier.

She keyed a new query. Where did the Skymaster go next? If anyone was on that flight, they had to be influential. Maybe Buckley flew them straight to Washington, D.C., or another covert location. If so, it could open a new thread—one tied to the real purpose of the flight. One tied to Whitmore.

Then she saw it.

The final note under "Destination" read simply: West—private.

Her stomach dropped. That could mean anything. A different state. A classified base. Maybe even another country. And why "private"? This was a military aircraft.

"What the actual fuck?" she said, throwing up her hands. "That's it? That's all I get?"

She stared at the screen, frustrated. Two aircraft. Two continents. Through an active warzone. Over seven thousand miles. And this was her next clue? West?

She scrubbed a hand down her face and dove back into the logs.

Another hour passed.

Still no record of the Skymaster's next stop.

But something else popped up—Collin Buckley had a relative still alive, living just a few hours away in Augusta.

Not an answer. But a direction.

Exhausted, she shut her laptop, packed her things, locked up the office, and made her way to the car. Tomorrow, she'd hit the road again.

She'd find that airplane—and whatever secrets it carried.

Twenty-Eight

In the morning, Jadene sent a text to Lilly telling her of her plans to travel to Augusta and chase down a lead. For once, Lilly replied in perfect English, no emojis: "I'll take care of everything. Safe travels, boss!"

Jadene read the text three times, then grinned. She was making progress.

As for the lead, it was Collin Buckley. The second pilot listed on the manifest who'd taken over for Gabreski once the Skymaster landed at Hunter Army Air base. However, he passed away in 1996.

Fortunately, Jadene was able to locate his grandson, Ronald Buckley. According to her search, he was a high school science teacher living nearby in Augusta.

Arriving unannounced was a gamble. But without a phone number, she had no choice but to make another long journey southeast of the city. And the roundtrip would consume most of her day, leaving her with too much time to think.

Beyond the names of a couple of pilots and a scattered theory about all of it, she had far more questions than answers. Was she closing in on anything tangible? Could any of this mystery be solved? Would she ever learn who was airlifted from Kraków and delivered to the United States? And for what reason?

She tapped a finger on the steering wheel.

It was Lilly's discovery, though, that troubled her most. Had someone inside Hitler's Third Reich intercepted the message? Could that person have been Arthur Whitmore, Sinclair's own grandfather?

A dryness filled her mouth.

Arthur was the reason for her investigation in the first place. But who was he, really? So many awful implications loomed. Was he fighting for the wrong side in a war that forever scarred history?

She liked Sinclair, but what if this all pointed to a vile legacy? Had she stumbled upon a hidden truth, one best left buried?

Or did Sinclair know his grandfather was a Nazi? If he did, why didn't he tell her? What purpose would there be in hiring her to confirm it? If Sinclair knew of Arthur's background, it was a burden he had to wrestle with. Why drag her into all of it?

Jadene scratched her chin. Or was there something else happening? Something she wasn't aware of? Could she be putting herself at risk if she continued?

Whichever way this played out, it left Jadene with three options. If she quit the case, Sinclair would demand that she return some or all of the money. He might even sue her. She couldn't afford any of that mess, and with his unlimited resources, it would mean the end of her business. He'd said the deposit was hers to keep—whether or not she found significant results—but she couldn't leave the case.

She could coast. Slow walk things and pretend to keep investigating. It would be dishonest, but if Sinclair knew the message's origin, he had first deceived her. But again, why? What purpose would lying to her serve?

The last option was to plow forward. Uncover everything possible, no matter where it leads. This would also allow her to keep the money and stay true to her promise.

Jadene nodded to herself. She'd remain on course, but set a boundary. If the information she uncovered came to a point where she could prove, beyond any doubt, that Arthur fought with the enemy, then she'd take her foot off the gas. She'd provide the bare minimum of detail, romanticize nothing, collect her cash, and be done with all of this.

She also wouldn't mention this dilemma to Lilly. While the girl was smart, Jadene doubted she'd connected everything or would understand its significance if she did.

At the next exit, she left the highway.

She followed the GPS map and, within a few minutes, found a cute neighborhood of mid-sized, detached homes. She made the proper turns as the GPS commanded and rounded into a cul-de-sac.

Nestled at the end was Ronald Buckley's home. An ocean blue, single-story, with ivory-white trim and a well-manicured lawn.

In its driveway sat a convertible white Lexus. The sporty vehicle told Jadene that either Ronald Buckley had no children or they'd grown and had moved out.

Jadene parked in the street, adjacent to the home's mailbox. She grabbed her notebook, exited her vehicle, and approached the home's front porch.

Nearby, a woman in a tank top and stretch pants pushed a baby stroller on the sidewalk. Jadene smiled at the exercising mother, who countered with a slight wave.

The porched entryway to the Buckley home was a charming space with two rocking chairs and a small, ornate table bearing a vase of freshly cut gardenias. The flower's fragrance filled the area with a welcoming scent.

At the moment, Jadene's entire investigation hinged on where Collin Buckley flew that Skymaster. Hopeful, she inhaled and pressed the doorbell.

Heeled steps approached, unlocked the deadbolt, and the front door cracked open.

"Yes?" a woman asked firmly.

Forty, Jadene guessed, and slender with long hair in a tight ponytail. It was hard to get a good look at her, though, as the home's dark insides obscured her facial features.

"Hello. Is this the Buckley residence?"

"Yes, it is. What do you need?"

Jadene stuck out her hand. "I'm Jadene Bowman. I'm a private investigator from Atlanta."

The woman ignored the greeting. The door held open just enough for them to speak to one another.

"What do you need?"

Jadene lowered her hand. "I'm following a lead on a case. Does a Ronald Buckley live here?"

"That is my father," the woman said. "Yes, he does, but they are away right now. Is there something I can help you with?"

Jadene swallowed. "Can we talk inside, perhaps?"

The woman glanced beyond her to the trotting mother and her baby buggy on the sidewalk.

"I am on my way out," she said. "I only have a minute"

"Oh, okay," Jadene said. "When do you expect him?"

She glared. "Not for some time."

This wasn't going as Jadene hoped, but she tried to maintain a friendly tone.

"Do you know how I can reach him?" she asked.

"My father is away on a cruise, unreachable," the daughter said, almost too quickly. "He and his wife will not be back for a week."

"Do you think I could get his cell number? It's important."

The woman's ponytail swooshed behind her head. "I am uncomfortable providing information like that to a stranger," she scoffed. "What is this about?"

She was a chore, but Jadene maintained a smile. "Well, it's actually about Collin Buckley."

"Collin Buckley?"

"Yes," Jadene said. "That would be, I believe, your great-grandfather. He flew during World War II."

She appeared uninterested. "I have never heard of any relative serving in the war." She shooed a hand outward. "Now, I really must be on my way."

The door started to close.

Jadene stopped it with a foot wedge. "Your ring," she said. "It's beautiful. Is that a ruby?"

The Buckley woman shot a glance at the jewel on her hand, but kept her weight against the door.

"Please." Jadene fished out a business card. "Can you tell your father I stopped by? And if he can, can he call me at his earliest convenience? I really need to connect with him, please."

The woman snatched the card.

"Thank you," Jadene said.

The door thumped closed.

Jadene rolled her eyes. "And have a nice day."

She stepped off the front porch, frustration bubbling. She'd come a long way for nothing. It was doubtful Buckley's daughter would even pass on her information. The woman was super uptight and annoyed.

This could turn into a dead end. But there had to be another lead to follow up on—something inside the strange telegram she hadn't uncovered yet.

The Camry struggled to start, but when it did, the check engine light blinked. Jadene drew a heavy sigh, praying she'd make it back home before any more lights came on, or worse.

Slowly, she and the vehicle sputtered from the cul-de-sac.

Twenty-Nine

"Thank you," Jadene Bowman said.

Rena shoved the door closed and locked it.

Attractive, the detective had a thin, athletic build with high cheekbones and chestnut hair. She and the woman were also about the same height, separated by only a handful of years.

Rena peered through the glass. The private investigator retreated to her car and, finally, pulled from the curb, disappearing down the street.

For now, she'd delivered a dead end. Without the location, the Bowman woman would never find what she was seeking. However, shutting down the sleuth's legwork left Rena in no better situation.

She examined the business card. Bowman Investigations. The address was familiar—the downtown area—and she would make the proper preparations. Doing anything in this quiet neighborhood wasn't possible. There were too many eyeballs. The busy-bodied woman and her baby, the other unknowns. The acquisition had to be clean. Her quest could suffer no pointless tangles.

Rena entered the kitchen, stepping around the blood. She searched the counter area, opened a drawer and found various cooking tools. Hardy scissors, oversized serving utensils, and an aluminum meat mallet.

She chose the mallet.

Seizing a dish towel, she paced through the area, unlocking the side kitchen door. Using the towel, she draped a glass panel above the door's knob, from the outside.

She swung the mallet.

The pane shattered, its sound deadened by the dish towel.

Rena returned inside and closed the door.

The bloodied man on the kitchen floor groaned.

She circled his body, twisting the ring on her middle finger. Every life and obstacle was collateral on a trail to uncompromising justice. Not just for her family, but for the millions. A path that demanded staunch resolve with no compassion. This was the way great things got done, and what her people expected of her.

She kneeled.

Ronald Buckley's eyelids fluttered.

She raised the mallet, steady and sure.

All in pursuit.

The hammer struck his skull with a sickening crunch.

His arms flailed, and his legs kicked.

She delivered several more blows until the thrashing man fell still—his eyes dull of life.

Things would have been easier had Buckley not been home. A man she'd already questioned and surveilled for weeks and who'd known nothing.

While the initial shot she'd fired did cripple Buckley, it did not kill him. However, shooting the man again, as she'd done after he invited her inside, was too risky in this quiet area. Neighbors, mothers with babies, and the general nosiness of bored suburbanites could foil her plans.

She seized a second dishrag from the counter, wiping away the blood spots from her hands and face. Then, she wrapped the mallet with the rag. She would dispose of these implements later.

She did not need to clean the area. The silicone on her fingertips obscured her prints, and her black halter dress quickly absorbed Buckley's errant blood spatter.

The police would assume a break-in.

Rena had made sure of it.

She carefully slipped out the kitchen's backdoor and rounded the home's yard to the street, careful not to disturb the broken glass.

The woman in the tank top and stretch pants trotted across the roadway, pushing a baby stroller.

Rena waited behind a row of bushes in the yard.

When the mother passed, Rena made her way to the BMW.

Now that she was certain Jadene Bowman was on the trail, it was time to plan the next step.

However, she couldn't do everything alone. Her exposure would be too great, and there was too much at risk for her to fail. She didn't relish using a local, but she couldn't be in two places at once.

Travis Floyd had proved predictable so far. His crude skills and handiwork were valuable, and he obeyed her like a dog. She hadn't shared the plans with him because of his criminal perversions—which was ironic, because those tendencies were precisely why he was valuable to her. But he was only useful when tightly controlled—left to his own devices, he'd ruin everything.

Slipping on her sunglasses, she started the BMW.

Her captive, he was nearly ripe. It was time to squeeze.

Down the street, the mother and baby strolled.

Had the young mom gotten a glimpse of her when she and the detective chatted in the doorway minutes ago?

Eyeing her and the baby, a thought came. A slight turn of the wheel is all it would take to shatter their simple world.

THIRTY

Travis Lee Floyd sat in his Bronco as rain pounded the windshield. This area was a retail zone of tiny shops and outlets. He'd parked down the street, far enough from his target to avoid being noticed.

Rena shouted through the phone's speaker. "Do it!"

Before Travis could reply, lightning flashed, and the call clicked off. He tossed the burner on the dash, fished out a snuff bottle from a pocket, uncapped it, and tapped a fat line on the backside of his hand. A quick sniff pulled the white powder into his nose, where it rocketed into his bloodstream.

He clacked his teeth.

From the truck's center console, he snatched his serrated Buck Knife. Pulling his silver belt buckle aside, he slipped the blade into a hidden sheath behind the medallion, concealing its handle under his denim jacket.

Low-rollers had to make their own opportunities. He was lucky to crack ten bucks an hour with two felony convictions—and punching a timecard would never make him rich. It was either the cards he was dealt, or a reckless hand he'd played long before he'd understood the game. Either way, he needed cash, real cash, to buy a new life. But no one would hand him shit—he'd have to take it.

And the only way to do that was to grind, stay hard, and when the opportunity came, he'd pounce and never look back.

He'd posted on EagerTask.com with an anonymous email and a pre-paid credit card to cover the eleven-dollar fee. The wording he'd used was simple: I solve problems, have own tools, cash up front.

It took time to get those words right. He had to weed out the simple and clueless for the first few weeks. An old lady wanted a quote to repaint her house, while another demanded he service their home generator because it was making a knocking noise and coughing out black smoke.

He'd responded to a few of them. Mow your own lawn. Build your own deck. Fuck your generator.

But finally, his post reached the proper client.

He'd first met a strange bald man, whose name he never got. The guy seemed like a shifty asshole. But that didn't matter—it was just an introduction. He'd be doing shit for a woman named Rena.

Auburn hair and a looker, for sure. Thirties, maybe. Rena had a killer body and a generous amount of chest. But no man like him wanted a dominant female, so he never bothered flirting with her.

Their meeting happened in a rundown diner where the coffee tasted like burnt rubber, and duct tape covered the cuts and cracks in the shitty booths. Rena slid into the seat across from him, removed her Dolce & Gabbana frames, and scanned the room before she locked eyes with him. "You come recommended," she said. Her silky voice had a foreign hitch. Travis remembered nodding, saying little, keeping himself mysterious. She'd laid out the basics, nothing too detailed, just enough to pique his interest. A downpayment of two thousand to start, with the promise of more cash as things progressed.

At the time, he didn't need to fish for details. Rena slid the entire advance across the table, along with a burner cell. "Keep the phone with you at all times," she'd said. But the money, the weight of the bills in his hand. That was all the motivation he needed back then.

But she'd fed him the job in pieces and parts. He'd been told not to ask too many questions. She wanted a base of operations, someplace off grid and remote. He lived in a rundown hunting cabin, way out in the boondocks. She'd said there would be a prisoner, so he built a cage. It would be the man at the airport, so he hired the two idiot food workers with means and access. When she'd decided there were too many witnesses, he didn't argue.

The work was exciting, but the pay was shit. There'd been no more cash since the two grand. Not for the kidnapping or helping dispose of those two jokers or the other shit Rena demanded. He wasn't some idiot, though she sure treated him like one.

Rena, the things she wore, the way she acted—she came from money. And this job, whatever the whole thing was about, he could smell dollar signs. She was holding out on him.

But this new task? She was taking advantage of him again, and he knew it. The same way punch-clock employers did when he'd tried to go straight. He had a record, and they could lowball him at every turn.

And yet here he was. Doing the heavy lifting and taking most of the risk. He was visible out here while Rena and her partner remained comfortably behind the scenes working on their scheme. A scheme he didn't understand and they wouldn't share with him.

Whatever the final take was, he wasn't getting anything close to whatever those two were raking in. And that fact pissed him off since this all began. The shares should be equal. In fact, he should get a little more. This whole thing smelled of bullshit.

There would be a time and place, and they would pay a heavy price for underestimating him. For now, he'd play the part and keep up his end of the bargain.

Outside came a massive lightning strike. Travis flinched at the loud boom. Around him, all of the streetlights extinguished, and the overhead traffic signal flashed red. Power had gone out in the entire area. Chalk one up for luck, he smirked.

Turning off the headlights, he shifted into drive and the Bronco rolled through the blinking intersection. With no one around, he drove up a few spaces and pulled to the curb.

He had to do this swiftly. The rain should also provide him cover. He drew the knife's butt from under his jacket. It wasn't the best weapon, but with his background, he couldn't upgrade without spending a thousand bucks or more on a scratched heater. And, if he was caught with a handgun, the cops would toss him back in a concrete box for three to five. Not worth it. He'd make do with the blade.

He popped his jacket's denim collar to obscure his face. Damn cameras were everywhere nowadays and that'd be the first thing the stupid cops would check.

He swung open the Bronco's door and hopped down from the cab. His boots splashed through puddles, the wet pavement slick beneath his steps. He made his way to a windowed doorway. A large, defunct neon sign stuck awkwardly against the glass, lifeless.

He scanned the area for any signs of life, but the rain-shrouded storefronts remained dim and empty.

A sly grin spread across his face as he reached for the handle.

THIRTY-ONE

Morning brought a steady downpour. With the Camry needing service, Jadene had no choice but to walk the city mile to work. She usually did so on foot but never in the rain. She slipped on her sneakers and recalled Sinclair's clever story as she laced them up when her phone buzzed with a text. Lilly would be late to the office but should arrive by 10 a.m.

Jadene shook her head. That meant eleven or noon, according to Lilly time. But that was fine. It gave her much-needed quiet as she was still far from solving this puzzle.

Lilly was probably still sleeping off whatever her Thursday brought her. An attractive young girl, Jadene liked her, but the unfocused Lilly was a long way from understanding the kind of discipline it took to manage a career in a professional setting.

Splashing along the sidewalk, she rounded the block at Sean's Vape, mulling over her progress. Investigation-wise, there was no verified way to know if she was on the right trail. Sadly, she'd had this same feeling before, years ago. Either she was closing in on solving this case or chasing ghosts and was far from the end. It was impossible to know which.

Still, she had to remind herself this wasn't about cracking the old telegram's message. Sinclair only wanted to understand the kind of man his grandfather, Arthur, was. That was the scope and what he was paying her for.

But, so far, nothing she'd come across had even mentioned Arthur. She couldn't prove or disprove he was on the Kraków flight. In fact, it was looking more likely he was nothing more than a rank-and-file Nazi radio operator whose only contribution to this entire mystery was to intercept an Allied communication and slip it into the hands of his confused grandson on his deathbed.

Jadene trudged down the alley behind her storefront and fished out her office keys. Shaking the drops from her umbrella, she entered and switched on the lights.

Despite the rain, she would also unlock the front door in case, by some miracle, a walk-in client showed up. But, really, it was more for Stan Roseman. She didn't want to leave the poor man out in the storm if he hobbled by to check on her.

She grabbed a cup of coffee and plopped into her chair.

The angry weather flashed and thundered outside, causing the lights in her office to sputter.

Last night, she'd laid awake thinking of anything else in the telegram that might help the investigation, recalling her meeting with Sinclair.

She eyed the telegram, cycling through what she'd uncovered so far. *Dakota Free Blue* was definitely a plane flight—at least two of them. But she'd hit a dead-end trying to locate its destination thanks to the unhelpful woman in Augusta.

Broken Castle could be a dwelling, but searching the phrase had gotten her nowhere. She'd have to revisit it at some point but decided to concentrate on the other terms first to see if they could bring more context.

Bay of the Montebello was either a city in the San Gabriel Mountains of Los Angeles, California—which was nowhere near the water. Or a city in Italy—which was nowhere near the water.

Whispering West meant almost nothing. Tommy had said the word whispering referred to a secret, a privy. But secret west? It didn't make sense.

Hermann was probably a name, she figured. But who? How were they involved? Without a first name, any probe was pointless.

A search of *Double Safe Haven* pointed to a romantic thriller released in 2013. Additional results led to a healthcare facility and another linked to a financial firm that urged its clients to invest in gold.

Little Ranch returned various photographs of farms and acreages throughout the United States. Some were charming, she had to admit, with big red barns and grazing cattle—but it was another rabbit hole. She found nothing conclusive as far as the investigation was concerned.

Powodzenia still meant good luck. With time running out, she could use a barnyard of that right now.

Jadene fired up her laptop, confirmed a few details, and noted others. She let out a heavy sigh, then confessed to herself she had no idea where to go from here.

Outdoors, an impressive crack of lightning cleaved the sky. Jadene bounced from her chair as trailing thunder rattled the building. The lights in the office blinked out. The glowing laptop on her desk hummed—but its internet connection went dead.

That strike was either a direct hit or had caused a significant surge. The power could be out for a few minutes or several hours. She crossed the empty office and gazed out the front window. The afternoon was coming, but the skies were a gloomy black-gray. Steady rain grew into a relentless downpour as thunder rumbled.

Across the wet street at Eva's Bakery, the neon "open" sign was dark. All electricity in the entire area was probably out, she figured. There wasn't a customer in sight, and the streets were barren, except for an old, black Ford Bronco parked near the intersection.

Jadene watched the storm for a long moment when a knock at the backdoor startled her. It had to be Lilly, caught in the torrential downpour. She was early—or on time—Jadene couldn't decide which. She paced through the office toward the hall to the rear.

A heavy fist pounded from the outside.

Jadene stopped in her tracks. That wasn't Lilly.

A prickling crawled up her neck.

The lights were still off. Jadene seized a long, silver letter opener from her desk. She didn't have a proper weapon because, despite the movies, there wasn't much need for guns in investigative work—especially with the kinds of jobs that came her way. Disagreements over spreadsheets and invoices usually didn't involve gunfire.

Although, Tommy had cautioned her. He'd told her to get a weapon. She gripped the ten-inch dull shaft in her hand, and a nervous flutter rose in her chest. Hopefully, it was nothing more than a delivery, though she hadn't ordered any supplies in weeks.

Pacing down the hall, her grip on the knife tightened.

Another knocking hammered at the door.

She inhaled and pushed the firebar.

The large passage creaked outward.

Thunderous, heavy rain poured. A gurgling downspout belched its overflow onto the asphalt. But there was no one. Clutching the letter opener, she stepped outside, beneath the overhang, angling for a better view.

A wet hand snatched her wrist.

THIRTY-TWO

Panicked, Jadene threw a blind elbow.

A powerful arm hooked her from behind, yanking her off the ground in one swift motion. Her pulse throbbed in her ears. She wanted to scream, but a large hand covered her mouth.

"Quiet," the voice urged.

She still had a grip on the letter opener, but her arms were locked to her sides. She torqued her shoulders but the hold didn't budge. With all her strength, she kicked a heel, striking a shin bone.

Her attacker didn't flinch.

"Please, don't do that again," he said.

The hold was unbreakable. Her ribs could be crushed at any moment.

"I'm not here to hurt you," he whispered.

She couldn't move. The grip wrenched to her waist was like a vise. It was fortunate she could even breathe.

The man carried her to the doorway, out of the rain.

"I'm sorry I scared you," he said. "But when I let go, please stay calm. Okay?"

With no other choice, Jadene dropped a nod.

The hand freed from her mouth, and the arm clutching her midsection released.

She spun, clenching the crude shiv, ready to strike.

Dressed in a dark suit and tie, Wes Holt and his clothing were drenched.

Jadene stared angrily. "What the hell are you doing here?"

Wes shot a glance up the alley, then to her. "You need to come with me," he said.

Jadene glared, her soaked blouse clinging to her skin. "Answer my question, dammit!"

"Miss Bowman," his tone was low and steady. "We need to go right now."

Raindrops coursed down her face, streaking her makeup. The letter opener held tightly in her hand as thunder rumbled in the distance. "Why?"

He seized her wrist, pulling her to his side.

"No!" she cried. "What are you doing? I'll stab you with this!"

His grip held firm. "Please don't. And please keep your voice down."

He dragged her down a wet, narrow alleyway. Puddled water splashed at her ankles, and the mush of mud sloshed beneath her sneakers. It was challenging to keep up with his hurried pace.

"Where are we going?" she demanded.

At the alley's ingress, Wes halted, his grip clenched around her forearm. Careful not to be seen, he checked the street and tugged her with him.

Her breath quickened. "Where are you taking me?"

Wes didn't answer. Instead, he hauled her across the avenue and into another narrow passage—one wide enough only for foot traffic—as rain soaked them both.

She hurried to keep pace, the letter opener still clenched in her hand—he hadn't taken it. She could jab him, but he'd asked her politely not to. Her mind spiraled. What was happening?

Wes ushered them down the corridor. Ahead was a parked Cadillac Escalade. Its lights flickered on and off. He halted, eyed the street again, then marshaled her to the passenger side. He yanked open the door, pushed her in, and rounded the vehicle.

She was too stunned to protest, sitting wide-eyed and breathless, her drenched butt sopping on the leather seat.

Rain rattled the Escalade's roof.

Wes leaped into the driver's side, started the vehicle, and swung a quick U-turn.

"Put your seatbelt on. Now."

Jadene glared. "Have you been following me?"

He reached across her lap.

"What are you doing?"

Wes jerked the strap over her midsection and clicked its buckle into place.

"What is all this?"

The Escalade's wipers lashed at the rain. He turned onto a main street, blew through a blinking red light, and raced toward the interstate.

The abrupt acceleration forced her body into the seat and made her nauseous. Jadene put a palm on the dash to steady herself.

Scanning the road, Wes said, "You're in danger."

A chill snaked down her spine. "Why? What's happening?"

He eyed the makeshift blade. "Please put that away. You won't need it."

The letter opener rested in her lap.

They raced down a side road. Steering with a knee, Wes stripped off his suit jacket and tossed the soaked garment into the backseat. The shedding revealed the holster strapped to his ribcage, which held a silver handgun the length of Jadene's forearm.

Glancing in the rearview, he turned toward the onramp, stomping the gas pedal. The engine revved. Weaving through the highway traffic, his eyes darted from the road to the rearview.

"I'm taking you back to the compound," he said. "You'll be safe there. Sinclair's in London."

"Safe there?" she said. "What's… what the hell is going on?"

But his attention held on the road, a road they were barreling down now.

"Hang on!" he shouted.

From the left-most lane, he tugged the SUV's wheel to the right, slicing across three lanes of traffic.

Jadene's insides went in the opposite direction.

The Escalade hurtled across the lanes, cutting dangerously close to a trailered big rig. An air horn blared, its deafening screech vibrating Jadene's insides as they slipped past the semi by less than a car length.

Easing up on the accelerator, Wes coasted the Escalade down the offramp. He checked the rearview. "I don't see a tail."

She'd caught a lash from the sharp turn and massaged her neck.

"We'll stay off the perimeter," he said. "Side roads are safer."

Jadene swallowed. Minutes ago, she was engrossed in her research, making headway at her desk, pecking at her keyboard, trying to solve Sinclair's riddle. The next second, she was whisked away by a man she'd met only once, dragged into an SUV, and evacuated from the scene like a politician under fire. Now, they were heading back to an enormous mansion with a courtyard fountain larger than her apartment.

"Here," Wes said, pressing a button on the dash. "This'll warm you up."

Heat radiated from the leather seat.

She held in a bubble of disbelief as the SUV's headlights clicked on. They were now on a tiny two-lane road that snaked through a forest of hulking, Southern pine trees. This was a route that Wes seemed to know well, and the slick road didn't seem to bother him one bit.

The adrenaline slowly left her system, her breathing coming under control. She blinked for the first time in what seemed like several minutes.

Her brain buzzed. What was Wes doing there in the first place? Had Sinclair ordered him to watch her? And what in God's name was going on?

The SUV sped through the downpour.

She kept the blade at the ready, squeezing its handle.

Driving through the rain, Wes glanced over. "Do you know a man named Ellis Martin?"

THIRTY-THREE

Frankie Peller couldn't boost a Honda Civic if the keys were in the ignition. But the skinny man had a knack for getting out of jail—having done it three times. While two of his attempts involved slipping out of the laundry facility, his final go used nothing but a toothbrush and a shitload of dental floss.

Working in complete darkness, Ellis felt for a piece he'd seen earlier. The rod cut too long for the section, the only stub in this prison that overhung its joint. He bent it side to side, the friction slowly weakening the hold. Hours passed, but the finger-sized chunk of rebar finally snapped free from the cage.

He coiled a lace around a pair of bars, tying the broken rebar to the end of the lace to form a makeshift lever. He torqued the apparatus clockwise until the first tack weld snapped free—a metallic pop that rang faintly across the room.

Ellis grinned, despite the sweat pouring down his face. He'd have to do this many more times to create a gap large enough to slip through, but he was getting out of here.

The door flew open.

He yanked the string and the twist tool free, jamming the parts under his thigh.

The light snapped on.

Rena stood in a tight, shoulderless black dress, her presence as sharp as a blade. "Where is it?"

Ellis draped his arms around his knees, feigning exhaustion. "Where's what?"

She stepped closer, her movements quick and purposeful, a tiny bloodstain visible on her calf. "I do not have time for games!" She jabbed a finger toward him. "You and that woman, you are working together!"

Ellis frowned. What woman? Her accusation made no sense. He was as puzzled now as he was when they'd dragged him here.

"I don't know what you're talking about," he said.

She circled the cage like a lioness hunting prey, her heels clicking against the floor. "I have been patient with you. Generous even."

Patient and generous? Ellis nearly laughed. Keeping him in total darkness, starving him, depriving him of sleep—it was anything but generous. She was trying to break him, stressing his mind and body like an interrogator would. But to what end? Nothing about this made any sense.

"But now, time is up," she hissed. "What I want from you is truth." She circled near, red specks dotted the skin near her ankle. "You will tell me everything, or this will not end well for you!"

"Lady, I have no earthly idea what you're talking about."

And he didn't. He wasn't working with any woman. Whatever they thought he knew, they were dead wrong.

What he did know was Belt Buckle—the wiry asshole with the knife—was probably a local. The truck, the accent, and the ridiculous crotch medallion were dead giveaways. This crappy cabin was probably his. Hillbilly hired muscle, taking orders from Rena.

But Rena herself? That was the real mystery. She was most likely the one in the shadows who'd shot the two food workers when he'd arrived. Fit, attractive—she didn't look like a cold-blooded killer. Then again, the best murderers never do.

"Do not deny!" Her forehead creased. "Lie to me, and—"

"This will not end well?" Ellis mocked. They'd already killed two people right in front of him and made me hide the bodies down a gully. This wasn't going to end well, no matter what he said.

Rena's lips tightened. She held up a sheet of paper, her eyes piercing his.

Ellis's stomach dropped.

She'd taken that document from his duffel bag. It was the case he was working—the reason for his trip to Alabama.

"You are involved with something well outside your understanding." She stepped closer to the cage. "Bay of the Montebello, where is it?"

Ellis stiffened.

Aw shit.

THIRTY-FOUR

Jadene furrowed her brow. "Ellis Martin?"

The rain lightened, and a mist covered the two-lane road.

She knew Ellis, or knew of him. Fifties, an ex-detective turned PI, he had twenty years as an investigator. A spotless record. Three or so years ago, he'd made a name for himself as an independent.

Using nothing but a grainy video and a partial license plate, Ellis tracked down a kidnapped infant from a hospital's maternity ward taken by a mentally disturbed woman.

The town's mayor gave Ellis a medal. Jadene recalled seeing his photo in the news, standing beside the thankful mother and her rescued child. A firm but friendly grin on Ellis's face.

Wes steered the road. "You're not the first."

"Not the first?"

Wes aimed a vent toward her midsection. Moderate heat blew against her wet blouse.

"We first hired Ellis," he said.

She slunk her shoulders. If Ellis had a head start on Sinclair's telegram—this mystery hunt—then she would never beat him. He had far more experience than she did. He was too smart and too damn good.

Jadene bit the inside of her cheek. "If he hired Ellis, then why the hell did he hire me?"

Wes stretched his neck, but his attention remained on the road. "Four weeks ago, I met with Ellis."

"You did?"

"Yes."

"Sinclair didn't meet with him? I don't understand."

"At the time, he wanted to keep the hiring anonymous. So, I found Ellis, supplied him the same telegram you got, and gave him a timeline of four weeks."

Jadene frowned. Was she the second choice? And why did Sinclair give her only five days?

"Then, ten days ago, we received a text from Ellis claiming the job was too tough and he had to quit."

"Quit? That doesn't make any sense," she said. Ellis had found a missing baby, for God's sake. Why would a man like that give up?

"I tried to contact him but got no answer. Sinclair wanted at least a debrief." He checked the mirrors. "How far did Ellis get? What did he uncover? Those kinds of questions."

The vent's warm air had already dried most of her clothes. "How far did he get?" she asked.

"I don't know. After that text, nothing. I never heard from him again."

Given Ellis's reputation, that didn't make any sense. What the hell was going on?

Wes steered past an intersection. "His wife filed the report, and I learned of it this morning."

"Missing persons?"

"Yes."

"But you said he quit over a week ago. Why did his wife only report him missing this morning?"

"Apparently, they'd texted back and forth for a few days, which wasn't unusual. But when Linda tried calling her husband several times, Ellis never picked up."

Jadene stiffened. How does an investigator go missing? A damn cop? And not just any cop, a hell of a detective with twenty years of service? A knot grew in her stomach.

"Last night Linda texted Ellis she was having Oysters for dinner."

"Oysters?"

"The response from her husband's phone read, "Enjoy them. I'll be home soon," and that's when she knew."

"A distress signal?"

"Right. Linda Martin is highly allergic to shellfish."

"Jesus. Do they have any leads?"

"His last known was Hartsfield, where they found his abandoned car in the north terminal. Security camera footage wasn't worth shit. Apparently, the cameras haven't worked in years."

"What about location tracking? His phone?"

"They tried. The texts routed through different towers."

"Where?"

"Connections vary. The pings came from La Grange, then Perry, and so on. All the way down to Dawson County. They were still pulling together the information when we spoke. Apparently, after each message, the caller removes the battery, and the GPS goes dark."

Ellis wasn't the type of man who would go joyriding with a 20-year-old. She tapped a finger on her knee. He was well respected in the community and as a private detective.

If this was an abduction and the perpetrators were on the move, was Ellis with them? Not likely. Too risky, too much exposure. No, Ellis was separated from the person who was traveling with his phone.

"Someone is driving around with his cell," she said.

Wes raised his eyebrows. "That's what the police think."

She tapped a finger on the dash. "Which means Ellis is being kept at another location, or…"

Wes tightened his lips, turning a glance to Jadene. "I tried to call you. But the phones are out, and I couldn't get a signal."

She shifted her jaw. "Okay, but you scared the ever-loving shit out of me. Why didn't you just use the front door?"

Wes kept his stare on the road. "I spotted an occupied vehicle down the street from your office."

"Occupied? And?"

"And it was in the same place I would be if I wanted to watch your comings and goings. I clocked it sitting there for thirty minutes."

But Jadene remained skeptical. "What kind of vehicle was it?"

"With Ellis and everything, I didn't want to take any chances. That's why you're in my taxi right now."

She repeated her question. "What type of vehicle?"

Wes cleared his throat. "A Ford Bronco."

She had seen the exact vehicle down the street, parked in the rain. A basic beater, cracked windshield, specked with red clay. But beyond that, she wasn't too concerned about it. That type of truck wasn't out of the ordinary for the area.

Though, Wes seemed guarded. She could sense he was holding something back. And him taking her from her office like that? It was like a huge overreaction.

She frowned. "What are you not saying?"

He stared out at the road.

Angrily, Jadene turned to him. "What is it? I have a right to know."

He dropped his shoulders. "I ran the plate."

"Of the Bronco? And?"

"And it came back mismatched. It belongs to another vehicle."

She huffed. "That's why you banged on my door and dragged me out of there? Somebody switches plates to cheat the system, and suddenly I need rescue? You're kidding me, right? Did Sinclair tell you to tail me? Is that what this is?"

"No, that isn't it."

"Then what is it?"

"Because the license plate on that Bronco is stolen." His expression turned stiff. "The plate belongs to a 2019 Audi A4, under the name of Ellis Martin."

THIRTY-FIVE

Ellis lowered his gaze. The telegram was short, and he'd memorized every word of it. Christ, this wasn't some old bust coming back to haunt him. This was about the Whitmore case. The wealthy man who'd hired him to find out everything he could about a relative. But the trail had gone nowhere, despite a ton of research and that fucking flight to Alabama.

Rena lifted the paper, the document rattling in her grip. "Who is Hermann?"

Ellis didn't look up. It all began with *Dakota Free Blue*—the plane flight—a phrase he'd picked up from a spy novel he'd once consumed. Tracking that flight was a pain in the ass and taken a whole week.

Though, despite his circumstance, he wasn't about to offer or confirm anything to this woman—not that he'd uncovered much—because fuck her and her shitbag partner. He lifted his chin.

Rena brushed a hair from her eyes. "You will provide me this information, or I will kill you."

"You're going to kill me?" he sneered. "Eat shit."

There were moments in his career, especially as a rookie, when fear gnawed at him. The fear of walking into an ambush, of responding to a domestic only to be met with a shotgun blast, or of pulling over a speeder and taking a bullet to the face. Those were his newbie nerves. Every good cop learns that the best they can do is prepare and anticipate. But the grim reality is when your number's up, that's it. No cop knows when or if that day will come. But once an officer accepts this, they transform from weakling to warrior. The shift is not just in mindset but in survival—embracing the unpredictability and stepping into danger with hardened resolve.

Rena lifted her chin, clamping a hand on the rebar.

He wanted to grab her fingers and twist them, savoring the ghastly screams. But he wasn't sure he had the strength anymore.

"You are not thinking of your wife," she warned.

Though Ellis was. The passcode he'd given for his phone was correct. Lying about something so easily verifiable wouldn't get him anywhere, and he knew that.

But since then, he'd had more time to think. His brethren on the force—neighbors and friends he'd made over the years—would never leave Linda alone with something like this going on. By now, they all knew he was missing. He hadn't come home from the airport. They'd hold vigil, probably around the clock, as brothers and sisters of the badge do for one another. Planning, searching, readying.

Rena and Belt Buckle wouldn't understand any of this. And Ellis would never let on about it, just in case they tried to use Linda as leverage again. Good luck, dipshits.

But something else bothered him. Something he couldn't figure out. How had this woman even known he was on this case? Had he triggered her attention somehow? The searches on his computer? He'd used a VPN and kept his IP address hidden. So how did they find him? Was someone watching him?

They'd kidnapped and trapped him here because they wanted information about the case. Whatever they were after, whatever that message led to, must hold considerable value. And these people wanted it bad.

A realization struck. Rena had to believe he knew more about the telegram than she did. In fact, it was the only reason he was still alive. But truthfully, he hadn't uncovered much—and if they ever found that out, he'd be face-down in the same ditch as those two dead food workers.

Rena's breath invaded the cage. "Tell me of Wawel Tower."

The question confused Ellis. He'd never heard of such a place. But his thoughts had already switched gears. He had to make her believe otherwise—it was his only move.

"I know the next clue," he lied.

Rena tilted her head, a curious gleam in her eyes.

If he could string her along, it would buy him more time. He could coax her into letting him out of this cage. Then, he'd be in control again. If he could do that, he could bait her and that hillbilly into a trap. Take them someplace under the guise of another clue. Somewhere like Schooley's—a bar loaded with off-duty cops. He'd step inside, toss his hands in the air, and shout, "This is a robbery!" All heads would turn, weapons drawn. Rena and Belt Buckle would soil themselves stiff.

Ellis fought a smile. "But if you want more, you've got to let me out of here," he said. "I can't help you otherwise."

Rena clenched a fist.

"You need my help," he spoke flatly. "And that's the deal."

She rose from the cage and glared down at him. Rage filling her eyes.

He didn't break his stare. This was it—a desperate bluff, the only card he held. One of two things would happen: she'd believe him and set him free, or she'd execute him on the spot. Either way, Linda was safe. That was his comfort, his peace.

He didn't move. He didn't speak. He just waited.

Rena said nothing for a long moment. Then, without a word, she flicked the light switch and slammed the door—casting him into darkness once more.

Thirty-Six

A girl glanced up from her desk. "May I help you?"

Travis frowned. Younger than he expected. Pretty with lengthy hair that fell past her lean shoulders. He drifted through the waiting area, grazing a finger along a dead TV screen.

"Good afternoon," he said.

"Our power is out," she announced. "But it should be back on soon."

Travis smirked. Of course, he'd known this. Several minutes ago a flash lightning had caused the streetlights to extinguish.

Because of the stormy skies, marginal light came in from the outside and diminished the deeper he entered the office. In its midsection were two desks, placed side by side. The girl sat at one using her cell phone as a flashlight.

He approached, admiring the papers on her desk. "What have you got here?"

Brushing a strand of hair from an eyelid, she said, "It's another case we're working on."

"Oh, really?"

"Yes, now what can I help you with?"

Travis scanned the papers. One contained a message of some sort with several handwritten notes. He tilted his head and reached for the pile.

"I'm not allowed to share that… please—"

He snatched a page. "What's this?"

She continued to protest.

In his hand was a photocopy of an old telegram. The page contained a dark jagged line on its right side and many strange phrases in capital lettering.

His eyebrows shot up. "Broken Castle?"

The handwritten notes surrounding the message had him curious. Who was Hermann? An individual, or part of the code? Bay of Montebello? LA or Italy? She had delightful handwriting, he smirked.

"Please, I need that." The girl reached across the desk.

But Travis pulled away. That name, Hermann. Rena had said it during one of her phone calls. Who was that? And what did these other phrases mean? Did this girl know? From the notes on the page, she was working on figuring things out.

Lilly rose from her desk. "Excuse me, these papers are confidential."

He gazed at her with a broad smile.

"I need that back," she implored. "Or I'm going to call the police."

"You have beautiful hair."

"What?"

Travis stared into her eyes. "Your hair is long and pretty."

She glared at him.

"And it will make this easier." He slipped a hand into his denim jacket.

"Easier? What are you talking about?"

Travis yanked a syringe from his pocket. He lunged across the table and snatched her by the hair. The girl screamed, clawing at his arm.

Wrenching her skull down onto the desk, he was unconcerned with finding a vein. He flicked off the cap, pricked her neck with the needle, and pushed the plunger.

The girl thrashed about, but it didn't help. He held her hair tight, and there was no way she was getting away from him.

Her fingernails dug into his skin. The rush of pain excited Travis. But, within seconds, the subdued girl grew weak and melted into silence.

The drug was his own unique concoction. A mix of cocaine, ketamine, and fentanyl. The ingredients were readily available on the street—and his dealer was more than happy to provide him anything he required.

He'd learned of mixing cocktails during his last stint in the sin bin. The cocaine, his personal drug of choice, provided an initial rush to his victim. However, it was quickly followed by the steady slowing of the heart. Next came the absolute shitstorm of euphoria created by the fentanyl.

To Travis, the cocktail's rush was like falling from a skyscraper into a bed of warm marshmallows. But, to the uninitiated, the trip was anything but enjoyable. Their bed, he imagined, was filled with snakes and spiders.

He checked her breathing—steady. She'd be out for hours. He'd only used half the syringe. He didn't want to kill her—not until he found out everything she knew.

Brushing a finger over her cheek, he admired her soft skin. She was a pretty little one. He'd bring her back to his cabin, as he'd done with the man. For now, he rolled the girl and her chair away from the desk.

His attention returned to his surroundings. Using the light from the girl's phone, he scanned the documents on her desk.

From the notes on the page, the girl was indeed deconstructing the strange telegram line by line. The same telegram that Ellis Martin possessed.

Rena, Ellis, and this girl—they were all after something.

But what?

Travis studied the document, his tongue gliding over his lip.

THIRTY-SEVEN

Wes steered down the wet road, lifted his phone, and his bicep flexed beneath his damp, tight shirt.

Jadene caught herself staring.

"Dammit!" he said.

She cleared her throat. "What is it?"

"No signal." A heavy sigh left his chest. "Man, this went to shit fast."

"What do you mean?"

"Mister Whitmore prides himself on sizing people up. Those he hires and those he associates with." He shook his head. "He trusted me, and I failed him."

"Failed? How?"

"Ellis was my pick. I selected him." Wes drew his lips together. "He has a solid reputation, and I figured he would get the job done. But him quitting like that, it didn't go over well. Mister Whitmore was angry."

"With you?"

"He wouldn't say it, but I could tell he was disappointed. He doesn't trust many people."

"I gathered."

"Well, if it's your job to get things like this right, failure doesn't look good."

"But that's not on you, I mean—"

"It is. Mister Whitmore holds me to the highest standard. He expects perfection and loyalty. To a man like him, precision, execution, and guarding his interests are valued over everything."

The vehicle turned down another sideroad, a familiar hilly section. They were nearing Whitmore's mansion.

"When the investigation fell through with Ellis, Mister Whitmore told me he wanted to go in a different direction." Wes's focus remained on their surroundings, checking the perimeter. "He aimed for someone eager, someone who wouldn't give up. I researched two dozen PI firms. Each of them an ex-cop, like Ellis Martin. All except one."

Her cheeks warmed. "Me?"

Wes nodded. "The others were good people I'm sure, just as Ellis. But career. They'd worn the badge, walked the beat, and solved some cases—which is great. But you had one thing that set you apart."

"I did?"

"You're the only civilian—you quit your day job and jumped into this profession with both feet. You set up shop downtown and went after it with everything you had, working your ass off to get clients."

Jadene recalled their meeting in the fireplace room, and Sinclair's tone when he asked her why she quit her daytime job. "To do something you love?" he'd prodded. It was odd to her that was one of the first things he'd said during their meeting. Now, it made total sense.

"He was very impressed by that. He said it reminded him of himself. Nobody handed you a thing. You just decided one day to go out and do it."

She dropped her gaze. Yes, but she'd romanticized the idea. And even that was the wrong word, given how ominously her interest in becoming a private investigator had all begun.

"Passion and determination. They can't be taught, and can't be bought. Those were his exact words. And you must be special because you were the only one he interviewed." Wes shot her a glance. "Mister Whitmore hand-picked you."

A rush of warmth and surprise filled her as the words sank in but were quickly followed by a wave of doubt. Had she really been chosen over everyone else? Could she, a nobody PI, live up to the trust Sinclair had placed in her?

Even still, she had one question that had bothered her.

"Why'd he only give me five days?" she said. "Ellis got four weeks, and—"

"It's Mr. Whitmore's timeline," Wes said. "I'm not able to share much—"

A beep sounded.

Wes grabbed for his cell. "All right, we've got a signal. I need to call in that Bronco's plate."

He dialed and put the call on speaker.

A man answered, "Lieutenant Hernandez."

"Lieutenant, Wes Holt. I'm sorry to call your personal cell, but I wanted to get the latest on the Ellis Martin case, and I may have a lead."

"Yes, sir," the lieutenant replied. "Good to hear from you."

As the two spoke, Jadene snickered. If she tried to get information on an active case from the police, they'd hang up. There were family consent rules, necessary and reasonable boundaries, data and protection laws, and the asshole factor. If she got the wrong sort of person on the line, they wouldn't tell her if the sun was in the sky.

But Wes Holt? He worked for Sinclair Whitmore. He calls a lieutenant's personal cell and gets a "Yes, sir" like they're best friends.

She wasn't sure if she was jealous or impressed. Nonetheless, after Wes relayed the plate, Jadene thought of something.

"Do they know when the last text from Ellis's phone came in?" she asked.

Wes relayed the question.

A pause, then the lieutenant said, "At exactly 1:02 p.m. this afternoon."

A shiver struck Jadene.

Wes glared her direction. "That's the same time I called in the plate, just before the power went out."

Her expression soured. "Wait, you said you couldn't reach me on the phone? And that's why you came to my office. But you were able to call in the plate? That means you were already there, why?"

He muted the call. "My job is to protect Mister Whitmore and his interests. When I got the news about Ellis missing, I wanted to check your area downtown. I wasn't even going to approach you, but then I saw the Bronco."

Jadene stared at him.

His expression turned serious. "And if you're wondering why I didn't approach the Bronco, there are two reasons. First, you are my protective priority. Second, it's a 1997 Bronco with stolen plates. The chances that driver is not armed are slim to none—and slim just left town. Which would have led to a shoot out on a rainy street." He tapped the sidearm on his ribcage. "And suspects with a bullet hole in their skull aren't usually too chatty. Make sense?"

Her mouth fell open. "Yeah."

He returned his attention to his phone. "Lieutenant, can you tell me which cell tower Ellis's last text was sent through?"

"Better than that," the lieutenant said. "I've got the tower's address. On Austell Road, in Marietta."

Jadene gasped. "Shit, that's right down the road from my office."

Wes and the officer confirmed the location again before closing the discussion. "Lieutenant, thanks for all your help. We'll call you if we come across anything else."

"We'll do the same, thanks Wes."

The call ended.

He steered off the main road and drove up the hedged pathway to the iron gates. The entry opened and they drove through, but as the gates came to a close, instead of continuing toward the residence, he pulled the SUV alongside the wall of boxwood and shut the vehicle off. The dash, the lights—everything extinguished.

"We need to hold here a minute." Wes's gaze fixed on the rearview. "I need to be sure we weren't followed."

Rain prattled the Escalade's roof. She gazed down at her hands, reflecting on everything that had happened. If Wes hadn't interceded, she would have been taken herself.

She touched his forearm. "I never said thank you."

He kept his eyes on the rearview. "You're welcome. But I didn't mean to frighten you. I was only trying to get to you out of there safe."

"I understand."

Wes inhaled, deeply. "Tomorrow, I'm going to retrace Ellis's steps."

"Where should we start?"

His head wavered. "No, no. This isn't a team exercise."

"But you need me," Jadene said. "I'm a detective, after all."

"You do what you do, and I do what I do. But you're not going. It's too dangerous. Besides, you have the case to work on."

"But—"

"Whatever you and Ellis are onto, you triggered something. There's another player in all this. Somebody who knew Ellis was active on the investigation, and now they know you're part of it, too. And, until I figure out who that is, I'm going to make damn sure you're safe."

He restarted the Escalade and shifted into drive. The SUV climbed the path, turned into the courtyard, and came to stop inside Whitmore's six-car garage,

Jadene unbuckled her seatbelt.

Wes popped from the driver's side, raced over, and opened her door. "The running boards are wet," he said. "Take my hand."

THIRTY-EIGHT

The Bronco growled along the interstate, its rugged tires ripping through the wet road. Travis sparked up a Marlboro, cracking the window to let the smoke dance away.

In the back, his captive lay limp, sprawled across the rear seats like a discarded doll. He'd bound her wrists and ankles together with zip ties—the huge kind used for HVAC work—which were impossible to break. Then, he'd fished out a heavy cloth painter's tarp from the Bronco's rear compartment and covered her from head to toe.

He'd grabbed two laptops and some papers from the office along with the girl. These would be his keys to unraveling whatever Rena and her partner were after.

Before he'd left, though, he'd knew his fingerprints were all over the place. The desk, the chair, and that TV on the wall. It left him with only one decision to cover his tracks, but it was the smart move.

As the Bronco's wiper blades swiped the windshield, Travis took a drag and blew out the smoke, savoring the moment. Approaching the city limits, a buzz on the dash caught his attention. His burner cell regained its signal, and that gave him an idea. At the next exit, he headed off the interstate.

The town was a pass-through for travelers and truckers, with three gas stations and several fast-food joints. However, a high, rotating sign appeared just beyond those.

Shelly's Motel boasted plush beds, free WIFI, and reasonable rates. The lengthy orange building was surrounded by dead grass and leafless trees. Nearing, he found a motel occupants had used the balcony as a clothesline, and hanging a week's worth of clothing over the wet rail.

Travis licked his lips. The place reminded him of a halfway house. It was perfect.

About two dozen cars sat in the resort's lot, each parked in front of its respective motel room. He turned into the area, eyeing various oil blots dotting the empty wet spaces. Next to a set of commercial garbage dumpsters at the far end, he found an out-of-the-way spot, slid into the space, and shut off the Bronco's engine.

Scanning the parking lot, every vehicle was at least five years old. However, a cobalt blue Sierra minivan, missing a hubcap, piqued his interest.

With his sleeping passenger secure in the backseat, he rechecked the Buck Knife in his waistband and exited the Bronco. Light rain trickled on his denim jacket as he approached the minivan.

The vehicle's rear window displayed a unique collage—a stick figure family carefully arranged by the owner. On the right was Junior, clutching a stick baseball bat. Beside the boy, a stenciled little girl with pigtails danced with childish glee. On the far left, anchoring the twosome, was Mom—her vinyl adhesive arm held in a friendly wave. Next to Mom, though, were the words "Position Open."

Travis snickered as he passed by, noting the room number in front of the minivan. He stepped from the parking lot onto a dirty concrete pathway, headed toward the motel's main entrance, found the door, and went inside.

Behind a counter stood a man in his mid-40s with shoulder-length, sandy brownish hair. He wore faded blue jeans and a Peter Frampton t-shirt specked with paint marks.

Travis secured the knife, ensuring its blade was latched behind his belt buckle and its handle hidden beneath his jacket, then approached.

"Good afternoon," the man in the Frampton shirt said. "What might I do you for?"

Travis dropped his shoulders and massaged his temple. "Man, I'm hoping you can help. My girlfriend, well, soon to be fiancé, really, we're… well, she forgot the WIFI's password, and now she's having a fit because the kids can't see their show on the tablet."

Frampton made his way over to a computer. "Little ones and those damn screens. Modern pacifiers, I tell you. What room y'all staying in?"

"Room 137." Travis let out a huff. "Yo, I'm real sorry about this. It's just that I can't get any peace at all."

"No worries. I get it," Frampton said, scanning his display. "The password is chunkymonkey."

"Chunkymonkey?"

"Yup. Lowercase, no space. Did you need me to write it down?"

"No, no. I think I got it." Travis turned to leave. "Man, thanks so much."

"Gimme a sec," Frampton said.

With the exit in sight, Travis halted. He slipped a hand beneath his jacket, to the underside of his belt buckle, and seized the knife's handle.

"Noticed here y'all just have the one key. Did you maybe need another?"

His grip released from the knife, and his mind raced. A key to her room? That could be fun. However, right now, there was another task he had to complete.

"Man, I appreciate it, but I think we're good," he said. "You know women, they like to be in charge."

"Don't I know it," Frampton smiled. "Well then, y'all have a good day."

"Thanks, man. You have a good day, too."

Outside, Travis returned to the Bronco. He grabbed a computer from the truck's cab and powered it up. But the screen required a password. He gave five attempts at gibberish, closed the lid, and seized the other PC.

The second computer did not require a password. When the home screen appeared, he struck the WiFi icon and pecked in "chunkymonkey"—lowercase, no spaces.

In the Bronco's rearview, the cloth tarp rose and fell with the sound of steady breath.

Travis's attention, though, lingered on the laptop's screen

Thirty-Nine

The ordeal of the last hour had affected Jadene physically. Following Wes, a kink grew in her neck and she worked a thumb into the tightness.

He brought them from the carport into a courtyard filled with blooming roses, then into an adjacent passage where they entered through a side door.

She was overwhelmed. The sprawling kitchen in Whitmore mansion was like something in a five-star resort. Warm butterscotch walls, stretching two levels, framed the enormous galley. In its mid-section rested three long butcher-block prep tables, each housing a wealth of pots and pans underneath. Several hefty stainless-steel refrigerators and freezers stood along the walls, including two glassed wine chillers. A bank of ranges, ovens, and four double sinks accompanied by at least two dishwashers, filled the outer perimeter. The place was a culinary factory ready to serve an army of guests.

Wes made his way to the chiller. "I caretake for Mister Whitmore when he's away," he said.

Jadene stood at the entry, wide-eyed.

Wes turned. "You can come in, you know?"

It was all so extravagant, and there was so much. Jadene wasn't sure she belonged here.

"You look like you could use a glass of wine." He smirked.

"Maybe two," she said.

Wes stepped from the chiller to a walled alcove. There, he scanned a selection of room-temperature bottles.

She made her way to the nearest prep table. The area was immaculate—everything had its place.

Wes uncorked the bottle, poured a red, and returned with two glasses.

"Where's yours?" she laughed.

He handed her a glass and raised his own drink to eye level. "To the comedienne."

Each sipped.

The velvety Bordeaux danced on her tastebuds, tickled her cheeks and finished with a warm, smooth quiver.

"Whoa, whoa." Jadene smacked her lips. "This wine tastes like world peace. What is it?"

"The kind that billionaires drink."

"So, it's not available at the Wine Depot?"

He shrugged. "It's not one of your boxed varieties, no."

They both chuckled.

"So tell me, Miss Jadene Bowman, how did you become a PI?"

Jadene lifted the glass to her lips and paused. "Can't a girl just enjoy her wine for a moment?" But the words didn't come out right, sounding overly rash. And that rendered the mood awkward. Still, there were reasons she wasn't ready to share that part of herself yet.

After a long silence, she attempted to change the subject.

"This kitchen is incredible," she said. "The house is…unbelievable."

Wes raised his glass. "Mister Whitmore has owned this estate for 30 years. Remodels parts of it every half decade—or whenever he gets a divorce." He flashed a frown. "I'd say we're about due."

"Oh, is he getting married again?"

Wes lowered his brows, and his voice went gruff. "I'm an engineer, Wes, and a damn good one! There'd be no cell phones without my satellites! But dammit, women are beyond reason!"

She laughed. "That was good. You sound just like him."

"He's a good guy, just doesn't have the best luck with women." He sipped his wine. "And call me crazy, but I don't think some of his admirers are after his heart."

She snorted. "You think?"

"Mister Whitmore says he's done trying to make someone else happy. He's focused on his companies and the success of his adult children nowadays."

"You call him Mister Whitmore. He doesn't let you address him as Sinclair?"

"It's not that."

"Because you're his bodyguard?"

"I protect his interests."

"His interests? Does that include me?"

He shrugged. "Today it did."

"It sounds like you really care for him."

"He's a remarkable man."

Jadene rested her glass on the table. "I know you're his caretaker and obviously his bodyman."

Wes straightened his posture.

"But is there some relation? I mean, are you his illegitimate son or something?"

He grinned. "Not afraid of direct questions, I see."

She rolled her eyes. "Good wine does that to me."

"Well, I look at it this way. Mister Whitmore is a once-in-a-generation mind. He's special. He's changed the world more than most could ever dream. And a man like that must be protected, wouldn't you agree?"

"Yes, of course."

"Every devoted career person takes a vow. Priests have their bible. Lawyers the law, and doctors have that oath…"

"Hippocratic."

"Thank you, Miss know it all."

She giggled.

Wes pointed to himself. "I have an individual who I've sworn to protect and serve."

"And you'd do anything for him?"

He flexed his cheek muscles, bobbing his head.

"And his interests?"

"And his interests."

She raised her glass. "And what if his interest needs a refill?"

"Then I suggest his interest scoots over to the bottle and pours it herself."

She gave a goofy smile. "Just testing your boundaries."

Wes cracked a smile. "I'd expect nothing less."

They both laughed.

She'd never met a bodyguard before. It was fascinating how sincere he took his job, and the pride of the trust placed in him. He was Sinclair's guardian, and there was no doubt he'd take a bullet for the man without thought of himself. He reminded her of a devoted soldier.

She gnawed her lower lip. He was also easy on the eyes and had a quiet intensity that made her feel safe—like a gallant, old-school presence. And his incredible loyalty to Sinclair was intriguing. Mixing business with pleasure was never wise, but she wished she had someone as dependable as Wes at her side. She could barely trust Lilly to…

"Oh God!" The color drained from her face. "Where's my phone?"

"Your phone?"

"My Goddamn phone!"

Wes produced his.

Jadene snatched it, thumbing at the numbers.

"What's going on?"

"Dammit! She's not answering!"

"Who?"

"She was coming in late, I…" Jadene gasped. "I forgot about Lilly!"

Wes dashed around the prep table, hooked her by the arm, and yanked the keys from his pocket.

FORTY

With the Bronco concealed behind the motel's dumpsters, Travis sat in the cab, working the keys on the stolen laptop. He'd never owned a computer but knew how to use one. He could've used the burner's browser but suspected Rena could be monitoring him. Besides, reading the larger computer screen was easier.

He tapped two words into the keyboard. Ones Rena muttered to the mystery man on her phone.

Wawel Tower.

An array of results lit the screen. Everything pointed to a location in Poland. He narrowed his eyes. What the hell was in Poland? Scanning the wordy links, he clicked one that looked promising.

Wawel Tower wasn't some high-rise. It was a castle. He studied the page. Apparently, the place was built on the banks of some river and finished in the early 16th century. Artist renderings showed soaring towers, a bunch of chapels, a huge cathedral, and a royal residence. All of the cartoon drawings on the screen were of people wearing tights for some reason.

According to the diagram, Wawel Castle had a massive wall around it. It reminded him of that city where the Pope lived—but smaller.

Gazing at the passenger seat and the stack of papers he'd boosted from the girl's workplace, he picked the telegram message from the pile. Scanning the page, one phrase stuck out to him: Double Safe Haven.

Rena, her secret phone calls, and taking that man at the airport—the whys of these matters did not concern him at the moment. Whatever this whole thing was about was high-dollar.

Travis scraped the stubble on his chin. "Those greedy bastards," he whispered. A broad smile stretched across his face. Rena didn't have the upper hand anymore.

The sedated girl in back stirred, then quieted.

Restarting the Bronco, he slid it into gear and cruised through the parking lot toward the street.

Frampton stood at the motel's entrance, paintbrush in hand, slathering another coat of paint. He threw a cheerful wave as the Bronco passed.

Snickering, Travis responded with a one-finger salute.

The Bronco rumbled down the two-lane road back to the interstate. Travis twisted a cigarette between his lips, lifted the burner, and dialed.

Rena answered, "Yes?"

"It's me," he said. "I have the package."

"Good. Bring her back to the cabin, and I will meet you there."

"Yeah, about that. We need to talk."

"Do we?"

"Our deal is no good."

"Our deal?" Rena said. "Our deal, which I am paying you for and which you have committed to, only has value if you continue doing what I need."

He wasn't sure what she meant by that, but it sounded like a threat. "I want to renegotiate."

"Renegotiate? How is that?"

"For starters, money," Travis demanded. "I want more money. And I want to know everything. By rights, I've been doing most of the work here. Whatever bullshit you're holding back from me, I want to be an equal partner."

"A partner?"

Travis squeezed the cell. "You heard me."

"And if I give you the money but refuse this partnership?"

"Then you're fucked, lady," he shot back. "I want cash now and a big cut of the final take." He checked his reflection in the Bronco's rearview. "A fifty-percent cut."

"Fifty?"

He scowled. "You heard me. And I don't care if you have other partners. I ain't seen none of them doing what I'm doing out here. So you'd better get them to agree."

"I see," she paused. "I will make a call. Smooth this over with my partners."

"You do that." He shook the tiny bottle between his fingertips. He had her right where he wanted her.

"I will not talk specifics on the phone. Meet me at the cabin. When can you be there?"

Travis checked the clock in the Bronco's dash, calculating his travel time. "An hour."

"I will see you in two."

Travis sneered. That would give him enough time to check out the documents he'd taken, do more research, and find out precisely what she was after—to better understand his take.

Then he'd define his demands. Whatever the number, it would be a deal she couldn't refuse because he had living, breathing leverage in his backseat. A precious asset.

It was almost too perfect.

"All right, be there," he said, ending the call.

Travis took another drag of his cigarette as the Bronco sped toward Willow Ridge. Smoke curled around the cab until the open window tore it from the Bronco's compartment.

Bossy Rena was pissed. A grin grew on his lips.

Things had changed. The idea of sharing plans and profits with a criminal like him probably made her blood boil. Before this, she'd seen him as nothing more than a tool, a pawn, in her selfish hunt.

He chuckled. He was the king on this chessboard now. That stupid prison psychologist would call this a shift in cognitive perspective. He'd outsmarted Rena, and she was powerless.

He flicked the smoldering cigarette out the window and glanced over his shoulder, a smirk playing on his lips.

FORTY-ONE

Jadene's hands trembled. Every call to Lilly went straight to voicemail. She tried again—same thing. Texted. Nothing.

They arrived at Jadene's office within minutes.

She aimed a finger. "Pull in front."

The SUV skidded to a stop. Jadene's door swung open, and she jumped from the Escalade.

"Wait!" Wes shouted.

But Jadene darted through the heavy rain and shouldered open the entrance where her expression switched to horror.

Her tiki paradise was a hellish scene. Thick smoke engulfed the waiting area. Terrifying flames leaped and twirled through the choking haze, bathing the office in a sinister, flickering light. Beyond, the desks where she and Lilly had spent hours together were now under siege by the relentless blaze. A haunting hiss erupted as fire devoured the big TV, the heat warping its once sleek surface and turning the Shetland gray walls into a dreadful, charred nightmare.

She sucked a deep breath, sprinting past the smoldering chairs, her heart thundering in her ears. Nearing the blazing inferno, she dropped low, crawling under the smoke.

"Lilly! Lilly!" she screamed. Her voice drowned by the fierce crackling around her.

No response came. Smoke seared her eyes. Tears poured. Blindly, she fumbled through the thick plumes. She ambled past a chair, then a desk.

"Lilly!" she cried again.

In the back hallway, flames bellowed. Ceiling tiles crashed down in angry chunks, a lethal rain of flame and ash. Frantic, she crawled—her hands sweeping the smoky air. As she came to Lilly's desk, she grazed something small and rectangular with her fingers and seized it.

The fire's fury grew. Heat swamped her. She pressed her face to the floor, gasping. The air scorched her lungs, forcing a harsh cough. Each breath became a battle. The air, thick and black, spun her head. A white beam of light raced past her. The flames closed in. She was trapped. Fire blocked the entry, and a wall of flames roared in the back. Her body grew weak and her vision blurred. She tried to crawl forward, but the smoke was too much, and she collapsed.

Everything went dark.

The memory cut through the smoke, sharp and sudden. College had her working part-time as a waitress, just like her mother. But to Jadene it was good exercise when she couldn't be in the pool as she was still on her feet. While the scholarship paid for books and rent, the extra she earned allowed her to buy her own cell phone and a few treats. One of those extras became a new dress, but it wasn't for herself. It was for her mother. A dark blue, short-sleeve V-neck with floral print.

Victoria was a beautiful woman with poor taste in men. So poor, in fact, she'd given up dating all together when Jadene was still in grade school. Instead, her mother resigned herself to working at the diner, reading, and doting over her daughter's swimming.

"Oh my gosh, this is so beautiful! However did you afford it?" Her mother's smile lit up her eyes.

It was Christmas break. Jadene had hidden the package in its own suitcase for the ride home, so as not to damage its big, curly red bow.

"Try it on," Jadene implored. It would fit, of course. They were roughly the same size. "You can wear it in the spring. It's a fun dress!"

"Oh boy, is it!" Victoria said, holding the garment with a grin. A happy moment. Jadene didn't know it then, but it was the last dress her mother would ever wear.

Like a firework, a loud pop pierced the air. Heavy stomping approached. Hands clamped her waist, hoisting her from the ground.

"Hold your breath," Wes demanded. Her body bounced on his shoulder as he raced them from the inferno. Outside, he propped her up on the curb, keeping a strong arm around her shoulders.

Drops of rain struck her cheeks, and she opened her eyes. "Lilly." A cough. "Lilly's inside."

"No." He held her. "I searched everywhere. I didn't find anyone else. Only you."

Jadene's tearful gaze met his. "You promise?"

Wes brought up his flashlight, nodding firmly. "I promise."

She held something—something she'd found it in the fire. Four sides. It was a phone. A breath caught in her throat. The scratches and stickers. It was Lilly's cell.

Anxiety struck. Lilly was supposed to be safe. Jadene was supposed to be watching out for her.

Next to her, Wes thumbed at his own phone, rain dribbling down his jawline. "I think the storm struck the cell tower. I can't get a signal."

But Jadene didn't hear him. Images of Lilly laughing and joking flashed in her mind. The work they'd done together. How they'd tracked down the first plane, which led to the second. There was such excitement on Lilly's face through every step of the hunt. And she'd texted Jadene three times during her trip to the records center.

Rain trickled down Jadene's face, a sob growing in her throat. Lilly—the girl who always showed up late, dressed however she wanted, loved her freedom, and had more brains than she knew— was gone.

Forty-Two

Was it a tactic? A ruse?

The BMW tore through the winding, tree-lined roads as Rena tightened her grip on the wheel, glancing at the ring on her finger.

Before the war—before the bombed-out roofs and barren cupboards—there was a life of quiet abundance. Peaceful. Full of promise. But then the marching men came, unprovoked and relentless, grinding everything to ash. The hamlet was erased. The laughter silenced. The small ruby on her hand the only proof any of it existed at all.

For her, it was a wound festering through generations—etched into her bloodline. A plague. It was up to her now. She was the last. Nothing and no one would stand in her way.

Ellis Martin would get one more chance to tell her what he knew. Her patience had run out—his deception wasted her time. If he remained elusive or provided no information, she would put a bullet in his brain. An inevitable fate, nonetheless, but it was time to force the outcome. His life was insignificant. They all were.

And she'd have done it already if not for one thought. What if the man did know more? What if he could lead her to what she'd been searching for her entire life?

She needed a clear head. Impulsiveness was never an ally.

Besides, right now, she had a new problem.

"Fifty?" She gnashed her teeth.

A steady hiss filled the call's other end. Travis Floyd, the stupid man who smelled of cigarettes, was traveling in his beat-up Bronco.

"You heard me," he barked. "And I don't care if you have other partners. I ain't seen none of them doing what I'm doing out here. So you'd better get them to agree."

Yesterday made it clear that the woman investigator was getting close. If this were a game, Jadene Bowman would make a formidable opponent. Showing up at the house, she'd found out about the aircraft, deciphering the clues in the Wawel telegramm, and the woman detective had tracked the flight, somehow, all the way to Collin Buckley.

But how was that possible? It didn't make sense to her.

Whether she and Ellis Martin were working together was unclear, but what was clear was that they were searching for the same thing.

What else did that woman know? Did she have knowledge of Hermann's identity? Or the location of Montebello Bay? Little Ranch? Could she fill in any useful gaps?

She tightened her grip on the phone.

In the immediate, things were going askew. Her once reliable errand boy had turned on her. His sudden declaration—his new demands—were troubling.

However, it left her curious. This ultimatum from Travis Floyd had not risen from thin air. The woman must have revealed something to him. A clue that gave him newfound courage for a powerplay.

Even if she agreed to provide him more money upfront, Travis Floyd wanted to be part of the hunt. This she would never give in to.

He was a wretched, white trash nothing. The kind she would never consort with if the need had not been vital. A criminal like Travis would never understand this quest, so she'd never shared it with him. It wasn't about material wealth. It was of honor and legacy, things a man like him could never understand.

No others had any rights, and his claim was ludicrous. This was owed.

But there was his cargo to consider. She could not refuse him outright because he had something she needed. But she had to play this tactfully. Pretend to be weak so he may grow arrogant, she considered. Draw him nearer to his comfort zone.

Her foot eased off the accelerator.

"I see," she said. "Let me make a call. Smooth this over with my partners." In truth, only one other knew of her actual undertaking.

"You do that," Travis sneered.

Rena moistened her lips. "We should not talk specifics on this call. Meet me at the cabin," she said. "When can you be there?"

"An hour," he said.

The BMW slowed, and she quietly pulled a quick U-turn.

"I will see you in two," she said.

Travis Floyd grunted. "All right, be there."

A click ended the conversation.

A short distance returned her to Willow Ridge, and the BMW bounced down the forgotten dirt road, concealed beneath a canopy of soaring pines. In a partial clearing, she drove beneath the tree line. Satisfied she and the car were hidden, she switched off the engine.

In the glovebox, she fished out the Makarov .380—the cold metal tight in her hand. Grabbing her umbrella, she stepped out of the car.

That pitiful cabin was a short hike away.

A childhood proverb surfaced as she mazed through the mud and towering trees—an omen of Floyd's impending betrayal: Cut the sitting branch before it turns to a snake and strikes.

She emerged from a thicket of trees, descending the trail toward the decrepit domicile, the Makarov tight in her palm.

Travis Floyd had shown his scales.

FORTY-THREE

Wes ran to the SUV and came back with a cold bottle of water. He twisted off its lid, kneeled, and cupped Jadene's hands around the plastic container.

"Drink this slowly," he said.

She sipped. A pink phone lay on the ground by her hip. Raindrops collected on its screen. Wes picked up the device and slipped it into his pocket.

Jadene's coughing erupted again.

"The smoke," Wes pointed. "We need to get you out of here." He brought her to her feet. "Let's go, right now."

"Lilly…" she gasped. Tears welled in Jadene's eyes as she looked up at him.

"Police and fire are the first calls." He put a hand on her shoulder. "But we have to connect to a new tower as soon as possible."

Jadene was dizzy. Wes opened the Escalade's passenger door, helping her inside. He strapped the seatbelt around her midsection and checked her eyes.

Sorrow gripped her insides, a pressure she couldn't shake. Her sweet landlord Stan entrusted her with his niece. A bright 19-year-old girl who she'd seen blossom with drive and focus in just the last few days. They'd connected over this case, and now she'd put Lilly in harm's way—leaving her vulnerable.

"Jadene?"

Tears streamed down her cheeks. She'd failed her friend.

The voice called again, "Jadene?"

Dazed, everything around her shuddered. The water bottle was cold. Outside, rain pounded. A vibration came. Heat grew on her back and shoulders. A sensation of movement.

"Jadene, are you with me?"

How did she get to work this morning? Why was this water so cold when everything around her was not? Where was she going now? Fingers caressed her neck. She flinched. A belt grabbed at her torso. The moving sensation stopped.

"Jadene, look at me."

The water bottle. The heat. The voice. The fingers on her neck broke into a soft kneading. It felt nice.

"Jadene, you've gone into shock."

The words were aimed at her.

"You suffered smoke inhalation. I need you to breathe for me."

An instruction.

"Deep breaths, okay?"

The plastic water bottle crinkled in her hands.

"Jadene, we'll do this together. Look at me."

She tried to grasp his words. Do this together.

She turned her head slowly. The muscular man stared into her eyes. His name was Wes. He was so handsome. She wanted to eat him with a spoon.

"Jadene, we're inside my vehicle. You're safe. But your brain isn't getting enough oxygen. You're breathing fast and shallow. We have to change that."

She fluttered her eyelids.

He caressed the back of her neck.

"Do what I do, okay? Big breath." His chest expanded, and then he exhaled. "Now, you do it."

She took a gulp of air, but her body rejected the oxygen, and she hacked a cough.

Wes ripped the water bottle from her hands. "Slow and deep," he commanded. "In through your nose, out through your mouth. But slow."

She did as he said. This time, there was no cough.

"Another," he said.

She struggled but held most of the air in her lungs.

"Keep going," he said. "Another."

A strange feeling, like an ice cream headache, swelled in her skull but then vanished. A heat blew across her body. It was from the Escalade's air vents. Her sneakers were wet. Vulcanization, Charles Goodyear—Sinclair's story. The telegram, the airplanes.

She reached for the water.

"Slowly," Wes said. "Drink it slowly."

She did.

"I'm taking you to the emergency room."

Jadene swallowed more liquid and took more deep breaths. The sensation in her legs returned.

Wes restarted the SUV.

"No hospital," she rasped.

"This isn't a debate," Wes shouted. "You're going!"

She raised her head gently. "What… happened?" Her voice came raspy. "I was so… dizzy."

The Escalade raced onto the interstate.

"Hypoxic shock," Wes said. "It does funny things to the mind. You were oxygen-deprived. How do you feel now?"

She pressed a hand to her chest. "Sore, but…"

"But what?"

The Bronco, the fire, they had to find Lilly.

"Oh shit!" she coughed.

"Deep breaths, all right?"

"But the phone!"

The SUV switched lanes.

"Lilly's cell." She pawed at her pockets. "I lost it!"

Wes turned to her, lifting a pink phone from his shirt pocket. "No, you didn't."

She snatched the device, thumbing at its screen.

"Jadene, are you all right? Should I pull over and—"

"No!"

"No?" he said.

"I need a signal!"

"We should hit a working tower any second. But—"

Panic clawed her insides. "Faster!"

Wes glared.

"She's wearing a smartwatch!"

FORTY-FOUR

Rena slipped off her muddy shoes and stashed her umbrella under the deck. She moved to the cabin's front door and quietly turned the latch.

A musty pine scent seeped inside. Dimly lit, the cabin's construction was haphazard, likely built by Travis Floyd, a criminal who never finished anything. Wooden planks made up the floor, but as the long boards neared the west side of the dwelling, the wood no longer matched in species or thickness, creating an uneven surface. About half of it was sanded, but large sections remained rough under her toes. The lumbered floor was unfinished, but three dented cans of polyurethane sat in a far corner, waiting to be spread.

Boxes filled with magazines, clothing, and papers were scattered throughout the house. She'd never opened any and could only guess at the illicit materials inside.

Hammers, wrenches, screwdrivers, saw blades, and other tools lay where they were last used, their edges dulled and surfaces speckled with rust. Most resting where last used, waiting for a hand that never returned.

A flat-screen television—the only item without grime or corrosion—hung crookedly on a wall, facing a dirty sunken couch, looking like someone had found it on the side of the road. Its cushions were the same reddish shade as the clay, muddy grounds outside. On the backside, a single spot, about the size of a hand, showed the sofa's once lavender hue.

Two bedrooms, a bathroom, and a small kitchen sat off the cluttered main area. The eatery held a three-legged table with a stack of cardboard boxes as its fourth leg. A single lawn chair, webbed with plastic bands and stained with clay marks, waited to seat its owner.

She paced down the hall quietly, timing her creaking footsteps to the heavy rain. She moved past Ellis Martin's room—a man she would deal with later—and entered the cabin's only bathroom.

The cramped lavatory was a testament to Travis Floyd's laziness. The facilities inside did not include a bath or a sink. Instead, the shower was a single pipe sticking from the wall with no spray head directly above a lidless toilet. Next to a naked drain sat two large, open garbage bags filled with trash and liquor bottles. The area was also home to an army of tiny buzzing insects. Thankfully, the drafty cabin's innards wafted away most of the odor.

She eased the squeaky door closed until only a narrow gap remained. From this vantage point, she had full view of the cabin's cramped hallway.

The second bedroom belonged to Travis, who'd padlocked its door shut from the outside. She had no desire to enter the room but could imagine its filth.

Headlights beamed through the grime of the bathroom window. He was here.

Rena remained silent. Next to the trash bags, a sickle sat on the ground. She examined its black blade.

Her quest wasn't just about justice—she had to admit—it was about balance. A long-overdue reckoning for those left behind, forgotten by a world too eager to move forward. But justice alone didn't pay debts or buy security. There were fortunes buried in the past, and she intended to claim her share.

History had always favored the ruthless. Empires rose and fell on the backs of the nameless many, and the strong preyed on the weak. That was the world's natural order, and she had no illusions about changing it. But if she played the game right, she could tilt the scales in her favor.

Ironically, this cynicism, this acceptance of the world's brutal truths, only strengthened her resolve. Hardship wasn't a curse—it was a test. One she intended to pass.

Her path was littered with obstacles, but she moved forward with the certainty of someone who refused to lose. The end had to justify the means. The outcome had to be perfect. And she had no patience for those who thought they could take a piece of what was hers.

Forty-Five

Dark skies poured rain. The Bronco bounced down the mountain's dirt road, its headlights piercing through the dense wet trees as it trekked toward the remote cabin.

Travis fished out a smoke. Rena would arrive in another hour to make him a partner and negotiate his new deal. That gave him time to unload and review things.

He parked in the muddy drive, got out, and circled to the rear door. There, he found the unconscious girl lying across the rear seat. Gently, he pulled back the tarp, exposing her head. Steady breath struck the hairs on his arm as she slept, and he swept a finger over her soft cheek.

He seized the two laptops and documents he'd taken from the truck's cab from the girl's office and carried them into the cabin.

Inside, he ambled through piles of boxes, pausing at the locked door of his other prisoner, Ellis Martin. From outside the partition, there was only silence.

He wrapped a knuckle on the door.

"Fuck you!" came a shout.

Travis grinned.

Continuing down the short hall, he fished out his key, undoing the deadbolt to his room.

Here sat his well-used king-sized bed covered in a stained, gray quilt. The mattress and box spring rested on a carved wooden frame sporting a black steel sunburst headboard. On the floor were several boxes containing clothing and keepsakes, surrounded by dozens of empty whiskey bottles he'd consumed to fall asleep.

Clearing a space, he placed the laptops and documents on the floor, setting them aside for later. He fished out the tiny bottle, cleared his nose, and took a bump.

Returning to the Bronco and its backseat, he peeled back the tarp, exposing the girl. She huffed and groaned, and her head lolled to the side as he hoisted her sleeping body from the Bronco.

The cabin door swung open with a nudge of his foot. Shouldering the girl through the entry, he passed the sagging sofa, paced around the boxes, and brought her into his room. He laid her on her back, arms out, on his bed. Sliding two zip ties from a pocket, he fastened her wrists to the sunburst headboard.

Travis held for a moment. Outside, droplets trickled on the cabin's rooftop. He watched the rise and fall of her chest, the soft sighs that escaped her lips, and the peaceful expression on her blushed cheeks. Enchanted, he combed his fingers through her long, silky, golden hair.

So fresh, so fragile. He blanketed her lower body with the quilt. As her captor, he was also her caretaker. However, right now, he had to attend to other things. Rena was on her way.

He would find out what they were after and use it to calculate his end. Whatever the take, it had to be high dollar—a fortune probably—after all, they'd hired him. And if the take was in the millions, he'd find a way to steal it all.

He pushed a few boxes aside and sat at his makeshift workstation. Plans and possibilities grew in his mind. He'd use the money for a new truck. One with four-wheel drive, a navigation screen, and

Bluetooth so he could play music from his phone. Plus, he'd get the complete luxury package with plush leather seats.

He would move away, far from this wooded nowhere, and reinvent himself. Get cleaned up. Start his own business. One where he could do the low-balling. Hitting the laptop's power button, he laughed out loud.

The screen booted to life, bathing the dingy cabin bedroom with a bluish glow. As the computer's tiny fan blew, a smile crossed his lips. The key to everything—his new truck and new life—lay hidden inside of this console.

A grunt came from the bed. His guest was stirring.

Rising to his feet, Travis made his way over. The girl. So pretty, so innocent. With money, could he woo her? Have her?

Cupping her hand, he knelt by the bed.

The girl blinked, her lids sagging.

Travis smiled.

"Where… what's happening?" she muttered.

Her face was so angelic. He couldn't wait to introduce himself to her.

Outside the door, a creaking sounded from the hall.

He spun.

A crack split the air.

Searing pain scorched his shoulder blade. A wetness grew inside of his jean jacket. Gasping for air, he slunk to the floor.

Forty-Six

Before the phone found a tower, Jadene scrolled Lilly's texts while searching for her smartwatch app.

A friend of a friend wanted to ask Lilly out. Another girl, who attended the same junior college as Lilly, complained about her parents giving her a curfew because she still lived under their roof. One of her friends texted wanting a consensus on her new hairstyle, and at least five others replied positively.

But Lilly sent a text this morning that caught Jadene off guard—because it mentioned Jadene directly. Lilly told her friend Maria how exciting the last few days at work had been, that they were investigating something important, and she may not reply to texts right away. Maria asked what it was, and Lilly replied, "Something cool."

A bittersweet pride filled her. She'd managed to reach the girl, who didn't seem interested in anything but boys and social media before all this.

As she held Lilly's phone, alarming dread swept over her. Tommy, the man at the bar, was right. The deeper the briar, the thicker the thorns. In the past few hours, her investigation of Sinclair's telegram had escalated from simple research and footwork to kidnapping and arson. A life was in peril, Lilly's life, and Jadene was to blame.

Her chest tightened. No pursuit was worth all this. Not to save her business and not so that some billionaire—whose grandfather was an actual Nazi—could sew up his past.

She turned to Wes. "I'm quitting. I can't do this anymore."

Wes drove with both hands on the wheel. He didn't say a word but, after a long moment, he bobbed his head in silence.

They drove quietly for another half mile until a vibration sounded from the console.

At the same time, a buzz rattled Jadene's hand. The cell phones had reconnected.

She scrolled the screen on Lilly's cell and found the smartwatch app. She prayed Lilly still had the device on her arm. Within seconds, a ping came.

"I've got it!" she shouted.

The signal was moving north, up I-575. Less than a minute later, Wes had them on the same interstate.

As she tracked the smartwatch's GPS signal, Wes called emergency services about the fire at the office and demanded dispatch alert Lieutenant Hernandez about Lilly's disappearance. He also asked the police to track the Escalade's position using something called V-TAR.

Following the smartwatch signal, they turned onto the Apalachin highway—a hilly, two-lane passage with light traffic. Despite the narrow roadway, Wes weaved them up the wet passage at almost 70 miles an hour.

Lilly's phone vibrated again.

"The signal," Jadene cried. "It stopped!"

"How far away?"

Her glance darted from Lilly's phone to the roadway. "I think, yes! Take the next exit."

Wes let up on the pedal. "Next exit?" he said. "This road doesn't exactly have signs."

He was right. They'd seen only unmarked roads the last several miles—some paved, some dirt, and most a countryfied, potholed combination. But wherever Lilly's GPS signal was pinging from, its direction indicated east of them.

"There," she pointed. "Take that one."

Wes turned onto the muddy trail. The rain was still pouring. The wipers sped their pace as the Escalade bounced over the slurry surface.

"All right, about a mile, maybe two. I can't tell," she said.

Going about 30 miles an hour now, Wes kept his eyes on their surroundings. The muddy trail was only wide enough for one vehicle and flanked by giant pine trees. Every so often, a low branch scraped the Escalade's sides.

In the passenger seat, Jadene sat wide-eyed, gripping the dash with one hand and Lilly's cell in the other.

"Fresh tracks," he motioned ahead. "Should we go that way?"

"No, keep on this path."

Wes did as she directed. The trail rounded a bend, changing its trajectory to an uphill grade.

"Aw, shit," he said. "We've got all-wheel drive."

"You mean four-wheel?"

"No, it's different. Power in this vehicle goes to all the wheels automatically. But it's not as strong as four-wheel drive. This is a heavy truck. I need to keep us moving. The ride could be rough. We don't have a low gear like true four-wheel drive, so if we stop, there's a good chance we get stuck in this muddy crap."

Jadene's insides jiggled. But with her adrenaline at max, she was focused only on finding Lilly and whoever had taken her.

Moving fast up the treelined ridge, the hill abruptly flattened, cresting to a blind summit.

"Woah!" Wes cried. He slammed on the brakes. The Escalade's rear end spun sideways. Wes braced his arm across her chest as they slid to a complete stop.

The Escalade had ascended into a hairpin turn. Had Wes not spun the wheel at the last second, they'd have launched over a cliff. He held his arm across her midsection.

"You all right?" he said.

"Yeah," she replied, breathless.

Wes tried to rock the SUV forward, but the tires got no traction.

Jadene peered out the windshield and pointed. "Do you see that?"

Wes took his foot off the accelerator. In the distance, through the rain, surrounded by overgrowth, sat a cinderblock-sided cabin. Parked in front of the boxy shack was a muddy, black Bronco.

A sudden flash of light erupted from a cabin window.

"Get down!" he shouted.

Jadene dropped, squeezing herself as low as possible to the Escalade's floorboard. Breathing shallow, every muscle tensed.

Wes drew a long, silver handgun from his holster, pulling back its slide with a metal clink. Steeled with purpose, his eyes met hers.

"Stay here," he said. "Lock yourself inside. Police are on the way."

She swallowed hard.

Wes threw open the driver's door, leaped out, and slammed it shut. She fumbled for the lock button, mashing it down three times. She wanted to tell him to be careful, come back in one piece, keep himself safe—but he was already on the move.

Using the foliage for cover, Wes slipped from tree to tree, clutching his weapon with both hands. Thunder rumbled with a deep, ominous growl as he disappeared into the undergrowth.

Another flash exploded from the cabin, followed by the sharp crack of a bullet striking nearby.

Jadene recoiled, curling low and tight. Fat drops drummed the SUV's roof, growing louder and more frantic. Cautious, she inched up in the seat, scanning the area.

In a blur, Wes sprinted toward the cabin. He fired three shots, their echoes splitting the rain-soaked air. Without fear, he bounded up the porch, charged the entry, kicked in the door, and vanished.

Trembling, all Jadene could do was wait.

FORTY-SEVEN

Rena drew the Makarov from her waistline, fingering its trigger. Outside of the unfinished bathroom, the cabin's door flung open with a crash, and heavy boot steps trounced over the planks.

In the shadows, she hid behind the door.

Travis Floyd crossed her vision, carrying an armful of materials. He halted in front of the room across from her.

She raised the Makarov and aimed at his skull.

He wrapped his knuckles on the door.

"Fuck you!" came a muffled voice.

Travis snickered before continuing down the hall, unlocking the padlock, and entering his bedroom.

Rena kept her breathing steady. He wasn't expecting her for another hour and had no idea she was already here, watching his every move.

Stomping down the hall, Travis passed and headed out the cabin's front door. Soon, though, his boots returned, heavier this time.

Rena gripped her weapon.

Travis passed the door's slot again. This time he was carrying a body. A blonde body.

She stiffened. Who was that woman? She'd tasked him with collecting the investigator, giving him the exact address from the business card Jadene Bowman provided. What the hell had this imbecile done? She opened the bathroom door as quietly as possible and craned her neck.

Travis laid the woman down on his bed, fastening her wrists to its headboard before clomping across the bedroom and out of sight.

Rena held, Makarov in hand. Only the woman lay on the bed. The downpour rattled the cabin's roof. She moved delicately into the hall, approaching the bedroom.

Thunder rumbled. The girl he'd taken was young. Unconscious, she lay on his bed, dressed in jeans and a white blouse. Her wrists were bound and secured to the headboard. She raised her head and her eyes opened. She pulled at her restraints with a grunt.

A second sound came from inside the room.

Rena held in the hall's shadow. Travis paced back to the bed, sitting on its edge and leaning over the bound woman. He touched her face and hair and whispered something to her.

Rena aimed. She didn't know who the girl was but wanted to be careful not to strike her, so she moved in closer.

The floor creaked. Travis turned.

She fired. The hollow, cracking discharge stung her ears. Travis Floyd did not move. A black stain spread on his jean jacket, left of his spine. He gurgled and gasped, sliding off the bed's edge onto the floor.

"Hey, what the hell was that?" The gunshot had stirred their prisoner, Ellis Martin, who was locked in the second bedroom.

Rena ignored him. Crossing the doorway, she held her gun at the ready. The woman on the bed screamed.

Travis was on the floor, holding his chest, breathless for air.

"Who is that?" Rena pointed the pistol down at him.

The dying man's eyes filled with fear.

"Who did you take?" she shouted. "Who is that?"

Blood seeped from a corner of Travis's mouth. "Detec… tive," he sputtered.

Turning to the blonde woman, Rena examined the restraints around her wrists. On the girl's left side, below the zip tie, a piece of jewelry wrapped around the girl's arm.

Her jaw clenched.

It was a smartwatch.

"You simple fuck!" She raised the gun, ready to fire into Travis Floyd's skull.

Near him, something caught her eye. A pile of papers on the floor. The top sheet appeared to be the same telegram she'd collected from Ellis Martin. This one, however, contained handwritten notes.

A noise came from outside. A vehicle. Someone else was here.

Moving to the bedroom's north window, Rena eyed the strange SUV. Who was that? Did Travis have partners? Had he told them what he'd found? Were they here to renegotiate his deal?

She raised her weapon, firing toward the vehicle. Quickly, she ran to the pile and snatched the telegram.

A trio of shots whizzed over her head. She ducked. The projectiles missing her by inches.

Heavy footsteps pounded through the cabin's main room— racing her way.

She sprang over the gasping Travis, slid open the bedroom window, and escaped into the rain.

FORTY-EIGHT

The twist torqued the lace, grinding tension into the metal. A sharp pop. The weld cracked. Ellis slipped a hand through the gap—not that it mattered yet. One fracture wasn't an escape. Not even close.

Even if he snapped enough welds, squeezed through the mangled bars, and got free, then what? He had no idea where he was. How far was help? From what little he'd seen outside, this place sat in the middle of nowhere. Miles of nothing. Could he steal a vehicle? Make a getaway?

He shoved the thought aside. First, the cage. Everything else came later.

He slid the apparatus to the next joint and wrenched—around and around—grinding metal, creaking bars, stressing the welds. The cage shuddered. Another twist.

The lace snapped.

The twist whipped free, ricocheting off the bars, clanking from one to the next before skittering to the floor.

Shit.

He fumbled, his pulse hammering in his ears as his hands swept blindly through the dark until he touched the fragment. He snatched it up—a sharp breath welling in his chest.

One more lace. One more shot.

Carefully, he looped the tie, threaded a rebar fragment through, and twisted. Clockwise. The bars groaned, bending inward. His grip locked, eyes unblinking, every muscle in his hands straining.

He could almost taste freedom.

Outside footsteps approached.

He quickly untied the lace and hid the pieces in a shoe.

A knock came. It had to be the idiot. Rena wouldn't bother.

"Fuck you!" Ellis shouted.

A low, sinister chuckle drifted through the door.

Yeah, that was Belt Buckle screwing with him again.

Returning to his work, he tied the lace around the bars. Carefully, he cranked the twist. The bar creaked. Pressure pulled at the parallel bars, stressing the weld.

Snap!

The second shoelace, his last hope, broke in half. He dropped his head, closed his eyes, and leaned back on the bars. He was never getting out of here alive.

More jostling came from outside the room.

Fingering the broken lace, Ellis sighed. He could try tying all the broken ends together. But what he needed was a shitload of dental floss. Frankie Peller, that slippery son-of-a-bitch, had the advantage.

Outside the dark room were voices. But he couldn't make out the conversation. Shouting, followed by a loud bang.

The hairs on the back of his neck rose. Was that gunfire?

"Hey," Ellis shouted. "What's going on?"

Had the crazy idiot shot somebody? Was he next? Sweat dripped down his forehead. He was a sitting duck in this cage. Using his feet for leverage, he gripped the bars and pulled as hard as possible. Kicking at the bottom, the metal cage rattled. But no welds broke. He was trapped in this coffin.

Fuck, this was it. Any minute, that door would open and they'd shoot him dead.

Raindrops filled the steady silence. The last moments of a man's life are often filled with regrets, missed opportunities, and mistakes.

Ellis fumbled with the broken laces. He should have stayed retired. Linda would never know how this all happened. In fact, she'd probably never recover his body. He'd be her missing husband, forever. Flowers on an empty grave.

Moments passed. A faint tap sounded at the door.

Ellis lifted his head.

The frame exploded into shards.

The door violently shot inward from its hinges.

A body slammed through the doorway, like a cannonball tearing through a wooden ship.

Light flooded the room as tiny particles drifted about.

"What the hell's going on?" Ellis shouted.

From the rubble came a familiar voice.

"Ellis Martin?"

Breathless, he answered, "Yeah?"

Wes Holt rose from the ground, grinning. "I have an order of oysters for you."

"Oh, shit, man." Ellis settled his breath. "It's good to see you. Let me out of this fucking thing, please."

Wes approached the cage, examining the contraption.

"Get back and cover your ears," Wes said.

Ellis squeezed to the far side, cupping his hands over his earlobes. Wes raised his pistol, nuzzled its barrel against the padlock, and fired. The steel lock blew into fragments.

He tore open the door, lowering a hand. The weary detective gripped his palm and emerged from his prison of welded rebar.

"Can you walk?"

"Give me a second." Ellis closed his eyes, stretching his back. Linda's smiling face appeared in his mind—the way she'd tuck her hair behind an ear when she took a sip of coffee each morning. His ragged breath calmed, and he muttered, "I'm coming home."

Wes placed a steady hand on his shoulder. "You good?"

Ellis cleared his throat. "I heard other gunshots."

"Yeah, you're not the only one he took." Wes pointed. "Come with me."

He led them from the room, down the hall, as Ellis limped behind.

Inside the second room, a groggy girl lay on a bed, half covered by a dirty quilt. She fought to keep her eyes open and massaged the red marks on her wrists.

Wes aimed a finger at the bed's far side. "We've got a KIA on the ground over there. It could have been my doing. I fired when shots came in my direction. But I don't see a piece on this guy."

Ellis approached the bed's other side. On the floor, in a pool of blood, lay Belt Buckle. His eyes stared lifeless. Ellis checked the wound in the man's chest, and raised his chin.

"That's close range, small caliber," he said. "There's no way your .50 Magnum did that."

"Can you ID him?"

"Unsub. One of them."

"One of them?"

"There's also a woman," Ellis said. "Slim, dark hair, early thirties. Foreign, I think. She's the brains. I'm thinking she was also the doer here." He paced to the open window and pointed. "I see muddy prints outside. Look fresh."

Wes cocked a round and handed Ellis the pistol, butt end first. "Weapon hot," he said.

Ellis seized the Desert Eagle.

Wes brought the girl up to a sitting position, felt her pulse, and checked her pupils. She appeared semi-conscious.

"Do you know your name?" he asked.

The girl's hair was disheveled, and her head slumped.

"Lil… ly," she slurred.

"All right, Lilly. You're safe now. I'm going to carry you outside."

"Mm-hmm…" came the soft response.

Wes raised Lilly from the bed onto his shoulder, and cradled her legs, hoisting them both upright. He, Ellis, and the sleepy girl entered the cabin's main room. Sirens sounded in the distance as the three made their way around the boxes and debris.

"Hold up," Wes said.

Ellis stopped.

"I need a favor."

Ellis chuckled. "Shit man, of course. Anything."

Wes took a deep breath. "We put another investigator on the trail after we thought you quit. Sorry about that."

"Can't blame you," Ellis said.

"Her name's Jadene Bowman." Wes inched a nod to the girl over his shoulder. "This girl is her partner."

"Oh?"

"I know it's a lot to ask, but the thing is, I need her to keep going. She's made so much progress. She's smart, tenacious. And I think with your help…"

"I'm out." Ellis turned his head, glancing toward the back room where they'd held him captive. "I'm sorry, but this one was… too much."

Holding the unconscious girl on his shoulder, Wes gave a nod.

"But you need her to keep going because of?"

"Right," Wes said. "She doesn't know the importance yet. I haven't found the right time."

Ellis thought on this. "All right, but one condition."

"Name it."

"This all turned into a shitshow for me, and there's three bodies that I know of."

"Three?"

"Two others they executed in front of me, outside in a ditch."

"Shit."

Ellis studied the big man. "If she's going to do this, she'll need full protection."

Wes flexed his cheek muscles. "Already under my wing."

"All right, then, I'll do what I can."

"Thank you."

With Lilly in tow, Wes marched toward the cabin's front door.

Ellis limped behind. He needed food and a shower. But first, he had to call Linda.

FORTY-NINE

Three squad cars and an ambulance arrived, but only the ambulance, with its treaded tires, made it up the muddy hillside. Overhead, a helicopter buzzed in the distance until a uniformed officer on the ground gave the all-clear and sent it away.

For the moment, the rain had stopped.

At Wes's urging, a paramedic checked Jadene's vitals and offered her oxygen. Jadene insisted she was fine and demanded they attend to Lilly instead. The paramedic shrugged an okay, and Wes relented, leaving to speak with the officers.

They'd found two more bodies in a gully not far from the cabin, and the police were trying to ID them.

Distant chatter revealed the kidnapper inside the cabin was dead. Shot by his partner—a woman—who'd escaped through the window, likely just after she and Wes arrived.

A uniformed officer asked if she'd seen anyone on foot. She hadn't. Before the rescue, she'd remained in the vehicle, eyes fixed on the cabin until Wes finally emerged with Lilly over his shoulder and another man, who turned out to be Ellis Martin, hobbling behind them.

From afar, Ellis was just as Jadene recalled from his photo, albeit with some injuries and dirty clothes from his ordeal. Distinguished and good-looking for his age, she wasn't sure now was the right time to introduce herself with all the questions and commotion going on.

Lilly was placed on a stretcher, assessed by the two paramedics, and given Narcan to counteract whatever was in her system. Jadene stood by her side, holding her hand.

Within minutes, the opioids in Lilly's brain were displaced by the medication, and she was alert and talking.

"Is that Wes?" she asked Jadene.

"The tall one, yes."

Lilly snickered. "Tell me you jumped him already."

"Lilly, you need rest. We shouldn't—"

"Don't change the subject."

"Please, stop," Jadene giggled.

Lilly's grin went devilish. "He's like a mountain man. I bet he could bench-press a Grizzly Bear."

Jadene laughed aloud.

"Muscles, and that perfect hair." Lilly's brows arched. "You never thought of messing it up?"

"You might still have some drugs in your system. I think you need—"

"Girl, you're a hot mamma. You need to break you off a piece of him."

Jadene blushed. Wes was a very handsome man. There was no denying that. But with everything happening—from the start of the case to Lilly's disappearance—she hadn't thought about anything outside those parameters.

"Okay, okay," she said. "Lilly, you have to rest. I need you to feel better. Okay?"

Lilly smiled. "All right. But you never told me."

"Never told you?"

"Yeah, what'd you find out at Buckley's?"

Jadene was just happy to see her friend safe again. The case didn't matter, and she hadn't told Lilly she was quitting the investigation yet—but would do so once she got better.

"I talked with his daughter." Jadene drew a deep breath. "But she didn't know anything, and I think it's a dead end."

"Ronald Buckley?" Lilly's forehead creased.

"Yes. Remember? The pilot's grandson. I went to his house and—"

"No, no," Lilly frowned. "Ronald Buckley doesn't—"

"Excuse me?" A paramedic appeared with a bulb and cuff hung around her neck. "I need to retake her blood pressure."

Jadene backed away from the stretcher as a soft hand touched her shoulder.

"Hey, I'm Ellis Martin."

He looked like he'd been tossed from a moving car. A black eye, a cut across his forehead, and a bandage on one of his hands. His cheeks held a week's worth of stubble, and his collared shirt was ripped at the neckline.

She had seen him earlier speaking with his wife on the phone. During the happy call, a tear rolled down his cheek. It was sweet, really.

Ellis was the pinnacle of her profession and well respected in law enforcement. The five officers on the scene went out of their way to introduce themselves to him. One of them even did half a curtsy when their palms met. To them, he was royalty.

She stuck out her hand, butterflies trembling in her stomach. "Bowman, Jadene Bowman." She cringed at her own words. Did she drive an Austin Martin? Did she drink Martini's? No, she was agent idiot.

Ellis didn't notice her embarrassment as the two shook. Instead, he pointed in Lilly's direction. "How's she doing?"

The paramedic replied, "Her cheeks are pinking up. With more fluids and some rest, she'll be just fine."

"Good to hear," he said. Then to Jadene. "Hey, can we talk for a minute?"

"Sure," she said.

As they paced away, Jadene waved a hand in Lilly's direction. But Lilly and the paramedic were in conversation.

Ellis led Jadene down the path toward the Escalade, out of earshot from the others.

"Three in black wrap, and one fled." He lowered his head. "Hard to believe I can't put anyone in handcuffs after all of this."

"I'm sorry they did this to you."

"Thanks." Ellis reset his feet in the mud. "I understand you're in the hunt now?"

Jadene paused. "I was."

"Well, I'm off the investigation," he said, facing her. "It's not really my kind of case, anyway. Plus, I can't put Linda through this anymore."

"Linda. How is your wife? Relieved, I bet."

Ellis exhaled. "She gave me an earful. My retirement from the force was the happiest day of her life. But I do miss it." He eyed the squad car lights flashing down the hillside. "But this case was my last."

"I'm sure she'll be happy to see you."

He huffed a chuckle. "I'll grab Italian on the way home. She loves anything with noodles." He looked toward the ambulance. "I'll keep it light. No point telling her how close this all got."

Simple and sweet. Jadene returned a smile.

"Although, I do have one question for you." He raised his chin. "Like I said, I'm done with all of this. But Sinclair Whitmore's telegram, I'm curious."

Jadene sported another grin. "You want to know how far I got?"

Ellis narrowed his eyes. "Very much so, yes."

FIFTY

At the trail's other end, Lilly was loaded onto the ambulance, and Wes was shaking hands with the officers. Caution tape was strung up around the cabin, and a policemen radioed in a call for the meat wagon.

With the chaos settling, debriefing Ellis felt right.

Jadene cleared her throat. "We started with Dakota free blue."

Ellis bounced a nod.

"Once we learned that phrase referred to an airplane, a C47 Skytrain, we scoured the flight logs online. Lilly quickly found a craft that took off and landed in the proper period."

"Lakenheath, 41-978?"

Jadene lifted a brow. "That's amazing. You have a great memory."

"Don't be too impressed." He pointed to the cabin. "I had a lot of time to recall my own research, over and over."

Her smile broke. "I'm so sorry you had to go through that."

"It's over, thank God. But please, go on."

"She and I tracked the flight from Lakenheath into Sussex, then Kraków. And then back to Lakenheath again."

"And you verified the transfer to the larger plane? And the flight to Lajes?"

"Right. And then we got stuck trying to find out where the Skymaster went after leaving Lajes."

Ellis dipped his head. "Same. I figured it flew from the Azores into the States, someplace."

"As did we. But no logs existed online, so I drove to Alabama to see if I could find out where that Skymaster landed."

"Max Air base." Ellis twisted his lips. "We were on the same trail, you and I, and these bastards took me from the airport when I returned to Hartsfield."

"Again, I'm so sorry this happened to you."

He raised a hand. "Please, I'm interested."

She collected her thoughts. "Then, in the log at Max Air base, I found Buckley's name, and—"

"Who?"

"Buckley. The other pilot."

"Other pilot?" Ellis said.

"Collin Buckley. A civilian. The guy who took over from Gabreski."

"Gabreski?"

"Gabe Gabreski. I think he started the whole thing and flew into Kraków with the C47. The logs confirmed he passed the trip's leg off to Buckley in the second plane."

"You saw the actual flight controller log? The one at Max Air base in Alabama?"

"Yes," she said.

"I waited in that place for almost three hours. The bald guy couldn't find it."

She lifted her shoulders. "A nice woman named Dottie helped me and brought out the original logbook. She found it in the back and said the facility hadn't scanned it yet."

Ellis shifted his jaw.

"Like I said, now I had Buckley's name and the tail number of the Skymaster. But I had to find out where the craft landed. My theory was it touched down someplace in the United States."

Ellis raised his eyebrows. "And?"

"And I found it," she said.

"No shit?" he chuckled. "You tracked an 80-year-old flight halfway around the world to the States? And you did this all in just over three days?"

A warmness filled her cheeks. It was nice to share this with someone who understood the difficulty of the investigation.

"You're a hell of a detective, Bowman."

She fought a colossal smile.

"What else?" he urged. "Don't hold out on me."

"I tracked the Skymaster to Hunter Army Airfield in Savannah. I found a log entry online and matched the tail number. But that's where things stopped. Nobody and nothing got on or off the plane in Savannah. The only thing the log mentioned was that the aircraft refueled and was headed west. But no destination was recorded."

Ellis gave a slow nod. "This Buckley, does he have any family?"

"I worked that angle, too," she said. "And I found a relative, but she didn't know anything about her grandfather's war service and, honestly, the woman seemed kind of disinterested. I gave her my card, but I think it's a dead end." She dropped her shoulders. "And we never found any manifest, so we don't know who was on either of the two planes."

Ellis grunted.

"That's it. That's everything I know."

"All right." He rubbed his chin. "I'm impressed. You got farther than me in just a few days."

She beamed with pride.

"But nothing on Hermann or the other phrases?"

"Just Powodzenia."

"Yeah, right, good luck…" he said.

The ambulance carting Lilly made its way toward them, and Ellis put an arm on Jadene's shoulder, walking them out of the way under a nearby pine tree.

"Wes tells me you're thinking of quitting?"

Jadene lowered her gaze. "This whole thing with Lilly, and putting her in danger. It all got crazy scary."

"I understand," he said. "Stow that for a minute, and let me tell you what I know."

"Okay?" She had to admit, she was a little curious. But it was unlikely anything he shared with her would change her mind.

Ellis eyed the trees, and his stare lowered to hers. "I know they smuggled something out. I'm not sure what it was, but I think we both know it has considerable value."

Jadene scratched at her elbow. Tommy had said precisely the same thing.

"And they hid it someplace. Someplace secure." He gazed down the cliffside. "When you restart your investigation, remember there are others, dangerous people, who are after whatever this is."

"Restart? I don't think I can, it's—"

"Nonsense." Ellis raised a palm. "You're an investigator. That's who you are." He pointed toward Wes in the distance. "Besides, you have protection."

She glanced toward Wes, who stood a few yards up the path.

"And there's something in the telegram you haven't checked out yet."

"There is?"

Ellis flashed a grin. "Bay of the Montebello."

"I did, though." She shuffled her feet. "There's a Montebello Bay in France. But why would they fly out into the middle of the Atlantic to Lajes Airfield just to turn around? And—"

"No, no," Ellis said. "Check it again. That phrase references an event. It's not the name of an actual bay."

"It isn't?"

A uniformed officer walked up the trail toward the pair, aiming a finger at Ellis. "Still need that ride?"

Facing Jadene, Ellis paced backward alongside the officer, and the two headed toward the squad cars.

"The day before Christmas Eve, 1941," he said, stepping farther down the hill. "The Montebello."

"What does it mean?" she called out.

Ellis tossed his arms into the air, shouting, "No way, Jadene Bowman. I'm not going to spoil the surprise."

FIFTY-ONE

"Why don't you sleep on it?" Wes urged. "Maybe we can talk about things in the morning?"

Evening rolled in as they pulled back onto the main road from the trail. Two officers had helped to push the Escalade from the deep mud. Wes thanked them with a firm handshake before escorting Jadene back to the vehicle.

Wes insisted she stay under his protection, demanding she be at the mansion. She was still in disbelief by the dead bodies, the kidnappings, and processing everything Ellis told her.

But as she rode in the Escalade, one thought worried her. Only a handful of people knew about Sinclair Whitmore's telegram. She and Ellis had signed an NDA, and after overhearing Ellis's statement to the police, it was evident he hadn't revealed anything to his captors.

Then, there was her circle. The only person she spoke to was Lilly. But it was unlike Lilly to betray Jadene in matters of business, and even if she had let something slip, that would never account for Ellis's kidnapping, which occurred long before she'd been given the case.

Was Lilly taken to leverage against Jadene? Was she captured so she'd reveal what she knew of the hunt? But how did they know she was on the case? How did they know Ellis was on the case?

The Desert Eagle sat in the center console, its cold metal glinting under the dim light. She drummed a finger on her knee. Could she trust Wes?

Her mind raced with questions. Who were the kidnappers working with? Chillingly, Wes was the most obvious suspect. She tried to recall every detail of the day, every word Wes had said. Her brows furrowed. He was also the only person with knowledge that both she and Ellis were on the case. In fact, Wes had hired Ellis himself.

Was it possible he was behind all of this? And who was the mysterious woman Ellis mentioned? Jadene wasn't with Wes when he'd entered the creepy cabin. In fact, he insisted she stay locked in the SUV.

The dead man they found in the room with Lilly. What if Lilly wasn't taken for leverage but taken by mistake? Had that enraged Wes and his partner? Enough to kill the man they found? And what about the mysterious woman Ellis spoke of? Was this a bizarre dispute between the three? Did the woman flee? Did Wes let her go before the police arrived?

Gazing out at the dark roadway, Jadene gnawed a fingernail. When Wes showed up at her office today, was everything he said true? Spotting the unlawful license plate on the Bronco? Not approaching the vehicle himself because of a possible rainy shootout? And Jadene's safety being his first priority? Was any of this true?

What if the man next to her was working both sides? Her mouth went dry. The potentials were stacking up. The Desert Eagle was within reach. But could she grab it, aim, and fire? Was she capable of killing?

Jadene took a long breath, closing her eyes. What if she was wrong about all of this? What if the man next to her was completely innocent? Was she overthinking things again?

First, if Ellis suspected Wes had anything to do with the killings or kidnappings, he would have said something when the two were speaking in private at the scene. Ellis Martin was trustworthy. That was indisputable.

Also, Wes didn't hesitate when she told him Lilly was in danger. In fact, she'd barely gotten the words out of her mouth before he'd whisked them out of Sinclair's kitchen into the SUV. He'd also saved her from the fire at her office, which she still couldn't believe.

But there was another question that could help her understand things, one that could give her a better idea of where Wes stood. And it was time she got an answer.

Jadene turned to him. "Why the five days?"

Wes stared out at the road.

"I've asked before, and you said you couldn't tell me. But if I'm going to stay on this case, I need to know. Or, you can take me back to my apartment right now. I don't need to sleep on things and don't want your protection."

Wes stretched his neck. "The five days is Mister Whitmore's timeline. He needs to understand everything you can find about Arthur. He's counting on you."

"You said that." She pointed a finger in his direction. "And I swear, Wes, if I have to ask again and you volley that bullshit back to me, you can pull over and drop me off."

He stayed focused on the road.

"I mean it," she said.

Wes drew a deep breath. "Because your investigation is important to Mister Whitmore and his company."

"His company? How?"

Wes activated the turn signal. The ticking echoed in the silent car. They were nearing the exit for the mansion.

"You don't know this," he began. "Because it's not public knowledge yet. But Whitmore Systems and Whitmore Dynamics will go public under a new company called Whitmore International."

"Go public? But what does—"

"He might not be able to keep it."

"Keep the company? I don't understand."

The blue hue from the SUV's dash lit Wes's profile. "Things are politically charged. The board is considering replacing him before the announcement is made."

"But…" she stammered. "But why?"

He stared ahead, not blinking. "I'm sure you know about Arthur Whitmore through your investigation. Who he was?"

A sinking sensation overcame her. This was about Sinclair's grandfather. His Nazi grandfather.

"Some on the current board want to see Mister Whitmore ousted. They say it's a bad look for the company. You and Ellis are his final hope, his hail Mary. He wants you to uncover something that might help him."

"How does this board know about Arthur? I mean—"

"Somebody figured it out, and I've got my suspicions. I've caught that son-of-a-bitch Iverson skulking around a time or two. Or it could have been discovered during a deep background check. I'm not sure. But there's a rumor among the group that Arthur willingly volunteered for the Nazis."

"Wait." Jadene raised a hand. "Hold on. Can't Sinclair keep the companies private? He has money. I mean, why does—"

"Money's not everything. Mister Whitmore is concerned about his reputation, legacy, and children. Whether the company is public or private isn't the central matter. That's just stockholder funding to him. But these accusations will destroy his name once the board meets." Wes cleared his throat. "Nobody will see him for his achievements. They'll tie Sinclair to his grandfather's past and tarnish his character."

A bad feeling struck Jadene. "You said the board's going to meet on this? When does that happen?"

Wes turned to her. "You already know."

A chill raced up her neck.

"Mister Whitmore's meeting is the day after tomorrow. It's a corporate image thing to them, and, under the bylaws, Mister Whitmore will be removed."

"Do they know about the telegram?"

"No, only Ellis and yourself do."

The weight of the investigation suddenly hit her. She had a little more than 24 hours to find something, or Sinclair Whitmore would be thrown to the wolves. Forced to give up his position in the companies he built, while his reputation became shrouded in sins committed two generations before the man was even alive. She closed her eyes. This was so unfair.

Wes dipped his head. "He doesn't show it, but he's beside himself."

"Hang on," she said. "Arthur was almost certainly conscripted. He didn't have a choice. It was eighty years ago, World War II, Nazi Germany. He either served or faced a literal death squad. Arthur can't be blamed, and Sinclair sure as hell had nothing to do with it."

"I agree. But to them, it doesn't matter. Corporate boards have a funny position on that kind of association. There's even precedent for it. They'll get rid of Mister Whitmore and say he retired. Then, they'll plan the initial public offering under a different name without him at the table."

"What do you mean it doesn't matter?"

"It may not even matter whether Arthur was forced to serve or volunteered. But, if, like you said, he was conscripted involuntarily, that's what Mister Whitmore is pinning his hopes on. If you can prove Arthur served against his will, he could argue the point. Though, it may not do much good."

"This sounds like blackmail."

Wes nodded. "It absolutely does."

"But if the board gets rid of him because of his grandfather, I can't change anything," she said. "What does Sinclair want from me?"

"I don't know," Wes said. "Maybe a miracle."

The SUV turned off the road, snaking up the long, private drive toward the mansion.

Fifty-Two

Wes hustled over to her door, and the two made their way from the garage, across the rose garden, into Sinclair's cathedral-sized kitchen. Wes unbuckled his holster and laid the weapon on a prep table.

Jadene held for a moment. Wes couldn't be involved in anything nefarious. His expressions, his words—for as stoic as he was at times, he held genuine concern for his boss, and it showed. An exceptional loyalty, and looking back on the day he'd shown incredible selflessness and courage. Wes was every bit the man he portrayed and she was embarrassed for thinking otherwise. Beyond that, he'd said the magic word.

She stood across from him at the prep table, her lips forming a gentle smile. "You know, you called him Sinclair."

Wes hitched his neck. "I did?"

"You did." She smiled warmly. "While we were talking about the board getting rid of him because of Arthur's past."

"I don't want to see him fail." Wes shrugged. "But all of this—your investigation and the board's decision—it's out of my control." He met her eyes with his. "I'm not going to pressure you. This is your decision. My job right now is to keep you safe until we learn more about what's going on."

Jadene gazed down at the table. The truth was, she wasn't sure what to do.

Wes paced to the kitchen's pantry and the wall of bottles.

"Wine?" he asked.

She could use a big glass. The day was exhausting, and her neck was stiff. However, her concerns about the case brought two competing thoughts.

First, somewhere out there, someone knew about the telegram. It might have been a person Ellis was working with, though they may never know for sure. Regardless, that person was a lethal adversary. Even more troubling, if the aircraft in the telegram did smuggle something out from Kraków—as both Tommy and Ellis theorized—this unknown person's actions now put the payload's value at two kidnappings and three murders.

Jadene was also gravely aware that if Wes hadn't shown up at her office when he did, she would have been taken instead of Lilly. And she didn't wear a smartwatch.

But second, despite the danger, she was fascinated by the research and stimulated by the hunt. Further, Ellis's commendation of her work instilled in her a new sense of momentum. She couldn't explain it. This was a genuine mystery and far removed from the background checks and bullshit claims depositions her other clients demanded.

She tapped a finger on the prep table. But there was still so much she didn't understand about the telegram, and time was running out.

Could she walk away from the case? She'd been wondering this all day. If she did, it probably meant the end of her business—even if Sinclair let her keep the money. Once word got out that she quit, it was doubtful she'd get another chance at a real case again.

Her gaze lingered on the prep table. Now that she'd had time to process everything, would leaving the case, at this point, make any difference? Would it lessen the danger she was in? It wasn't like she could announce to whomever this murderous person was that she'd given up and that they should leave her alone. She was still in the same peril whether or not she stayed in the hunt.

Her only real option was to keep investigating, see where it led, and try not to get herself killed. Besides, Ellis had given her another clue. And, apparently, she'd gained the protection of a personal bodyguard, who was currently offering her a glass of wine.

A smile tugged at Jadene's lips. "Do you have a computer I can use?" she asked.

"Sure," Wes said. "They've made up a place for you, and there's a laptop in your quarters."

Yes, right. She'd been so deep in thought that she forgot she was a guest at The Whitmore Waldorf.

"Well, if you don't mind, can you show me to my quarters?" she grinned.

"Does that mean you're not quitting?"

"It means I need some time to think," she said. "If that's okay?"

Wes led her from the kitchen, up the river of stairs, and down a long hall. Everything on the upper level was just as lavish as the main floor, with artwork, tapestries, paintings, and more. It was like trespassing in a museum.

"Here you are," he said, opening a tall double-doorway.

She stepped into the mammoth bedroom. The scheme was royal blue, and everything inside appeared plucked from a romance novel. A lush Persian rug ran most of the floor, with a collective of tasteful, ornate chairs arranged in front of a fireplace. A four-poster bed—a pillowed cloud of comfort—rested cornerwise, facing a bank of floor-to-ceiling windows.

But her attention remained on something else. In the distance sat a beautiful Queen Anne desk with a large laptop on its surface. She approached the workstation, kicked off her shoes, sat, and clicked the computer's keys.

Wes stood by the door. "Are you hungry?" he asked.

But Jadene was already engrossed, scanning the information on her screen.

"All right," he said. "I'll leave you to it, then."

The bedroom doors closed, and he vanished.

Thirty minutes later came a knock.

"Come in," Jadene said, scrolling the laptop's screen.

Wes appeared with an enormous silver platter.

"The kitchen whipped up some nibbles if you're interested." He set the tray on the desk beside the laptop.

The platter was filled with cheeses, crackers, and bread. All of Jadene's major food groups. Surrounding the spread was a rim of cigar-sized chocolate cookies.

She picked up a cracker and chuckled. "You really don't want me to quit, do you?"

Wes glanced away, sheepish.

"All right then," she said. "Sinclair's telegram, the original, can you fetch it? I need to show you something."

Wes grinned. "I'll be right back."

FIFTY-THREE

Wes returned with the tin, handing it over.

Sitting cross-legged in the desk chair, Jadene opened the metal box, unfolded the half-sheet, and placed it next to the laptop.

TELEGRAMM   KRAK (tear)
NL 17 JAN 1945
URGENT STOP BROKEN CASTLE STOP DAKOTA FREE BLUE
STOP WHISPERING WEST STOP BAY OF THE MONTEBELLO
STOP LITTLE RANCH STOP HERMANN STOP DOUBLE SAFE
HAVEN STOP POWODZENIA

"Grab a chair," she said. "I need to bring you into the loop on all this."

Wes brought over a seat as she began explaining things. The telegram came from Arthur, Wes already knew, but she explained how seven-year-old Sinclair received it from his grandfather on his deathbed.

"He didn't tell me that. He only said the goal was to find a way to clear Arthur's name," Wes said.

"It wasn't easy for him," Jadene said.

Despite their closeness, some things remained unshared between Sinclair and Wes. It was probably easier for Sinclair to deal with her, and perhaps the main reason she was chosen.

"When you hired Ellis, what were your instructions to him?" she asked.

Wes leaned forward. "I gave him the telegram and told him to learn all he could about Arthur and report back."

"He gave me the same direction," Jadene said. "But whatever this is, I haven't found any connection to Arthur. My guess is he intercepted the communication. I'm not sure if he had any other role than that."

She grabbed a slice of cheese from the tray and took a bite before realizing her hunger. Wes waited patiently while she chomped it down.

"All right, the first phrase is Broken Castle. I'd researched a few structures in and around Kraków, and there were a number of them, but—"

"That's a citadel," Wes said.

"A citadel?"

"A fortress. A place with structure and defense. A military base."

She studied him. "And how do you know this?"

"I spent some time in greens."

"In the service?"

He dipped his chin. "And the term, broken, I think it means the place was breached. Broken into."

She mulled this over. "Broken fortress?"

"Right."

"Interesting." She remembered Tommy's telling of the Army Group Centre and how the Soviets overtook the Nazis. Without more information, though, they could spend all night trying to locate whatever structure this was and still be uncertain. Instead, she made a mental note and moved on.

Though she also found it curious that Wes didn't elaborate on his service. He just moved past it like a forgotten memory. But she didn't want to make things awkward and didn't press him.

"Okay, let me skip around." She pointed to a phrase. "Hermann might be a person, but we haven't found anything. Nothing solid on Little Ranch or Double Safe Haven either. But Powodzenia means good luck, which may have been a message for the pilots."

Wes scanned the telegram, bobbing his head.

"But the key phrase was Dakota free blue." She explained that the aircraft flying into Kraków—an active warzone at the time—picked up someone or something and then flew back to the UK. "There, the pilot switched planes to a four-prop C54 aircraft, almost double the size as the plane that flew into Kraków. And it took off west, to Lajes Air base."

"In the Azores," he said.

"Right again." She smiled. "After a refuel, the flight continued west. Tracking the tail number, I found it landed in Savannah, Georgia."

Wes turned to her. "At Hunter?"

"You know your bases."

He grunted.

"I found the controller flight log, but it didn't reveal much. Like in Lajes, the aircraft landed, refueled, and switched pilots from military to civilian without anyone else disembarking. Then it took off again."

"Where was it headed?"

"That's the thing," she shrugged. "The log only recorded "Private—west" with no other details, until Ellis mentioned something."

"Ellis?"

"He gave me another clue." She switched tabs and brought up a map of the United States. "Which brings us to our next phrase," she said. "Bay of the Montebello."

"Where's that?" he said.

"I thought it was an actual bay, but it's not."

"It isn't?"

"Nope."

"Then what is it?"

"That's what I've been figuring out," Jadene said. "On December 23rd, 1941, just weeks after Pearl Harbor, an American Union Oil Company ship was transporting crude from California to Canada." She pointed to the screen. "A merchant ship named the SS Montebello."

"A steamship?" Wes rose, turned his chair backward, and reseated with his chest against its hind end. "And the ship met with the plane somehow?"

"No."

"I don't get it."

"That's the crazy part. A torpedo struck the Montebello and sunk her."

"A torpedo? Ours?"

"No, it came from a Japanese submarine, traveling from Japan to California at a slow 24 knots. That's who sunk the ship."

"You're kidding?"

"I know, right?"

"Casualties?"

"None. Would you believe all the men aboard the Montebello survived?"

"No kidding?"

"But the incident wasn't well known to the public because of wartime censorship. So it wasn't widely reported, and certainly nothing about the cause of the Montebello's sinking. The public would freak out if they knew an actual Japanese sub was lurking off the coast firing torpedoes."

"I would imagine."

"Domestic attacks were also suppressed by the military to keep troop morale intact. But not this one."

"I don't understand."

"Because there were no casualties, news among the troops spread fast." She aimed a finger at the telegram. "That's why it's mentioned here."

"I'm still not making the connection."

Snagging a cigar cookie from the tray, Jadene bit its crunchy end. "Oh man, these are good."

"Billionaires know their snacks." Wes grinned.

She clicked the keyboard, and a map of California's central coastline appeared. "The Montebello's sinking occurred near Cambria, a seaside village. Six miles from shore, that's where the ship went down."

Wes eyed the topography. "All right, but what does that have to do with the airplane?"

"Remember when I told you the flight was going west?"

"I do."

She chewed. "I think this shipwreck is a marker."

"A marker?"

Jadene aimed her half-eaten cigar cookie at the screen. "I believe the aircraft landed somewhere around here."

Wes's gaze swung from the screen to hers. "Then we have to find it."

FIFTY-FOUR

Three slices of cheese and two cigar cookies later, they'd searched every air base from Los Angeles to San Francisco. However, they could not locate the C54's tail number.

Jadene slumped in her chair. "I thought for sure we'd find something. I don't understand."

Leaning back, Wes stretched his arms. "Are you certain it landed at a military base?"

"Why wouldn't it?"

"Well, Buckley was a civilian, right? A pilot, but a civilian pilot, right?" His broad shoulders rose and fell. "Could he have touched down at a public airport?"

Wes had a strong point. Jadene had been so wrapped up thinking it was an air base because the C54 was a military plane she'd never considered it landing at a civilian airstrip. They changed focus and searched every public airport they could find for the next few hours.

However, surprisingly, this was far more difficult than tracking down military bases and related flight logs. At least most of those records were public.

With civilian airports, they ran into two problems. First, the finding of any comprehensive list of airfields in 1944 was hit-

and-miss. Second, it was nearly impossible to find any flight controller logs.

"This is hopeless," Jadene said. "We're never going to know where that aircraft landed."

Wes took over on the keyboard for a while, but his luck was no better. Their exhaustive search yielded nothing but dead ends and growing frustration.

Jadene's usual determination waned, and she paced the room. "I know it touched down out there, somewhere. It's the only reason for the Montebello phrase. It had to." She returned to the desk and sunk into the chair, where the laptop's screen glowed, casting shadows across her face.

Page after page turned up nothing.

"This is like chasing a damn ghost," Jadene said, tapping a finger against her cheek.

Straddling the chair, Wes slipped a finger under his shirt collar, pulling in a whisk of air. He looked toward the windows, where the first hues of dawn streaked across the skyline.

"Maybe we're approaching this all wrong," he said.

Her reddened eyes drew on his. "What do you mean?"

"We've been assuming the plane had to land at an established airfield, right? But what if it didn't? What if it landed somewhere more… isolated?"

She straightened in the chair. "You mean like a private airstrip or an unregistered landing site?"

"Exactly," he said. "This was the mid-1940s, and there had to be plenty of makeshift runways."

She stroked the back of her neck. "That could explain why we haven't found any records. But I don't know. How do we even start to look for something like that? And the C54 was a big plane that needed 3,500 feet of runway to land. I mean…"

"Well, it's not impossible airstrips like that existed."

"Yeah, but if the area were abandoned, even something that size would be grown over by now."

"That's my point," Wes said.

"Your point?"

"The only way to find out is to explore the spots."

"You mean, like, check out satellite photos?"

He hitched a brow. "That might work, but the best option would be to narrow down a few possibilities and talk with the locals."

"You mean go out there? To California?"

"I think it's the best option."

She huffed. "That's not possible. We'd need to chart places, get tickets, make the trip, and hope someone can help us. There's no way we can do all of that before Sinclair's board meeting. We'd have to get very lucky and…"

"Look, we can do some of that in the air. Scope out the landscape and find spots that might be long enough. Make a list, that kind of thing, right?"

"Yes, but let's be practical."

"Practical?"

She seized the laptop and started to type. "I bet same-day tickets are astronomical."

"But—"

"I know what you're going to say," she said. "Sinclair's a billionaire. Don't worry about it. But I do. If we spend a ton of money and come back with nothing, which is like a 99% probability, it's hard to explain to an employer. Even someone like Sinclair."

He tried again to interrupt. "Jadene—"

But she continued thumbing the mouse and clicking keys. "Maybe if I find the cheapest airline and we fly coach, and—"

Wes put a hand on her shoulder. "Stop."

She looked up from the screen.

"You can be exhausting, you know." He smiled. "And your nose gets all crinkly."

"My nose does not crinkle."

He grinned. "It does."

"If we're going to do this, we can't waste any time. We'll have to—"

Wes pressed a finger against her lips. Then, he fished out his phone and dialed.

"Mister Levin, Wes Holt. We're on our way." He locked his eyes on Jadene. "California," he said, pausing. "Forty-five minutes? All right, then. Thank you, sir."

The call ended.

Jadene stared at him.

"Sorry, I didn't mean to cut you off, but Mister Whitmore's jet leaves in less than an hour."

FIFTY-FIVE

Grand pine trees, their branches tangled by twisting ivy, lined the two-lane road. A whisper-thin fog draped over the leaves and needles, crowning the treetops with a ghostly veil.

Twin iron gates scissored upward at the path's far end, unveiling a hidden lane that streamed up a distant hillside. A black Cadillac Escalade with darkened windows rolled silently through the open passage.

As it approached, a familiar face emerged through its windshield. Jadene Bowman, the investigator, sat in the passenger seat alongside a driver—an unknown male with sizable shoulders and dark hair.

Rena had parked the BMW in a secluded patch of a neighboring road, hidden mainly by the draping shrubbery. Inside, she held low, watching the SUV pass before starting her engine. Slowly, her car crept from the bushes and followed.

Travis Floyd had taken the wrong woman and, at the same time, allowed others to track him to his cabin. He was an imbecile who'd almost cost her everything. He'd gotten sloppy and selfish, but his betrayal was not wholly unexpected. The man's demise was always to be.

The large SUV turned onto the Interstate at a junction, heading south. Two vehicles behind, Rena did the same, blending in with the early morning traffic. They sped through downtown, onto the highway, weaving through the skyscraper city until wakes of traffic slowed them to a crawl.

On the massive interstate, seven lanes of cars inched forward, moving in a collective waltz. When an unexpected path cleared, several sprung from their lanes, revving and jostling, before the dance of slowness quickly resumed. Rena feathered the pedals, always keeping the Escalade within eyesight.

Travis Floyd had managed to acquire a second copy of the telegram. Ellis Martin also possessed one, but that copy did not contain the handwritten clues of the second sheet. It had come from Jadene Bowman's office, and the name of Sinclair Whitmore appeared, circled on the top of the page.

A businessman and a technical industrialist, Rena learned. But whatever that man's connection with all of this was, she did not know. However, she was determined to uncover the relationship and didn't need to wait long before spotting Jadene Bowman and her driver this morning.

The tempo increased, and the motoring dance accelerated. Lengths away, the Escalade switched lanes and moved onto the I-20 junction, heading west.

Rena and the BMW snaked behind.

A few miles later, the SUV broke from the highway, turning toward the Fulton County Airport. Several stop lights later, the Escalade entered the facility, drove into the parking area, and found a space.

Behind, Rena and the BMW kept their distance and slid into a spot several lengths away.

Jadene Bowman and her companion left the vehicle, clutching respective carry-ons, and strolled into the main terminal building.

Rena waited in her car for several minutes. Wearing a black knee-length skirt and blouse, she tossed a white pashmina over her shoulders, slipped on her sunglasses, and seized her handbag before exiting the vehicle.

The crisp morning air brushed against her skin. Making her way across the asphalt, she entered the terminal's glass doorway. She trekked down a short hall, approaching a red-headed woman seated at an information desk.

"Good morning," the clerk said.

Rena nudged the sunglasses up the bridge of her nose, ignored the woman, and kept her stride.

This small, private airport didn't hassle travelers with the usual ticket counter and security foray—unless one was flying a commercial charter.

Rounding a bend, she approached a large seating area facing a wall of floor-to-ceiling windows. Half a dozen passengers, most in business attire, sat in random spots, engaged in their smartphones. Clutching her handbag, Rena approached the threshold of glass and steel, taking in the scene outside.

A light fog drifted over the tarmac. On its surface was a world of bustling steel birds, from prop planes to sleek private jets. Some rolled about, readying for the skies, while others sat resting their wings for the next journey. Hustling between the aircraft like bees circling a hive was the orchestrated chaos of ground crew and carts.

Rena scanned the runway. It didn't take long before she spotted Jadene Bowman and her companion ambling toward a Gulfstream. In front of the craft, a man in a black cap stood near the stairs and waved them forward.

The two climbed aboard.

Rena fished out her phone, keyed the jet's registration number into a flight tracker app, and a slew of details appeared within seconds—including the Gulfstream's destination. She closed the app and turned toward the exit. Clutching the phone, she thumbed a number. It was time to collect from the man who'd offered her anything she needed.

"Hello?" came an answer.

Rena passed the redheaded clerk without a glance, whispering into the phone. "It is ironic," she said. "But we need a plane."

Fifty-Six

Jadene ascended the stairs. She'd never stepped onto a private jet. The experience was foreign to her—like she didn't belong.

The cabin's interior radiated warmth. Half a dozen caramel-brown leather seats bordered the aisle. Farther aft, a couch-style booth with an inset mahogany table led to a built-in bar. Nearby, two mounted flatscreens displayed diagrams of their awaiting journey on opposing bulkheads. Everything looked comfortable and spotless.

"Mister Whitmore used to fly out of DeKalb," Wes said, entering the fuselage behind her. "But he enjoys driving through the city, admiring the buildings."

Jadene hadn't blinked since she'd boarded.

"Yeah, okay," she said.

"Take a seat, and I'll check on things up front."

"Yeah, okay."

Wes chuckled, leaving to speak with the pilots.

Jadene paced down the aisle, found a seat, and sank into its cozy cushions. She hadn't slept since last night, and with the eventful day—the kidnappings, the fire, and everything else—the plane's plush seat was incredible. But she had only a few hours to scout possible landing sites for the C54. She removed the loaner laptop from the bag and powered it up.

Her phone buzzed with a text, followed by a photo. Lilly was home from the hospital, sipping an energy drink—which Jadene was sure the doctors advised against—wearing pajamas and a wide grin.

Jadene asked her how she was doing after the ordeal, and Lilly said she was fine and getting rest. Then, Jadene told her she and Wes were on a jet, heading out to California, hunting down the next lead.

"California?" Lilly responded. "What's there?"

Jadene explained things, and to anyone else, it would've sounded batshit crazy that they were flying across the country, looking for the remnants of a runway based on a ship that went down in the Pacific almost a century ago.

But Lilly's excited response came in all caps, "COOL!"

Something else occurred to Jadene. Stan was right to be concerned about a young girl coming into her own, especially with things at home being as free and loose as he'd let on. But in Jadene's view, Lilly was just Lilly.

She'd also seen a significant change in the girl in the last few days. Oddly, all it took to get her going in the right direction was some responsibility. Something challenging. It excited her. Lilly crushed every task Jadene had given her in this case, going beyond in every instance. In fact, she wouldn't be on this plane right now without Lilly's help. Lilly should probably whittle down the boyfriends to one or two, but she was young, and she'd figure it out soon enough.

The phone buzzed again.

"Did you kiss him yet?"

Jadene laughed out loud. "Lilly, stop!" she texted.

"I want juicy deetz when you return!"

Jadene blushed. Lilly being Lilly. "Bye-bye," she responded.

"Safe travels, boss."

Wes returned. "I think they're ready for us. Buckle up."

She set the laptop and phone aside and fastened her belt. Seconds later, the Gulfstream taxied onto the runway, throttled up, and roared down the tarmac. Her stomach lurched. Outside the aircraft's large oval window, the ground transformed into a shrinking mosaic of roads, rivers, forests, and fields. Soon, the jet was enveloped by clouds, like a cocoon in the sky. When they leveled out, the only other passenger on the plane rose from his seat.

"My name is Wes Holt, and I'll be your onboard steward this morning. Something to drink?"

For Jadene, this was all so unreal and only the second time she'd been on an airplane. The first was a business trip to Kansas on a budget carrier, where she sat crammed in a middle seat and queasy for three hours. She'd consciously avoided flying after that. But here, she had plenty of space and her own flight attendant. A smirk tugged at the corners of her mouth.

Wes went to the bar to fetch them water while she brought up a map of California's coast on the computer. Starting at Morro Bay, she noted a few possible fields and mysterious parcels that might have been used as landing sites. Something inside her told her this area was the destination of that C54.

But the coastal mountain terrain didn't provide many possibilities, and a knot tightened in her chest. This entire search was a needle-in-a-haystack outing. Still, she wrote down several locations in her notebook for the next hour and tried to stay positive.

Wes handled transportation particulars at their destination. They'd land at San Luis Obispo airport, grab a rental, and drive up the coast to check out locations.

"With an aircraft that large, we'll find where it touched down," he said. "We need to talk with folks. It could be a private strip that's been around forever or an old field. Somebody has to know."

Jadene wasn't so sure. What if they found nothing? Her investigation had led them here, and it would be her fault. Moreover, Wes—who believed in her more than she did in herself at times—

would be disappointed. Not to mention Sinclair and the looming implications to his business if she came up empty-handed.

She wished Lilly was with her right now for support. Any discovery, or lack thereof, from here on in would be entirely on Jadene's shoulders.

Hiding her insecurities, she and Wes chatted a while longer until, somewhere over Arkansas, Jadene closed her eyes.

Wes brought a thick blanket and draped it over her, then settled into the seat beside her.

FIFTY-SEVEN

The jet touched down by early afternoon, Pacific time. A black Denali waited near the terminal. Wes loaded their bags into the rear compartment. The shoreline skies were overcast as they drove north along the Pacific Coast Highway. The two-lane road meandered through winding curves, flanked by rugged cliffs on one side and the deep blue ocean on the other.

At lower elevations, waves crashed on sandy shores, salt-laced air drifting through Jadene's open window. The coastline was picturesque and serene—the closest she'd ever been to a vacation in her adult life.

Time was running short. Jadene had the day to connect Arthur Whitmore to something in the telegram. She needed facts on his character, yet even finding the landing site might not reveal anything about Arthur.

Wes insisted on driving, which was fine by her. They stopped at various shops and outposts to speak with the locals.

In Morro Bay, a gas station attendant—barely twenty, with long nails—rolled her eyes at Jadene's questions—and every other customer in the store. No help.

Next, Jadene tried a bookstore where the anxious owner knew nothing about any abandoned airport or runway but wanted to sell her an aviation guide.

When they reached Cayucos, she visited a cabinet shop, hoping for better luck at a family-owned business. However, the friendly staff couldn't help her unless she wanted to remodel her kitchen.

Finally, up the coast in Cambria, Wes spotted a lone open sign in an empty strip mall just off the highway.

"Is that a beach town dry cleaner?" he chuckled. "I bet you'll be the highlight of their day."

She gazed at the storefront. He was probably right. Whoever worked there likely didn't have much going on and might welcome a visit, even if she had nothing to press.

The SUV turned off the PCH and exited a side street across the empty parking lot. They stopped at the storefront, and Jadene stepped out.

As he'd done at every location, Wes remained in the vehicle. It was her preference. His size was intimidating, so she left him behind to keep sources open and candid. Wes reluctantly agreed.

A man with long, ashy blond hair sat watching television inside the dry cleaners. Feet propped on the counter, he seemed startled when the door chimed with a visitor.

Jadene knew precisely how he felt.

The place was a basic dry clean facility. Brown carpet in the entry area, no chairs, a standing dress form for alterations, and a long counter in its mid-section. In the rear was a garment conveyor, lightly filled with plastic-draped, hanging clothes.

The man bounced to his feet and strutted to the counter. He was in his mid-30s and wore a gray t-shirt with a nametag that read, "Benny."

"Hey, hey. Good day?" he said.

Benny had a deep, dark tan and a crooked smile. He looked like he belonged out on the water, straddling a surfboard—not stuck inside.

"Hello. I'm Jadene Bowman. I'm a private investigator." She handed him her card. "Did you grow up in this area?"

Benny seized her offering but didn't answer her question. Instead he stared at her card, reading it aloud twice.

She raised an eyebrow. A few things behind Benny's counter drew her attention. A vape stick and a half-eaten bag of Doritos rested near a chair. Also, he was watching a television show featuring an animated golden-haired character in a martial arts costume.

She chuckled. It was the middle of the day, and Benny—a grown man—was binging anime. He was also baked beyond the chips he was eating.

Flipping his long hair aside, Benny's voice came slow and mellow. "Is this about the owl?"

"The owl?"

He scratched at his nose. "I keep telling them there's an owl. It's pooping on the cars. Doing it for months, but they're not doing anything about it. Comes every evening. And I try to go after it, whack at it with a broom." He reenacted it—all elbows and chaos. "But it comes back."

An image of stoned Benny chasing an owl with a broom around the parking lot emerged in Jadene's mind. It took everything she had to keep from bursting with laughter.

"I'm sorry to hear that," she managed. "But no, I'm not here about the owl. I'm here on an unrelated case."

Benny's eyelids sagged. "What do you need?"

Jadene wasn't sure if she had his complete focus, but she'd give this a shot. "Did you grow up around here?" she asked again.

Benny bowed. "Sure did. Working here since I was in high school. Pays the bills, man."

"It's a fine shop." She placed a hand on the counter between them. "Listen, I'm looking for an airport, really a runway, that might—"

"San Luis is closest to. Cabrillo highway, the PCH, will take you straight to it." Benny pointed left, then right.

"Actually, I'm looking for an old landing strip that might have been around here in the 1940s?"

"The 1940s?" Benny scratched his chin. "Whoa, that was a time ago." His red eyes tried to do the math before they became stuck, staring at the ceiling.

She was in a different dimension than dear Benny. "Yes, a runway," she said loudly, snapping him from his daze. "It would be a long stretch of land, semi-level. About 3,000 feet or so. Possibly paved at one time?" She held to make sure he was taking in what she was saying. "Do you know of anything like that around here?"

Benny smacked his lips as if tasting the words.

She tried not to giggle. If Benny's attention locked on the ceiling again, she may have to go elsewhere.

But then, to her surprise, he gave a half-lucid response. "Way too hilly. Mountains everywhere. Plus, I never heard of one. I've lived here all my life." He eyed her. "Why are you looking for one?"

Jadene was half curious about how he'd respond and said, "I think a plane might have landed here in 1945."

Benny's mouth dropped. "Really? In 1945? What kind of plane?"

"A big one," she said. "A Douglas C54."

"Ah, a Skymaster. World War II. Okay, okay."

She was astonished that Benny, a dry cleaner in a beach town, knew that a C54 was called a Skymaster and used in World War II.

"It'd need a bit of runway," the drycleaning pothead said. "Figure half a mile or so?"

Surprised, she said, "Yes, just over half a mile." This guy was beginning to grow on her.

He stroked his chin. "If you're looking north-coastal, between here and Monterey, I don't know if you'll find much. But, you know, Hearst has one."

"Hearst?"

"Hearst Castle," he said. "The rich guy. He used to fly in all kinds of guests back in its heyday. Presidents, actors, musicians. All of them partied up there."

Hearst Castle was just up the way in San Simeon. Jadene had seen its landing strip—which was long enough—but not built until 1946. That was too late to accommodate the mystery flight she was searching for.

"Yeah, but I don't think that's it," she said. "Can you think of any other place where one might have existed?"

Benny squinted. "Hearst area used to have a pair of runways up top. Higher, near the Castle."

Her skin tingled. "It did?"

"Yeah, the old one." Benny grew a broad smile. "Charles Lindberg and Amelia Earhart used to fly in there. But…"

"But what?"

"But I don't think any C54 could've landed on the old runways." He lowered his head. "They weren't but a thousand feet or so, and I don't think they were paved or anything."

Shit—Benny was right. No large, four-engine plane could have landed on less than a quarter mile of dirt.

Did the crew switch to yet another plane? That was indeed possible. However, if they moved passengers and cargo to a smaller craft, they could have touched down almost anywhere. That made every air base from Savannah to the West Coast a landing site for the transfer, and it could take months to find those logs—if any existed.

Jadene was close to a breakthrough, she had to be. This coastline was directly near the *Bay of the Montebello* incident, but she'd never make sense of the telegram without knowing where the hell that plane landed. A tightness grew in her shoulders.

During the elongated silence, Benny snatched a chip, and his attention drifted back to his television.

Jadene's smile soured. "Thanks, Benny."

He tossed a wave without turning. "Have a swell day."

Dejected, Jadene left Benny to his snacks and Karate cartoons.

FIFTY-EIGHT

Back in the SUV, Jadene grew quiet, wondering if they'd made this trip for nothing. She didn't want to let Sinclair down, yet it all seemed impossible. Now, she'd deluded herself into thinking she might find some long-forgotten runway used by a plane that flew halfway around the world eighty years ago.

She shifted her gaze to Wes. If it wasn't for him, she'd have suffered significant smoke inhalation or worse if he hadn't pulled her from that fire in her office. He was a selfless guardian like no one she'd ever met before. Lilly, Ellis, and herself all had him to thank for their lives. Yet, he was unassuming and humble, as if saving people was an everyday occurrence for him. And there he was, dutifully steering her like Sancho Panza to her next field of windmills, where they'd inevitably find nothing.

Maybe it was jet lag, or a sense of debt to him, but she broke the silence.

"My mom," Jadene said quietly.

Wes shot a glimpse toward her.

"You'd asked me how I got into this. Why I left the 9 to 5 world and became an investigator." She sighed. "It was because of my mom."

"Your mom wanted you to be a PI?"

"No," she said. We didn't have much growing up. Dad vanished before I was born, but that was okay. She and I were close."

He nodded.

"For fun, she'd take me swimming at the city pool. She used to say I was in the water more than I was out. She teased me that there was never a dry towel in the house."

"Sounds like you were a regular Mermaid."

"Pretty much." Jadene readjusted the seatbelt strap across her midsection. "That led to the swim team in high school. I competed, but I didn't think it would lead anywhere." She shook her head softly. "My senior year… I wish you could have seen my mom's face when I got three scholarship offers. There was pride, shock, and relief in her eyes."

"That's wonderful," Wes said.

Her stare drifted downward. "But my junior year of college, she came up to see me compete at a meet. She did that every once in a while, you know? She used to call me her favorite daughter—even though I was her only child—and she'd sit in the stands cheering as loud as she could."

He smiled. "I bet she did."

"Anyway, it was the state finals. I don't remember who my University was competing against. I just remember being excited for my mom to show up. We hadn't seen each other in a few months." She cleared her throat. "I waited at the Bean Spot, this little coffee place on campus. It was a sort of ritual with her and I. We'd get drinks and chat and stuff, but that day, it got late. She hadn't shown, and I had to head to the aquatic center for the event." Her jaw clenched. "I looked for her in the stands. And when the meet was over, I wandered the lot to see if her car was there."

Wes frowned.

"The day after, I filed the missing person's report."

"Oh, my God," he said. "I can't… I'm so sorry."

"Somewhere along the route, my mom just vanished."

"Did they track her phone? I mean…"

"She didn't have a cell. Heck, I could barely afford one back then." Jadene rubbed her hands on her thighs. "It was just the two of us for so long. It's not something I imagined could ever happen. Nothing felt real."

Wes touched her arm, squeezing softly.

"I'm sorry," he said.

She lifted her stare. "I quit school and spent all my time searching for her. Hounding the detectives to the point where they stopped taking my calls. But I knew, I just knew something bad had happened." A soft breath escaped her lips. "I was desperate. I retraced the route she took. She hated driving on the Interstate, so I searched every sideroad multiple times but found nothing. Not a trace."

"That had to be painful."

"The worst part was the silence," Jadene said. "I researched cases of missing persons. It became a second job. I wanted to learn everything I could. That led to consuming shows and blogs. I'd completely cut myself off socially. I just thought that this couldn't be it. My mom couldn't just disappear, and me not find her. You know? It couldn't end that way."

Wes slipped a caressing hand over hers.

She stared blankly out at the road. "Apparently, she'd left early that morning, before sunrise. My mom was excited to see me. But it was raining. The road was slick. She'd misjudged a turn." Jadene paused, letting out a slow breath. "Three years later, nearly to the day, a couple of hikers found the wreck in the Chattahoochee River. Police say there was no water in her lungs. From the submerged wreckage, they think she died instantly."

"Jadene, that's awful."

She bobbed her head. "You would have loved her. She was funny, strong, and a really good lady. She taught me everything I know. And I think, maybe, I do this PI stuff now just to keep her close, you know?"

"I get it, I do."

She pursed her lips. "Until this case, though, I was about to close my doors for good. I'm still not sure I'm cut out for all this investigation stuff."

Wes released her hand. "Can I make an observation?"

"Observation?"

"You might have gotten into all this because of what happened to your mom, and I'm so sorry for all that. But I think you're more than capable. What you've done already, working through things in Sinclair's message. Tracking that aircraft. Shit, we'd have never found Ellis and Lilly without your quick thinking. And you've done all this in such a short time. It's amazing, truly." He flashed her a glance. "You're a damn good investigator, and I think you're right where you should be."

A smile blossomed, and her eyes grew misty.

For the next few minutes, they drove in silence. The two-lane highway came to near sea level. The change was a welcome break from the mountains they'd driven through all morning, and the entire north-south coastline was visible when they crossed over San Simeon Road.

"You say this is where the Montebello went down?" Wes pointed toward the ocean.

"Along this coast, right. I couldn't find an exact location, but I know the tanker sank right out there."

"It's incredible they all survived," he said.

"Yeah, it went down six miles from shore. It was the break of dawn, too. And it's good that the sun was coming up when that torpedo hit their ship because…" She spun in her seat, glancing back at the two-lane thoroughfare.

"What is it?" Wes said.

Bringing up her cell, Jadene thumbed at its screen. "Pull over."

"Pull over?"

"Pull over!"

"All right, all right." Wes steered onto the shoulder and came to a complete stop.

Jadene seized the rearview mirror, angling its direction for a clear view behind them.

"Holy shit!" she shouted.

"What?"

She unbuckled her seatbelt and jumped from the vehicle. Outside, she raced up the highway's shoulder several yards.

Wes switched off the key, got out, and tried to follow. There wasn't much traffic as Jadene jogged down the highway's shoulder.

He called out to her, "What are you doing?"

She stopped, spun on a heel, and shouted, "Son of a bitch!"

"Jadene, what's going on?"

She raised her arms toward the sky—a giant grin filling her face. "Son of a bitch!"

"Jadene?"

She raced back in his direction.

The two met on the side of the road near the vehicle.

"What the hell's happening?"

"What do you notice?" she said, excited.

He tilted his head. "A crazy woman standing on the side of the road, yelling?"

She laughed. "No! What do you notice around here?"

"Here?"

She pointed toward the hills. "We've been traveling through the mountains, up that pretzel of a road all morning. But suddenly here—right here in San Simeon—everything is flat on this coastal stretch of road. Flat and straight. And there's not a mountain or any old trees around."

He scanned the landscape.

"It's the straightest stretch of road we've been on all day," she added. "Like perfectly straight."

"Okay, but what…"

She pointed down the highway. "How long?"

"How long?"

"This path—this insanely straight path, up until it curves ahead. How long do you think it is?"

Wes eyeballed the roadway from north to south. "Got to be a solid mile. We can check it, but I'd say at least."

"That's almost twice…" she muttered.

Checking for traffic, she skipped into the road.

"What the hell are you doing?"

"What's your shoe size?"

Wes looked down at his feet. "A twelve, but—"

Jadene hustled back, grabbing him by the arm. "Start at the divider, go heel to toe. Let's go."

Wes did as she asked, measuring the width of the highway. When he reached the shoulder again, he stopped.

"Total width like forty feet, I'm guessing."

"The wheelbase was just under 25 feet."

Wes took a step back. "You can't possibly think—"

Jadene aimed a finger at the asphalt. "Those sky jocks would have loved the challenge!" She raised her cell. "And did you know California State Highway 1, the PCH, officially opened in 1937?"

Wes gazed down the long stretch of road, bobbed his head, and grinned. "Well, son of a bitch…"

FIFTY-NINE

The runway Jadene was searching for was right under her feet. It couldn't have been more fitting.

This portion of the Pacific Coast Highway was straight, relatively flat, and stretched from San Simeon Road—headlong, parallel to the coast—for a solid mile. A skilled pilot would only need a clear sky and a steady stick. The asphalt was plenty long enough. The plane wouldn't have much width to land, but men like Gabreski wouldn't let that stop them. In fact, they'd fight one another for the chance to attempt it. Patch or no patch, bragging rights were everything to those guys.

Bay of the Montebello. It was brilliant.

"I never would have seen it," Wes said.

"If they did land out here, this is the only place it could be," she said. "It makes so much sense."

He agreed.

But in an instant, her excitement faded. Now what? If the large aircraft touched down here, where was the proof? Did the passengers disembark? Where did they go, and why? What about any payload? She hadn't figured out the rest of the telegram's riddle nor made any tangible discovery up to this point. It was all theory.

Names, tail numbers, flight logs, even this supposed runway. She had nothing physical.

As the two returned to the rental, she tongued a cheek. They were missing something. Wes started the Denali and pulled back onto the PCH.

Eyeing their surroundings, the uniqueness of the topography struck her. Not only because this section of the PCH was flat enough to land a plane but also because there was nothing but nature out here—a beautiful coastline—with one exception.

San Simeon extended from the mountain range down to the oceanfront. However, but for a handful of ranches, less than 500 residents currently lived in the area. The bulk of San Simeon was treated like an enormous preserve, untouched by developers and subdivisions.

This was because, over a century ago, a very wealthy man inherited most of the acreage. And he built an incredible, secluded estate on its hilltop. Nothing else was around for miles—affording the manor unheard of privacy.

"Woah," she said.

"Woah?"

She grabbed Wes by the arm. "Ellis said if that aircraft carried something valuable, they'd need a secure hideout, right?"

"Right?"

"Well, we just passed one of the most isolated and secure places this side of Fort Knox. And I think…"

Wes laughed. "All right, I'm turning around."

If her theory of the Skymaster landing here held, that residence would be less than two miles from this makeshift coastal runway. Of course, it may all be a long shot, but the next solution to her mystery could be right up that mountainside.

Wes spun a U-turn as she brought up her cell, typing furiously. It was bizarrely fitting that this particular estate became her next step in the hunt. She keyed her query and hit enter.

Construction began in 1919, making the compound relatively modern. An extravagant Spanish-Mediterranean estate, San Simeon's Hearst Castle was a rich man's Shangri-La. The compound had four immense "homes" and more amenities than most could imagine. Two pools, one indoor and one outdoor, whose volume totaled half a million gallons. Gardens, tennis courts, a movie theater, a ballroom, a dining hall, and some of the finest arts and antiques in the world.

The media tycoon William Randolph Hearst passed away in 1951. In 1957, the family donated Hearst's San Simeon properties and surrounding lands to the state of California for financial and preservation reasons. Today, the area exists as a state park.

Though, in the 1940s, the place was a private fortress. Plus, it was built on top of a mountain.

Jadene licked her lips. That combination of security might very well be the *Double Safe Haven* the telegram referred to.

As Wes drove up the road to the Castle's visitor center, she added "Hearst Castle" and "William Randolph Hearst" to every word and phrase she'd memorized in Sinclair's telegram. But no correlation appeared.

Did Sinclair's grandfather know Hearst? What about the other name in the message? Did Arthur know Hermann, who knew Hearst? She swiped through website after website on her phone. How did this all fit together?

They parked. Wes pointed to the white A-frame building at the end of the lot.

"Guess we take the tour, then?" he said.

Jadene didn't say anything. She now had an entirely new set of challenges. If someone or something was taken to Hearst Castle, how would she ever find it? Should she be looking for a guestbook or another marker? Surely, anything from 1945 had been discovered and taken by now.

A wave of angst washed over her. She had to find something to link Arthur Whitmore to Hearst. Some relationship between the two men had to exist.

Beside her, Wes unstrapped the holster from his ribcage.

"They might frown if I have this on me." He grinned. Carefully, he opened the Denali's center console, and placed the weapon inside.

SIXTY

Jadene unbuckled and opened her door. It was mid-afternoon. The overcast skies had burned off, and an offshore breeze struck her shoulders.

She and Wes trekked across the packed parking lot toward a large, welcoming Mediterranean building. Beyond the entrance center, up the mountain, sat Hearst's sprawling Castle with soaring palms sprouting at its peak.

Questions danced in her mind. What were they looking for, and would she know if she saw it? Wes handled the tour particulars while she continued through the building's corridor, past the gifts and memorabilia. Outdoors once more, she strolled into the center's open-air patio.

Here, tourists of all ages, from couples to kids, pointed up the hill, excited. Easily more than a hundred people jostled to take photos and videos of the wondrous structures on the mountain's summit.

Jadene scanned the grounds. In the distance, Hearst Castle stood tall against the backdrop of the blue sky.

It was like gazing upon a bygone era. The distant estate felt removed from everything—from the war, from the telegram. A relic wrapped in sea wind and distance—elevated, isolated, impenetrable.

She wandered the area, a mild wind tickling her cheeks.

According to her hasty search, William Randolph Hearst had left the compound for the last time in May of 1947, closing the first publicized chapter of American celebrity and opulence. That was around the same period as the flight from Kraków—but the connection—if there was one—eluded her.

Something smacked against her shoulder.

"Excuse me!" a man barked.

Lost in the beauty around her, Jadene had bumped into a tall, slender man, and caused him to spill his coffee all over the front of his blue blazer.

"Oh my gosh. I'm so, so sorry."

The man fished a white cloth from his pocket and dabbed at the mess on his jacket. A nametag on the left pocket read, "Gerald Beckett, Tour Supervisor."

"That was completely my fault," Jadene confessed. "I didn't mean to bump into you."

"No one's fault really." Gerald managed an uncomfortable smile. "Let's blame it on Leonardo da Vinci and his dreadful discovery of fluid dynamics, shall we?"

"Again, I'm so sorry."

Dabbing at his blazer, Gerald arched a nod. "Please enjoy your time here at our Little Ranch."

A shiver struck Jadene. "What did you say?"

Gerald Beckett carried himself in an interesting manner. He looked like a tour supervisor if there ever was such a guise. His receding salt-and-pepper hairline complemented his pointy nose. The only spots on his uniform and shiny shoes were the droplets of coffee Jadene had caused.

Holding the cloth against his lapel, Gerald straightened his posture, gazing down at her. "That is a term Mister Hearst used when referring to his home here in San Simeon."

She looked at him, blinking hard. "Little Ranch?"

"Yes. You have excellent hearing, even if your sight is compromised," he sneered. "Little Ranch was the playful magnate's attempt at humor." He outstretched a hand toward the hillside while his other held the cloth against the wet spot on his blazer as if wounded in battle. "Clearly, Hearst Castle is anything but little. Undoubtedly, the term's ironic undersell amused Mister Hearst."

Gerald had perfect diction with a hint of snobbery in his tone, like a practiced combination of annoyance and confidence. She wanted to ask him about the name *Hermann*, but Wes arrived with two tickets.

"Tour 11," he said, approaching Gerald and her.

Gerald's brow arched. "Eleven? Wonderful, you're part of my entourage." He turned to Wes. "It seems your lady friend here has trouble with the concept of personal space. Please ask her to mind her step, as the décor and furnishings of this century-old Castle cannot be replaced with a quick trip to Ikea."

Wes glanced at Jadene.

"Our transport leaves in three minutes," Gerald added. "While I shall cherish our little bump and greet, if you'll both excuse me, I need a moment to recover from my recent showering of Espresso Romano."

"I'm sorry again."

Gerald marched off, dabbing at his uniform.

"What was that about?" Wes chuckled.

"Oh, just making friends," she said.

"Here." He handed her a brochure. "This came with the tickets. It's information about the Castle."

She opened the guide, which included details and a map.

Hearst Castle's living quarters totaled almost 100,000 square feet, spread among four colossal dwellings. That footage didn't include amenities or outbuildings, and beyond that, the total estate grounds covered more than 80,000 acres.

The two made their way toward the shuttle lines.

Jadene worried again that she had no idea what she was looking for. Were the answers in a guest book, or hidden someplace in its archives? If persons were smuggled from Kraków, would there be any record of their arrival here? Probably not. Whoever or whatever was on that plane was brought here in secret—but which phrase in the telegram connected her to the who or what of it all? As they waited to board, she cycled through the telegram's phrases again.

Broken Castle—She had a pretty good idea this referred to Hearst Castle itself. It was a fortified outpost on top of a hill, and she and Wes were about to take the tour. But she couldn't find any record of anyone breaking into the place if the word broken meant it was breached, despite many search attempts.

Dakota Free Blue—Definitely referred to the plane leaving Kraków. Its final leg, she believed, landed right on the PCH here in San Simeon, California. Who or what was on that aircraft was still the biggest mystery.

Whispering West—The direction of the plane flight. They couldn't get anymore west unless they swam in the Pacific.

Bay of the Montebello—For sure this referenced the Japanese torpedoing of the Union Company Oil tanker in 1941. That shipwreck provided the marker for this area.

Hermann—A name still unidentified. Probably an individual and Jadene's best bet was to ask snooty Gerald to see if he could link it to this location. Cracking this clue might connect her to Arthur somehow.

Double Safe Haven—Denoted Hearst's mountainside compound. It protected whatever secrets were flown here by its elevation and fortification.

And, thanks to Gerald, she now understood *Little Ranch* was Hearst's nickname for the decadent Spanish-Mediterranean castle he'd erected.

Still, three references to Hearst Castle? Why so many? One should have been enough.

The tour bus opened its doors, and visitors stepped onboard. Wes, her handsome, six-foot-two guardian, got on first. She approached the doors, glancing at the distant castle.

There was a mystery up that hill. An answer to Sinclair's telegram, and she'd have to scour the property to find it. There were four homes, two pools, and thousands of acres to search—and roughly two hours for her to find anything, shepherded by a guided tour.

Or, one of the greatest engineers in modern times, Sinclair Whitmore, would lose control of his business empire and be forever tarnished by the deeds of his grandfather. A man Sinclair had only met once as a child. On top of everything, she'd lose her fledgling PI business if she didn't come up with any objective evidence.

As Jadene climbed the shuttle's stairs, Gerald glared at her, picking specs of lint from his fresh blazer.

Inside the tour bus, Wes beckoned her to the seat beside him. Lumbering down the aisle, she passed rows of seated tourists anxious for the tour, until a woman swiftly grabbed her by the wrist.

"Please sit here," she said.

Jadene froze. The woman's face was hauntingly familiar, but the brunette hair was new.

"Take the window seat. The view is much better here." Cloaked under the woman's scarf emerged the barrel of a black pistol. She shoved its muzzle under Jadene's ribcage.

Legs weak, Jadene crossed into the row, and sank into the seat. On the woman's lap lay a copy of Sinclair's telegram. Jadene's terrified gaze locked on its final word, *Powodzenia*.

Good luck.

SIXTY-ONE

Jadene trembled. Bitter iron filled her mouth. She'd never had a gun pulled on her before, and her insides churned with terror and disbelief. She fell into a restless daze.

"Please stay in your seats," the mic'd-up driver announced. "Our journey up the hillside will take approximately 15 minutes."

The tour bus rumbled up the hill.

"Do not turn around." The woman's voice was barely above a whisper. "We have not been properly introduced. My name is Rena."

A vague memory flashed. Lilly on the stretcher. She'd said something that Jadene never sorted. A chill raced up her spine.

Jadene had met this strange woman before in her search for Collin Buckley—the second pilot. The woman claimed to be Ronald Buckley's daughter. But when Jadene asked for her help, she was met with unpleasant disinterest.

The bus driver was still speaking over the intercom, but Jadene's thoughts became tangled in panic, and she couldn't hear a single word.

Petrified, she held her stare forward. There had to be a way out of this. Her best bet was to text 911 to Wes. Stealthily, she snaked her hand below the bus's side panel to the rear pocket of her jeans. She brushed against the phone with her fingers.

However, a disturbing thought struck. How had this woman followed them across the country? It wasn't possible. Yet, a cold realization grew—there was no other explanation. It had to be Wes. He'd been playing both sides all along. She wanted to turn around and scream at him, let him know what a devious bastard he was. And to think she'd let herself develop feelings for him! He'd been working her from the beginning—softening her up during her first meeting with Sinclair, sharing that glass of wine, making her feel special.

Her shoulders tightened. Sinclair probably had no idea that the man he trusted—his bodyguard, with unfettered access to him, his house, his jet—was a backstabbing murderer.

Jadene withdrew her hand from her back pocket. Texting would do no good. But she promised herself whatever happened next, she'd find a way to let Sinclair know that Wes couldn't be trusted.

But at this moment, she'd fallen right into their trap.

In the seat next to her, Rena glared.

"I will need that cell phone," she said.

Jadene's face went pale. She wanted to shout for help but knew it would end badly. Instead, she slid out the device and handed it to Rena.

On her middle finger, a gold ring with a glowing, red oval ruby sparkled. Its sophisticated Art Deco design spoke of another time, vintage, rare, and strikingly unusual. The piece's quiet, commanding elegance was a sharp contrast to the deadly woman who wore it.

They were headed to Hearst's estate, where there was a better chance Jadene could mount an escape. For now, she'd sit quietly, keep herself calm, and hope the gun pressed against her mid-section didn't go off.

Rena whispered, "Tell me what you are searching for."

The paper in the woman's lap—the photocopy of the telegram—contained Jadene's handwriting. They'd stolen it from her office, the office they'd tried to burn down after kidnapping Lilly. But if she was working with Wes, wouldn't she already know why they were here? Something wasn't making sense.

The gun jabbed her stomach.

"What are you after?" Rena said again.

"I don't know," Jadene whispered.

"You must know. You found a clue. Something is here, what is it? Tell me."

"I'm telling the truth."

"No, I do not think you are."

Jadene was confused. For the past two days, Wes was always around her. She hadn't hidden anything from him because she believed she could trust him. But was he truly playing both sides, or was something else going on?

"Why have you come to this place?" Rena said.

Making the woman angry with a busload of innocent people around was a bad idea. Jadene could never live with herself if something terrible happened. They'd already killed three people. Instead, she'd placate her, give Rena whatever information she wanted until they deboarded. Once they were out in the open, she'd get a ranger's attention and run to safety the first chance she got.

"Bay of the Montebello," Jadene said. "That was the marker."

Rena glanced down at the photocopy, then back at her captive. "Here, this bay?"

Jadene explained as calmly and quietly as she could about the attack on the tanker and the sinking. She did her best to recall every detail, hoping to buy time as their vehicle crisscrossed the mountainside, ascending toward the hilltop estate.

"What did they take?" Rena asked.

Jadene wasn't sure how to answer that, but she did her best. It might have been personnel, she explained. It might have been cargo. It might be a combination of both, but she didn't know.

"I think you are lying," Rena said. "I think you know what they took from Wawel."

A shiver struck Jadene. Wawel—that word—unique and familiar. Early on, when she'd started the case. It was a medieval castle in Kraków, Poland. Wawel Castle. But with the adrenaline coursing through her body, she couldn't recall any other details.

The tour bus slowed and the pistol pressed at her side. They'd arrived at the hilltop, and would begin offloading shortly.

"Remember to stay with your guide, and within the roped boundaries at all times," the driver said. "It's a beautiful day here at San Simeon's Hearst Castle, and I hope you each enjoy your tour."

Clapping erupted.

Jadene flinched.

Rena's breath struck Jadene's ear. "You may be thinking of making a run. But I warn you, do not fuck with me." She gestured to the rear of the bus. "Or my man will kill your companion."

Jadene turned, and her stomach tightened.

Three rows behind, Wes sat rigid. His face was as pale as hers, and trickles of sweat rolled down his cheeks. Next to him sat a bald man with beady, black eyes, who glared back at her.

It was the unhelpful stick-in-the-mud from Max Airfield, Karl Riggins.

SIXTY-TWO

A metallic chill pressed into the small of Jadene's back, forcing her forward. She moved her legs unsteadily, ambling down the cramped aisle.

Excited chatter from other passengers filled the cabin, eager to offload. Ahead, a silver-haired man smelling of strong aftershave meandered to the door. Tipping his Calloway sun visor, he smiled at Jadene. She did her best to return the greeting despite the gun stabbing her in the spine.

Somewhere behind, she imagined Wes in the same predicament. A rush of thoughts flooded her mind. Max Air base. The flight controller log. The one for Lajes Airfield. It wasn't digitized, as Dottie had said, and the only way to see its contents was by appointment. Max Airfield's Assistant Curator Karl Riggins somehow knew about the secret 1945 flight from Kraków. He was gatekeeping the information, tracking anyone who requested its viewing.

First came Ellis Martin. Like Jadene, he was searching for the aircraft's tail number. Ellis had said he'd met with a bald man who'd told him the log was missing, throwing him off the trail. Upon his return from Max Airfield, they abducted him at the airport. Next came Jadene. By a stroke of luck, she'd met with Dottie instead. Karl had been on break. Anxious to help, Dottie showed her the log, allowing Jadene to trace the flight to the U.S. That entry was essential in making the connection here to San Simeon.

Rena and her scarf-covered gun were never more than a quarter step behind Jadene as they stepped from the bus. Wes exited likewise, followed by Karl Riggins and his casually folded jacket concealing his firearm.

A ranger with a crewcut, dressed in a khaki shirt, stood nearby. He possessed no sidearm, and why would he? Hearst Castle was a family-friendly attraction, and tourists weren't supposed to arrive at gunpoint. If she signaled him for help, Wes would pay the price. If she tried to escape, both she and Wes—and possibly the ranger— might get shot.

The four hung back, pacing behind the other tourists up the trail to a set of sprawling stairs ascending to the castle's West Terrace. The manor's hardscaped grounds were unlike anything she'd ever seen, drawing gasps from the onlookers. Jadene wished she could enjoy them.

Ahead, female-figured columns served as light posts, peeking above the elevated pathways like keepers. Long rows of neatly trimmed hedges stretched the walkways, and the path at her feet was constructed of perfectly patterned, elegant tiling. The terrace was like an outdoor room, with the vast blue sky as its ceiling. Stone railings encircled the area, giving it a Romanesque feel. Over its boundary came an expansive view of the rolling hills and distant Pacific Ocean.

Despite the area's magnificence, Jadene's palms were moist. Could she escape? Jump over the rail and make a run for it? What about Wes? What might they do to him?

"Group eleven, over here, please." Gerald counted heads as many gathered around him. His final tally came to twenty-two. Jadene, Wes, and their two armed companions circled on the outside, away from the larger group.

Providing a lifted brow in Jadene's direction, Gerald cleared his throat and the crowd hushed.

"George Hearst acquired the San Francisco Examiner as compensation for a gambling debt in 1880," he announced.

"Hell of a win," someone said to scattered laughter.

Unamused, Gerald continued. "A few years later, his son William began managing the newspaper and learning the business. But when George died in 1891, William decided to dominate the news market and hired the best writers at the time." Gerald strolled past a line of hedges, and the crowd followed. Rena trailed Jadene a few feet behind, and bald Karl held Wes under the fold of his jacket at gunpoint.

"These writers included Ambrose Pierce, Julian Hawthorne, Jack London, and even Mark Twain."

A tourist shouted, "Tom Sawyer, Mark Twain?"

"Evidently, we have a scholar among us," Gerald replied. "Yes, that Mark Twain." The group continued down the walkway and past a beautiful tiered fountain at least twenty feet high. A dull jab struck Jadene in the shoulder blade, causing her to wince.

Gerald addressed the moving group. "Under William's management, these talented writers enjoyed competitive salaries, flexible working hours, and printed bylines on page one—which, while commonplace nowadays, not many papers afforded to their writers at that time. It wasn't long before the San Francisco Examiner overtook the market." He stopped, glancing over the crowd. "Developing a taste for success, Mr. Hearst began acquiring other newspapers nationwide."

"Guess he had the money," came a shout.

Gerald stared at the man in the Hawaiian shirt before continuing. "Mr. Hearst also poached talent from other papers. Writers and editors." He lifted a finger. "This obviously soured his competition, which led to a fierce battle with another newspaper, the New York World, run by Joseph Pulitzer."

"Pulitzer?" a voice said. "The prize guy?"

Gerald shot a curt nod. "Yes. Pulitzer the prize guy."

"I knew that," came a response.

Gerald huffed. "Academics, all of you."

Someone snickered.

"In a clash of words, Hearst and Pulitzer tried one-upping each other by printing exaggerated headlines in their respective papers in an effort to gain readership. The stories contained outrageous claims and opinions without research to back them up. They called it yellow journalism." Gerald grinned. "For our younger and more technology astute, it was tantamount to your clickbait—but with newspapers."

"Ahh," came the crowd's collective response.

"Hearst and Pulitzer fought like this for months, escalating things to the point of a newsboys strike in 1899. Overworked young men seeking a fair share of profit from the booming feud."

A hand went up, and Gerald pointed. "Yes. Woman in the dizzy, polka-dot dress?"

"This fight. Hearst versus Pulitzer. Who won?"

Gerald straightened his tie, eyed the faces, and said, "Well, you're not standing at Pulitzer Castle, are you?"

The crowd erupted with laughter.

Gerald led the group through a passage toward a giant outdoor pool surrounded by elevated porticos. As the cold barrel struck her back, Jadene stepped forward, fearful of any misstep.

A muffled thump—like a hammer striking a nail—broke the air.

An iron grip seized her forearm. Wes yanked her into a gap, up a narrow stairway, and they broke into a breathless sprint.

Darting from the hedge line, they crossed a garden, zigzagging through the grounds toward a large stone building. Heart pounding, Jadene moved as fast as she could but had trouble keeping up with

Wes. When they rounded a corner, an outbuilding appeared with a wooden door. He wrenched it open, pushed her inside, and yanked the door closed.

"Quiet," he said, out of breath.

Dark and windowless, Jadene felt for a light switch as Wes held at the door. Finding a toggle, she flicked it. A single bulb lit the small, shed-like space.

On a far wall ran a network of wires feeding an electrical box. Pipes extended across the ceiling, crooking into and out of the room in all directions. This was some kind of utility room. Its only door was the one they'd come in.

Feet from her, Wes held a shoulder against the wooden door, his right bicep dripping with blood.

Sixty-Three

"What… what happened?" Jadene said, shaking with adrenaline.

"Quick," Wes said. "Find a cloth—something I can rip."

A cleaning cart with bottles, brushes, and dusters sat in the far side of the room. Jadene searched the supplies and snatched a cloth rag.

"Here," she said.

Wes split the fabric with a harsh rip, sweat glistening down his cheeks. Next, he tore his dress shirt to expose the bloodied area, probing at the gash.

"Entry and exit," he muttered. "Missed the bone."

A wave of dizziness swept over her as Wes's blood-stained hands worked the injury with practiced precision.

He slung the rag around his bicep. "The same damn arm," he whispered. Then he turned to Jadene. "I can only get a half-hitch. You're going to have to tie the knot."

The bulb flickered above, casting long shadows in the small room.

"But how did this happen? Why are you bleeding?"

Wes squinted. "I was shot."

"Shot? What? How?"

He pulled at the torn skin, widening the gash. "The bald guy's pistol. It had a suppressor. Sounded like a nail gun. Kind of a thump."

Jadene had seen cuts and bruises before, but nothing like this. The gory wound was a black chasm that bore into his skin. Taking a deep breath, she clutched the ends of the cloth, trying not to panic.

"Don't tie it yet. You'll have to cinch things first." Wes gestured at the area. "I'll hold the bight while you yank down on the cloth."

A steady stream of blood trickled from his arm. At the opening, whitish bits rose under his skin. Jadene was light-headed and glanced up at him.

Concern grew in his eyes. "You all right?"

Her throat tightened.

Despite his own pain, Wes gave her a smile.

"I'll talk you through this, okay?" He faced her, gaze steady. "I'm leaking a little blood. Now, there could be a rip in my artery."

She drew a sharp breath. "A rip?"

"We need to apply a tourniquet—but we can't stop all the blood, or I could lose my arm. We just need to slow the flow, okay?"

She trembled. "Okay."

Wes grinned. "It's called a partial occlusion. Just enough to reduce the hemorrhaging, the pressure. This is so the arterial tear doesn't get any larger, and I bleed out."

She gulped. "Are you going to be okay?"

"With your help, I'll manage."

But Jadene wasn't so sure. The injury was bad.

"Talk to me," Wes said. "It'll keep your mind busy. All right?"

He was wounded, and Jadene needed help to get through it? She took a calming breath. Catching sight of something on his upper arm, she said, "Your tattoo? The blade and—"

"Army, Operational Detachment."

"Army?"

"Delta," he grunted.

He'd mentioned he'd spent time in greens but didn't elaborate.

"Is that like Special Forces?"

Wes lifted his head. "Yeah. They taught us to kill with popsicle sticks and survive eating worms."

A gag rose in her throat. "You ate worms?"

Wes licked his lips. "Tasted like slimy chicken."

She broke into a laugh. The sound of his voice was comforting. She narrowed her eyes and worked the knot. He was leaking a little blood. She could fix that.

"How long were you in for?" she said, seeking his gaze.

"Two stints." Wes bent his arm to check the dressing. "Second one, we were out on a classified mission."

"Classified? So you can't talk about it?"

"Not the where or why. But we got hit in an IED explosion. Tore up this arm." He motioned to the scar running up his wrist. "But my partner took a piece of shrapnel to the stomach. He was in bad shape. Communications were cut off. Our primary and secondary rendezvous points were no good, so we headed into the woods to aid and recover."

"What happened?"

Wes winced. "We waited three days, freezing, in the snow. My buddy was getting worse, and I knew he couldn't hold out much longer. So I held until nighttime, stripped down to my t-shirt and drawers, strolled into town, and made a phone call."

"You did?"

"Pull down on it, kind of hard, all right?" He gestured to the bind. "Don't stop until I tell you, and I'll hold the middle."

Jadene did as he asked. Once they had the proper tension, he pressed his fingers over the strap to keep it from loosening while she knotted things.

"I made a phone call and gave command our location." Wes grimaced as Jadene tugged. "The good news is we made it home. But, they gave me my walking papers after that."

She finished the tie. "What? Why?"

"Violation of procedure. I'd used an insecure line to make that call." He patted the bandage. "I took full responsibility."

"But you saved a life?"

Wes dipped his head. "Anyway, I'd had my fill of the forces and military politics after that. And that's when Sinclair took me in." He let his wounded arm fall to his side. "Been with him half a decade now. I try not to be overprotective, but the guy was there when I needed a job. I pretty much lost who I was when I was discharged, and was kind of drifting. Know what I mean? I'll always be grateful to him."

She understood that mire of loss. A year after her mother vanished, Jadene returned to school to finish her degree. But she was standoffish. She no longer swam competitively, and after graduating, wandered into a career she didn't enjoy. Only years later, she finally got closure when they found the wreckage of her mother's accident. But to her, it was more like that tragic missing piece snapped her back into taking charge of her life. The sudden layoff at her company was the final push.

It was clear where Wes's deep allegiance to Sinclair came from. She'd misjudged him. He wasn't involved in the kidnappings or the murder of that man at the cabin. She would apologize to him properly when they got out of this mess.

Wes held his bicep and rechecked the dressing. "We need to figure out if the coast is clear," he said. "I'll crack the door open, and you try to get a look outside. Okay?"

She moved to his left.

"Here we go."

The door groaned.

"Nobody right," she whispered.

Wes widened the opening.

Rena appeared several yards away, across the courtyard, searching the bushes. Her gun was concealed against her hip.

"Shit!" Jadene whispered. "She's out there."

Wes inched the door closed.

"Did she see you?"

"No, I don't think so."

He returned his weight against the door. "They took my cell."

"Mine too."

"We'll hold in here until she's gone, then we can get help."

"Okay," Jadene said.

Wes put an ear to the door as she remained silent. A moment later, he said, "I hear something."

Faint footsteps approached outside. A hand turned the knob, but Wes kept his body against the panel.

A knock came.

"Hello?" a voice said from outside. "Is anyone in there?"

"Gerald?" Jadene called.

"What's going on in there?" he shouted.

"Gerald, are you alone?"

"Of course I am. His voice filtered through the door. "But that is a restricted area, and you're not permitted to be there."

Wes whispered, "They must be gone, but are you sure it's him?"

"Madam, I need you to end this tomfoolery. You've already cost me a blazer today."

"It's him," she said. "We should—"

Wes held against the door. "Wait a minute."

She waited behind him.

His expression softened, and he gazed into her eyes. "If I open this door…"

"What is it?"

"You've made so much progress. What you've uncovered in just a few days. I can't—"

"Wes, you need help. I appreciate it, but we don't have time."

He lowered his head. "You said everything led here, right?"

"I think so, but—"

He gaze rose. "When we leave this room, I'll separate us somehow."

"You'll do what?"

"I want you to sneak off."

"What do you mean?"

"Didn't you say you needed to wander around, check things out?"

"Yeah, but—"

"I want you to find something. A clue, whatever. Get yourself to that next step."

"Next step?"

"This is a huge place." His eyes widened. "They'll never find you."

A cold intensity filled her. "But Wes, we're—"

"I owe Sinclair a debt. It's something I'll never be able to repay, not to a man like him. Not unless you can finish this."

For as strong and reserved as he was most of the time, Wes had his soft spots. Inside of the man was an incredible heart and tremendous loyalty. He was also so protective—not just of Sinclair, but of her—even when she believed he might have ulterior motives. Through it all, Wes never wavered.

A profound and compelling sense of duty seized Jadene. Now, she owed him a debt. This man had saved her life—twice. She stared into his eyes.

"All right, I'll do it," she said.

A smile grew on his face. "If you're caught, they'll toss you in jail," he said. "But don't worry, I'll bail you out."

Gerald pounded the door.

She chuckled. "I may not get far before they slap the cuffs on me."

Wes raised his eyebrows. "Think of it as a big game of hide and seek. A real chance to investigate," he said. "If anyone can find something, it's you, Jadene."

A warmth filled her cheeks. "And you'll spring me, right?"

"I'll bring a bottle of wine when I post your bail."

She chuckled. "The good stuff?"

Wes grinned. "The kind that billionaires drink."

"Deal."

Another knock at the door came.

"Ready?"

She bent a gentle nod.

"One more thing," he said.

"What?"

He leaned down and kissed her.

Her heart fluttered. His lips were surprisingly tender. When they parted, he flashed a wide grin.

"Something I can remember you by when you're in the slammer."

She blushed a laugh.

"All right, wait for my signal and then take off. I'll distract this guy. That should buy you some time."

"Okay."

Wes backed away from the door and turned the handle.

Outside stood Gerald with a confused look on his face.

"I'm sorry," Jadene said, pointing to Wes. "He injured himself. We had to find a first aid kit, and—"

A gun pressed to Gerald's ribcage.

Jadene's stomach dropped.

An icy whisper cut through the silence.

"Make a sound, and all three of you will die," Rena said.

SIXTY-FOUR

Jadene hovered in the shed's doorway behind Wes.

Rena's cold eyes locked on hers. "Where is it?"

Karl appeared, aiming his weapon at the pair. "The two of you, out, now!"

Slowly, they stepped from the maintenance shed. Tall hedges concealed this area from the rest of the estate. They stood off the tour's main lanes, hidden west of the manor. No one could see them here.

Jadene was positioned between Wes and Gerald. Fear had overtaken the tour director, and his hands trembled. He'd left the group looking for her and Wes, and now he was trapped between guns and confusion.

Clutching his arm, Wes's shirt was soaked with blood. The binding they'd tied around his bicep was holding, but he needed help.

Rena's scowl turned to Jadene. "I ask again, where is it?"

A second time under a gun's aim, yet Jadene's mind sharpened. She was powerless against their weapons, but Rena's question gave her confirmation. They were in the right place, looking for an object at Hearst Castle. Whether it was another clue or the endgame, she didn't know. But given Rena and her companion had followed them across the country, Jadene suspected the latter.

"I don't know where anything is," she said.

"You are lying to me," Rena snarled. "Take me to what I seek, or I will kill one of these men!" She raised her gun.

Wes's stare snapped from Karl to Rena, then back to Jadene.

"Run!" he shouted.

In a split second, Wes shoved Jadene aside and charged Karl, bowling him into Rena. The two men crashed over the hedges as Rena fell backward, tumbling to the ground.

Jadene bolted with Gerald close behind. They sprinted across manicured lawns, weaving through shrubs. Something whizzed past Jadene's ear, and she ducked. A statue splintered under a bullet's impact.

Yards behind, Rena had returned to her feet and mounted a pursuit.

Racing through garden paths, Jadene and Gerald weaved around ornate sculptures as more projectiles zipped past, missing them by inches.

"This way," Gerald shouted. He pulled ahead, surprisingly spry, and zipped around a corner. She followed.

Above the foot chase, the massive shadow of Casa Grande loomed, its towers and terraces watching the action below. An archway near the main home's foundation appeared. Gerald led them to a side door, heaved it open, and the two slipped inside.

A narrow stairwell coiled into the darkness below.

"Down here!" Gerald's voice reverberated through the dim corridor. He rushed down the passage as Jadene's footsteps echoed close behind.

Between breaths, she huffed, "Where—?"

"The cellar," Gerald panted.

Two towering steel doors stood at the stairwell's base, each ten feet high. Gerald led them inside and closed the passage. Flicking a switch, he lit the room with a soft glow.

A chilly, musty scent embraced them. The space was a massive basement—a wine cellar—walled floor to ceiling with dark wooden racks.

Catching his breath, Gerald said, "This area was built during prohibition." He placed his hands on his hips, taking in a long breath. "Unfortunately, the bolt no longer functions."

Jadene worked to contain her breathing. "It doesn't?"

"No. The mechanism was removed long ago for safety." He cleared his throat. "But if we can bar the entry, we might hold them out a while."

Around them, each rack held rows of dusty wine and champagne bottles. Most shelves were encased with Plexiglass to protect them from touchy tourists. Around the area, exposed floors and thick stone walls carried the coldness of the earth, keeping the collection at a perfect, steady chill. This cellar was a protected sanctuary where time paused, allowing each bottle to mature undisturbed.

"Help me here, would you?" Gerald moved to a midsection of open shelving and began removing bottles from its lower ledge. They cleared the shelf and he pulled out its arm-length wooden shelf board. Returning to the steel doorway, Gerald wedged the board between the door's inner rails to prevent anyone from entering easily.

"It may not hold for long," he said. "We need to get the word out."

"The word?"

Gerald fussed with his phone. "I can't get a signal down here, though we should be safe for a bit."

She pointed to a second passage deeper inside the chamber, beyond the shelves of bottles. "What's through there?"

"That passage leads to another storage area, but there is no exit." He gestured around the room. "They blasted this chamber into the mountainside below Hearst's main residence. From top to bottom, we're surrounded by solid limestone. The only way in or out is the way we came in."

But she worried for Wes. Beyond his heroic attack that allowed her and Gerald to escape, Wes had a significant injury. Any loss of blood could put him in real trouble, and she couldn't do anything for him inside this room.

Gerald checked his watch. "Normal rotation sees a check-in every hour or so. We shouldn't need to wait long until a ranger arrives."

"So, we wait," Jadene said, gazing at the cellar's limestone walls.

"We do." Gerald fixed his tie and blazer, looking curiously in her direction. "Now, you must tell me. Who are those people? And why did they attack your friend?"

SIXTY-FIVE

They were stuck here until help arrived. The last few days' events circled in Jadene's mind, and, believing she had nothing to lose, she explained to Gerald that she was a private investigator hunting down a lead.

"In 1945, a cargo plane possibly landed nearby, which led us here, searching for clues," she said. "We were on the tour, like everyone else. I was trying to see if I could spot something. It was a long shot, I know. But maybe a marker or…" she trailed off, shaking her head. "We had no idea we were being followed."

Gerald nodded—as if the San Simeon compound regularly entertained this kind of lunacy from its guests. Then, he said something peculiar. "If you're being followed, you must be close to something."

Jadene sighed. "If we are, I have no idea what it is. This all began with a weird telegram."

He narrowed his eyes. "A telegram, you say?"

Rattling off the phrases, Jadene tried to keep them in order—though she was unsure it mattered.

Gerald paced in a circle, cradling his elbow, touching a finger to his chin. "Interesting," he muttered.

She explained everything over several tense minutes. The period of the war. The Nazi retreat. The aircraft that flew out. Tracing it over the Atlantic. The landing in the US and the pilots she believed were at the helm.

She reiterated everything she knew of the telegram, concluding, "This may sound far-fetched, but I think a Douglas Skymaster—that cargo plane—landed on the PCH, just down the mountain here."

She left out the part about the four copies now in circulation—scattered among people with their own motives, and none alone revealing the full truth.

Half expecting Gerald to laugh in her face, she waited for his reaction.

Eyeing the ceiling, he remained silent a long while.

"Now, that's a hell of a story," he said.

She braced for his laughter.

But Gerald's expression softened, and he turned his gaze to hers. "Before my position here, I was, by trade, a professor of historical architecture." He gently pulled at the knot in his tie. "I do this now because I still enjoy teaching. Seeing that glint in the eye when I share something that fascinates the unsuspecting mind." He chuckled. "And now you, Miss Jadene, despite our rough start, have supplied me with that same spark."

"I have?"

He raised his head, cleared his throat, and spoke as if giving a tour. "The visionary behind Hearst Castle was a woman named Julia Morgan," he crooned. "A normally male-dominated field, especially in 1919 when construction of the grounds began. But she held a brilliant understanding of architecture, infusing a mix of Spanish, Mediterranean, and Gothic elements into her designs. In doing so, she created for Hearst a timeless, iconic mansion."

She listened intently.

"Julia Morgan even oversaw the design of this very wine cellar." He outstretched a hand. "And, as you can see, there are almost 3,000 bottles on display here—most Bordeaux and Burgundy. It has the capacity to hold over 20,000 containers. Although, Mister Hearst was not himself a big drinker."

She scanned the walled assortment. Many vessels contained wine, but others were mixed into the collection, which held liquor and various spirits.

Gerald pointed to the cellar's entry, now secured by the shelf board. "Ostensibly, it was safely secured by those heavy doors due to the 18th Amendment. The one outlawing the manufacture, sale, and transportation of alcohol."

Yes, prohibition was a strange time in this country.

"But Mister Hearst also sought to limit his guests' consumption. He, himself, held the only key to this cellar. Not even his staff had access." A frown creased his forehead. "But his biggest challenge was, of course, Marion."

"Marion?" Jadene said. "Marion Davies?" She'd learned a little about Hearst's affair but didn't absorb much because she was focused on finding a connection with Arthur Whitmore.

Gerald gazed up at the ceiling. "Although Hearst married Millicent Wilson, who bore his five children, she and William grew apart. Millicent took up residence in New York while he spent more time here in San Simeon with his mistress."

Married rich guy has a young girlfriend. Jadene rolled her eyes.

"Mister Hearst met Marion at 19. She was a theater player." He raised a finger. "However, as a recipient of Hearst's excessive wealth and connections, she was promoted as a film actress—though it didn't end well."

Curious, and because it kept her from thinking the worst for Wes, Jadene said, "What happened?"

"Regrettably, Hearst interceded in Marion's career—like an obsessed baseball parent, screaming at Junior from the stands."

She cracked a smile. Gerald used unusual similes.

"Hearst overspent on Marion's film productions, overexposed her through his media empire, put her on magazine covers, and flooded all his newspapers with her interviews and pictorials. He even suppressed negative reviews of her work, and the critics reviled him for it." He dropped his shoulders. "Though, despite her talents, Marion Davies never genuinely hit the big time, as it were."

Jadene frowned.

"Hearst created smoke, hoping the world would see fire. But they never did." His expression turned glum. "Blotted with the stain of nepotism, Marion often turned to alcohol."

A strange sadness overcame Jadene.

He gestured towards the shelves, a shadow crossing his face. "Legend has it, these steel doors were not installed just to foil the law during Prohibition. They were to shield Marion from her own demons."

Even at Hearst Castle there was tarnished history. It made her think of Sinclair and the looming question of his grandfather's past. If the worst came out, he would lose his company, and the Whitmore name—his children—would endure the ramifications.

"This telegram," Gerald said. "You mentioned a name? Would you mind sharing its spelling?"

Jadene did so.

Gerald stepped back to the steel doorway—the one he'd barred with the wooden board—and turned to her. "You noticed the second corridor in the back of the cellar?"

"Yes," she said. It was a slimmer doorway—the one she'd asked about earlier, wondering if it contained an exit. Gerald had said it did not.

"That, too, is a steeled vault door. It's difficult to see now because it's partially obscured." He clasped his hands. "But it is a safe within a safe."

"A safe within a safe?" she repeated.

Gerald stepped to the side, pointing at something above the board he'd wedged to keep the wine room's entrance from opening easily. Something embossed across the belly of the cellar's enormous ten-foot black doors.

Jadene approached, her brows bent in confusion. Directly above his finger, an inscription appeared in small, gold lettering.

A gasp of shock escaped her lips.

The engraving read, "The Hermann Safe Co."

"This door to Hearst's wine cellar," Gerald beamed with an outstretched hand. "I believe we may be standing inside of your double safe haven."

Sixty-Six

Leaving the Hermann steel door behind, Gerald moved past the wine shelving toward the cellar's second threshold, deeper into the hollowed space.

Jadene followed, her chest pounding. Was this really happening? Had she found the *Double Safe Haven* in the telegram?

While this second steel door was open, its entry was protected by a hinged panel of Plexiglas. Tourists could view the room, but only from the outside.

"If something was taken, my guess is it's in this area—where entry's forbidden," Gerald said.

Jadene peered through the acrylic. It was a smaller, oddly shaped space. Shelves and bottled spirits lined its fortified limestone walls. She touched the padlock near the handle. So close. Maybe the next clue was in there—if she could only get inside.

"Well, you've already cost me a blazer today." Gerald fished a set of keys from his pocket.

"We're going in?" Her voice trembled with excitement.

Gerald winked. "I told you, I'm intrigued."

He keyed the lock, slid the bolt from its keeper, and swung open the Plexiglass door.

A dry puff of air struck her face—cool, stale.

"Aside from cleaning, this area's been undisturbed since Hearst's passing," he said.

She bit her lip. If something had been left here all those years ago, someone would've found it by now. Unless they already had—and just didn't know it.

She stepped inside, her gaze drifting over the bottles, scanning each tattered label, wondering if one held an answer—or another message, cryptic as the telegram.

Across the faintly lit room, Gerald scanned bottles too—just as drawn in as she was. A hush fell over the limestone chamber, broken only by the soft clinks of shifting bottles as they searched.

"Did Marion have a favorite cocktail?" Jadene asked.

Hunched over a shelf, Gerald answered without looking up. "No, she drank anything and everything. Like a shirtless teenager on spring break."

Jadene chuckled.

Moments later, he spotted something on a high shelf. "That's curious."

She stopped her search. "What is it?"

"Although Marion did not have a preferred drink, Mister Hearst did."

"What was it?"

"Aristocratic ale."

Jadene squinted. "Beer?"

Gerald pointed to the top rail. A lone beer bottle stood at the apex of the shelf, flanked by dusty wine and whisky containers.

"When it came to food and drink, Mister Hearst was a man of simple taste."

The bottle sat too high, its label lost in the shadows—too faint to read from below.

"Can you boost me?" she said.

Gerald frowned. "We need to be careful. These shelves here are almost a century old."

"Of course." Her smile was broad but uncertain.

Gerald cupped his hands. "Very well, then."

Jadene lifted a leg, bracing against the wooden ledge for stability. He hoisted her up, and she reached toward the bottle.

She felt along the upper rail, grazing something at the base of the bottle with her fingers.

A taut wire—invisible from below—ran a short distance behind the shelving.

On impulse, she pulled her hand back, tugging the wire.

A crack echoed through the room. Then came a faint wisp of air.

"What was that?" she said.

Gerald lowered her, turning toward the hiss. "I hear it, too."

The whistling grew loudest near the lowest shelf as they searched for the source. Jadene pointed to a tiny spot behind the collection of bottles.

"Is that a hole?" she said.

Gerald slid several bottles aside. About waist high, they discovered a breach.

She reached a hand toward the crack, touching its opening. "I don't think that's stone," she said.

Gerald dropped to one knee, peeled off his jacket, and tossed it aside. He reached under the shelf and pried a loose chunk from the wall. He held the piece in his hand, eyebrows arched.

"I believe this is plaster," he said. "Roughed and painted to appear as limestone."

"Camouflage?"

The corners of his mouth twitched. "Curious."

Jadene tore off another small section, and examined it. Then, Gerald ripped off another chunk. Before long, a rectangular cavity appeared under the lower section of the shelf.

"It looks like an opening."

Gerald eyed the breach. "That may be a tunnel."

"A tunnel?"

"It's not entirely impossible. Remember, this cellar was excavated using dynamite. It could be a natural vein, or something else."

"Something else?"

"This is pure conjecture, but it's long been rumored excavators built tunnels beneath the castle grounds. For what purpose would be unclear, but…"

"But what?"

Gerald pointed. "But I believe you just found one."

Jadene peered into the dark hole under the shelving. A torn telegram's cryptic clues, a phantom aircraft, kidnappings, murders, and all of it had brought her here. She tightened her lips. She couldn't stop here.

"I'm going in," she said. She expected Gerald to argue, tell her to wait for the rangers, but he didn't. He, for whatever reason, was as curious as she was.

"Wait." Fishing a penlight from his pocket, he handed it to her. "You'll need this."

She took the device and shone it into the opening. The space was large enough for her to fit through, but even with the penlight she couldn't see anything but darkness on its other side.

Flat on the stone floor, she inched under the shelf through the plaster gap in the wall. Crawling on her hands and knees over the stone and dirt, she entered the passageway and found the cavity had more than enough headroom for her to stand.

The air inside the tunnel carried a slight breeze—and it was much drier than the musty cellar.

"I'm moving around this corner," she shouted.

"Be careful," Gerald hollered back.

Pacing forward through the rocks and earth, the only light came from the device in her hand. Moaning wisps of air grew into a low howl, nipping her cheeks and playfully tussling with her hair. She trekked deeper into the passage.

Gerald's calls were barely audible now. Fifty or more feet into the tunnel, the corridor took a sharp turn, and she came upon a fork.

One direction was more of the same—a rocky shaft, eight to ten feet high, wide enough for her to hike along its stony trail.

She raised her penlight, sweeping its beam at the cave's ceiling. Strangely, a pair of strings ran parallel to one another, the length of the shaft. The strings were attached to a series of circular buttons, knotted every ten feet or so. They led to a bend she could not see beyond.

Following the mysterious strings above her head in the other direction, she made her way down a dark corridor to a wider hollow. Above, cobwebs clung to the cave's mouth, dangling in a delicate veil of threads.

A breath caught in her throat.

Beyond the curtain of spider silk stood a series of rough wooden boards, spiked into the limestone—blocking an entrance.

SIXTY-SEVEN

Inside the secret passage through Hearst's wine cellar, an unbroken wind yawled through the ghostly tunnel. The dry, cold air sent shivers through Jadene. In her grasp, the penlight struggled against the darkness as earthly particles swirled in its beam.

This was no natural cave. Someone had carved it, blasting its honeycombed path into this mountain. But here, the walls were unfinished and coarse. Fractured, scattered stones littered the path at her feet. This space was created without considering aesthetics—crude, hasty, and out of need.

Whisking the spiderwebs aside, Jadene gradually drew into the corridor, her steps echoing through the hollow tunnel. In the shadows, the horizontal wood planks loomed before her. Each board butted against the other, creating a barrier about six feet high and half as wide. Their wooden faces were weathered with grooves and dark cracks, bearing the scars of time, and fastened to the stone wall with heavy, rusted spikes.

It was a tomb of sorts. Near eye level, between a pair of boards, a tiny root from the cave's ceiling crept downward, vining over the lumber through the butted edging, snaking into whatever lurked behind.

Jadene stretched out a hand.

From behind her, footsteps approached.

Her adrenaline surged. She was not alone.

Gerald stepped from the shadows, grinning.

"Historians are, after all, explorers," he said, brushing dirt from his shirt.

She exhaled in relief.

Gerald examined the cave's planked wall using the light from his cell phone. "What have we here?"

"I'm not sure. It's some kind of barricade." She scanned her penlight along the partition. "We might need a crowbar to…"

Gerald grabbed hold of the timber, yanking at its center.

The wood cracked easily.

"Guess we don't need that crowbar." She chuckled.

"Weathering." Gerald eyed the broken pieces. "Swelling and shrinkage over many years." His light shined over the boarded area. "If this blockade is as old as I believe, it's a wonder the wood held this long."

Jadene yanked at a plank. Its brittle center crumbled as she tore at it, and shards of wood fell to the ground. Gerald did the same from the other side. Soon, the two opened the corridor and shined their lights into the large, cavernous hole.

Before them was a dark cavity. But with almost no light, the scale of the void was impossible to understand.

Gerald fiddled with something on the wall.

A sharp snap cracked the air.

The penlight slipped from her hand.

Connected by two wires that snaked in from the tunnel, a garland of light sockets dotting the chamber's walls came to life. Old, incandescent bulbs bathed the enormous cavern with the glow of an eerie sunset.

"Remarkable," Gerald said, standing near a metal switch.

"Woah," Jadene added.

Their voices echoed through the immense stone hall. It was several times the size of Hearst's wine cellar, and its enormity reminded her of Sinclair's keeping room.

On the dirt ground, in neat rows, sat thousands of packages. Each was concealed in a milky, dusty covering. Most pieces were stacked waist-high like dominoes against the cave wall and as far as Jadene could see. Some were small—the size of a shoebox, while others were taller than herself and bulky. But each piece was shrouded in the same translucent covering, from the meager to the monolith.

It was a secret warehouse. One crafted into the side of the limestone mountain, using Hearst's wine cellar as its only passage.

Jadene retrieved the penlight and slipped it into her pocket. Approaching a row, she knelt next to a procession of parcels.

"Careful." Gerald pointed to the parallel twin wires running along the wall behind her, feeding the orangish lights. "That's old knob and tube electrical wiring, protected only by a thin cotton cloth. And it's not the best insulator of electricity. Heaven only knows what kind of current is running through it."

Undeterred, Jadene bent, reaching for an oblong piece about knee-high, and brushed a line of grime from its face. Bits of dust fell, revealing its milky, flexible exterior.

"This looks like plastic," she said.

Gerald came to her side, gazing at the flat panel clutched in her hands. "I believe that is polyethylene."

"What's the difference?"

"Between your household trash bag and this crude plastic here? I'd say about a hundred years."

The thick covering crinkled beneath her fingertips.

Gerald seized a piece about the same size as Jadene's from the pile. Examining its face, he said, "Rather curious, though."

Jadene chuckled, gesturing to the untold aisles of parcels surrounding them. "Which part, exactly?"

"I mean, the process to produce polyethylene was costly back in its day."

"It was?"

"If memory serves, synthetic sheeting wasn't even commercially available until the late-1950s." Gerald drummed a finger against the elastic. "Even then, it wasn't as if one could run out to Costco and buy a roll of it."

"So someone made this special?"

"I'd say someone mass-produced a batch of this plastic canvas specifically to wrap these items." He lifted his chin. "Unusual."

It was clear these stacked pieces had been bundled to protect them from the moisture and dryness cycles in this cave—to guard them from the same environmental damage suffered by the boards sealing the cavern's entrance.

Jadene eyed the area. "What are all these?"

Gerald tilted a nod. "Only one way to find out."

Taking a large rectangular piece, Jadene carefully poked a fingernail through its flexible film. Seizing both ends of the plastic, she ripped the sheeting down its middle, revealing its face.

The tour supervisor's mouth fell open.

"Oh my God," Jadene said.

Gerald paced to a bulky piece, pulling off its cover to reveal a life-size marble sculpture.

"Oh my goodness," he said. "I don't believe it."

Grabbing another parcel, Jadene peeled off its dusty plastic cover. "Wait, wait," she said. "I know this one. I don't know how, but it's familiar."

Gerald leaned over her, touching its frame with two gentle fingers. "That's because the medium is textured and thick-layered."

His wide eyes met hers. "And the man who created it had a signature, bold style."

"Who?"

His soft gaze came unblinking. "Vincent van Gogh."

An icy tremor raced up her spine. If this was an original work by the artist, its value had to be insane.

"What's it worth?" she gasped.

Gerald pursed his lips. He motioned to the first painting she'd discovered, portraying two women seated in a garden with uncanny, sophisticated brush strokes. "I'd say at least as much as that Renoir you uncovered."

"Holy shit!"

"Yes," Gerald added. "Holy shit."

Jadene became dizzy. There were thousands of pieces here. Each packaged and protected, hidden from the rest of the world. Had the pilots smuggled all of these from Kraków? Was this why the flights were kept so secret and Sinclair's telegram so cryptic? It was apparent no one had entered this chamber since its construction. But why were these artworks abandoned? Was this an elaborate heist gone wrong? Gently, she tugged another parcel from the row.

Gerald paced to a corner, eyeing an olive-green container on the ground. It was an old military ammo box, smaller than a loaf of bread, and wasn't covered in any plastic tarp. He dusted its top, and lifted the container, cradling it with an arm.

Springing the latch, he yanked open its lid. Inside, he found a compass strung through its bail, a rusted bowie knife, and an old, handwritten note penned with hurried scribbles.

Lifting the fragile paper from the ammo box, his breath hitched. He hurried back to Jadene, pressing the note into her hand.

"You must read this," he huffed.

The paper's texture was strangely familiar to her fingers. However, before she could read the words on its surface, a shuffle of footsteps echoed across the cavern's passage.

She and Gerald turned.

A silhouette emerged from the grotto's mouth, stepping into the amber light. A dark stain blotted the figure's right arm.

It was Wes Holt.

The hard muzzle of a pistol shoved against his temple.

"I see you found all they have stolen," Rena said.

SIXTY-EIGHT

Stumbling into the chamber, Wes's shirt was soaked with blood. His face was pale, and the tourniquet around his arm had come undone.

Rena and Karl followed behind, clutching their guns. The bald man approached the van Gogh, pawing at the painting.

"Magnificent, and it's in perfect condition," he said. "I know just the buyer."

Gerald bounded toward him. "Please be careful."

"Not another step, tour man." Rena took aim.

"Madam, we must notify the proper authorities and—"

"Your authorities have no right!" she shouted.

"But these are priceless artifacts."

She squeezed the trigger, firing a shot above Gerald's head. Scattered stones from the ceiling fell to his feet, and he cowered in retreat.

Rena spun the weapon to Wes. "Get over with those two!"

He staggered through a row of dust-covered packs, holding his arm, wincing with each step. Jadene rushed to his side, seized the rag on his bicep, and retightened the band. A new gash, above his eyebrow, oozed with blood.

"What did they do to you?" she whispered.

"Tried to give you more time," Wes grimaced. "Paid the price."

Rena shouted, "No speaking! All of you, in the corner!"

The only exit was the way they'd come in—the tunnel's rocky opening behind the armed duo.

Jadene, Wes, and Gerald stepped closer to the limestone wall. The amber bulbs lighting the chamber produced a tense, low hum. The frail wires running along the cavern's walls had begun to droop slightly as if weighted by the heavy current running through them.

Across from their position, Karl crouched on the floor with his back to the group, ripping the synthetic cover from several parcels and mumbling anxiously.

Surveying the large chamber, Rena announced, "For decades, many have searched. And here they are, safe and sound." She stroked a dusty bundle with the tips of her fingers.

Jadene eyed the area. Given the two secret plane flights from Kraków, the huge cache in this chamber made sense now. However, no phrase in Sinclair's telegram hinted at anything like this. Yet Rena knew about this massive hoard of valuables all along. But how?

She and Gerald held their hands in mid-surrender as Wes clutched his bloodied arm.

Rena paced toward the trio, a side of her mouth twisting upward. "You are the one, the one who solved this?" She fixed her eyes on Jadene. "I knew it would have been wasteful to kill you at the Buckley home."

A knot formed in Jadene's stomach. This woman in front of her had no qualms about murdering her partner at the cabin and had probably killed the innocent Ronald Buckley as well. Jadene glanced at Wes and Gerald. Unless she thought of something, Rena would shoot all three of them and leave their bodies in this forgotten chamber.

But if she could keep Rena talking, she might be able to convince the woman to let them go. And even if that didn't work—it might buy enough time for a park ranger to find their trail. However, if that ranger came unarmed, it would only add another hostage to the situation—or worse. A heaviness grew in her chest, but she had to do something.

"Yes," she said. "This is my investigation."

"Investigation?" Rena sneered. "You make it sound virtuous when I know greed brought you here."

Jadene exhaled, her posture dipping. This all began because she was looking to clear the character of Arthur Whitmore. She never expected to stumble onto anything like this. But explaining that to this angry woman might only make things worse, especially if Rena figured out that Arthur himself had worn a Nazi uniform. In fact, that detail might provoke another bullet—one that wouldn't strike the rocks above her head.

"I didn't know what we'd find. We—"

"These are bloodstains, not treasures!" Rena shouted.

Beside her, Gerald mopped the sweat from his forehead with his tie. Wes hunched, a hand pressed over the injury in his arm. The color in his face was fading by the minute. He needed help.

Karl dashed to a new section, excited to continue his inventory. Gently peeling the plastic from a thicker parcel, he unveiled a leather-bound manuscript.

Flipping through its fragile pages, the bald man muttered, "The codex? Magnificent."

Jadene held her palms steady. "We're not here to take anything. I was only following the trail of my investigation." She motioned to Wes and Gerald. "These men had nothing to do with it."

Rena leveled the gun at her chest. "Then you dug up the past without understanding any of this!"

Deep rage came in her words. This woman was somehow connected to all of this—to the war—to the tragedy of the past. But how?

Everything around them in this chamber, the paintings, the sculptures, were stolen. Jadene closed her eyes. She had a strong idea of the answer. For many, the wounds still ran deep—Tommy's words echoed in her thoughts. Though, if she could convey a sense of empathy, she might get the three of them out of this alive. However, she'd have to remain compassionate and choose her words carefully.

Taking a hard swallow, Jadene lowered her hands a half measure. "I understand what your people went through." She held a steady gaze on the woman's eyes. "And I'm deeply sorry for those dark times, for the cruelty. It is unimaginable. To have everything that matters—family, home, the very essence of your culture—torn away in that war. I can't begin to grasp what you must be feeling right now. All of this, stolen." She inched a step forward. "But you must understand, we aren't here to take anything from you. This is your history, borne of the persecution of your people, and I promise I will do everything to help restore—"

"Persecution?" Rena's laugh came cold and hollow. "You are a stupid woman! You follow clues yet know nothing. Instead, you assume?"

Jadene shook her head slightly.

"Your ignorance insults me." Rena's icy glare swept over the three. "I should kill you each right now."

A breath caught in Jadene's throat.

Rena approached. "You do not know why I am here, do you?" She held the pistol tight in her hand. "This is betrayal."

"Betrayal?"

Rena angled toward her. "You wish to save your friends? Then see if you can solve this puzzle, detective. Let us see how good you really are." She motioned to the items the bald man on the ground was picking through. "Your country is the thief—the one who stole. Now, you tell me the reason." A sharp grin crossed her lips.

Jadene's pulse raced.

"I will give you two guesses—two solves of my purpose, my reason for this claim." She waggled the gun. "Two strikes, as in baseball."

Karl's attention rose from the package he was tearing open, a trickle of moisture dangling on his upper lip. "Baseball has three strikes."

Under the tawny light, Rena's expression darkened. She aimed first at Wes and then shifted the gun's barrel toward Gerald. "On the third strike, her body hits the ground alongside her companions."

Sixty-Nine

Rena jammed the pistol against Wes's skull.

"Your answer in sixty seconds, or he dies!" she shouted.

Hunched and bleeding, he looked up, terror on his face.

A coldness gripped Jadene. She'd known this selfless man only a handful of days. But in that short time, she'd learned he was incredibly loyal and protective. She'd felt like an asshole for thinking he would deceive her.

Beside him, Gerald, the innocent tour guide she'd unwittingly dragged into this mess, shivered with fear. And now both men might die if she didn't crack this psychopath's riddle.

Her strength faltered, knees threatening to buckle. A flash of her mother's face seared her mind. Missing with no trace. Jadene helpless to find her. Her mother's face—last seen in a coroner's photo— seared her mind. She'd spent years blaming herself for not finding her sooner. Years wondering if she'd been too slow. Too stupid.

She drew a deep breath. She couldn't reverse time, go back and save her mom. Those were emotional illusions. And it had taken her a long, long time to come to grips with that.

But this was different. She needed to think—remember the details—recall everything of the last few days. Most of all, she had to put her emotions aside.

Rena had provided clues. Several clues. If Jadene could assemble them logically, she might save them. Her heart thumped in her chest. She had to save them. The alternative was unthinkable. She paced in a circle, cycling through her research.

"Where are you going?" Rena barked.

But Jadene was deep in thought. First, the reason—the purpose. Rena's glare. It wasn't sadness. It was anger. These artifacts had come from Kraków, but the woman's reactions made it clear she was not Polish or Jewish.

That flight from Kraków. The men who swooped in and took this chamber of artifacts. The objects uncovered so far were of varied mediums, styles, and periods. She blinked. The relics hadn't all come from Poland. No, they were amassed, brought together, before they were put on that airplane and flown here.

The Nazis—they'd stolen them. Raided homes, took valuables, and ran without honor. They'd accumulated this stolen trove. And the Third Reich's plundering happened all over Europe.

But Rena had used the word "owed"—yet every country was owed. By the war's destructive sixth year, when the C47 took off, the Nazis had occupied and looted over twenty countries. Jadene curled a finger and tapped her palm. Poland, Norway, France, Denmark, the Netherlands, Italy, Romania—she could recall most, but not all of them. Why, though, would Rena believe she had any more claim to these items than they?

"Thirty seconds," Rena shouted.

Wes stood frozen, subdued by the woman's weapon pressed to his forehead. Gerald held beside him, sweat dripping down his cheeks. Nearby, Karl ripped open packages like it was Christmas, oblivious to the execution about to unfold.

Jadene circled, muttering under her breath.

Rena had also used the word betrayal. This could mean wherever Rena was from—whatever country—they may have had an agreement. A pact. An accord with Germany. If that were the case, it left four countries. The United Kingdom, France, the Soviet Union, and Italy.

Jadene halted. A detail, right in front of her.

A recollection grew. It was one of the darkest chapters of World War II, yet until she'd researched this case, she'd remained insulated from understanding its gruesome scope. And, it was an event known chiefly for its failure.

And that ring. That vintage ruby red ring. This wasn't about money for Rena, this was personal.

Jadene gazed across the tiers of artifacts, each meticulously stacked throughout the chamber. Could this be the reason for Rena's vengeance? For her claim?

Bloodstains, not treasures. Treasures robbed by the Nazis before they broke in retreat. Retreat before the Soviets moved into Kraków.

Jadene's hands trembled. Tommy was right. The beaten and conquered never forgive. Never.

"Ten seconds!"

"Please!" Gerald cried. "You don't have to do this!"

Jadene's palms moistened. One name. One answer. It hit like a jolt—sharp, sudden, and final. If she was wrong, Wes would die in front of her. But if she stayed silent, she'd carry that failure for the rest of her life.

In that moment, she understood—this wasn't about justice or history. To people like Rena, stealing cultural artifacts wasn't theft. It was payback.

Rena steadied her weapon, finger brushing the trigger. "Five, four, three…"

Betrayal. Retaliation. A broken deal. Every detail clicked into place. Jadene's head snapped up. Her voice cracked through the hollowed cave.

"Barbarossa!"

SEVENTY

Rena's gaze narrowed. "What do you know of Barbarossa?"

She pulled the pistol away from Wes's face. He sagged with a sigh.

But Jadene steadied herself. The danger hadn't passed—not with this woman's unpredictability. She had to keep the three of them alive. Steadying her gaze, an idea formed.

"I know of Hitler's betrayal, the treaty," she said.

Rena blinked. "Nineteen-thirty-nine."

"Yes, but Germany broke that agreement and attacked your country."

Rena paced, her steps echoing on stone. "An unprovoked slaughter." Her words etched with a pitch of pain. "They did not care about human life."

Jadene studied her face, the lines of anguish carved deep. "It was an abomination," she offered softly.

Rena let her arms fall limp, her voice barely a whisper. "They burned our homes to soil."

Jadene's stomach churned as the imagined the desolation. Operation Barbarossa was the largest wartime invasion in history, an unstoppable wave of death and destruction. It was also the Nazis' first direct assault on the USSR, in the summer of 1941—a brutal campaign that lasted six bloody months.

"The attack on your country was unconscionable," Jadene said.

Rena raised her head. "Four million invaders left nothing but death."

Jadene nodded slowly. The facts unraveling in her mind. From the Black Sea to the Baltic, Hitler's tanks and troops plowed through the unprepared Soviet Union, obliterating everything in their path.

"A Holocaust by bullets." Rena's voice was slow and hollow. "They took the food, let my people die slow."

As Tommy had termed it, the Reich's collective mindset was absolute evil. Hitler himself had conceived the idea, thirsting to wipe the Soviet people from the map—just as he planned for the Jews, Romanis, the infirm, and others.

The Soviets would lose more than 25 million souls in World War II, more than any other country. Nearly five million people were killed during Operation Barbarossa alone. Most of the deaths were defenseless civilians. The enormity of the suffering tightened her chest.

"But they made a fatal mistake."

Jadene frowned. "The weather."

"Never attack our Russia in winter." Rena flashed a bitter smirk.

It was a lesson Hitler should have learned from Napoleon when the French tried to topple Russia in 1812. But a savage winter entombed the countryside, and his forces were stopped. With over half a million French troops invading Moscow under his command, less than fifteen percent survived and returned home, devastating his military.

Hitler's arrogance repeated history. This time known as the Soviet Union, the Nazis attacked on the same grounds. But after a half-year of slaughter, the December heavens took mercy on the Soviet people. The Nazis couldn't run supplies to their troops once snow and cold enveloped them, killing a sizable number of enemy troops by weather alone.

Until this case, she'd only held a vague understanding of the battles, the bravery, and the atrocities. She'd read about them, knew the numbers, but she'd never understood the viciousness, the actual loss of life, or the courage.

Rena angled down the aisle, her pistol gleaming at her side. "My ancestral village. Many fled. My Babushka, a child then. Irina. Her parents stayed behind to protect the land. It was all they had on this earth. But they did not, could not know what was coming…" Her voice cracked. "Their village annihilated, burned to nothing. No graves, no names. Only ash."

Jadene caught a flicker in her eyes, a fragile glimmer built of love, ache and grief. But then it was gone.

"They gave Irina the only trinket of value they had." She lifted her hand. The ruby ring caught the faint light, glowing like a drop of fresh blood. "Her parents were killed, but she fled with the others. Yet they could not keep her. Irana was a burden, a child with no family, and no name worth risking lives for." Ren's eyes tightened. "Strangers took her in."

Something in her expression. It wasn't only anger—it was raw, personal, bottomless.

"What did Irina get?" Rena's voice rose, jagged. "A life of suffering. Raised by hands that beat her. Betrothed to a drunk, a cheat. A future as empty as the graves her parents should have had." She stared unblinking at the weapon in her hand. "That life became my mother's inheritance. And hers became mine. A legacy of nothing. Three generations of pain, stitched into our blood like some cruel curse." Her knuckles whitened around the pistol.

The air shifted, thick with unspent rage.

"And why?" Rena thundered, stepping closer. "Why did my Babushka have to crawl through life scraping for bread, for dignity, for a place to rest her head while your country turned its back? Why did my ancestors die while yours feasted on its neutrality?"

Jadene recoiled. "What? That's not—"

"We bled more than any!" Rena shouted. "Millions of my people massacred and starved while America and its precious Allies sat and waited." Her voice laced with venom. "You knew what was coming. You knew! But you did not care. Not until your own interests were hit in the harbor did you act—but only after months of butchery in my homeland!" She drew the pistol toward Jadene. "Those in Kyiv, Moscow, Leningrad—an attack which your countries could have stopped."

The accusation hit like a slap. Jadene's breath hitched, her mind racing. It wasn't true—America hadn't abandoned them, hadn't even entered the war until later. Rena was distorting things. Jadene was taken back. And something else Tommy had said now made complete sense.

"I don't think it's fair to—"

"Fair?" Rena barked, cutting her off. "What is fair? Was it fair for my Babushka to lose her innocence, her childhood? Was it fair for her children to receive nothing but pain and hunger? No. There is no fairness. There is only survival." Her voice grew to a growl. "And for that abandonment, for the silence of your country while mine burned, I claim restitution!" She gestured wildly toward the treasures in the chamber. "This art, this history—they all belong to me now. My country, my family. To the bloodlines cursed by your apathy!" She aimed the weapon toward Gerald and Wes, "And if you wish to live, you will stay out of our way."

Jadene narrowed her eyes. There was no honor in this. What had happened to Rena's family was horrifying, but this wasn't justice. This was greed. She and Karl weren't reclaiming history—they were scavengers looting what wasn't theirs. But she also knew there was no point in arguing with this woman.

Unaffected by the goings-on, Karl was one aisle over, squatted and unpacking. He'd stacked several items aside, cherry-picking the war booty and piling pieces near the cavern's exit.

Rena stepped to a marble statue, unveiling its milky white plastic. She stroked the contours of its surface, muttering, "Beautiful."

Across from Jadene, Wes clenched his fists. It was clear he was thinking the same thing she was—they would never leave this place alive. But the most endearing thing about Wes was also his biggest fault. He protected those he cared about, even if it meant sacrificing himself. It was his nature. But he wouldn't stand a chance against two armed opponents—not with a bullet in his bicep. It would have to be her.

She turned to the statue. Stillness gave way to focus—a feeling she hadn't known since competition, when her toes curled over the starting block.

"I understand now," Jadene said. "All of this is for your people."

Wes shot her a confused glance.

Jadene glanced toward the statue, then to Wes.

Immediately he seemed to understand. He turned to Karl without a word.

Lugging another painting to his booty pile, Karl said, "How do we get these out of here?"

Rena's lips curled faintly. "Why do you think I left them alive? They are both leverage and labor."

Karl snorted. "Perfect."

During the exchange, Jadene inched beside the tall sculpture opposite Rena as Karl whisked past Wes and Gerald, returning to the row he was picking from.

Rena pointed to an aisle. "I want only the best pieces. Pushkin would be proud."

They would never get out of this alive. Jadene set her feet, tension coiling in her legs.

SEVENTY-ONE

Rena ogled the statue. A marble masterpiece that took the breath away—towering proof of her triumph. Stolen and lost in the tides of a war, borne from a twisted empire. And while the West had stood idle while her people burned, she would claim this stolen past. A fitting trade.

Rena closed her eyes.

Months ago, the man had reached out to her. He'd read about her interest in war artifacts in the vlogs she'd posted for Pushkin. The museum encouraged outreach. But when he'd sent her photos of an old telegram he'd found, she knew.

A plane flight later, they met.

Oddly, the suited man with the wet hair sought only information about the sender of the telegram. He did not understand the document, nor did she offer to educate him. For him, it was information. To her, it was everything—the critical piece mending decades of stories she'd heard as a child. Embellished, misremembered, passed from one to the next.

Mariupol. A simple port by the sea. Back then, home to hardworking fisheries and proud people, surrounded by farmlands. Idyllic, shared, unspoiled. But it was a place that no longer existed. Not in any way that mattered. It had been shattered once by the war of her ancestors, when Nazi shells had turned the streets into trenches and fire devoured whole families. All but one of her elders had perished.

Now, decades later, the city burned again, caught between forces that saw land but never lives. The latest battle claimed her entire living family. The cycle never ended. History was a beast that came to feast, and it never left a meal unfinished.

This hardened truth forged her into a predator.

She was not Ukrainian. She was not Russian. She was an enraged Mariupolite. A suffered people, trampled. Fodder for wars they had nothing to do with. Now, she had sacrificed too much, bled too much, to allow anyone else to take the glory.

Surrounded by the spoils in this cave, so much was going through her mind. Yes, this all began with a different intent—the agreement was simple. She would return anything she recovered to Pushkin, solidifying her place among the gallery greats. An unselfish bid to the homeland. But she was not that naïve girl from those war-torn shores any longer.

She had evolved. She had not hesitated to do what needed to be done. Every turn had led her to this impossible bounty where so many had failed.

She glanced at the bald man picking through the spoils. Unearthing these valuables in this cavern seemed fitting. America, with its self-righteousness, had let her elders suffer as they watched from the safety of an ocean away. It was just one more reason to despise them.

Yet, an alluring thought consumed her. So much was here. Far too much to just… give away. She had pried open history's vaults with precision and a ruthless hand. She deserved more.

Discreetly, she could sell some pieces to those who understood their worth. Others she would keep. Why should the blind be trusted with works of genius?

Of course, she would grant the museum a few pieces. Selected works to secure her plaque on their walls. Perhaps one day, they would teach her name in schools. The daughter of Mariupol who reclaimed reparations of a stolen past.

A surge swelled in her chest.

This was not fate—it was design.

She could never return to the job or her native dirt. But neither held meaning anymore.

Though, tales of her achievements would echo through the ages despite the West's inevitable condemnation. Let them call her a criminal, a thief—such petty labels would never diminish the grandeur of her accomplishments. Wealth would be her armor.

She brushed the marble's chilly shell with her fingertips. Exquisite.

"How do we get these out of here?"

The bald man clumsily grabbed another piece for the haul—a painting, marvelous no doubt, given the counterfeiter's meticulous training. Unlike the convict Travis Floyd, Riggins had been bold enough to attempt a forgery in her own museum. A still-life, passable to amateurs. But her eye was too sharp for that. The brushwork was substandard, the lines muddied—an overworked imitation of a master. Still, his ties to the underground made him valuable. And for now, he remained useful.

But he'd raised an interesting question. She had three loose ends at the moment. The woman investigator whose legwork had led here—onerous, bright, and familiar with her city's atrocities. The injured man with large shoulders who seemed to have an affinity for the investigator, and the awkward gentleman in the blazer.

They were unexpected obstacles. But obstacles could be repurposed. Now that she had what she had come for, killing them would be simple and efficient. However, they might be handy in the immediate—as a matter of logistics.

"Why do you think I left them alive?" she said. "They are both leverage and labor."

With three hostages as leverage for transport—they would have no choice but to meet her demands. Her escape would be legendary.

A snicker came from the bald man. "Perfect."

She would change much in a short time. The West would call her a villain, a thief. But let them scream from their safe shores. They had abandoned her city, her people—now, she abandoned their judgment. They would honor her name—fear it. Her victory would resonate long after her detractors had faded into obscurity.

Rena Volkova would be remembered.

"I want only the best pieces," she said. The splendid statue loomed before her—it would fetch a fortune. "Pushkin would be proud."

A brisk wind tussled her hair.

SEVENTY-TWO

Jadene drove her shoulder into the marble statue with all her weight. The sculpture tipped forward.

Rena whirled too late. The heavy monolith toppled, striking her square in the chest and driving her backward. Her body pancaked between the falling statue and the electrical wires, arcing the current.

The result was immediate. Flashes flared. Rena's mouth opened, but no sound escaped. She thrashed helpless against the wires. The chamber's lights flickered violently.

Mounting his own attack, Wes pummeled Karl with a left hook, sending him to the ground. A muffled shot cracked. A bullet hissed past Jadene's ear as she dove for cover.

Sparks crackled, the lights flashed like a strobe fire.

Wes rushed over, pulling Jadene to her feet. Gerald followed, and the three ran for the tunnel as the entire cavern plunged into darkness. Breathless and panicked, they scrambled through the rocky passage, blindly searching for the way forward.

"Wait," Jadene whispered. She yanked the penlight from her pocket, shining its unsteady beam. With both men close behind, the three rounded the passage toward the wine cellar.

Each wiggled back through the hole under the shelving when they reached the tunnel's end. Once Gerald was on his feet, he urged Jadene and Wes from the secondary area into the main cellar, swinging shut the acrylic door behind them.

Jadene huffed a breath. "Do you think that'll hold them?"

"Not to worry," Gerald huffed. He wrapped his knuckles against the panel. "It's an inch and a half of polymethyl."

Wes held the band on his arm. "Bulletproof."

Gerald slid the latch into place, clicked the lock, swung the outer steel door closed, and smiled triumphantly.

"Let's see them try to get out of that," he said.

Jadene tightened the rag around Wes's arm, cinching it firmly. The fabric was soaked with blood, but her hands held steady as she worked to secure it. Reaching up, she placed a palm against his cheek to check its warmth.

"I'm fine," Wes said. "Been in worse shape."

Gerald ushered them toward the stairs.

"Truly astonishing," he said. "I'm still having a time wrapping my mind around…" The tour supervisor stopped.

"What is it?" Jadene said.

Gerald eyed her, curious. "Inside of that chamber, I gave you something. Do you still have it by chance?"

From the pocket of her jeans, she fished out the paper.

"If it's all right with your injured friend, I'd like you to read that before we head upstairs, where I'm certain all manner of Ranger will hound us with questions."

"But—"

"I assure you, madam, it is worth a moment," Gerald said.

Wes gave her a nod.

Jadene opened the crumpled sheet. She drew in a sharp breath and her knees grew weak.

This had all been so strange. Her first real case. Things she'd never expected. Her meeting with Sinclair, a reclusive man with a past he couldn't escape. All his achievements, everything he'd built for his family, tainted by a wretched secret. An appalling war. An unwelcome heritage. Living with a past he couldn't shake.

The fluke chance. Her business nothing more than a sliver of space downtown with a stupid neon sign she refused to plug in. Help from a friend, a stranger in a bar, a quirky woman who taught her about planes and pilots during the war, and a teenager who taught her about herself.

But it was Sinclair who'd given Jadene the most. Her life interrupted by her mother's death, a career she'd drifted into, an existence she was floating through day to day. She'd tried to change things, but even after becoming a PI, she'd slipped back into a melancholic routine. Unchallenged, uninspired, and indifferent.

She now figured Sinclair had known from the beginning about the tragedy that ended her mother's life. After all, she'd never have gotten through the gates if he didn't already know all about her. But he never brought it up, never turned things awkward. Instead, he'd given her the chance to prove herself, to finish something on her own terms.

The close calls, the danger, the things she'd learned along the way. It had all changed her.

Now, she had the truth—answers to mend Sinclair's life.

Tears stung her eyes as she studied the torn, scribbled note. A signature. A symbol. A quiet rebellion passed down through blood and time. And now—hers to protect.

She smiled, not for what had been found, but for what still could be made right. Sinclair's grandfather—his words—it all made sense now. The next step was clear—but she couldn't take it alone. She turned to Gerald and gave him a warm hug.

"Very gracious of you." He smiled. "But I only opened the box."

She chuckled. "Gerald, I'm not letting you out of my sight." She hooked Wes by the arm, leading the two men toward the steps.

"Wes, do you have a contact who can grant me access to Sinclair's email servers?"

"Email?"

"I need full access permissions. I want to check something out."

"I'll make a call," he said.

Ascending the stairs, she placed a soft hand on the guide's shoulder. "Gerald, have you ever flown on a private jet?"

"Madam, I don't think I…"

"I can assure you it's top-notch," she said.

The tour supervisor held in the stairway, a twinkle of doubt in his eyes. "But I shouldn't just…"

"Nonsense," Jadene said firmly. "It'll be fun."

SEVENTY-THREE

Sinclair Whitmore sat at the boardroom table with his head in his hands. Maxine Sheehan, Pat Goler, Jerry Palmer, Sean Fritz, and Greg Ratcliff stared his way. Senior Vice President Kenneth Iverson and head counsel Andy Mulligan were at the table's other end.

Palmer fixed his tie and leaned forward. "Unpleasant as it is, we must take a vote."

Sheehan and Fritz bobbed their heads.

The boardroom's doors swooshed open.

A broad-shouldered man with his arm in a cast entered and announced, "Miss Jadene Bowman, of Bowman Investigations."

In a royal-blue summer dress and Bondi sneakers, Jadene strolled into the room, holding her leather notebook.

"What the hell is this?" Fritz demanded.

Ratcliff adjusted the glasses on the end of his crooked nose. "We're conducting official business," he declared.

Wes Holt gave Sinclair a single nod. "Sir, she has important information."

Grumbling from the others erupted.

Iverson rose, over-bleached teeth gleaming. He slicked a hand across his damp hairline. "Sir, this is a closed-door session," he said, giving her a once-over that made it clear she didn't belong.

"Mulligan?" Sinclair eyed the man at the end of the table in the paisley tie.

Mulligan held out an empty hand. "Sir, uh, you own the far majority of the company. If, as Mister Holt says, Miss Bowman has important information, it is the board's duty to take that into consideration before any potential vote."

Jadene stepped inside, followed by two men and a woman.

"My colleagues and I have some news," she announced.

"What news?" Sheehan grumbled.

"My news is confidential. However, if I do receive my client's permission to reveal my findings, I don't believe there will be any vote today."

"What? Who is this woman?" Fritz demanded.

"This is ridiculous!" Palmer shouted.

Sinclair pounded a fist. "Oh, shut the fuck up, both of you!"

The room went silent.

Sinclair eyed Jadene's feet. "Love the sneakers."

She grinned. "Their rubber soles are quite handy."

The billionaire chuckled. "Yes, you have my consent."

Jadene eyed the room. "I was hired to examine a document held in the Whitmore family for several decades. A document that, I believe, speaks to the heart of your discussions today."

"Who are these people?" Goler said. "They have no standing."

"They are employees of mine," Sinclair barked.

Jadene pointed to a flat panel on the boardroom's south wall. "If I could have the screen, please."

"Connecting now, boss." Lilly Weller wore a long tweed skirt and a white button-up blouse. She took an empty seat at the table, flipped open her laptop, and an image of Sinclair Whitmore's telegram appeared on the boardroom's large screen.

```
TELEGRAMM                                    KRAK (tear)
NL 17 JAN 1945
URGENT STOP BROKEN CASTLE STOP DAKOTA FREE BLUE
STOP WHISPERING WEST STOP BAY OF THE MONTEBELLO
STOP LITTLE RANCH STOP HERMANN STOP DOUBLE SAFE
HAVEN STOP POWODZENIA
```

Mulligan lowered his spectacles. Palmer, Sheehan, Fritz, Golen, and Ratliff stared at the screen, confused. At the other end of the table, Iverson toyed with his cell phone.

Pointing to the words on the monitor, Jadene began. "As you can see, this document includes a dispatch type, part of a location, a date, and seven phrases sent with urgency."

"What is this?"

"What you're looking at is a telegram, sent on the indicated date." Jadene pointed to the screen. "During World War II."

Iverson glanced up from his phone. "Intercepted by whom?"

Jadene rose her chin. "This dispatch was sent, not intercepted."

"It was?" Sinclair said with surprise.

Jadene gave him a nod.

"By whom?" another asked.

"By a German," Jadene replied.

Gasps from the board members erupted.

"But who, precisely?" Iverson shouted.

A vibration came from the cell phone in Jadene's dress pocket, but she ignored it. "Oh, I think you know who," she said.

"Tell us, I want this on record," Iverson demanded.

Jadene looked to Sinclair, who returned a slow nod. She sent a quick wink, and straightened her posture.

"Arthur Whitmore was indeed in Hitler's military at the time," she said. "And I can confirm that he sent this message."

"This is absurd!" one cried.

"We can't delay this any longer," Goller shouted. "If word gets out, the value of the IPO will plummet!"

Sinclair shouted, "Stop worrying about your damn shares and let her finish!"

The chatter ceased.

"Thank you, sir." Jadene stepped toward the table. "As each can see, there appear coded phrases in the telegram, which my team and I were able to decipher."

"Decipher?" Sinclair leaned forward. "All of it?"

Wes shot his boss a grin.

Jadene stepped to the monitor, aiming a finger at the screen. "The message's location, as you can see in part, is Kraków, Poland. The country first attacked by Germany in 1939." She flashed a frown. "The Nazis would occupy Poland until their retreat in January of 1945 when Soviet forces drove them back to Berlin."

"Soviets?" Palmer said.

"Our Allies during the war," she replied.

Mulligan gestured. "What's that before the date. NL? What does that mean?"

"No limit," Lilly grinned. "Messages over radio and wire like this were usually priced per letter. But since this was a military communication, there was no limit on its length."

"Interesting," the attorney said.

Jadene shot Lilly a smile.

"This is a waste of time," Golen said, sternly. "Can we get back to our vote?"

Jadene ignored the woman. "The date of the telegram is significant because it represents an interval between the Nazi retreat, and the Soviet forces moving into the country to secure it."

"Why does that matter?"

"Because an aircraft flew into Kraków during this period."

"What?"

"How do you know that?"

Jadene pointed to the message in the frame. "The phrase, Dakota free blue, indicates that an aircraft took off from Kraków."

"Wait, wait, how do you know this?"

"Please," Sinclair said. "Let the detective finish."

Jadene continued. "Because the term Dakota is field slang for the type of aircraft. A Douglas C47 twin engine cargo plane."

"Whatever for?"

"We're getting to that," Lilly chimed.

"Through great effort, my colleague and I identified the aircraft in question."

"You did?" Sinclair said with surprise.

"Through a process of elimination, Lilly and I cross-referenced dates and times to nearby air bases in the United Kingdom. We found a single, matching aircraft, correlating its takeoff and return times to an air base."

"Which one?"

"Lakenheath Royal, in Suffolk, England."

Mulligan nodded along.

"From what we gathered, someone or something was picked up from Kraków and flown back to Lakenheath."

"Is there a manifest?"

Jadene raised a finger. "We later came to find that leg of this flight wasn't finished in the UK. A second aircraft, a larger C54 Skymaster, continued the journey, leaving Lakenheath bound for Lajes Airfield in the Atlantic."

"Where?"

"However, we lost track of the flight until a visit to an airfield archive put us back on course." Jadene paused. "But this is where we unknowingly ran into trouble."

"What trouble?" Sinclair said.

She turned to him. "Seeking out that flight number triggered another party searching for the same thing."

"It did?"

"It appears someone at the facility was gatekeeping a particular log from Lajes, waiting for someone to come searching for the detail on that Skymaster flight."

"Someone else? I don't—"

"My friend Ellis Martin was put onto the same case several weeks prior. And I will let him explain."

Ellis stepped forward, wearing a jacket and tie clipped with a stylish steel bar. "Yes, sir. After I visited Max Airfield, I was followed. Perpetrators abducted me on my return trip at Hartsfield."

"Who?"

"I don't want to detract from Miss Bowman's chronicle of events here, and I'll share more later. But rest assured, the suspects were identified and paid for their crime," Ellis grinned.

Sinclair frowned a nod.

"After that, thanks in large part to my friend Ellis, we deciphered our next phrase." She gestured to the screen. "Bay of the Montebello."

"Where?"

"It turns out this was not an actual location but an event." She circled the table. "On December 23, 1941, an oil tanker, The SS Montebello, was struck with a Japanese torpedo off the coast of California."

"California?"

"Right off the central coast."

Sinclair eyed her. "But the ship, it sank?"

"Yes, it did," Jadene said. "Miraculously, all crew survived without significant injury." She turned slow, her gaze drifting from one face to the next. "And that event, while censored in the media to keep domestic panic at a minimum, was widely circulated among the armed forces. This is, I believe, how it became a marker in this telegram."

"A marker for what?"

"Our Skymaster's landing."

"Landing?"

"I could not find any airfield or logs to confirm a touchdown. However, Wes and I traveled to the area to search for clues. And we deduced that the flight landed on the PCH, in San Simeon."

"That's not possible."

Jadene raised a brow. "Not only was it possible, I assure you, it did happen."

"Bullshit," Iverson barked. "Where's your evidence?"

Lilly keyed the laptop, and a map appeared on the flat screen, showing the long stretch of road running along the oceanfront.

"As you can see, the straight length of the treeless route from Lilly's map shows more than enough runway."

Gasps came from around the table.

"Fine," Iverson said. "You tracked an old plane and where it landed." He scoffed. "Where is all of this going?"

A tall, slender man in slacks and a fashionable blue vest stepped from the group. "I believe I can answer that," he said.

SEVENTY-FOUR

"My name is Gerald Beckett, and I am head of Visitor Experience at Hearst Properties."

Those around the table eyed him curiously.

"I've only known Miss Bowman and Mister Holt a short time. And, while, my initial introduction to Miss Bowman still weighs on my mind, we quickly became acquainted."

The two eyed one another, and Jadene gave him a playful wink.

"Miss Bowman's efforts in tracking this flight led to our coastal property. Land which the Hearst family purchased in the 19th century." He picked a spot of lint from his lapel. "The aircraft in question, we now believe, which landed on the PCH was loaded with unconventional cargo."

"Cargo? What cargo?"

Lilly brought up a photo on the large monitor.

"The first phrase, Broken Castle, we now understand refers to a walled compound in Kraków, Poland, which sits along the Vistula River," Jadene said.

"Wait, a moment ago, you were talking about cargo?"

"Let her finish, would you?" Mulligan said.

"This series of medieval structures, known as Wawel Royal Castle, was built in the 13th century."

"A castle?" Golan turned to the others. "I'm not sure where this is heading. Strange plane flights, cargo, a castle?" He huffed. "Honestly."

"We believe the cargo we found were items looted by Nazi forces in and around Poland, during the war," Gerald said. "And they collected them at Wawel—"

"Looted?"

Jadene bowed a nod. "A war criminal named Hans Frank, who controlled Poland's occupation at the time, used Wawel Royal Castle as his headquarters. Frank was later executed after the Nuremberg Trials, but it is widely understood that he and his men robbed the lands, gathering the valuables at the fortress."

"What valuables?"

Gerald raised a palm. "If you permit me, I will share a partial manifest of what we found in Hearst's compound." He cleared his throat. "From what I am told, my team has only been able to catalog a small percentage of the trove thus far, and there remain thousands of items to peruse."

"Thousands?"

"Please, please," Sinclair quieted the group.

Gerald cupped his hands behind his back. "Paintings include Jan van Eyck's Annunciation, Bruegel's Adoration of Magi, Dürer's self-portrait, and several works by Rembrandt and Caravaggio."

Every head around the table shook in disbelief.

Gerald shot a glance at Jadene. "And a long sought after piece, which I cannot name at the moment for security reasons, by the 15th century painter Raphael Sanzio da Urbino."

"Raphael?" Mulligan's expression went pale. "The Raphael?"

Gerald raised a brow. "If you mean the man who painted virgins in the Vatican while bedding half of Rome, then yes—the Raphael."

"Jesus Christ," Fuller exclaimed.

The others gasped.

Sinclair, though, nodded with a grin.

"Most of these found paintings were presumed lost or incinerated by the Nazis. And various artifacts of royal lineage were also recovered, including the Golden Chalices of Kings Władysław II and King John II, a bevy of crowns and crucifixes, and hundreds of jewels and ornaments taken by the Reich during the war." He raised a hand. "But I must also point out that while the cargo may have been brought to Hearst property, it is doubtful that Mister Hearst himself knew of the cache's arrival or its keeping."

"How could he not?"

Gerald gestured to the screen. "You must understand that for decades Hearst Castle itself was under constant construction and renovation. As well, furnishings and works of art were flown in from around the world, on a near daily basis." He shrugged. "An aircraft landing near the property may not have raised any suspicion, and it was normal for all manner of trucks and trains to offload goods meant for the estate during these times."

"So, nobody noticed?"

"I'd say that's likely. Especially if the aircraft landed at nighttime. My bet is the artifacts were unloaded and the plane took off again under the cover of darkness." He shrugged. "Stopping traffic on either side of the hill would have taken a couple of men, probably dressed as road workers. And none of this would have raised suspicion, given the highway's new construction at the time."

Palmer shook his head.

"My guess is the heavy door manufacturer—the name Hermann, which appears in the telegram—may have been communicating with someone, or a partner. Or, it may have been a collective of workers on the property who aided in the endeavor." Gerald bent an eyebrow. "Though I'm afraid I'm without hard evidence to verify this."

"Wait, wait, wait." Ratcliff raised a hand. "They stole these items from Kraków?"

"Appears so," Iverson smirked.

"This is outrageous!" cried Fritz.

"And that document, Whitmore's family document, directly ties… this is worse than I thought!" Palmer shouted. "Not only was he a Nazi, but a thief!"

"We have to vote, I'm calling for the motion!"

"There's no way we can let—"

Ratcliff pointed a finger at Sinclair. "This may be interesting, but the fact remains your grandfather was part of the worst regime of modern times. We have to be realistic about all of this. You claim he was forced into service, but I don't see any real proof. And now this thievery, it's an abomination."

Jadene glanced at Ellis. The detective fished a ball from his pocket, tossing it in her direction, and she snatched it from the air.

Every head turned to Jadene.

"Stan Lee Roseman, my landlord, is an incredible man," she said.

"Landlord? What is all this?"

Jadene scanned the room and smiled. "Stan volunteered for two tours in Vietnam as a medic. Unfortunately, during his last tour, his helicopter went down in Saigon."

Sinclair shot a glance of concern.

"The crew sustained minor injuries, but Stan was seated near the gunner's doorway. When the cabin rolled, it caught his leg under the frame, shattering his lower leg."

Fritz scowled. "What the hell does this have to do—"

Wes put his large hand on Fritz's shoulder, squeezing.

Fritz recoiled.

Ellis chuckled.

"Stan's injury was patched in the field at a MASH unit," Jadene continued. "Though, the damage to his leg was permanent. He was then deemed unfit for duty and honorably discharged."

She rolled the golf ball Ellis tossed to her across the center of the table. When it reached Sinclair, he snatched it, eyeing her strangely.

"You see, every recognized military has fitness and operations standards. Even during times of forced conscription," Jadene explained. "However, if a war drags on long enough, a country begins to run out of able-bodied individuals—and this was the case for Germany in 1943. That is when they lowered standards to draft less able soldiers. Anyone from 16 to 60. Even those with poor vision, less physically fit… and individuals with flat feet—a condition that runs in families." She paused, studying their faces. "I have read, however, that regular use of a golf ball for arch stimulation can help alleviate discomfort." She winked in Sinclair's direction.

Clutching the golf ball, Sinclair raised his chin. "So, Arthur was forced to serve?"

"That doesn't matter," Golen said. "This is about image, about the head of this organization and its association with those travesties. We can't—"

Wes glared his way. "She's not finished."

"However, because of Arthur Whitmore's disability, he did not see combat. Instead, he took a position as a radio operator, and during that time, he sent the message you see on the screen now."

"We know this already."

"That only proves he's party to this unbelievable crime!" Golen cried.

Others rumbled similar statements.

A notebook slapped the table, causing every head in the room to spin Jadene's direction.

"We also found something else," she said.

SEVENTY-FIVE

Patricia Golen's tone was sharp. "Whatever it is, it doesn't change the fact that this entire ordeal is a poor image for the company. I mean, honestly, the association alone is beyond the pale."

"Here, here," someone added.

"Quiet!" Sinclair barked. "I want to hear what she has to say."

Fritz folded his arms, as did Palmer. Golen's jaw tightened while the other two board members scowled.

"The final piece literally has two parts," Jadene said. "Wes, if you would, please."

Wes slipped a tin container from under his arm, resting it on the table. Carefully, he opened its lid and brought out a yellowed, torn document. He held it at eye level, turning its face toward the board members.

"What you see now is the original telegram from 1945. The same letters, the same phrases you see on the screen. You'll also notice it is torn precisely where the scanned copy on the flat screen shows damage lines."

Mulligan stepped closer, fussing with his glasses. Iverson's attention broke from his phone.

Holding the olive green ammo box, Ellis set it on the table beside Jadene, and then returned next to Gerald.

Jadene unlatched the ammo box. "In ancient Egypt, there was a practice—"

"Ancient Egypt?" Ratcliff sighed, eyes sweeping the ceiling. "Where's this fable going now?"

"Indulge her." Sinclair gritted his teeth.

Jadene smiled. "The Pharaohs and the talisman."

"The what?" Frits scoffed.

"Like the Pharaohs, soldiers often leave pieces of themselves behind," she said. "A memento to both mark the end of something and to protect it."

"And?" Ratcliff said, annoyed.

"Along with the cargo artifacts, we found this box of trinkets." From the ammo box, she pulled out a field compass, handing it to Sinclair. "If you would, please read the initials on its backside?"

Sinclair's breath hitched. He turned the compass over, running his fingers across the engraved initials. "AJW."

"Who?" one said.

Sinclair swallowed hard. "Arthur Johann Weissman."

Jadene touched his shoulder. "Your grandfather?"

Sinclair's moist eyes fixed on the compass.

"So he changed his last name to hide his roots?" Sheehan scoffed. "Typical."

Fritz pointed. "Finding that only proves he was part of the heist. I'm not sure what you're getting at here. This changes nothing."

Wes paced toward Jadene, placing the torn original telegram flat on the table. As he did so, she removed a second item from the ammo box, smoothing its folds.

The printed top center of the divided document displayed the Holy Roman Empire's Imperial Eagle, clutching a wreathed swastika. Large, bold black letters read TELEGRAMM with several small, typed German phrases.

Palmer uncrossed his arms. Golen leaned forward with a frown. Others craned their necks for a better view.

Jadene slid the two torn pieces to Sinclair.

Sinclair reached for the papers. He pressed the halves together. The edges matched perfectly. The telegram, after eight decades, was whole again.

He trembled, hands unsteady. For a moment, he didn't speak.

A hush fell over the room.

"My God," Sinclair finally whispered.

A collective gasp came from the others.

"That piece—the telegram's matching half—was also found inside of this box," Jadene said. "Would you please read the handwriting on its backside?"

Sinclair lifted the new half and a tear broke from his eye. "To their new guardian. Please keep these treasures safe so that many will enjoy their beauty." He wiped a cheek. "Faithfully, A.J. Weissman."

The room went silent.

"Loyal, not lost." Jadene smiled, then pointed. "There's a drawing under his signature. Do you see it?"

Clearing the moisture from his eyes, Sinclair squinted. "Is that a flower?"

"Yes," Jadene said. "It's a symbol. A rose."

Sinclair froze. His lips parted, but no words came.

"A rose?" he finally whispered.

She stepped to the center of the room. "Arthur Weissman, later Whitmore, was forced into Hitler's military against his will. But he never ceded to the movement, and in fact, he resisted."

Sinclair stared at the document. "Arthur… resisted?"

Jadene nodded. "He was part of The White Rose."

"The resistance?" Mulligan said.

"Yes. Smuggling information. Sabotaging the Reich from the inside."

Sinclair ran a hand through his hair. "And all this time, I thought—"

"That he was one of them," Jadene finished.

Palmer's expression went curious.

"Started as a student gathering at the University of Munich, the opposition to Hitler and his policies grew to include many anti-Nazi members within the military. Members who provided coordinates of enemy troop movements and target locations, sending secret communications across battle lines to the Allies." She locked eyes with Sinclair. "Your grandfather wasn't a Nazi. He was working against them. This document and the recovered artifacts prove that he, in fact, is a hero."

"Extraordinary," Mulligan said. "Was Arthur on the aircraft?"

"No," Jadene said. "He would immigrate to the US in the early 1950s, once laws were relaxed."

"So, he didn't know the where this cache was himself?"

"Doubtful," Jadene said. "Collin Buckley, the plane's final pilot, was probably the only one who knew. His return flight never landed. No records. He simply vanished."

"And the secrets of this resistance operation died with him?"

"It appears so," she said. "Until Arthur Whitmore's half of the telegram came to light."

Iverson gave a quick shake of his head.

Drawing a phone from her dress pocket, Jadene scanned its screen before setting it aside. "And speaking of resistance, the people Ellis and I encountered during our search—"

Sinclair wiped his eyes. "Who were they? I want to know."

Jadene motioned to Lilly, and a map of Poland appeared on the boardroom's monitor.

"I was always curious about the timing." Jadene brushed a wrinkle from her dress. "That sliver of time, January 17, 1945, when the Nazis left the area as Soviet troops were moving in. Why would they fly a plane in? What could be worth risking so many lives?"

"I think we all know now," Palmer said.

"At the time, many Soviets soldiers saw the recovery of any valuables in the hands of the Nazis as fair game. The fact the looted items came from museums and private collections didn't matter to them. They saw only payback."

"They wanted to steal it?" Sinclair asked.

"Yes, but a handful of brave souls risked everything to keep these treasures safe." Her finger raised. "Yet, decades later, someone was watching. They knew somebody took a priceless cache from Wawel Castle."

Sinclair's expression grew angry. "Who?"

"A woman named Rena Volkova. An employee of the Pushkin museum in Moscow. She'd spent years hunting down these artifacts. She believed she was entitled to their recovery because of wrongs done to her family during the war."

"You said there was another?" Sinclair said.

"Yes. An art forger and smuggler named Karl Riggins. He'd somehow weaseled his way into working at Max Airfield. We believe their plan was to steal what they could, and sell the pieces to the highest bidder."

"Where are they now?"

Ellis stepped forward. "According to the ranger's report, Karl Riggins was found in the locked cellar, alongside Rena Volkova— who's body was still twitching from the current."

Sinclair's eyes went wide. "The current? I don't—"

Jadene giggled. "That's a whole other story. But they're both in custody and won't be causing any more trouble."

"Incredible."

Ellis nodded to Jadene.

She took in the faces around the table. "But even these two could not have done this without help."

"Help?"

She lifted her chin. "Someone tipped them off. Someone else knew about the telegram. Someone with their own agenda was running interference, long before Ellis or myself were on the case."

Sinclair frowned.

"At first, my instincts were mistaken…" She flashed a glance at Wes. "But then I wondered who might have the most to gain from all this. Who had the means? The incentive?" She lifted the cell from the table, pressing its screen.

At the table's other end, a pulsing vibration erupted.

Heads turned.

Iverson swept the number to voicemail.

Jadene smirked. "Didn't want to take my call?"

The VP's face went flush.

"This cell phone was in the possession of one Rena Volkova." She handed the device to Sinclair. "You'll find a series of text messages sent from this device to Randall Iverson. The two were in contact for months. Evidently, he'd found the telegram in your home, and my bet is he's also the one who leaked your lineage."

"That's not true! This was about preserving and protecting the company. They weren't, I wasn't—"

"Ellis, if you would please," Jadene signaled.

"I love this part." Sporting a broad smile, Ellis approached. "Randall Donald Iverson, you are charged with conspiracy, accessory to kidnapping, murder, and being a first-class asshole."

"No, no!" Iverson shoved his chair from the table. "I put years of sweat into this place! I should be running the company—not this silver-spoon son-of-bitch and his kids!"

Ellis snatched an arm, yanked him from the chair, seized his other wrist, and torqued both hands behind his back.

Iverson squealed. His slick hair flopped as the handcuffs clicked tightly around his wrists.

"I miss that sound," Ellis snickered. He bucked a knee into the backside of Iverson's leg, ushering him from the boardroom. "Let's go, you stupid bastard."

Fritz shouted, "I don't believe this!"

Similar reactions followed around the table.

"I vote we adjourn for the day," Sheehan said. "This is too much."

"I second the motion," Palmer said.

Jadene slipped a manila folder from her leather binder. "Please, if I could keep your attention, we have one final matter."

"It's too late. The meeting is adjourned," someone protested.

Sinclair motioned to the attorney.

Mulligan shrugged. "Bylaws grant you, Mister Whitmore, the power to call any session you'd like."

Jadene smiled at Sinclair. "C'mon, it'll be fun."

The billionaire chuckled. "Did you bring more handcuffs?"

She held up the folder and smirked.

Sinclair gave a sharp nod. "Since all board members are present, I hereby call a special session."

"Session called," Mulligan said.

"Second not granted," Ratcliff shouted.

Mulligan turned to Jadene. "Is your information time-sensitive?"

"Very much so," she said.

"There you have it. The board is now in session," Mulligan called to the others.

Jadene wasted no time. "Voting to oust a CEO is serious business, as each of you knows. And before my turn as an investigator, I reviewed and analyzed contracts, negotiating to resolve disputes between parties."

"What in God's name is she talking about now?" Sheehan grumbled.

But Jadene didn't waver. "I submit to the majority holder a list of email communications showing every board member colluded with Iverson to replace the CEO of Whitmore Dynamics and Whitmore Systems, Mister Whitmore, before any vote." She handed Sinclair the folder of documents. "As such, these improper communications reflect a lack of transparency and accountability, and constitute blatant acts of undermining, eroded confidence, and a breach of trust by the board."

Mulligan cracked a laugh. "Oh, she's good."

Lilly grinned, and Wes chuckled beside her.

Sinclair exhaled sharply, flipping through the emails. "So this is what you all were up to?"

The silence stretched.

Palmer looked away. Sheehan cleared his throat.

Sinclair closed the folder, his scowl melting into a crooked smile. "You people are so fucking fired."

Shouts, finger-pointing, and insults erupted.

Sinclair Whitmore leaned back in his chair, a wide grin spreading across his lips. He looked at Jadene and mouthed, "Thank you."

SEVENTY-SIX

The next morning, Jadene found the remnants of her Tiki Paradise in soppy shambles. Quelled smoke drifted in the air. The waiting room was puddled with water, and its sea-blue carpet was completely charred. The chairs, the desks, and several of the file cabinets were damaged beyond repair. The once-vibrant Shetland-gray had peeled away, revealing scorched walls beneath. Ceiling tiles had also collapsed in several places.

Two men Stan hired busied themselves dragging out damaged furniture to an alley dumpster. Incredibly, though, one particular item had weathered the flames.

Stan pointed to the neon light leaning against her storefront. "Your sign survived, but you'll need to plug it in to be sure."

Eyeing the large Bowman PI display, a tiny grin grew on Jadene's lips. "I'll definitely do that," she said.

"I know a place in Dalton for the carpet. We can find the same color there if you'd like."

She was still absorbing the shock of it all. "I'd like that very much."

Stan steadied his cane on the sidewalk. "This all looks worse than it is, really. The fire was mostly in the entry area. We'll rip out the sheetrock and repaint. Of course, it'll take a while."

"Stan, you've been so gracious. I don't know if I can ever repay you."

Lilly skipped around the corner, wearing jeans and a t-shirt.

Nodding with a grin, Stan said, "You already have."

The young girl grabbed Stan in a bear hug, then threw her arms around Jadene. "I'm here to help," Lilly said. "What can I do?"

Before either could answer, her phone rang. Swiping the screen, she answered, "Bowman Investigations, Lilly speaking, how can I help you?"

Jadene was awestruck.

Lilly strolled away, holding the phone to her ear. "Sir, let me take down your information." She fished out a pen and a small pad from her back pocket. "You said your name was…?"

Stan grinned. "The busy little bee already forwarded your calls. And, you know, she's talking about a degree in criminal justice at the University." He tapped his cane on the sidewalk. "But she wants to stay near so she can still work with you."

Jadene smiled. "Absolutely. She's a hell of a girl."

Stan grinned. "She's becoming one."

A shiny, black Lexus GX pulled to the curb.

"Who's that?" Stan pointed.

The vehicle parked and the engine cut off. From behind the driver's side stepped a strapping man in charcoal trousers, a collared shirt, and a tie, wearing a shoulder brace and a wide grin.

A glimmer danced in Jadene's eyes.

"Good morning." Wes gave her a quick hug, then reached for Stan's hand. "Wes Holt."

"Stan Roseman."

"Ahh. I've heard a lot about you, sir," he said. "And thank you for your brave service."

"My duty, my pleasure," Stan replied. "I also believe I have you to thank for keeping our girl safe."

Wes shook his head. "Not at all, she's the hero."

Nearby and still on the phone, Lilly tossed a wave to Wes.

Wes reciprocated, then returned his attention to Jadene and Stan. "Mister Whitmore extends his gratitude once again." He handed Jadene an envelope. "He awarded you a generous amount of Class A shares in his new company."

"What?" She stared at the envelope. No one had ever given her anything like this—not because she deserved it, not for any reason at all. For a moment, she didn't feel broke or behind. She felt seen.

Wes shrugged. "He wanted to ensure you were well cared for."

Her fingers closed around the envelope. "Tell him… thank you," she said, barely above a whisper.

Lilly bounced back to the three, excited. "We've got a case!"

"We do?" Jadene turned to Lilly.

"This attorney was, like, referred by some other attorney. And he's got a missing witness he wants us to track down before they need to appear in court." She raised her writing pad. "Says he'll pay whatever Whitmore did."

Jadene chuckled, shaking her head.

"It's our third call today!" Lilly jeered.

"Sounds like you're going to be busy," Stan said, before stepping away to speak with a cleanup worker.

Lilly pointed to the SUV. "Hey, nice ride."

Wes hitched his tie. "Oh, yeah. That's not mine."

The two women stared at him, puzzled.

Wes broke into his Sinclair impression with a gruff voice. "An investigator needs a good set of wheels. Don't you agree, Wes?"

Jadene's eyes widened in shock. "Get the hell out of here!"

With a broad smile, he tossed her the keys.

"Oh my God!" Lilly squealed.

"Also, Mister Whitmore will be overseas this summer." Wes said. "He invites you and any guests to stay at his residence for the season."

"Really?"

He grinned. "Mister Whitmore wants you to be near your office while it's being renovated, of course."

"But her apartment is only, like, a mile away."

Jadene stomped her foot. "Shut up, Lilly!"

"And," Wes turned to her. "I'll need a ride back to the residence if you don't mind."

Jadene grabbed his arm. "Will there be wine?"

He squeezed her hand. "Nothing but the good stuff."

Thank you for your review!

Appreciation

In our Brave New World of Huxley beeps and buzzes, settling into a book feels like a forgotten refuge. Thank you for choosing mine.

To my wonderful wife—a beautiful, patient woman who understands the trash will get taken out... just as soon as I eke out a few more words.

To my friends, Shell and Rob, who've read so many drafts they're never quite sure which book they're in anymore.

To my high school history teacher, Mr. Siglala, who thought I wasn't listening.

To the heroes: Francis "Gabby" Gabreski, Thomas A. Baker, and the countless others who inspired parts of this story.

To my grandfather, who walked out the door one day to volunteer for World War II—because he loved his country. He probably should've mentioned it to Grandma, though.

And with deepest respect—to the Greatest Generation, and to every person who has worn the uniform since. You are the best of us.

www.ingramcontent.com/pod-product-compliance
Lightning Source LLC
Chambersburg PA
CBHW021216220726
48287CB00015B/1418